Burning Desire

Burning Desire

*The Psychopath and the Girl in
Black Prada Shoes
Part I*

M. L. Stark

Copyright © 2020 by M. L. Stark.

Library of Congress Control Number: 2020902256
ISBN: Hardcover 978-1-9845-9360-3
       Softcover 978-1-9845-9359-7
       eBook   978-1-9845-9358-0

All rights reserved. No part of this book may be reproduced or transmitted in any form or by any means, electronic or mechanical, including photocopying, recording, or by any information storage and retrieval system, without permission in writing from the copyright owner.

This is a work of fiction. Names, characters, places and incidents either are the product of the author's imagination or are used fictitiously, and any resemblance to any actual persons, living or dead, events, or locales is entirely coincidental.

Any people depicted in stock imagery provided by Getty Images are models, and such images are being used for illustrative purposes only.
Certain stock imagery © Getty Images.

Print information available on the last page.

Rev. date: 08/22/2020

To order additional copies of this book, contact:
Xlibris
UK TFN: 0800 0148620 (Toll Free inside the UK)
UK Local: 02036 956328 (+44 20 3695 6328 from outside the UK)
www.Xlibrispublishing.co.uk
Orders@Xlibrispublishing.co.uk
798600

CONTENTS

Introduction: The Shady Lizard and the Woman ix

Chapter 1: You Consume Me in Your Dark, Devious Terror 1
Chapter 2: Blindly I Trust Him 8
Chapter 3: Suddenly He Rips Off My Thong 12
Chapter 4: Doctor and Patient—Déjà Vu 24
Chapter 5: The Doctor's Foot Fetish 43
Chapter 6: Dragging Me into His Darkness 49
Chapter 7: Family, Love, Deception, and Lies 56
Chapter 8: Birthday, Fishing, and the Doggy-Style Knee Chest 63
Chapter 9: Her Angry Body Language 82
Chapter 10: Time is Just an Illusion 89
Chapter 11: The Exotic Dream 93
Chapter 12: A World Full of Two-Faced People 102
Chapter 13: A Seductive Sneaky Hour, and the Tattoo 109
Chapter 14: Revealing the Letters 124
Chapter 15: Hidden Shades of Doctor Bates 136
Chapter 16: Chiringuito and Gentleman Jack 150
Chapter 17: Where do you Come From? 160
Chapter 18: Viagra, Sex, and the Magic Wand 168
Chapter 19: The Angry Bird's First Morning Song 178
Chapter 20: Secrets and Lies 186
Chapter 21: I Do Nothing Wrong. You Do! 201
Chapter 22: Trust, Scams, and Women 213
Chapter 23: The King of Israel—The Chosen One 226
Chapter 24: It's Sheer Magic in Israel 244
Chapter 25: The Ping-Pong Game 262

Chapter 26: Let's Get Floppers Money, Babe 274
Chapter 27: The Shady Angel on the White Horse In Macau 289
Chapter 28: Roll of Fat, and Honeymoon Under the Cherry
   Blossom Tree... 298
Chapter 29: He Consumed my Soul... 310
Chapter 30: Who is that Handsome Bastard? 314
Chapter 31: Reflections from Kate 331
Chapter 32: The Puppet Master... 343
Chapter 33: Now I'm a Bloody Secretary!.. 362

I'm grateful to everyone who supported me in my growth throughout a difficult process in my life and helped to make this book a reality. Writing is certainly not an easy task!

Thanks to my family, childhood friends, and their families for putting up with my obsession with travelling the past years. Thanks for being my children, giving me grandchildren, and being loyal and supportive throughout my difficult time. You are all essential to me. My best childhood friends, you are like a sister and brother to me. Your parents are the parents I dreamt of. Thanks to friends in Jutland, to the many distressed women I spoke with and people I met during my worldwide travels. A special thanks to my two private chauffeurs in England, listening to my story.

Thanks to Mr Dexter Lopez, my publishing consultant at Xlibris, for the massive support. You gave me the final kick and showed rock-solid belief in the book.

A special thanks to Daniel Esparza, USA for the permission to use your stunning artwork as a book cover.

A special thanks to digital artist Elena Dudina in Spain for finishing the book cover and social medias.

Mr Drake Lucifer Bates, thanks for allowing me to love you. Fortunately, you failed in bringing me down, although you took away my dignity. My life was never the same, but I learned from your evilness. I truly loved you. The only thing I regret in my life is the many good things I did for you.

Enjoy the reading!

INTRODUCTION

THE SHADY LIZARD AND THE WOMAN

> It is my ambition to say in ten sentences what others say in a whole book.
>
> —Friedrich Nietzsche

It's more than difficult to get this all down on paper, because I want it to be authentic. I wish to rationally sense life as Mary experienced it with her 'lounge room lizard'. All the names of the characters, the establishments, and the places have been changed. The story is fictional, but it contains ideas based on real events.

There is merely one problem! How to tell it in ten sentences? It can't be told in a few words. Sorry, friends! However, ten sentences might be easy to read. So, let's jump to it. A wise man once wrote, 'Screw it. Let's do it.'[1] So I did it! In my new process of life, I can add one more quote by the same man: 'Do not be embarrassed by your failures. Learn from them and start again.' Thank you for the push. It gave me a new beginning.

Living near the beach and walking it day and night, is my dream. Falling peacefully asleep with the windows open to the gentle sound of the waves crashing on the beach. Letting the blue moonlight shine

---

[1] Sir Richard Branson.

through the window and watching the glittering stars in the clear night sky, while relaxing in my bed. My decision to finish the story began when I moved into my new apartment, in the first row of homes facing the impressive sea of the English Channel. It provides a striking view from the vast balcony and is barely fifty metres from the dark blue sea and the golden sand, presenting its many small colourful typical British beach huts. Each hut has its own precise shade ranging from burnished orange to icy blue, to depict a 'sunrise to sunset' scheme.

The first night is wonderful peaceful and as I wake up to a warm August summer morning on the south coast of the United Kingdom. The Sun is shining through my window as it awakens me at ten o'clock in the morning, while I'm still resting in my silky white sheets, warmly tucked around my naked body, and stretching my limbs as a lazy cat, because I have no desire to get up. After rubbing my eyes, I sit upon my bed to let the blood flow through all my veins, and I look around in the room in confusion. Oh, my goodness! Boxes in every corner. The balcony door is open, and I sense a pleasant fresh and cool sea breeze sneaks into the room, while I'm listening to the sound of the crashing waves reaching my inner ear with a pleasing calmness, and I think, *Why not?*

Leave the boxes and start writing a new book or finish the other ones I'm working on. I know my life is rather unreal, because I was heartbroken for a long time, and have not had the time or psyche to finish them. Being loved one day and completely upset the next turned my life drastically upside down. The man I love often tells me, 'Trust me. I love only you. We are meant to be' or 'We will be together for the rest of our lives'. I'm devastated because it's not as he promised. It's all a lie! The many red flags slipped past my attention about him being a dangerous person. It's difficult to imagine and comprehend if I'm going to have a life without him, because he is the best thing that I believe has happened to me. Too late, I figured out the meaning of the phrase 'lounge room lizard', but I believed him and trusted him with my life. That could be the biggest mistake I ever made in my life, pondering if he behaves like this to every woman he meets on his path. What gruesome things will I eventually be able to reveal?

Why is it so important to use the expression 'lounge room lizard'? This expression is usually a reference to lounge musicians, but most often in a negative sense. Such a person has the character of a medieval, ordinary man, who looks charmingly good, and resembles a dehydrated, oppressed lizard, which romantically is involved with a wealthy woman. He is typically shown as a well-dressed man and frequents surroundings where the rich and famous gather. He is the type of man who will seduce a wealthy woman with his flattery and deceptive charm. Oh, golly gosh! Do you believe it? He has so much charisma and is extremely convincing and pretends to be a first-class trustworthy charming person. I have never met any person so full of good ideas as his. It's amazing how the chap can captivate people in front of an assembly, by being so enchanting with his skills and high energy.

Trust me!

Those were the main words during our time together. Later, various problems began to arise, with his many calculating plans, when his professional approach or his projects usually started to awaken a great deal of speculation—though often, it was too late to see through the disguise. So, did I do all my research too late? Was I excruciatingly conned, because I loved him blindly? A Russian proverb says, 'Love is evil. You can fall in love with a goat.' In other words, love is so blind, and the pretty headless chick becomes blinded.

The phrase 'lizard' presumably relates to the cold and insinuating quality of the reptile. It has sharp claws like an eagle, which is unscrupulous when snatching the next victim. It's usually a distressed woman, whom he wants to lure into marriage, and maybe Mary was such a sorrowful pretty little doll. He eagerly tries at the early stage to seek some benefit from her, because he never married the previous one. Will he succeed? The woman usually has valuable possessions and money that the lizard man can profit from, and the more naive, unhappy, and helpless she is, the better for him. Then he strikes with his nasty sharp claws into her vulnerability and misuses her to the last drop, without any empathy or remorse. He chillingly torments her until she is severely wounded, like a helpless animal lying in the gutter, abandoned and helpless in its misery! Why does such a person so? Will she discover if he is a maliciously cunning narcissistic artist, an evil psychopath? A bloodsucking leech who sucks the last blood out of others. Has he done so through his entire life? Some say he is a person who completely lack of self-discipline and respect for obligations, rules, and social norms. Others say his speech patterns are repeated lies, with mood swings that are almost impossible to see through. Though, Mary trust this stunning man, even she sometimes sees that he has the flawless ability to bend the facts, and often he says it always someone else's fault. That is his best play, so no matter what, that's how it's done.

It's never his fault!

CHAPTER 1

You Consume Me in Your Dark, Devious Terror

> Loving you was like going to war; I never came back the same.
>
> —Warsan Shire

Let me present myself to the reader. My name is Mary, and this story is about a delightful, funny, dramatic, and sorrowful part of my life. I'm often told that I'm too sensitive, too gullible, and too helpful, with great empathy and plenty of affection for anyone. By enduring a more in-depth of my mind, heart, and soul, I finally discovered the strength to find the truth about myself and my previous love life. Why did I allow myself to be a prisoner in a miserable life? I did find the root of why I repeatedly let myself be ill-used, but why could I not say stop when others exhausted me? I never stopped loving them, and in time, I forgave almost everyone who harmed me, physically or mentally. Forgiveness is vital for me, so one does not inflict more unnecessary emotional pain. And hatred of other people did not work so well for me, because I can't hate.

There are different opinions about me, while some say I'm crazy, naive, and foolish. I've lived a long time with emotional pain and a broken heart and allowed those I loved unconditionally to mistreat me badly. There are many questions, which I scribbled on paper, and in time, I became strong and realised that I'm only human, a completely average person, and can love and respect others in a healthy way. Life gave me a valued gift—to be able to forgive and forgive myself—but it doesn't mean others forgave me for my mistakes. That is sad, but then it is their problem, not mine.

* * *

Doctor Bates, I am so glad that you picked me up from my sadness, although I later became disappointed. Well, I must say, heartbroken! Ever since you captured me, you have given me multiple malicious kicks in my ass. To illustrate, millions of uppercuts in my face. OK, they were not physical but psychological, but every time I got on my feet again, I got another nasty punch from you, when you assured me, 'Trust me.' 'I love only you.' 'You are my beloved Mary.' You called me 'babe', 'baby', 'little girl', 'MM', and many other sweet nicknames. How cute is that? But darling, dear, you succeeded in taking my self-esteem and self-confidence. I used to believe men could be caring and loving, though my life was never the same again because you tried to break me. But luckily, you failed, and I still have some sanity left. The best part is that by trying to break me, you made me immensely strong. Perhaps you I will forgive you for the nasty things you have done, but your devilishness will never be forgotten. I loved you with deep passion and gave you all my support for years, providing for all your daily needs and business projects, because you are not capable of earning or holding onto any money yourself.

I learned a lot from all the evil you did. Most of all, you gave me the final inspiration to grab the magic pen, and I let it write most of what happened down on paper. Incredible how clever the pen is. It tells me you're a narcissistic, calculating psychopath. That is tough medicine to swallow, but that's what you truly are! It has been an immensely hard decision to remain in a relationship with you, which often did not work decently, but I truly love you. My darling love, I wonder if you are worth any of it, because you did your best to systematically to destroy me year after year. I try to keep up my courage and positive spirit by searching for the necessary peace in my life with you. Thus, I pay a huge price for the choices I make, and I don't deny I'm not always able to figure out the long-term costs of my decisions. Instead of finding myself in a pleasant life, with love and peace, I found you, but sometimes everything goes wrong. I know that I obviously can't get wealth and happiness at the same time, so I seek the love of the last man in my life, instead of the wealth. Well, darling dear, life with you sometimes ends up worse than I hoped for, as my total trust in your help and at times the false love I sense is a realisation that I can't understand.

I have no idea if you suffer from a bipolar disorder, when I notice how it affects your mood, which can swing from one extreme to another. If you don't know what it is to be bipolar, let me enlighten you. It used to be known as manic depression, where the person can either be very low and sluggish or feel astronomical and overactive. In some of your phases, you can often feel ecstatic, having ambitious plans and voluminous ideas, and then spend sizeable amounts of money on things we can't afford. Sometimes you lose all your energy and become easily annoyed, that's where I don't understand why your lying increases, and run faster, like a chased rabbit. You often feel extremely creative, but you regularly see or hear things that convince you of things that are not true. Therefore, I believe you turn everything around in your favour, then everyone else is always wrong and to blame for what happens. You managed to convince me, well done; you're smarter than me. But maybe at the end of the day, I'm perhaps smarter than you, because when things went wrong, you said 'it is always your fault Mary' so I thought it must be me who is wrong, not you. Who is right? Who is wrong?

You quickly caught me up in your disturbing personality, as a bug caught in a spiderweb. Sadly, by then, it was too late for me to have any imaginable chance to get away. Thereafter, you consumed me in your manipulative, dark, shady terror by making me promises of a better and happier life. Though I always had enough physically to cope with everything that was required of me, I lacked the strength to cope with the destructive and devious mental abuse you exposed me to.

When my world looked the blackest and scariest to me, I tried to heal my soul through my Christianity. This was when you, playing a smiling and charming man, came into my hopeless life with promises of rescue.

'I'll get you out of the rough sea. Sweet Mary is about to consume you fully.'

Did my love for you then turn out to be my worst enemy, instead of your rescue and the love you promised me? Was it genuine, or was I subjected to the serious grim darkness of a manipulative hell? Did you disgustingly insult my sacred religion and used it against me? I speculate if I allowed you to exploit my weakness, for you to tear me to pieces, because I could no longer see who I was. I speculate if it was you or I who was mentally ill.

Your sudden mood swings and some of your, I ponder if they were false declarations of love. Thus, they can be draining and often end with a surprising explosion of negativity from your hidden shady side. If I mention something that doesn't fit into your agenda, you are outraged. The many promises that came from my new best friend—were they only a play on your part? Perhaps you are the perfect puppet master, who can control the strings on your new pretty toy doll, when you play the role perfectly, as well as any Oscar-winning actor. At times I wonder if there is only one agenda in your head: to drain and viciously undermine me mentally and take the most from me, until I stand on the edge of the cliff, ready to commit suicide. I wonder if you are a dangerous lizard man, and if I too late will find out what your agenda is for me. Sometimes you achieve your creepy, crooked, and draining plan, when you dump me in the nearest gutter, because you always want me to come crawling back to you, as a submissive, helpless, beaten little dog, begging for your forgiveness and love.

Next you like to use my submissiveness to support you with everything. And when I block that financial support, you get tired of me trying to find your next victim or if it not succeeds you to find another woman, you try to get me back, so such a game almost costed me my life. Darling, I truly could have used your help at that time, but where were you?

Your convincing—and fake—expressions of feelings kept me from seeing the many red flags before it was too late. Do you have any respect for me or others or is it all about you, and not about us?

'You can't do anything of value in life. You're worth nothing.' You often told me.

So, I convinced myself it might be true, with the many repulsive words I heard. Sometimes they are often easier to believe than the rare good words a person hear. Am I unwise? Can't I see the woods for trees? Is the ocean so big, that I can't see the water? I'm not sure if I'm living with a, dangerous, harmful, self-absorbed sociopath.

So, darling, perhaps it's about time for me to get going with my life. I have decided, if I put on some red lipstick and black mascara, dress nicely, fix my hair sexy, put on my black Prada shoes, and go out to a nice pub. There are hundreds of men out there who will appreciate someone like me and my sweet smile. I know there are still many great men looking at the blonde Danish woman with her amazing, gorgeous smile. Are you ready to lose your ultimate chance for a great life with a woman who unconditionally love you? I will not cry over you because no man is not worth my tears. Though I wonder if I'll regret the many good things I'm doing for you and all the forgiveness I always give you. I don't know, yet it might be the best thing to do, so I can live my life in peace.

As you know, from my time as an infant, I quickly discovered that crying for loneliness doesn't help, and there are never any loving people to comfort me. Childhood pain has not taught me to master mental terror and manipulation but has taught me to *give in to the power of others, to men as you*. I don't protest because I don't know how, and I'm often scared when I do the opposite of what people and you want from me. So, I obey them, as I obey you.

* * *

Based on my background, I hope the reader will understand my life choices, including the wrong ones. Hopefully, with this first part of my story, people will try not to be intimidated and used as I was. I hope that you can say no to your abuser and keep your own promise of that no. It can be difficult. I know! I truly believe there are many women like me, who are quietly forced into such systematic exploitation, and are badly manipulated by male psychopaths. Did you know there are more male psychopaths than female? Scary! Three out of four psychopaths are males. Chilling!

Many women keep on going back to their abusers, though you should *not*, but try to fight for your dignity and leave the scumbag in the gutter instead. I know it can be hard, but the predator deserves to be there, and *not you*. My fear of being left alone in darkness of loneliness scared me, and the dudes terrifying strategy will be occurred repeatedly, for years. Dear reader, be aware of *red flags*! Don't accept psychological or physical violence, because it will hurt and damages you, as it did to me. I wish I had learned to turn my back to such horror in my life before it was too late, stepping out of such lunatic's train tracks. I'm certain I'd have come much further, without so many injuries on my soul, as well I should have searched for help to make my life good again. But I didn't! It's shameful, embarrassing, and I have before been suicidal, though I managed to get out of it myself, however it was difficult. But I'm a survivor!

When you read the story, perhaps you will understand it all. How I mentally became of what was required of me: a trusting person who never questioned what people did to me and who couldn't see evilness in humans. Why should I? I'm not evil! Perhaps you will have a deeper understanding of why I'm spiritually weak and why I can't say no to others. Often I'm asked, 'Why did you accept this physical and psychological domination and manipulation in your entire life?' I don't know, but I hope there is an answer in the scribbling on my torn-up paper and I will find out why a cruel person can ruin another person's life. Letting my pen floating with the black ink on the paper made me realise if I continue such a horrid track, it will be as letting the rest of my happiness fall into a deep, devilish black hole. I want to be released from my previous pain, so I can continue with a fresh, blissful life, and never let any person ever hurt me again. Maybe it's better to live alone than live with the devil, so I wonder if I will learn the lesson.

It's not a secret that this journey has been challenging to relive it all again, during my research, looking at pictures, reliving god and bad memories, and steering the quivering nervous hand with my pen on the paper. Many of my hidden and suppressed memories were rediscovered in my search through photos and correspondences, and then again during the writing process, where I unearthed difficult conditions and facts, from being born and became a strong adult person.

This is a part one of the *Burning Desire* trilogies, though in the end, I hope you will have a complete picture, however, it's not about pity but about the understanding why humans can be so mean to children and adults. My mistakes taught me to stay solid and take care of myself, as I will use my future positive energy in a better way. I will not use it on cynical and psychopathic persons or on people who drain the goodness and love out of my kind heart and mind. I don't need to become tough to survive, nor do I need to change myself, but I must learn to be realistic with my life. I must maintain my genuine quality, which makes me true to who I am: a loving, compassionate, and honest women. I have realised, the happiness and love I see in movies do not exist. They are found only on the screen, and I'm sure by the reader, who also wants a cheerful ending.

Take care of your life, and nurse it with your self-respect! Don't let others destroy you, because you are worth so much more than the psychopath. I wish you a pleasant reading with this dramatic, loving, tough, heart-breaking, and funny story.

> Three things cannot hide for long: The Moon, the Sun and the Truth.
> —Gautama Buddha

CHAPTER 2

BLINDLY I TRUST HIM

> 'Why not?' inspired the enthusiastic and wild hope. It is a sign of courage and an optimistic attitude to life. I still have much to gain from chanting to myself, every time I face a sign of weakening courage or an overwhelming challenge.
> —Karen Blixen

Where does it all begin? In the past, present, or future? This is the beginning of the end. Who can say where it all begins? Is there even a beginning, or is it all doomed to be the end before it begins? For a long time, I considered whether I should or should not write about my past life with Drake Lucifer Bates, both the good and the evil. Tell about my grim childhood, my frustrating youth, my almost happy, though unsecure marriage, and then there was the ultimate love with Drake! You might think during the reading, *Oh my Goodness! She must be naive, blue-eyed, and unwise.* It's OK. Despite the fact you don't know me, you might be right! When viewing back at my past with Drake, yes, even with my marriage to Paul and my horrible childhood, I seem exactly as what you are thinking, but I don't mind you having those thoughts. Because it's so true! So, I forgive myself for being gullible in my past and in this important thus also crucial process of seeking the truth. So, are all my dreams then turned to shame, because of those people and the last man I loved, who had killed the dream I dreamt?

This is about dating a genuinely spine-chilling sociopath, one who swindled himself through life. A self-absorbed, lying person who used people and whom I forgave too many times for his immoralities. Why did I fall in love with him? I don't know, and I didn't know everything back then of what I know today. He is handsome, charming and persuaded me that he could help me through my personal struggles and save me from my unwise thinking; a foolish suicide attempt. Swiftly, I was captured in his sticky web when he promised me, I would get a better and perfect love life with him, so he tried to persuade me to complete a divorce and wanted to help me, day and night, writing divorce letters and agreements. A perfect settlement with "my ex-husband to be" would, of course, be great. Who doesn't appreciate good help and advice? So, will this become my future with Drake? Shortly after we met, we discussed it all, and in his eagerness he wanted more from me, as soon as my divorce and settlement were finalised. His wish would be of great benefit for him because he knows about the financial aspects of my divorce, which could end up with a pretty nice sum for me. But there is one main thing that could make it somehow troublesome; According to Danish law, everything would go in my husband's favour if I approved Drake's suggestion. My ex-husband would no longer be liable for paying further alimonies, so I would lose many years of regular income. Worse yet, I didn't research if Drake was married or not. Perhaps I'll face an immense surprise, though I figure out he likes to date other women behind my back, when I'm not nearby. Was he worse than my own husband?

'Shame on you.' I said, 'you know how I feel about adultery.'

'Babe, they are only business associates. Good friends.' He denies every accusation I bring up. 'I only want you. No one else.' How sweet of him, so I trust his words, with my good, trusting heart. I worship him, and my burning desire was to have a loving man, so he won my compassion with his enormous intellect, his glimmering charm, and his handsome features. Will I find out what lay behind the dark shade of Doctor Drake?

Well, according to Ernest Hemingway; The best way to find out if you can trust somebody is to trust them.

So, I carelessly trusted him! It would be bizarre of me to think of him as a sociopath, with me as his girlfriend, even there was a part of him that made him so mysterious and exciting as a character. He always presented himself with a public persona of normalcy, and when I first met him, at my best age, I thought he was normal; he seemed wise and educated, with a great personality. He looked psychologically healthy, and he was seductive, handsome, and charming. He had all the aspects I fancy in a man, and he came off as a well-speaking and polite person from the first day we met. I had no idea at first what he was up to, and I believed I was a clever-thinking woman who could see through such men. However, I got thoroughly caught up in his intrigues, since, I believed he would help me with my annoying medical condition, and I began to look up to him. He seemed to be intelligent and friendly, so I thought he must know what he was doing for me as his patient. I felt he possessed great empathy for me, and something vastly magical happened around him, because he appeared energetic and funny and had a trustworthy job. In the early stages, I felt he would become my saviour, my star, with his openness, embracing arms, and amazing understanding, which captured me. Then I began to catch on that he was inappropriately flirting with me; he was a doctor, and I was his patient. But I kept telling myself he was a moral, kind, elderly gentleman with nothing wrong in him. It had to be a joke, so, I ignored his flirting, because he is harmless. Though, as Gabriel Garcia Marquez quote says; Everyone has three lives: A public life, a private life and a secret life.

It's inevitable that we go through all three stages, and so did I, because when I meet Drake, I'm in an awful, vulnerable situation and doomed in my marriage. Thoughts of divorce is often racing through my mind, because there are too many other women interfering in our life—one of my husband's Paul's three lives. My life is an extremely petrifying mess, with naivete, goodness, and potential loss of life, as I am suicidal, because to me it seems as the easiest solution, so no one can hurt me anymore. Selfish? Yes! Yet I want to survive, so I begin to believe everything this handsome doctor tells me. Trusting him with my fragile life, I don't see what he is capable of as he seems to sink into a mania of manipulation and deception. Trusting Drake with my fragile life, I don't see whether he is like Dr Jekyll and Mr Hyde, who is capable of evilness. Have I become blinded to the truth, as a foolish woman, and can't grasp the dominating, insistent, false part of his personality?

Shortly after I begin treatment in his clinic, I experience something unexpected and I'm utterly upset! I don't dare to say a word. Yet because of my good heart, I possess the gift of great forgiveness, so I forgive him for his insult. Is it wrong?

However, I believe I have found someone I can trust, someone who will care for me, someone who will respect me.

'Babe, I only want you. No one else. I love you from the deepest part inside my heart,' he often tells me, mesmerising me with his many hot loving words. Christ! It's amazing the love declarations he can give, which make me fall in love with him even more. I want to believe the best in him because he has some decent parts as well, and not to mention he is also hilarious. I think I have found someone I can trust, someone who will love me, someone who will respect me. Perhaps the total love he has promised me has entirely blinded me, so I don't spot any early warning signs, and being blindfolded by his influence, believing he is intelligent, caring, and loving. I'm trapped in what I believe is love, and yet there are many *red flags* I don't see. He has arms made of steel which are impossible to escape from, and perhaps everything is too good to be true.

'Mary is naive,' many will say. No! I believe I'm a vulnerable, trusting women whom others to easily utterly uses, controls, and psychologically abuses. I don't know anything about psychopaths, sociopaths, or narcissistic behaviour, but maybe I'll figure it out what I can expect from such people. Though, I find out it is all a play to them, and you are the victim who gets netted like a fly in their foul web.

This story is not about being a scorned woman, but it's about observing it all from above and from a healthy perspective, to realise what can happen. Will I ever be the same, and will I possibly learn my life's lesson?

CHAPTER 3

SUDDENLY HE RIPS OFF MY THONG

> It's amazing what a human being can endure, as long it feels there is a meaning to the adversity or the suffering.
> —Søren Aabye Kierkegaard

Perhaps, it might have been best to leave my past life in my head. As my own little secret thoughts, because there are many good and loving memories, but worst of all, there are so many bad ones as well. Most of the time, it's a curse and a devilish experience that I cannot escape, and sometimes it can pull the teeth out of any normal person. Normal, decent people who respect others do not do as what I'll endure in my life with a man.

In my quest for a meaningful life, I participate in many voluntary projects, which do me worthy, when I work among poor people who have it far worse than I do, and it gives me a more profound sense of love and care for people and animals. I perceive that many suffer more than I do, although I can draw several parallels between our respective lives. My aid work is about supporting children, young people, elephants, and other threatened rare animals. I love saving dogs in Third World countries by feeding them and giving them medication, and those I find many of on the streets or in the mountains. Puppies, as well as mummy and daddy dogs, get the best aid I can give them, as it is an essential mission for me, during a period when I have mixed feelings of living in happiness and walking around in my own hell. Learning of the doomed fates of many of those I meet puts everything into perspective for me. I discover the importance of the many different religions with which humans enrich themselves, as they believe in their own gods or goddesses. My deep belief in my Jesus and the Virgin Mary is a faith from which I can get optimistic answers to my many questions about happiness, hell, and deeds, which torment me. Soon I discover the good aspects of Buddhism, Hinduism, the Koran, and Judaism during my travels to different countries and my pilgrimage. In my religious search for knowledge, I am enriched by the ancient Greek gods, who provide amazing inspiration for my life. The main thing in all the religions is, yes, will you believe it? Everyone needs love and care, and it's something unusual and seldom in my life.

Tears run down my cheeks when I glance at the picture of the man I love. It stands on my bedside table even though I know it is a bad idea to keep it, but I will not cry over a man who treats me inhumanely— or is it because I'm angry with myself? I had allowed myself to get into an extreme situation, in which I trusted and loved a person unconditionally. Am I angry because I tell too much about my life and my many hidden secrets of my childhood and marriage? My anger grows when I find out there do exist evil predators, disguised people as human figures, like the devil, who walked on earth. Yes, you are right, and maybe it does sound somewhat disturbed. But on the other hand, it's all excruciating and dramatic.

I don't know what to do with myself, I ponder. Gently I wipe my tears away from my cheeks and toss the stupid picture into one of the moving boxes standing in front of me. It has totally exhausted me, yet I still doubt who is responsible for all this chaos. Him or me?

I turn my inner meridian clock several weeks back to where it all began—the first meeting and perhaps the happiest and possibly also the darkest, gloomiest period, when I again have a treatment session with Doctor Bates at his clinic in Spain.

* * *

I have been here a few times before, and its three weeks after I met Doctor Bates the first time in his clinic on that breathtaking day in August 2010. Though today is a specific gloomy day when the scariest thing happens and the day I fear the most. Humbly, during some of my first visits, I had told him about my suicide plan, because I was completely unable to cope with my life anymore, and I was terribly depressed and weak.

Both of us have a week before been Denmark, of course separately. I'm with my husband, and Drake is together with his secretary somewhere else, but now he and his secretary and me are back in Spain again. Paul stayed in Denmark with the kids, because of work and their school. Drake and I have arranged a new visit at his clinic the day after my MRI scan at the local hospital. When I'm arriving at the clinic, I'm in an awful condition, with the feeling of knives constantly stabbing my body. My neck feels locked, my head is pounding comparable to a furious drummer, and the agony is severely increased. Ouch! I can't figure out why, and I have not been in this much misery since my back surgery several years ago. However, I expect he can help me because I trust him, and he has promised me so.

Drake is pleased and intensely welcomes me and shows great joy over my return. Wow! He looks great, with a vast, loving smile on his face. I reciprocate his smile and reach out my greeting hand to him, and in confidence, I enter the room and sit down on the chair in front of me so we can talk.

Swiftly, he turns around towards the door, locks it, and leaves the key into his pocket, which I find rather unusual, and I get a weird feeling. He has never done this before, so a nervous thought runs through my brain: *Help!*

'Eh, why did you lock the door?' I ask as I gaze at him with a fat question mark solid printed on my nervous forehead.

'Oh, no worries. It's because it is the weekend. I don't want any others to disturb us. You get it? I mean, while I am treating you.' He smiles, sly and convincing.

'Huh? But you've locked the front door. I suppose nobody else can get in?' I'm scared, wanting to demand that he unlock the door. *Now!*

But somehow, I can't, and he gazes at me with devilishly eyes. His expression clearly hints at a sinister motive.

'Umm, you never know who will come while we are alone. Others have a key to the clinic.'

'Ohhh, ahh-ha, I see.'

'Yeah, the cleaning staff will come during the weekend. Oh boy. It won't be so smart to have the door unlocked. Phew, not good as you're lying on the treatment table with no clothes on.' He smiles oddly, gazing at me with a peculiar mystique. His smile is slicker than usual, but I swallow his explanation and trust him.

Awkwardly, I unbutton and unzip my pants to take them off.

'I'm not sure if I shall take off my blouse.'

'Yes, of course.' He stares at me eerily, confirming this item must also come off. Uncomfortably, I stand only in my pink lace bra and thong, and so is his rule every time. After I laid my body on the table he begins his treatment, with smooth, light, gentle strokes, almost in a caressing and loving way.

'Jeez, it was such a horrible break in Denmark.' He at the same time tells me, and I can tell he wants sympathy, wants me to feel pity for him.

'Huh? Really?'

He blabbers as a wild chatting parrot, but I try to ignore him, by not asking to many questions, by only saying, 'ahh! Ohhh, yikes, eyh? Doh, or a-ha.' Then I try to watch his moments, but mostly I wanted him to shut up.

Swiftly, the room becomes hushed when he stops yakking. Somehow, I sense that he is puzzled, thinking of something, which bothers me, while he seems much clammier, as a predator, ready to attack. It is repulsive and weird, even more so than usual, as he scowls intensely and creepily at my big breasts and half-naked body the entire time. His body language seems villainous and then he begins to be extreme flirtatious with me. He has never been so intense before, and I begin to fear him. My panicking thoughts run through my head: *How can I get out of the room if he hurts me? No!* A shudder goes through my body. I feel utterly lost! *Oh my God! No, no! Surely, no. I'm certain he can't do this to me!* I'm afraid. Should I scream? *Good Lord! And the fucking door is also locked! Shit! The damn key is in his pocket!* Runs anxiously through my head.

Desperately I gaze around in the room to see if there is anything, I can defend myself with. Damn! Nothing! *I will kick him in his balls or face.* Christ, my heart jumps up to my throat. More fear and chills run through my mind. *What do I do? Can he see my heart is galloping out of fear?* My breathing gets faster, and I try to control it so he can't see my fear. What shall I do?

'Oh my God. You are absolutely a lovely woman. Jeez, and beautiful,' he shouts bizarrely and unexpectedly. I become even more frightened, so my heart jumps, going a hundred miles an hour. Perfectly created in his mind, he starts his grandiose and cruel plan. He gives me a devious gaze, smiles slickly, and blinks with his long black eyelashes, seeking the perfect way to attack. I can see the predatory glimpse in his eyes, and I want to jump off the table. Instead, I freeze in fear, and at the same time, he rapidly puts his handheld treatment device with a quick movement on the table beside him. I go into a *tremor*! Douchebag! How he managed to do it so quickly I have never comprehended. But within a split second, he rips off my thong, then pulls down his own pants. Grabs me, pulls me out to the edge of the treatment table! Spreads my legs and sticks his purple-headed warrior into my dry vagina. Petrified, I'm now lying there wearing only a bra, and go into immediate distress. Complete fossilised, I become as an unmoving plastic doll. Damn it! What he has suddenly done to me is exactly what I feared, because he is hurting me. It's identical to a horror movie, where I'm trapped in a death machine, being raped by a man I fully trust, and whom I believe wants only the best for me. Is it a fetish he has? Does he get hard when he treats patients? I wish I knew beforehand. I'm shaken and in my motionless state, I get the worst flashbacks of merciless memories from my time as a teenager, when two men raped me. One of them was a well-known porn actor, and the other a singer. The day they died, I felt liberated from their torment. Damn cursed man whores! Those men's actions made me feel powerless, the way I now feel with Drake at his clinic.

Dear reader? What do you think? Do you have any idea of how it feels, being cruelly raped? Deep inside my heart, I sincerely hope no one has ever or will ever experience such cruelty or horrifying physical or psychological abuse. And now the scenario repeats itself with my doctor?

Fucking pigs!

Drake's selfish, fast, back-and-forth movement inside my vagina is a violent, rough, speedy cannon shot only for his own pleasure. There is *no* love or tenderness in his rape when he bangs inside me with his sexcalibur. *Asshole!* This is not lovemaking but narcissistic brutality, a dark hell of burning fire. Everything is only for his own benefit, to get as much as he can get from my vagina. He didn't even have the decency to ask me first if I wanted to bone with him. Oh, no, he takes, with greedy lust, what *he needs*. I'm only a piece of delicious meat on his table as he consumes me. What is the difference between his cruel sexual act and what the other men had done to me? Nothing! All of them screwed me against my will. The horrors flare up in scary, scorching flames again as he harshly pumps in and out of my dry front bottom. The scenario, the sequence, and the fear are the same repulsive experience, which I once chose to forget about, but it is impossible to completely forget in one's lifetime. What shall I do? Scream? Who will hear me? Nobody! We are alone in the building, and by the way, the door is also *locked*. No one can hear the scream, nor could they back then in my younger days, down in the gloomy putrid cellar. Drake has created his own horror scene of terror, as were it a Hitchcock play! The sense of déjà vu is chilling.

But how did he get of his pants so quickly? He must have prepared it while he was sitting on his chair, whereas I could not see what he was doing with his other hand. Loosen up his belt. Opened the button and zipped down his zipper without me seeing or hearing nothing. Can it be so?

In my ice-covered Lolita state of mind, I haven't realised what to do while this selfish monster is pushing his nasty little baby organ inside me. Surprisingly, someone pulls the door handle, and Drake becomes terrified. He glares at me and puts his hand over my mouth so I can't scream, and I get claustrophobic and can't breathe. Next, he indicates with his index finger on his lips that I shall be completely silent. In his state of panic, with his pants below his ankles and his hand over my mouth, he mysteriously kicks the chair behind him because he is about to fall. It makes a terrible noise. *Crash! Bang! Boom!* But it does not prevent him from continuing the sex act, and he restarts his violent back-and-forth movements, one hand over my mouth. Outside, I can hear someone talking, trying several times to push the door handle. They continue knocking firmly on the door, but I still don't know who it is, while I'm glaring at the door from my eye corner, hoping they will unluck the door. It gets hushed and they disappear, then Drake heaves a sigh of relief. I'm still terrified and don't dare to move myself a millimetre out of the spot. In the same moment, he gets his orgasm he falls flat on my stomach, with a weird, weak, sobbing voice, whispering to himself, 'Oh … Mom.'

Yuck! What the fuck? What is that about? I can't believe it's true, musing, *I must have heard it wrong!* He is exhausted splayed-out on my corpus, as this other fat guy did back then, as a drunken and self-satisfied dried lizard. I can't explain what happens next, but a few minutes after, Drake apologises for his actions like an angry chit-chatting parrot.

'Oh my God! I'm so sorry, sorry, sorry. I have never done this before with any of my patients. Can you forgive me?' he begs.

'Huh?' I only stare fossilized at him, while my mind ponders: *What do you think?*

Ugh!

Next, he has the audacity to command me something odd. 'Ahem, do not to say anything to anyone. Not even to your husband.'

'Eh? A-ha. Ohhh.' I stare speechless at him and can't find any words for his selfish act. I'm dumbstruck. Stupid, bogus, plastic American!

He pulls up his boxer shorts as if the action hasn't disturbed him diddly squat. *Arrogant bastard!* He thinks only of his own well-being and the reputation of his clinic, not of me, his offended victim. Then he pulls up his bright canvas pants, zips up, buckles up the button, locks his belt and smirks satisfied at me. The dude has a wet spot on the front of his pants. Gross, right where his 'skin flute of a rotator stick' is positioned. Disgusting! I want to give a proper uppercut to his face, but I don't dare. He is a strong man and can crack my neck with the greatest of ease. I'm more than scared thinking of that.

'Eh ... uh ... wet spot ... eh ... on your pants, uh ... right there,' I stutter in my scared condition and shakily I point at his crotch, as he stares at me, surprised.

'Oh yah, I see! It's because *he* began crying with eagerness in my slacks. Wow, it was while I was touching you. Ha-ha, ha-ha.' He laughs broadly as it's funny.

'What? Crying?' I ask, upset, and he gladly continues his self-important speech.

'Oh, yay. That's why I got so excited. Yay, I wanted to feel your lovely, tight, wet pussy.' He smiles slyly, but in my wordless frustration, I want to kick him in his ugly balls!

'Huh? What?' Pig ass! Come on! For sure, I'm not wet—it's a dry pussy! Miaow! I scream in panic in my head, and he smiles and licks his lips at the same time. My angry, crying mind ponders in the same second: *I know my vagina is tight, but I'm not wet! Fucking loser! Grab a plastic doll next time.*

'He is thinking so much about you. So, striking, your soft skin is. *Willy* happily wakes up,' he says cheerfully.

Jesus Christ, such a knucklehead!

I stare dumbfounded, and he glances at me, 'Ha-ha, ha-ha,' laughing as if it's funny. Is the act a naturally allowed fuck game for him? Suspiciously and angrily I stare at him, resembling a stupid woman who doesn't know any better.

What the fuck is this crazy cowboy toast talking about? Willy! And it also wakes up? I ponder in frustration. For the first time in my life, I've heard a man calling his trouser snake 'Willy', a monstrous thing that *wakes up* and *is crying*! How bizarre! So, clown-like to give his cock a boy's name and talk about it as if it has a unique personality. Is that normal for men? Come on, boys. Help me out! I hear people call the beast the 'bandit', the 'flute', the 'slam-bam', 'bad boy' or 'shorty' but never 'Willy'. It sounds as a children's story. Ha, ha, ha, yes, 'Willy the nasty cat'. Yes, ho, ho, ho, he can't even brag about the size. Hmmm, 'Shorty' is much better than 'Willy'.

'I'm so sorry. My bad. Pardon me,' he sobs, though I can tell it isn't genuine.

'OK, OK, easy now,' I'm trying to calm him. But I think, *you are a disgusting Andalusian mountain goat!* and I only want to get out of there and no longer listen to this creepy dude. 'Now I need to go to the bathroom.' Finally, he lets me get up. I'm holding my private parts in my hand, and immediately as I get up, all his ejaculated buttermilk runs down into my fingers. Holy shit! I'm about to barf and can't get out of there fast enough so I can squeeze the rest of his nasty cum out of my vagina. Plop! The splash lands right away in the bidet, and I open the shower nozzle and rinse my private parts as best I can. Gross! I need to get all his nasty prostatic juices and the piggy smell of his sticky spunk out of me. Now, you might think man milk doesn't smell, but for me, it stinks and is disgusting. My entire body is shaking, and I don't know what to do with myself. It's as if men who enter my life's path think they can do what they want with me and take as much as they like of the delicious little 'herring on the Christmas table' (a Danish special cold fish). Yikes, and every time it fits *them*, and not when I accept it!

Hallo there! I ponder, *I'm not a take-it-yourself-free lunch or grab bag, am I?* My sobbing mind screams. I can't go to Kate, because she isn't here, so I have no idea what to do. I fear him! Keep in mind, I'm alone in a foreign country, and I'm afraid the police will not take me seriously if I turn him in. Furthermore, will they believe me? No one will! Waste of time and effort, and it will be his word against mine. The villains always win. Shall I tell my husband? Oh, no, I don't dare. Besides, our relationship is a living inferno, and Paul will not believe me. My head is spinning with crazy thoughts, and I don't dare get out of the bathroom, because I can't escape from the clinic.

* * *

In reconsideration, I sincerely regret never reporting any of these dirty, rotten twatwaffle's. I bet that Drake will claim that I gave him permission to screw me. Slam bam, Alabama! Another devious fuck in my head, and unquestionably, these would be his exact words. I wonder if the guy is totally lost. So, please tell me, what will help? So many thoughts run through my brain. Besides, he has plans of leaving the country, so I bet the police report will end up in the trash. Yes, everything will be forgotten. Out of sight, out of mind.

What do you think? Is it rape or not? Yes! In my opinion it's a serious assault. Regardless of whether I'll forgive him or not, it's a violation against me. And he'll for sure get away with it. Why? Because of his manipulative, well-thought-out, sneaky plan he has for me. Damn, he managed to shut me up. Has he done so with other women before? And my fingers are itching on the keyboard to reveal something gruesome, though you must wait until you have read the story. Will it be scary? Well that's what I must find out during my writing of the story, so let's continue.

*   *   *

I finish my doings in the restroom and walk back into the treatment room again. His false excuses begin to resume.

'Sorry about that. But you are so lovely. So, tempting.' The weaner giggles with a slight smirky smile on his lips.

Perhaps I should have considered the people I involved myself with, might be your next question? You are right! But then this story would never have been told, and it was also a bad time in my life, so I didn't. As my life collapsed in my marriage, I submitted myself to the stronger authority, and this time, it was Drake who used his vast weight and control he had over me as his patient.

Fucking fool! I shattered yell in my head, glaring angry at him.

He was ice cold, as a snake, and pretended if as nothing has happened. I'm so embarrassed that I feel like hiding myself in a dark gloomy mouse hole, because I think the whole intermezzo is my own fault.

'I can't resist you. And your beautiful body.' He smirks.

Clown!

I don't sense any real remorse in his voice. Flabbergasted, I stare at him while the chit-chatting, irritating, stupid parrot keeps on yakking. 'Please forgive me?' he casually mumbles. Then I notice it's all in English, which conveniently comes to the surface for him. Blah, blah, blah! I wonder why? Can the piglet not find the proper Swedish words for his stupid excuses and his vile crime? I have lost my tongue, realising what he is capable of, when he during this treatment session, went too far. Then I put my clothes on and hand him the rape dough for the rape treatment.

'Unlock the door. I want out of here *now*,' commanding, while I want to run *fast*.

'No, no, no. You shall not pay for today. The treatment is free.' He smirks.

'Free of charge?' Once again, I stare at him dumbfounded while he continues his yakking parrot speech.

'And by the way, you are not finished with the treatment.' Then he waves his hands stupidly in the air, as a chicken with its head cut off.

No! You damn beast, you are right! You are fucking me instead of giving me the treatment!

Dear reader, now you are probably thinking, 'Yes, of course, she must not pay.' But no, no! Not me! I'm not his private little whore, and don't require these kinds of *free* treatments. The cockroach unlocks the door, and I throw the eighty rape euros on his table and want to leave. But this freaking nasty dude is too much and has the audacity to invite me for lunch.

'Let's go down and get some food. Have a beer at the tapas bar,' he suggests. Creep! How tasteless he is.

I will gladly buy you a bottle of insect spray, your nasty maggot, I angrily muse. Most of all, in that instant, I have the angry urge to slam him with a scorching frying iron pan in his handsome face.

'No!' I scream and stalk out of the clinic.

* * *

So, all you wonderful and lovely women around the world. Report your predator! Don't ignore it, because it's not worth it, keeping it a secret or not acting. The risk of lifelong self-indulgence will be sitting within your soul, and always remind you and will never be forgotten. This is not a healthy ability, I must advise. You can't erase it, but you can help yourself to do the right thing. Unpleasantly, I still have my nagging deep down my soul, even though I have survived several nasty crimes against my life.

In 2019, a Danish article noted, 'It is estimated that approximately six percent of the Danish population, has been exposed to forced sex. About sixteen percent of the victims are men, while eighty-four percent of the victims, are women. In most cases, the victim knows the offender.'

'In 2015, in America, one in five women and one in seventy-one men will be raped at some point in their lives. Nearly one in ten women has been raped by an intimate partner in her lifetime. Ninety-one percent of the victims of rape and sexual assault are female, and nine percent are male.'[2]

This is to the many women and men who experience such a horrifying crime. *Not OK!* I wonder how the statistics are in other countries around the world.

Let's now tell the actual story of how my acquaintance with Doctor Drake began.

---

[2] National Sexual Violence Resource Centre Info & Stats for Journalists—Statistics about sexual violence.

CHAPTER 4

Doctor and Patient—Déjà Vu

> The patient has suffered from depression, ever since she began consulting me in 1989.
> —Unknown, *Hilarious Doctors' Journals*

My first meeting at the clinic was the 3rd of August 2010, so I certainly did not meet Drake in 1989. Such nonsense he wrote about me in his doctor files, so I was pretty sure he had made a mistake. Oh, my goodness, he did it so often, so I wonder if it also had happened with many of his other patients. I laughed over his crazy stupidity and his burgeoning memory loss, pondering, *was that what he was suffering from?*

Damn it!

When I think of how he was able to do what he did, I'm extremely disappointed. For three weeks ago I thought he was an appropriate, trustworthy, and pleasant man, but things aren't always as they seem in the many jolly endings of love stories. Damn it! Especially when I backtrack my latest love moments to that year, because it was about to smash me big time when I met him for the first time that summer.

* * *

I naively believe in all the many joyous love stories I watch on TV. Therefore, I know I must make some significant choices with my life this year. I'm hoping my life can be more euphoric than it is and not because of the doctor or my husband but mostly for myself.

I'll turn back three weeks, where strange and mysterious things happen in my female head after I meet Drake that first day. Somehow, he situates some strange ideas in my little not-knowing-any-better female intellect. Without me truthfully realising it myself, he has quickly become a disruptive element in my life. He puzzlingly begins to twist around with my mind from the first day, though I don't notice any wicked red flags that shortly thereafter will appear in front of my nose. I should be much more aware of them, but quite frankly, why think about red flags? I don't have any bad intentions and no reason for involving myself emotionally with a total stranger. I want help with my health condition, and that's the reason I began attending his clinic.

Drake possesses an amazing personality and is more charismatic than my husband, Paul. So, I almost fall over backwards when I meet this stranger for the first time. Quickly Drake chants all the right and most exciting things to me, which I never hear from Paul. I find Drake humorous, appealing, and exciting, even if he has the tendency to brag a little too much. Nevertheless, he gives me lots of compliments on how great I look and how smart and witty I am. So, as any other woman who is searching for personal acknowledgement, I swallow it all uncooked and with the greatest pleasure. It's the sweetest honey in my mouth, with his many sugary words flying like ecstatic buzzing bees around in my brain. I feel as the happiest woman in the world, who has captured the attention of the most amazing man on the planet. He succeeds in giving me a great sense of fulfilment about myself, so I begin to look at myself as a totally different person, feeling great and amazing. But it's not a 'free present' or 'at-no-cost' performance, as it has a price I don't know about. It begins when he becomes interested in knowing as much about me as possible, about my at-the-time 'ill-fated' life.

Suddenly he tells me, 'You are a woman who breathes fresh air into my boring life.'

'Wow! Fresh breath? Ha-ha,' I joke, but what does he mean? Nevertheless, I'm captivated by his magic. But let's begin where my condition began for the first time, when I meet this illusionist of a doctor, and when two doomed people get some 'fresh air!'

A warm summer day in Spain, two days before I met Drake and when I decided to do something new in my life, a good friend Cliff recommended Drake to me. By a coincidence he told me about this fantastic person who might be able to help me with my problem, so I immediately call the clinic for an appointment. *Why not? It can't harm anyone if I try*, I muse. Next, I am convinced it will be helpful for me to try alternative options for treatment, though I have no idea what this magician of a specialist does or how. Out of curiosity, I grab my red Bang and Olufsen phone and call the Harry Potter clinic.

'SW Clinic. This is Kate. How may I assist you?' a woman kindly says.

'Is this the clinic where the famous Doctor Bates performs miracles?' I joyfully ask, then briefly explain my problem, hoping they can help me.

'Ha-ha, just a moment.' she sweetly laughs back, then I hear her asking something to a man in the room. 'I have a new client on the phone. She is asking if we can treat a neuroma?' Then she begins to laugh. 'Ha-ha, ha-ha. Also, she wants to know if it's correct you are performing miracles?' There is dead silence for a few seconds on the other end of the phone. 'Can we help her or not?' she asks the physician once more.

'No problem at all. We can handle anything. Yah, ha-ha even everything. Ha-ha, and yes, I'm a magician,' the fella proudly yells. Kate asks him some more questions concerning me, but I can't hear all his answers when he replies. I have an odd feeling inside when I hear his first words and the rasping sound of his kind speech. I begin to tremble as a minor earthquake and cannot figure out what is happening inside my body and mind. Weird! While I'm waiting for a fast reply from Kate, my thoughts fly insanely, resembling thousands crazy confusing particles in my head. *What's going on? I know this voice.* I'm so sure and become so convinced it is true. No matter what, I must meet the doctor, and the sooner the better.

Wow! I knock myself down like a feather with the odd feeling I suddenly have in my brain. In the same instant, I sense it as a strong déjà vu, as if I truly know him or I have been in the exact same situation before. But of course, I know it's not possible that I ever have seen the Harry Potter chap before.

'Hello?' I ask.

'Just a moment,' Kate replies. 'I need to verify what other info he needs before I make an appointment with you.'

'Eh, I believe for some few years ago.' I pause, thinking.

'When did your problem begin?' She pauses. 'Hmm, I also need your name and address.' I give her my full name and addresses for Spain and Denmark.

'Hmmm, yes, I'm sure now. Hmm, because it came one year after my back surgery. Well, yah, three years ago.'

'OK, it's no problem. We can talk about the rest when you come.' I can hear her turning some pages, probably in her diary. 'Just a second. I've to look in my diary. We are so busy all the time.'

I reason, *Wow! This must be a successful and responsible clinic.*

My thoughts are interrupted when she quickly comes back to me with an answer.

'OK, how about the day after tomorrow. He has a small window there. Are you available?'

'Just a moment. Eh, What time?' I pretend to be looking in my diary as if I am a busy, yea, an important person.

'He has time during the morning. It's at eleven o'clock.'

'Huh? Really? That's fast.'

'Yep! How does it fit into your plans?' she asks. I don't hesitate one split second.

'Ok, yes, yes … great. Of course, I can. Thank you so much. I'm glad about it. Ciao for now. See you the day after tomorrow,' I cheer, then slide, relieved, back onto my sofa.

'See you soon. I'm looking forward to seeing you,' Kate responds and hangs up.

In relief, I toss my phone next to me. She must be his secretary! *Stupid!* Why do such crazy thoughts run through my head? I'm totally eager and exhausted over this experience and are excited to see if the wizard can help. I suffer from this irritating pebble, and I feel as the character in the 'Princess and the Pea' (a fairy-tale story by H. C. Andersen). My orthopaedic surgeon discovered it after an ultrasound scan some years before. I have tried all sorts of different treatments with several different doctors in various clinics. Jeez, I am so tired of all this running from one clinic to another. Oh gosh! The worst thing is the many painful cortisone injections and it hurt like motherfucking shit in between your toes. I have tried different kinds of insoles and so much more of yucky useless stuff. Nothing helps. It's all a waste of money, and I gradually become more frustrated walking on this nerve-wracking knuckle of a pebble. The crunching feeling is so painful on my forefoot, so I'm more than willing to do whatever it takes with regards to treatment. So that is what this magic Harry Potter doctor apparently can provide. I'm certain you have tried something similar if you have had upsetting medical conditions. You are ready to do anything and pay whatever you must do just to get rid of your vast pain. Well, I'm pleased with my appointment and need to wait only few more days before I will meet this mysterious 'déjà vu' doctor. The days are awful, and they can't go by fast enough. 'The snail is coming. Who knows when it arrives?'[3] Christ! It takes ages before it reaches the forest, presuming a car doesn't run it over, and as the snail survives, I do too until the mysterious Tuesday.

    I prepare myself for this glorious morning and wake up early, which is unusual for me, because I love to sleep and snooze until at least ten o'clock in the morning. Despite that, I get up and make myself a quick cup of coffee, then grab my mug and step out onto the rooftop to burn my first cigarette, while I carefully slurp the hot coffee and watch the Sun's final rising over the peak, but I can barely see the ocean. I have not the slightest idea of what to do with myself. Next, I'm extremely confused about how to style my hair, fix my makeup, and choose my clothes. When my morning ritual is done, I move on to the bathroom and stare weirdly into the mirror, while undressing myself, and then

---

[3]   Russian proverb.

jump into the shower. Whereas the water is drizzling, I muse, *it's probably best to tone down the makeup. Nothing too cheeky.* Somehow, my thinking is always the most sensible when I'm showering. The enjoyment of the steamy pouring water over my nude body makes me calm. Every centimetre of my tanned figure is checked for wildly growing dark hairs, including my legs and toes. Awful! I go into a tremor! Some disgusting black wilderness on my flesh pops up. Grrrr! So annoying, backtracking my thoughts that I had several cosmetic laser treatments years before to remove those ugly, unwanted hairs on my legs and armpits,. Mostly those disgusting ones in my groin and female parts. I went nuts about this wilderness in the jungle, and back then, I wanted to get the wild undergrowth removed from my so-called Venus mountain (pubic bone). It appeared sexy afterwards because it ended up with only a small and straight hairline of short-cut hair, resembling a mohawk right on top of the pubic bone. Sexy girl, and my husband loves it, because it provides easy access to the pearl and for his love stick to find my hot cave. Oh my God! Can you imagine searching for a tiny little pearl in a wild scrubby forest? It's as looking for a needle in a haystack, with my husband needing to drill his phallus through all that wilderness of long hairs. So, I got rid of the gigantic mane, yet it still drives me crazy when tiny wild unwanted growths appear. It cost me a fortune to get it done, and unfortunately, it also resulted in some severe burns to the sensitive area, because the stupid laser wench did it all wrong. However, I'm lucky it didn't end up with any scars, so I forgive her, but it's never forgotten, and I never went back for anymore treatment.

Gently, I remove the wilderness, wash my hair and body, jump out of the shower, and wrap a towel around my wet mane and another around my body. Then I get my teeth scrubbed like crazy, so my gums nearly begin to bleed as a bloody massacre, so I rinse my mouth with lots of mouth wash and spit it out again in the sink. I perform this routine several times a day, usually before I go somewhere, because may God forbid if I ever smell bad out of my mouth, so every third month I go to the dentist to get my gums cleaned.

Awkwardly I'm gazing in my closet, *hmmm, what to put on,* then I decide to grab some casual clothes, without appearing too provocative or fancy. Next, I slip my slim, well-trained body into the tight-fitting summery garments of a pair of bright, tight jeans, and a beautiful white top with some delicate lace which fits perfectly with these jeans. My tanned feet are slid into a stunning pair of sandals, covered with lots of glittering white and red Swarovski gems. Finally, the complete 'Mary package' ends up with my hair styled up into a cheeky random tuber behind my neck instead of the braid I had originally decided on. In my opinion, it looks quite good with those many loose, light tuft of hair, randomly hanging down along my ears and neck. It shows that my hair is long and gorgeously coloured in bold, light tones, recently done by my hairdresser whom is an absolute darling and does such a great job with my hair. The makeup ends up in some light, mild shades, as the colours is radiating stunningly and perfectly against my face. The purpose is to make the completed style seem randomly, as if I have not given it any special thought. *Sneaky!* What is the chick up to? you perhaps will think. Nothing, because that's how I normally am. I never go outside my private space without styling the complete pretty doll.

As I finish this morning ritual, I am ready to enter a novel world of hope for an efficient and proper treatment of my annoying condition, that of my damn foot. But first I need to do one more thing before I leave. Some quick puffs off my fag! Shut up! Disgusting! And I smell comparable to an ashtray from the horrible tobacco flavour. Even though I smoke, I dislike the smell and taste of tobacco, but smoking is my only comfort at this or in this horrible time of my life. A quick rinsing with mouthwash to remove all traces of the smelly odour, solves the problem, and off I go.

It's boiling outside, so I take off the hardtop on my black convertible Mercedes sports car, drive off, and resemble a happy million-dollar babe in her flashy car. The drive to downtown is ten kilometres away from my apartment, to my first meeting at the clinic. I don't have any idea what to expect from wizard, so my feelings end up in a complete mess. What to consider? What to believe? What do I tell the warlock? Strangely, the feeling that I know him swirls in my head, but I don't know him at all! Crazy questions strike my head, stupid and not necessary, but something weird is going on in my body and mind.

Fifteen minutes later, I am at the parking lot close by the clinic, though it's a bit early, but better to be timely than to be late. I will not contribute to delaying someone else's program for the day. Belt up! Hooray, I'm so lucky to get a parking spot right in front of the clinic, because yikes, I tell you, normally, it's totally impossible to get a spot downtown. I get the car parked, then fix my windblown hair, roll the hardtop up, close the windows, and lock the Mercedes with a single touch of my remote control. Beep, beep—the auto gives a confirmatory light sound that it's locked. Elegantly I turn to the parking dispenser, buy a ticket, return, and put it inside my windshield. Just to be sure, I glance one more time to see that it's at the right spot, and I lock the car again then gaze in the direction I must go. I ponder, *what is awaiting me? Is this doctor perfect?'* I have not Googled him or tried to figure out who he is, so in theory he can be a quark, fantastic, arrogant, well-educated, or even a fraudster. But I trusted Cliffs opinion about Doctor Bates, so I seize the opportunity. Elegantly I move my corpus in the direction of the clinic's front door, though I'm far too early for the appointment. While I quietly move towards the entrance, I'm considering, *well, I can sit down at the café below, and grab myself a coffee before I go up.* I decide to snatch the coffee and some icy water, then automatically, my hand slides into my black Prada bag and seizes the fags and my pink lighter, to light myself a smoke. Panic grabs me, *shit, my mouth is rinsed with mouthwash.* I'm about to kill the delicious odour with a horrible cup of Spanish coffee with yucky condensed milk. Gross! My heated brain receptors begin to hunger for the taste of the cancer sticks on the table, so I panic—whether to snatch a fag. *Easy, be calm, Mary,* I tell myself. *Your gums recently got a proper clean-up with the toothbrush. The tongue is brushed,. Your mouthwash has been through your mouth many times since this morning.* So, what can I do? I keep on ruminating this way as a heedless, irrational chick. *No, No, No! Leave the ciggy. Put them back in your bag,* my rational brain yells at me. *Grab the fag! Next, take a piece of gum, after you have drunken your coffee,* the little red devil lures me from my shoulder. Oh, golly gosh! At the same time, my head panics again.

Holy moly, what if neither Kate nor Drake smokes? Or drinks coffee … What if they will think it's awful. Eww gross, if I smell of tobacco on my fingers and face? Honestly? Why bother? But those kinds of things unfortunately turn up often in my head when I meet new people. No one can know I'm a smoker, because I'm embarrassed that I smoke, so I often try to hide this miserable addiction until I know whether those around me smoke. And why is it so damn difficult for me to stop this crazy tobacco habit? It's even more difficult to be a smoker in the twenty-first century than in my younger days, when everybody had a fag in their hand.

Why the coffin nails end up in my bag again, I don't know, so instead, I drink my coffee, chew a piece of gum, and spit it out in the nearest flowerbed. I'm damn nervous about what is going to greet me when I gaze at the door in front of the building which I'm about to enter. Slowly I lift my right hand to the doorbell, yuck, it's greasy, so I use the backside of my knuckle of the index finger and carefully press the button of the bell, jingling up to the clinic. A friendly female voice asks in Spanish, 'Hello, who clink the bell?' Luckily, I speak some Spanish.

I do not know why my thoughts fly around in my head resembling a little hummingbird who is not able to find its nest, as there is a strange feeling in my stomach, with millions of tickling butterflies swarming around in my belly. My heart pounds rapidly, though there is no reason for these strange reactions, pondering, *how stupid. It's only an exanimation.*

'Hello, I've an appointment with you now.' I'm invited in with a hum in the speaker, indicating the door is open. I gently push the door inwards with the back of my butt, considering the lift and next I'm glaring at the stairs leading up to the second floor. Which shall I choose? I take the stairs, because it's good exercise for the body and keeps the butt in the right position and the legs free from cellulite.

Everything happens for a reason, I next muse for a moment, and maybe it's fate, or perhaps it's my destiny or some fresh choices in my life. Perhaps because of some unpleasant things forthcoming—lesser people's agendas or a sacrifice I must pursue at any cost. I don't know yet that everything has a reason and that this meeting will have a tremendous cost and effect on my upcoming life.

I find the brown carved entrance door, push it with my shoulder, and enter the clinic, while being welcomed by the secretary, who I assume is Kate.

'Welcome to the clinic. Nice to see you.'

She shows me to the waiting area, where I sit down for five minutes, then she comes smiling back, talking friendly with a previous patient. 'Take care,' she says in Spanish to the woman, and next, she glances at me, kindly telling me, 'He is ready to see you. You can come with me now.' And points in the direction of the treatment room and continues talking, 'Please, come in,' as she opens the door while I'm ten steps behind her. Wow, how friendly she is, and how relaxed. The second before I step into the room and notice him, I feel a peculiar feeling through my body and mind, which is unexplainable. The man's voice says something to Kate, then my heart starts pounding with a fast rhythm. Déjà-vu. My body becomes comically warm, and my legs begin to shake, as were they jelly. But everything happens for a reason, and I'm excited and nervous at the same time about the next mysterious phase in the unknown forthcoming. His voice does something marvellous to my supposedly prior memories. When I take my first step into the room, I notice the handsome man sitting on his office chair, tilting his head and glancing sweetly at me. Déjà-vu. *I've seen that tilting before, but where?* I muse. At the same time, he seems surprised to see me, as if he knows me. *His surprised way of glaring at me seems familiar. But from where?* I muse again. He smiles a gorgeous, stunning grin, gets up, and walks towards me. Oh my gosh, the way he shimmers at me with pleasure and straight into my green eyes. Does he know me? So strange! Yet I'm so amazed and warmed by his catching eyes, something I haven't seen in any other man before. Okay, silly girl, at least not of what I can remember. The excitement of not knowing if I know him rises, and the question from two days earlier is triggered. I grasp I don't know him! I cannot connect him to anything in my past. But why several Déjà-vu? Then I pause, take a deep breath, and settle my mind back to normal. Yet something magical happens when I offer him my hand,

and slowly it slips into his palm, while he takes it gently and squeezes it with tenderness. It was not a normal handshake. Gosh, it was magical. Wow, I have never experienced anything resembling this before, while I feel a warm softness from his palm that I don't understand. What is happening to me in this instant? A mysterious and enigmatic squeeze spreads as strange sparks travel from his palm to mine.

'Hello, my name is Mary,' I say, smilingly.

He won't let go of my palm and watch me intensely, while our palms are melting together into one unit as he now stares at me strangely. Does he know me from somewhere, since he behaves like that? I glance shyly aside, as if I am seeing at something else in the room. In the same moment all this cosmic behaviour happens, I immediately sense his warm, flirtatious hand even more when he puts his other palm on top of mine and twists it slightly downwards. Nervously I pull my hand to myself and stick it anxiously into the pocket of my jeans. His eyes are intense of a nice brown colour and seem gentle and smiling. I am captivated by people with brown eyes, and now his amaze me too, however they somehow show some sorrow and tiredness. Philosophic as I am, I begin to analyse why his glare is so inviting and flirting? Most of all, my belly rumbles with this strange sensation that I know the gentleman, and it is a huge mystery to me, but I have no answer. In the second I meet him, I muse, *where have I met him before?* I'm sure somewhere in the world, because I know his gorgeous rasping Clint Eastwood voice. Then there is something special about the way he gazes at me, as if is he Sean Connery or Michael Douglas. Oh, I adore Sean and Michael, because both have such an amazing foxy glare and is so gorgeously hot. The way the doctor clutches my hand sends me somewhere, to a magical, mysterious space, and it's unexplainable what he does to me in that short instant.

He presents himself with an abundance of polite manners as Doctor Drake Lucifer Bates. No idea who he is! The name does not ring a bell, and I also know straight away I've never met a person with such a strange name before. The name 'Drake' makes me think of a dragon. Oh no! 'Lucifer' I know from my faith, and it reminds me of the fallen angel sent to hell by God. The devil? Holy cow! Goosebumps run chillingly along my spine, but I don't know if they are good ones or bad ones. *Never judge a person by his name or looks*, I ponder. Maybe his mother didn't like him and therefore gave him such distressing names. Anyhow, I will not rule out meeting him before, perhaps related to my husband's work, because we participate in so many significant business-related events with important people. While I stand still in my own misty, creepy thoughts, I haven't heard a word of his reply.

'What can I do for you, Mary?' Standing there frozen in my confusion, I pay hardly any attention to him and his question.

'Hello, where are you? What can I do for you?' he repeats in Swedish. In the same moment, his rasping, delicious voice gives me a wakeup call from my mysterious daydream. I realise I can't have met him because of my husband, since he speaks Swedish, then I start to jabber as a crazy, insecure fool.

'Oh … hmm … you see … hmm … I was operated on a few years ago at a private hospital for sudden back pain after swimming in a pool,' I stammer weirdly. 'Yep … hmm … well … hmm … and just over a year later, I get these peculiar pains in my left foot.' Drake listens intensely to my explanation and gazes deeply into my eyes while I continue in an awkward confusion. 'Hmm … well … yea … it seems almost as … hmm … yes … as I have a tiny stone that is constantly pressing underneath my forefoot. There, close to my toes.' Swiftly, I push my sandals off and point at the painful area. 'Here … yes … right there it is,' I stammer and continue foolishly with my cracked explanation. 'It's so weird … hmm … I can hear a strange crunching sound coming from there when I press it,' I mumble embarrassed.

'Ha-ha, ha-ha. Funny explanation,' he glances at me smilingly, as if it's funny, and laughs.

'Well, it's not funny to me. I am trying to be serious.' Oh, sugar dear! I'm about to faint because of his gorgeous appearance and smile.

'Sit here on the table. Let me have a look.' Gently, he takes my foot into his hands and stares at it. In the same second, I begin to muse why I am having this sensation that we have met. Did we meet in a previous life? I know his voice—that's for sure. I have had the déjà vu experience! I felt a strange connection when he reached out for my hand. Gosh almighty! And now, when he holds onto my foot in his tender warm hands, I sense that hundreds of years ago, he performed the same movement, giving me the same touch and glare. Early eighteen hundred? I can't figure out what the connection is between us. *Weird! Truly mysterious!* I meditate. Though I have experienced déjà vu before with other people I met, never could I explain this ability. Sometimes I can also see things in the future or see an episode of something that has happened, often I've a strange stomach feeling of what happens to another person, but I mostly overrule the skill. In the old times, you got burned for it and were called a witch. Was I a sorceress? Ha-ha, there is always a reason for everything. There is also always a price for what you chose to do. The saying goes through my witchy mind, then he interrupts me with a new question and his intense magic dazzle.

'Is it here where it hurts the most?' He squeezes the painful area.

'Yes … ouch… yew, that's the exact spot.' I'm about to kick him in his handsome face, but instead, I tell him about my previous treatments. 'It has been scanned several times. All other doctors told me it's a neuroma.' He listens carefully to my explanation.

'Aha, hmm.' while he tenderly holds my foot in his hands and caresses it with his fingertip on the plantar part having his thumb on the upper side.

I try to ignore it. 'Oh yeah … I have also had several cortisone injections. Ouch, directly into the nerve. Damn, and in between the toes. But nothing seems to help.'

'Oh my God. That must have hurt badly. Where did you get the injection done?' he asks gently, eyeing at me with a strange blinking expression. Virtually flirting.

Sweet Jesus, he reminds me of a cute baby deer. Wow, is he like that to all his patients? I consider.

'Yes, right there it is.' I'm pointing with my finger to the foot and continue to tell him about my many treatments. 'Ugh, I tell you, those injections actually *hurt so damn much*. Damn, yes, as a pounding devilish pain,' I answer

Sweetly he glimpses at me with those cute deer eyes and smiles.

'The orthopaedic spoke about an operation. Uhf, I'm not so keen on that,' I continue anxiously.

'Hmm, I understand. The injections are not good for you. They destroy too much of the good tissue.' He caresses again with his fingers over the problematic area. 'I'm also certain it's a neuroma.'

'Really? How can you know?'

'Let me first scan it. Then I can find the exact point. Just a moment.' He turns on his scanner, takes a bottle of gel, smashes some freezing cold ultrasound mass on the foot, and scans it at many different angles. Kate sits in the background of the room, listening to what is going on. Then she asks him some professional questions and enters the information into her computer. I don't understand anything he is saying when he abruptly shouts out of the blue, 'Oh my God! Now I see something strange.

'Huh? Eh? Eyh? Is that right?'

'Oh, yea, something which should not be there.' His outburst scares me.

'Is it a cancer nodule?'

'Ha-ha, no worries. I can help you.' He smirks, and I stare with fear at the scanner, not knowing what he has found.

'I promise you. I'll fix this for you. You will be good as new again. It's an easy kind of work to fix,' he continues without giving me any further explanation. I feel relieved and take a heartfelt breath, considering whether I will continue with treatment. The odd sensation in my belly doubts whether his promises are true. No one else has been able to help me, so how can this Harry Potter magician swing his magic wand and make such a promise? But I must decide between the operation, in two months, or Drake's promise.

'Okay, let's begin the treatment—if you have the courage to do it,' he smirks and interrupts my considerations. 'At the same time, I also believe it will be a good idea if I adjust your back. Oh! Perhaps also your neck.'

'Hmm, I'm not sure. Why?'

'Ohhh, as the problem may well come from your lower back. And your neck after your many car accidents,' he says proudly, which surprises me.

'Many car accidents?' Where did he get that idea from?

'You've definitely had a whiplash,' he concludes.

'I haven't the slightest idea what you are talking about.' Hasn't he listened to me? 'I told you my problem came from a swim in the pool.' Jeez, to me, it appears he is taking it for granted I will immediately let him treat me. 'You haven't even explained what the whole treatment plan is about.'

'I'll explain in a second.'

'I don't know what whiplash is.'

'It comes from your car accident.' He smirks.

'I said it was only *one* accident. It was more than thirty years ago.' I correct him. He stares annoyed at me.

'Oh! Well, let me think. What I do is the best.'

'Why is that a reason for the little pebble under my foot?'

'I'm the best in human anatomy.'

'It makes no logical sense.' Clearly, he is irritated at my questioning his skills. I don't even know the after-effect of what he will do to me. What will the complete package cost me?

'I'll help you. Such a beautiful woman who needs my help.' He smirks, and rapidly, he convinces me to do the treatment. Honestly! I must admit, I believe he is my last hope after so many fantastic stories Cliff has told me. So why not give it a chance? Still, I was not expecting Drake's back and neck treatments, which he plans for me.

'I still don't understand what my neck and back have to do with this pebble in my foot?' I glare nervous at him with a big question mark.

'Don't you worry your pretty little head about that.' He smirks. Sexist! Woman oppressor! 'In a moment, I'll examine your neck and back.

'But why is that necessary? I have no problems in my neck and back.'

'I'll give you some qualified answers, afterward,' he brags.

'I'm sure everything is fine.' I don't want to tell him I do occasionally have back pain, when I've been working too much.

'Remember my swim accident. You know, few years ago,' I express hesitantly. This seems to irritate him even more, and he responds rudely, which I don't like. His speech becomes unpleasantly strict.

'Okay, let me just check it.' He growls. 'Then we can exclude it. If necessary,' he commands briskly.

'What if it will be dangerous?'

'It's not! I treat the foot first. No worries. It will all be good again. I know what I'm doing. Trust me,' he barks, and I dare say nothing.

'Are you sure?'

'Get down from the treatment bench. Sit on the chair in the middle of the room,' he growls. 'Then I can examine you.' He becomes friendly again and smiles. He rolls my head in different directions—left, right, forward, and backwards—to see whether there is a proper movement or if it's stuck somewhere in my spine. He doesn't say anything.

'Okay, stand up. Open your trouser button.'

'Huh? What? Why?'

'Just do as I say. Then turn around with your back towards me.' He scoops down my waistband a little, pushing and pressing several spots on my lower back.

'Lift your right leg. Yep, okay, now lift your left leg.' He is silent other than those tiny piggy sounds coming on occasion.

'Hmm … hmm … mumble … grumble … weeeelll …'

'Oh dear! I still don't understand the link between my neck, back, and foot.'

No answer, so I suppose this goofy guy knows what he is doing. I must trust him. I'm in his power! Trust is properly the most dangerous thing I can give away!

'May I ask, what have you figured out?'

'Not now.' Goofy grumbles.

'Hmm, when I did the surgery a few years ago, the surgeon removed my disc.'

'What? Why? Don't you have any disk there?'

'Oh, yeah. He inserted a movable implant in my lower back.'

'Oh, okay… hmm… What kind of implant did you get?'

'Hmm, if I remember correctly, hmmm, it's a movable disc replacement. I think it's a relatively new method.'

'New method. How so?'

'It's only used on few other patients with back worsening disc problems. I'm not certain if it's a new treatment,' I reply smartly and continue.

'I do not understand.'

'I think it's a titanium thing. I'm then able to move the spine in all-natural directions.' I'm clearly no expert, but I'm trying to sound clever.

'I have not the slightest idea what model this is. I will do my best to take all the precautions off any treatment in that exact area,' as he continues his examination. 'Why did you have the surgery in the first place?'

'They told me it was necessary.'

'Why? Have you never consulted any physio?'

'I did physio for a while. It didn't help.'

'What about a chiropractor?'

'Well, I've actually done some chiropractic. Nothing worked.'

'Have you tried an osteopath?'

'I don't know what an osteopath is. That I've not tried.'

'My field is occupational therapy. As physical therapy focused on injuries and rehab. It's better as and osteopath. I treat mostly back, neck and shoulder problems. You must do that as the first thing!' he slickly concludes.

'I have done some special rehabilitation.'

'Argh! Damn! For heaven's sake! Surgeons are always so quick to put people under the knife. Even before all other solutions are tried out,' he thunders with a brusque and grumpy expression. He for sure, has a lot of antipathy towards other doctors and surgeons. I've not understood if he is a chiropractor or an osteopath, but I don't care if he can help me.

'So, what do you find out?'

'You have a bad whiplash.'

'What?'

'Yay, phew, this is affecting your upper and lower vertebrae. You are stuck in the topmost C1. And C7, which is the lowest parts of your neck.'

'What is a vertebra? Sounds as a women's bra.'

'Ha-ha, that's the one I have to loosen up. With my special technique,' he insists.

'So, how can you help me?' I ask when he finishes the pre-examination. 'Also, what have you else decided to do with my neck and spine?'

'I do it with this equipment,' he points at it, 'as well, I'll do the manipulation of your neck. And your spine.'

'Wow, sounds dangerous.' I am scared. 'What are those machines for?'

'It's not dangerous; nor does it have any side effect at all.'

I stare curiously at the machine, next to me. 'I've never seen or heard about such a machine before. Does this neck thing hurt? I've never tried it,' I peep, and feel he is getting upset with my questions.' He scowls at me and thinks I don't trust him. But trusting him is important to me, which is why I'm asking so many questions.

'Eh? What? Oh, I'll explain and show you in a minute,' he says briskly, and suddenly his voice breaks, adopting a much nicer tone, smooth and lovely.

'Lie down on the bench.' I lie down on my back. 'Argh, no, no. On your stomach.'

'Okay ... okay.' And I put my head in the hole of the table.

'Oy, with your feet towards me. I'll fix the foot first,'

His voice rapidly changes from smiling and gentle to annoyed and brusque, until it quickly returns to sweet and sometimes a little sly. It confuses me tremendously during all my questions and his answers.

'Several years ago, I learned the skills of this new subject.' He opens with his bragging about how successful he is and has been for many years with his treatment protocol in Spain.

'Oh!. Interesting,' I mumble.

'Yay. Hereafter, I decided to use it together with my other treatment protocol.' He seems nice and highly knowledgeable in what he does. 'I'm the best. The only one in this country doing such bone and soft tissue treatment.' He briefly explains what the machine does and what effect it has on the body. I don't understand any of it.

'You see, I'm the expert. I have worked with my skills for nearly forty years.'

'Oooh. Wow!'

'Yea, so *trust me*. I know what I'm doing,' he defends himself, bragging in the extreme. Sweet Jesus! I realise his self-confidence doesn't fail him at all, and he has managed to boast about being the best and only doctor in Spain who can treat me.

'Blimey! That's fantastic. Indeed!' I shout as I sense he feels he is the best practitioner in the entire world.

'I'll help you. Trust me. Such a pretty little girl needs my help.'

'Strange, I've never heard about such treatments before. And never of you.' But he seems to be a great doctor, so maybe what he's telling me is all true. Who knows? We will soon find out!

CHAPTER 5

THE DOCTOR'S FOOT FETISH

Never trust advice from a man in the throes of his own difficulty.

—Aesop

The doctor has a different agenda for me, and from the moment he greets my hand and presents himself, I feel comfortable in his presence, but there is something mysterious about him.

'Well, Mary. Let's get started. OK?'

'As you wish.'

'I have full control over it. I know how I want to treat you.' He smirks and flutters his Bambi eyelashes. I turn my head and glance at him, when he initiates the treatment. With me positioned on my stomach, he gently, carefully, and calmly moves the weird device in his hand, while his left hand has a tender hold of my left foot, as he is holding the machine's treatment head, pointing it directly on the plantar part. Then I hear the first clicking wave, hitting as a nerve-racking painful shot on the underside of my forefoot. Afraid, I jump up as an angry pistol shrimp.

'Yeow, for goodness' sake! Damn that hurts!' I scream as it hits me with an unexpected blow. I almost give him a knockout blow, using my other leg as a weapon. Lucky for him, I don't connect with my prey and hit him straight in his face or stomach. However, most of all, I wish the effect is powerful if I *do* kick him. Aching me like that, he deserves to be laid out on the floor, paralyzed and no longer able to move and hurt me.

'Ha-ha. Come on. It can't be that bad.' Smilingly, he gawks at me and continues his sadistic treatment with no warning.

'Oww, ouch, fucking hell,' I swear once more. 'What the hell are you doing? It hurts like crazy,' I roar, and I try, as an eel, to twist my body so I can get up and leave the clinic. Impossible! The bloke keeps on holding firm and irritating my ankle.

'You must lay still. Otherwise, I can't aim the area I'm pointing at,' he irritated demands and I obey the sadist and remain grudgingly on the table for his nasty work.

'Honestly, what are you doing? Are you giving me electrical shocks?'

'Calm now. No worries.' The dude grumbles.

'Do you know what you are doing? It hurts so badly.'

'I know what I'm doing,' he angers.'

'How long will this take?' I am angry and worried, and I have lost my faith in him.

'I'll turn down the energy.' The next instant he is nice, and the treatment continues with less pain, so I calm down. The next blow is a surprisingly wicked outburst coming from him out of the blue.

'Whoa! Look, Kate. Mary has such a sweet, tiny foot, like yours.' With a rapid movement of distress, I turn my head in shock. I almost fall from the table but manage to grab on the side before I tilt over the edge. Eyeing flabbergasted at him, I muse, *Oh my golly gosh! Did he say what I just heard?* I want to kick and knock him out; which I should have done a few minutes ago. Unexpectedly I notice how he tilts his head at a specific angle, smiles kindly, and glances intensely and flirtatiously straight into my eyes. *Where in the heaven's name is all this coming from?* I muse and shy turn my eyes towards Kate to see her reaction. She is boiling inside with anger as she hammers the keyboard on her computer, and her angry red face is like ripe tomatoes. I glance confused at Drake again, nervously meditating, *Excuse me? Honestly, Doctor Dickhead, such things you can't say. I'm your patient!* but don't dare to say it out loud. However, at the same time, I'm also sweet-talked by his comment and the sugary way he glimpses and smiles at me. I simply can't figure him out. Neither can I figure out if she is merely his secretary or his wife. While he continues the treatment, he asks many questions about me and Paul. Oh, crikey! I don't want him to know that much about us.

'I understand you—and especially your husband—are famous hotshots,' he surprisingly says.

'What? Why do you think so?' *Where has he heard such things? The thoughts go through my confused head as I stare at him quizzically.*

'I read some articles about him.'

'Well… oh, I don't know if you could call him a hotshot?' I comeback, shy and embarrassed. Puzzled, he gazes at me again.

'Well, he is obviously a good earner,' he comments bizarrely.

Strange chap! I silently reflect, next I answer him 'Okay! Who has given you such an enlightenment?' *Not me!* So, my brain swirls and becomes confused in my tiny female head. I have not the farthest idea why he is behaving like this and asking such questions, as I'm finding it unusual from a doctor to his patient. I hardly ever see any doctor, but I know my GP is not like Drake. I have never experienced such conduct before.

'It must be so nice for you to have a summer residence here on the South Coast?' The chit-chatting parrot don't stop. 'I can see from your address you live in an expensive area!' the singing bloke continues, faster, resembling a rapper rushing to get his words out of his mouth. I turn my head again, and, gosh, he smiles so sweetly nearly flirtatious at me.

Shut up, so cute. 'It seems to that you know more about us than I do.' *Jeez, has he Googled us?* I feel intimidated, and out of curiosity.

'Are you happy? Sorry, I mean, with the apartment?'

I turn my head again and notice his smirking smile, then respond smilingly and well-behaved. 'Yes, I'm thrilled with it,' *but not my private life*, I muse and continue, 'Mostly it's me coming here. I have done that for many years. I've been here for some months so far.' I pause a second to consider what I more I want to tell him.

'Oooh, how lovely.'

'Oddly, I've never seen or heard about you and Kate before. Gasp, but it seems to I have been here many years more than you!' It's a weak reply, and I gasp deeply and nervously, while he examines me as I try to continue. 'How long has—'

He rudely interrupts me in the middle of my sentence.

'Ohhh, when are you going back again?'

'Well, hmm, I haven't decided yet.'

'Yea, it's so typical! I see! Rich people always have so many pleasures!'

'Whoa! What a strange comment.' What does this goofy dude mean by *rich*?

'I suppose you have an extended summer holiday.'

'Huh? A longer vacation? I'm not on vacation.'

'Yea, perhaps longer than many others have from work?' He strikingly smiles, and I muse, *Strange observations*.

'No, no, no, it's not like that. Ha-ha, I have free all year round,' I wittily reply and burst out in laughter together with him. Kate casts us a harsh glare as a cranky bull.

'Okay, I fully understand now. So lucky you are. And fortunate that you can afford it. Well, I'm almost done. I'll continue with your back. Next the neck,' he cheerful explains as if this is completely natural.

The treatment session is almost over. The first thirty minutes have gone faster than a racehorse can run, then he starts his manipulations of my neck and back. Not that I still understand what it has to do with my foot. However, he is convincing and tells me it's necessary, so I allowed it.

'You see, Mary, this is how the body is connected as a whole system. No doubt, you suffered whiplash after your accident. Yea, from younger days,' he tries to convince me, but I honestly don't understand his conclusion. Christ! For some strange reason, he gets it all wrong in his head, saying I have always had back issues.'

'Ay, that was not what I told you earlier.' He manages to adjust my neck. 'Aya caramba! Are you a sadist? Ouch, it pains me too much.' He smirks while it is sending unpleasant signals through my body. Out of agony, I want to smack him in his face, but I don't. Instead, I grab his hand and pinch it!

'Well, you are too stuck.'

'Damn, it goes through my upper shoulder. Aw, aw, and down to my arm. Shit, and now to all my fingertips.' I'm shaken! I'm terrified!

Afterwards, it is time for my back. Oh, my poor life. I never asked him to help kill me. And to top it off, he is unsuccessful at treating the lower back, despite all the hard work.

'I've decided not to do more on your neck and back today. I can instead advise you to come again. It is important that you come as soon as possible,' he suggests.

I notice Kate's mood has changed from kind and accommodating towards me to surprisingly vicious and jealous. Something must have annoyed her during Drake's treatment session, and she stares at me oddly. Angrily she hands over the bill for the therapy, breeding the text: 'First, study of patient; ESW-treatment of foot. Manipulation of neck and back. Net cash: 180 euros.'

I almost fall over backwards.

'Whoa! That was expensive.' But no one told me the price beforehand. So, no matter what, I must pay the damn dough for a sadistic treatment in hell. At the same time, I remain surprised and speculate about her sudden anger. I haven't the farthest idea why she suddenly treats me in such a ruthless manner.

'Can I pay by credit card?' I kindly ask, as I grab my card from my slender purse and hand it over to her.

'No way,' she growls rudely. 'You may not! We accept only cash payment.'

Gloomy money, I muse. Normally I never carry that much money in my purse, so I stick my hand into the bag again to see how much coinage I have. Luckily, there is precisely enough cash, so I hand her a mixed bundle of banknotes and then glare at Drake.

'When do you want me to come back?' I question him.

'Can you come again tomorrow?' he says with a smirk.

'That quickly? That seems fast. But okay. What time?' I notice his smirk again.

'Great. Come in the morning. Do we have time around ten?' he glares at Kate, then glances at me again and jokes, 'OK, if it fits into your amazing vacation program?' And laughs at his own joke.

Come on dude! I ponder, bemused, but I accept the appointment.

CHAPTER 6

Dragging Me into His Darkness

> There's a sucker born every minute.
> —P. T. Barnum

At this early stage, I have not realised what kind of an artist Drake is. A con artist? I must first learn a difficult lesson before I realise how many suckers are born into the madness and darkness of this world—and that he might be one of them. In my faith to him, I'm wise enough not to completely trust a person as him. However, I come to the appointed session this morning at ten o'clock. Kate is still mysteriously angry at me, and not as kind as she was yesterday. On the other hand, he welcomes me instead, with warmth and kindness, taking my hand into his soft warm palm, and gives me a gentle, almost loving squeeze, then smiles in a sweet and mildly sensual way.

'Well, sweet Mary. How has it been with your *cute little foot* today?' he begins, then sits down on his chair and writes down some notes on a piece of paper. This is supposed to be my medical journal, and it looks strange and unprofessional, but at least he writes something down. *Kate will properly bring it up to date later when she is at her computer,* I muse gladly.

'I haven't noticed any change at all,' I reply truthfully, disappointed.

'Okay, jump up on the table. Let me scan you again.' With a rough movement, he again smashes some cold gel on my foot, and a freezing coldness shot along my spine, as I shake for a second. The way he holds my foot and scans it, it's as he is in love with it. What is he doing? Though, I try to avoid my speculations by talking to him.

'To be honest. Hmmm, I think it hurts a lot more today than yesterday. It feels as I'm walking with a heavy lump of lead,' I dare to say while he continues scanning it.

'Grumble, hmm, oh. Good that you are honest. You must be. It's dark and scary when people are dishonest,' he grumbles, leaving me to ponder this mysterious sour answer. 'Well, I'm also going to be honest with you. I'm convinced there're many positive things already occurred. I can see the pebble has notably flattened. Yea, even diminished.' He smirks, and I have a weird feeling. Is he lying to me? He seems to be proud as he tells me about the news.

'Turn your head. I will show you how to see it on the scanner.' Oh, my ... he smiles so charmingly, then I turn my head to the scanner.

'I don't get anything out of it.' What knowledge do I have reading these strange grey, black, and white pictures on the screen? Instead, I firmly believe his words even though I am in enormous pain. Trust is an important thing for me, so I trust him.

'OK, are you ready to continue?' he asks with a stunning smile on his face, then I allow him to carry on shooting me with his exciting equipment. I speculate why he is turning up the intensity. He gives me a creepy yet gentle gaze, as if he is doing this on purpose, testing the limits of my pain.

'Does it hurt?' he tested me with false pity.

What do you think, you piece of shit?

'Ouch, yea, it's more painful than yesterday,' so again, I want to kick him to the underworld. The harder the kick, the better. Where I a horse, I would kick him right in his stomach and face. What a mess that would be. I giggle as I imagine him lying flat on the floor, kicked black and blue by ten horses. Somehow, it is as horrible as what he is doing to me, and next, I wish he was bleeding dead on the floor. I don't want him to think I'm a stupid chicken, so I wrinkle my nose at him. From my childhood, I've learned to handle my pain and that no man shall ever hurt me again. So instead, I just occasionally swear when things get too painful.

'Shit, and yes, of course it hurts. It's not nice. Can you do something about it?'

He lowers the intensity of the energy, then smirks at me, blinks his eyelashes slowly, and continues with his 'electrifying' treatment.

He's behaving the exact same way as the day before, maybe a bit slicker. Somehow, he is strangely flirtatious and caresses my foot. It's more as he is petting me, turning to see how I react when I occasionally turn my head towards him. Does he suffer from foot fetish?

'I'm done now. Open your pants. Shove them down a little bit,' he commands.

'Oh, I thought you were done. Why do I have to open my pants?' I ask nervously.

'I will examine your lower back again. That's why.'

I shove down the pants a little, then he begins to palpate me and comes up with some new body issues I'm supposed to have.

'You have several lumps in this specific area. On your iliac crest.' I can feel him press hard on top of some bones.

'Where? What is that?' I don't understand any of what he said.

'Here. Yes, I can feel them. Right there. It's as a big, tough lump.' He presses hard on it again. 'Not good. This is what causes back pain. I'll fix them now,' he decides without asking me, and begins the treatment, using that nasty, insane energy from the bloody machine on the sore spot, hitting my lower back bones.

Fucking bastard, I ponder, and then jump several times, as were I an angry pistol shrimp, shooting cannonballs on my prey. After five minutes of his obscure cruelty, he finally stops.

'Phew. Are you done?'

'Yep, you can get up now. Sit on the chair in the middle of the room,' he commands.

'What are you going to do now? Aren't we done?' I scowl worried.

'No, no, I'm not finished. I have to check your neck.' The moment he says neck, *Klong! Crash!* He swiftly just performs the same nasty twist and turns my head without warning and is adjusted painfully.

'Ouch, damn,' and I grab his hand and pinch it. 'Shit, you must be a sadist. That hurts damn much. It's the same shitty feeling. As being electrified from my neck, shoulder, and arm. It goes all the way down to my fingertips,' I fume, and then the treatment is over.

'Can you come again in two days?' He glances at me begging me, then pauses and stares at Kate as a sneaky man who has something to hide. 'It would be great if you could come in the morning,' he asks while he gives me a smashing flirtatious glimpse. What is the sneaky chap up to? It became clear to me I got caught up in his intrigues and begin to catch on that he is inappropriately flirting with me; phew, him as a doctor and I as his patient. But I kept telling myself he was a moral, kind, elderly gentleman with nothing bad in him. It-had to be a joke.

'Okay, I can. What time?' I ask, certain the treatment must have some effect. With that in mind, I give him another chance. At the same time, Kate erupts as a volcano. As a massive firecracker, she burst out in rage and nearly falls off her chair. Something set her off when she heard him propose another appointment in two days. I don't have the slightest clue why her reaction is so fierce, and I stare at her with surprise.

'You can't do that,' she scolds him. 'You know we have plans on your birthday.'

Drake spins and gives her a fierce, determined stare, then his eyes burned with anger, and he hisses, 'Honestly, behave yourself, Kate. What's the matter with you? It's not a whole-day arrangement.' He pauses, glances at me with a smirk and continues, 'when I *ask* Mary to come back that day, she will come back. No matter what arrangement we have. Is that understood?' He turns his head towards me again and smiles mildly, next his smile turns downwards sourly when he stares at the grumbling Kate again.

'Why can't you do as I say? Make the appointment, Kate. No reason for panic. Wow, such rude behaviour.'

Reluctantly, she makes the appointment with me, writing the date and time on an appointment card and handing it over to me in irritation. I feel simultaneously drawn towards him and scared shitless of him. This is where I find out, when the handsome doctor begins to sink into his mania of manipulation and deception. I cannot believe he is capable of such evilness. Her fearless reaction on top of it all worries me. Why would she be so angry and irritable at *me*! Straight away, it makes me more nervous. How will she behave in my future treatments? She's as a wild black panther, set on fire, ready to sink her long, sharp claws into my flesh. Next, I imagine she will rip out my heart and tear me into millions of pieces. After I pay her, she fearless raises her forefinger at me and points in the direction of the door, indicating, *get out!*

'Yes, the door is there. You can find your way yourself,' she yells. But *why me?* What have I done to deserve such bad treatment from her?

I put on the rest of my clothes, grab my bag, and reach my hand out to Drake to say goodbye. Silently, I slip worried and embarrassed out of the room with a strange bad taste in my mouth. I feel Kate's behaviour is unprofessional of thinking, but I somehow feel it's my fault. Does Drake flirt with other women as well, or is it just me? I have not the slightest idea. Is there something wrong in their relationship, private or business-wise? And so, what? What does it matter to me? Not my problem! But somehow, I feel sympathy for Kate, having seen Drake's peculiar and strange performance in the clinic, and I feel doleful feelings for her. After all, he let her down on this special day, something which I can easily relate, as my own husband often does the same to me. Mostly by changing plans or failing to follow through with an arrangement I've looked forward to, sometimes for a long time. At the same time, I also feel sorry for him, though Kate is entitled to get angry, but *not* at me, but be angry at Drake's unethical and uncivilised treatments upon me as his patient. Maybe he only is trying to small talk with me in a clumsy way, and she is mistaking this for flirtatious. Perhaps he wants me to see and feel sorry for him so he can win my sympathy? Too many excuses and questions swirl around in my head, but anyhow, he must take responsibility for what he has done today. Don't hide in your own shady darkness, and don't drag me into this horrendous darkness of yours, I ponder and haven't yet realised what his plans are for me.

Trusting him with my fragile life, I therefore don't see he might be as Dr Jekyll and Mr. Hyde, and quickly I become blinded to *his* truth, as a foolish woman, and can't see the dominating, insistent part of his personality.

After this horrendous issue, I go through the waiting room and into the ladies' room, and relieved, I let my water slip into the toilet bowl. When I'm finished, I wash my hands and left quietly out the door, running down the stairs, and begin to muse, *what in heavens name am I doing here? They are crazy at this clinic—most of all, him.*

Outside, excruciatingly hot weather greets me. Over my right shoulder, I glare for a vacancy at the café below the clinic, but the café is almost fully occupied, though I see a small table with two white plastic chairs close to the road. I'm not certain I want to sit there without any parasol or shade, but I flop my butt on the chair and order a sandwich, some water, and a cappuccino. Swiftly, the cappuccino arrives together with my water. The thought that it is usually served in the reverse order runs through my mind, and it takes ages before the sandwich arrives.

Out of the corner of my eye, I abruptly see Kate and Drake, both stomping angrily out of the entrance door, next, passing my table. I can clearly sense that she is still moaning about something and does not so much as notice the shadow of my presence. But Drake smilingly and unexpectedly walks towards me.

'Looks cosy. Are you having some lunch before you head home?'

I smile. 'Well, might as well do it now while I'm in town.'

'Well, no matter what just happened up there, it is great to meet you. You are a lovely breath of fresh air.'

'What do you mean by that?' As I'm glaring strange at him.

He continues chatting in a hyper and ecstatic manner. 'I so much look forward to seeing you again. In two days, okay? Have a great day.' He gently takes my hand, slides his palm into mine, squeezes it softly, and lifts it to his heart. Then he goes off. Content and ecstatic, he walks elegantly towards Kate, as I notice that she has stopped at the pedestrian crossing, waiting for him. Curious, I observe him strolling away. Jeez, his way of walking is captivating, so he appears graceful, firm and sexy, almost as if he is floating on a white cloud. Oh dear! Silly me,

I'm captivated, staring to see if he grabs her hand, because my curiosity needs to be satisfied. Are they husband and wife?

Holly Moly. Why am I prying like this? I feel completely heedless, but somehow, I can't let go, so I keep observing them, as a Russian spy, glaring to see where their car is parked, and it's on the opposite side of the street. Kate gets in on the driver's side, and he sits next to her. She starts the car, puts it in reverse, and backs angrily out of the parking lot, and speeds away in the direction of downtown. My female hormones are flushed—sudden hot flashes and palpitations—and I then I feel cold. What is going on in my silly head? Why do I have such crazy reactions? Quickly I let my thoughts go in another direction, towards Paul. Oh, my sugar dear! I miss him quite a lot.

After drinking my coffee and my bottle of water, finally, the waiter comes out with my sandwich. I gnaw on it with pleasure and rinse it all down my throat with another bottle of liquid. Ten minutes later, I pay my bill and go to my car. It is boiling hot, when I plant my still aching body on my cognac-coloured leather sports seat, so I roll down the windows and the hardtop. Strange thoughts rush through my mind as I drive home, pondering, *jeez, what a day. What a weird experience.*

Dear friends—for I believe that is what you have become to me by now—you are probably thinking, *Mary seems to be smart. Not naïve. Nor fragile. Surely, she must see through Drake's game. Something does not add up correctly with his behaviour.*

However, if I had already seen it by now, there would be no more story to tell. No, Mary does not yet see the complete picture—his tricky plot, his manipulative spider web, and does not see she is a little fly buzzing dangerously closer. His first game is about to begin in earnest, the deep darkness of his evil agenda. He needs to make several big moves to weaken the position and assure my compliance, a cruel play against a weak and breakable woman is about to begin. Will she soon end up as a character in his drama?

CHAPTER 7

Family, Love, Deception, and Lies

> Families are the compass that guide us. They are the inspiration to reach great heights, and your comfort when we occasionally falter.
>
> —Brad Henry

Restless I wander around in my Spanish summer residence, thinking of Drake and Kate's bizarre behaviour. My mixed feelings over him and my own marital problems confuse me. To get my mind on something else, I start cleaning all the rooms after my boys' and husband's vacation, many weeks before. Sadly, the holiday has been awful, which makes me sorrowful, as the bad turbulence between Paul and me arose during those two weeks, which was a nightmare. Again, I've discovered that he has an affair, and desperately, I try to stop it, but he denies it and comes straight to my face with so many lies. Thousands of excuses, when he always stays on the phone with the concubine, or when his phone jingles, he mysteriously disappears into another room. Then it's not possible to hear what he talks about—not that I want to know it, but it's his pattern of sneaking away that annoys me. He normally never does so when his conscience is clean. The pattern is always the same, and the thought strikes my mind: *The call girl must sincerely miss him a lot, since she constantly phones him, from early morning until late at night.* But as Helen Rowland quoted; Every man wants a woman to appeal to his better side and his nobler instincts—and another woman to help him forget them.

'Why do you always walk away when the phone clinks? You normally never do that when it's business related,' I politely question him. He becomes more nervous and restless than usual when my question arrives straight to his face. He often needs a few extra seconds, sometimes minutes, to think about his response to me.

'Such a strange performance.'

Normally he gives a quick answer to everything, when he is telling the truth. When he lies to me, I always know, because I'm sensitive to people's lying and their awkward conduct. He always scratches his ear and nose in a typical manner. I have learned to recognise these moments over our twenty years of marriage. Sometimes I truly want to burst out in laughter when he begins to rub his right earlobe. Oh boy! Next, he uses his right-hand forefinger to rub under his nose. Finally, he squeezes the nostrils and tip of the nose with his right thumb and index finger. Identical movements and an unchanging procedure, every time. It's imprinted onto my brain and eyes, as a movie that runs repeatedly in my head. With his beautiful Safire-blue eyes, he will stare down, then to the left, and then the lie arrives, and next, the rubbing and eye movements. The lie is always a long, incoherent explanation, usually impossible to understand. I have witnessed these reckless apologetic stories so many times. Sometimes he tells me it's because of confidential cases.

'Mary, it's overtime hours!'
'Bullshit!'
'I don't know when I will be home.'
'Gibberish!'
'I've a board meeting at 8 PM, today.'
'Baloney! Why that late?' More lies on top of all the other lies, and so, the charade goes on, the entire spring and summer. Awful!

What a nightmare! Lying bastard. My anger can no longer be expressed in reasonable words, nevertheless, I adore my family, and I'm proud of them all. I love my husband unconditionally, and I have a unique relationship with each of my children. I feel I have achieved something great with them as a loving mother and wife, something my mother and father never achieved when I was a child. I wanted to break the evilness in our family and walk in a different direction, most of all, to provide a better life. It will break my heart deeply, into thousands of pieces, if I ever lose the complete package of my dream. The dream of having an all-embracing, idyllic family life, like those I see in American movies. That is essential to me. But my entire life suddenly seems full of many *full-sized ugly lies*! Again, with another woman of the street is interfering in the happiness I believe I have with my husband. I hate it! Or rather, I am disgusted by it, because I'm not a hate-filled person. But lies, unfaithfulness, untruthfulness, and abuse are things I can't deal with. Despite what Paul does to me, I keep on loving him deeply in my heart and won't let go of him for anything in the world—especially not to another strumpet. So, I keep on forgiving him, and he is totally forgiven.

I can also feel how it affects the boys, because their mood is not perfect this summer, and it makes me sorrowful on their behalf. They must suspect something is wrong, but how shall I talk to them about this little harlot. I don't know. They are too young to comprehend such betrayal from their father, and I have no intention to paint any bad pictures of such a nympho an him in their mind. I do not want to show them that he is not what he pretends to be, and not the man they look up to. The children and my dogs are my comfort when things occasionally falter, but this time, no one can ease my pain. You will probably think again—and I don't blame you— 'Why isn't she at all pleased? She is Danish, and Denmark is the happiest country in the world!'

'Ha-ha, yea, right!'

I wonder who can tell me, under which are we to measure such happiness? Welfare, I suppose! In my mind, no one speaks about unhappiness in their private life. Is it taboo? So, for me, enough is enough, with Paul's chicks! This is the last straw! I decide after the family goes back that I will no longer think about his deceptive affairs and lies. I'm more than delighted he is back in Denmark, go to your little trollop, I anger, though I still love him immensely!

At least I can have some peace and quietness in my life. I have even considered devious plots 'to put an end to it all'. Selfish? Yep, you are right in your observation. It's pure selfishness in my mind and absolutely against my religion even to think about it. For the last couple of months, I harboured the crazy idea of killing myself. Yet I don't know how to do it, and I'm unsure I want to. It's so confusing, frustrating, and miserable that I barely hang together in any proper pieces. My inner struggles, pain, and broken heart surrender to a devilish plan, and Satan sits on my shoulder and keeps on pushing me. It's all dark deceptions and fucking gloomy flying lies from all those men who so far have intruded upon my life. Why don't I hate men?

I don't know how to hate. Dear Jesus, believe in me, because I believe men also are a great gift from God to women, just as women are a spectacular gift to men. But I imagine it's more the exception to the rule in the twenty-first century that everyone remains faithful in their partnership. For me, it's not acceptable, and as Mother Teresa, quoted; Love has no meaning if it isn't shared. We have been created for greater things—to love and be loved. To love a person without any conditions, without any expectations. Small things, done in great love, bring joy and peace. To love someone, it is necessary to give. To give, it is necessary to be free from selfishness.

I'm still madly in love with Paul, because he is unconditionally my lover, my soul, my best friend, and my life companion. So, I will accept his apology if he dares to tell the truth, but my trust is at this point denied because we are no longer in a truthful relationship, where we can tell each other everything and anything. Our lives are no longer built on 'no secrets and no lies'. Instead, I try to put myself together and get the best out of it, or I will die trying.

To forget my sadness, I spend the entire day washing the beddings, hanging it up on a washing line on our big roof terrace. It takes few hours to dry, then I can take it down again. I want all the bedclothes to be ready when my daughter, Sandra and her boyfriend, Tony soon arrive. One week's summer vacation with them will do me well, and

I'm looking forward to it, because I need their presence and some fun experience with them. Drink some chilly beers and icy wine, go to the overcrowded golden beach and crack tons of hilarious jokes. We always laugh a lot together, sometimes so much that we can hardly stop. One time, I peed my pants because I couldn't stop laughing. Gross yet comical.

Sandra has known Tony for a while, and the wedding bells are about to ring. She seems to be a wise person, with a sturdy personality, and she doesn't mind calling a spade a spade. She can usually sense if something doesn't quite fit into the agenda of life, and is surely the most honest person I know, being very similar to me. I experienced her honesty during our week together here, despite she implies I am immensely naive, and probably for a good reason. Shortly after their arrival, I take her to Drake for a treatment session for her back problems. From the moment she meets him, she expresses to me.

'Mom, what's wrong with this old man?' Sandra questions.

'What do you mean?' I'm dumbfounded over her outburst.

'No, thank you! Never expose me to this fraud again. Such a quack.'

'Old? Quack?' Staring flabbergasted at her.

'Yea, he acts as he is Jesus. He fumbles blindly through his treatments. Jeez, then his massive false stories.' Her anger surprises me, and I go into distress. 'Yuck, they're are creepy—as is his general manner. He is full of lies and deceptions.'

'What has he done to you?' I worried.

'Such a stupid, self-centred, selfish show-off. Christ, the old timer has no idea what he is dealing with.'

Her comments, smashing straight into my face, are perhaps the biggest red flag yet.

'I hope not you are too deeply involved with this dandy. You must stop your treatments there,' she advises me. But I do not heed her warning.

'Why? I don't see it in the same way as you do.' Though, it surprises me when she confronts me so harshly with her next words, giving me no chance to speak.

'Why do you look up to this chappie? Jesus, mom, you speak so highly of him.' She pauses a second.

'Eh? Huh? What?'

'Yea, this buddy is full of himself. And full of bullshit!'

I almost fall backwards, gazing at her with bewilderment, then she waves with more red flags!

'Mom, this dude is out of touch. He thinks he is the centre of the universe.'

'Oh dear!' Her opinion is set. Danger!

'Mom, his senses are detached from reality. Megalomania! Watch out for him. He is dangerous,' she warns me.

'Dangerous? I haven't noticed those things about Drake.'

'He's a nasty old dawg. Eww, he's gross. With a gloomy soul.'

'Aha. Okay, maybe he is a little weird. But he's also nice,' I unmotivated defend him, having given up trying to defend myself.

'Are you in love with him?'

'I think perhaps there are things okay and decent between him and me.' Can I not see it? We speak no more of it.

I'm delighted at Sandra's successes in life and the great connection we have as mother and daughter, by being the best buddies in the world. She has a successful job with enormous opportunities within the financial world, and she has always been a perfect, diligent student. At the same time, she has plenty of time to be a humorous, sparkling rascal with friends and family. She was that way as a child, as teenager, and now as an adult woman, for me amusing when I think back.

Oh boy! Yes, I still wonder why Sandra and Linda, one of her girlfriends in their teens set fire to a playground. I'm not so sure this specific episode is one of their best moves ever. Oddly, both girls got away with it, as they did not harm anyone or do too much damage to the playground. Sandra is always full of fun, even behind her occasionally fussy, serious character. She is tall and a beautiful girl, with lovely blue eyes and long, bright hair. Her clothing perfectly hugs her sleek body. She is not afraid to give it an extra touch, with a pair of delicious high-heeled designer shoes, like Prada or Christian Louboutin. Mostly, it's black leather pumps with red soles. Yes, indeed, we have the same taste, and sometimes we even by the same pairs' shoes or clothes, independently of each other. We often laugh over that when we proudly show each other our purchases.

Tony is slightly quieter and calmer, with both legs well planted on solid ground. I must admit it: he is every mother's dream for one's daughter. I adored him the first time I met him, and fell he is the best thing that has happened to Sandra and our family. The first time I met him, I immediately approved, when he and his friend Pierre came to visit Sandra when she was bedridden after her back surgery. When they rang the bell, I opened the front door to her apartment, wow, and for the love of God! I immediately became a sly matchmaker, thinking, *He will be a great catch for Sandra.* That day was the first time she and I saw Tony, a handsome young man with sparkling clear green eyes and short dark-blonde hair. He was dressed in the latest fashion, appearing stunningly on his trim 190-centimetre body. When he entered the room, she almost fell out of her bed of surprise, eyeing at this handsome man. Ha-ha, I was certain she immediately fell in love with him. Her blue eyes shone passionately with a heaven full of sparkling stars. We enjoyed each other's company for several hours, and it was as it was the most natural thing, as if we were old friends over many years. He is such an easy-going fella to talk to, with a wonderful, special, hilarious laugh.

A few weeks after their first meeting, she began to date him more frequently, which I was pleased on her behalf. She needs—and deserves—a good guy as him. I never have doubted it for one second that he and I clicked well together and that I had the best son-in-law I could ever wish for. My wishes and dreams for her were successfully accomplished, and the next year, hopefully they will get married. I'm glad for her and my perfect family but saddened by my cheating husband, so now, because of Paul's betrayal, we are about to ruin it all for the entire family.

CHAPTER 8

BIRTHDAY, FISHING, AND THE DOGGY-STYLE KNEE CHEST

> 'If you don't stop chasing the ladies, you won't live long.'
> 'Such nonsense. I'm in great shape.'
> 'It may be, but one of the ladies you chase is my wife.'
> —Unknown

The days go by so fast from my first to this upcoming treatment. I'm busy preparing many things, as well as thinking about the man at the clinic. Where have I seen him before? Weeks before I met Drake, I had a weird dream, and mysteriously, it keeps on coming back. It's something about a man, a house, 1840 or 1850, someplace in the Caribbean or maybe Asia. I'm not sure if it's related to Drake's voice or the way he takes my hand when he greets me. It's still a huge mystery, and it haunts me, as it's trying to tell me something about my forthcoming.

I do not take it too seriously that I am suddenly dreaming about another man, after all, my marriage means everything to me. Temptation is not a weakness of mine, and I'm fully capable of being faithful. All I want is honesty, love, and loyalty from my man and myself. Therefore, cheating and chasing this phantasm of a handsome man from my ghostly dream is not an option. Although I cry, complain, and whine about all the things that make me hopeless. However,

I'm hooked on this exotic spot, in my ghostly dream, with plenty of happiness, and to the idea of a man who loves me for my good heart and the women I am. Truthfully, I still want to give my husband one more chance before destroying our life. So, the dream is a fantasy, one of many other hopeless romantic delusions I can remember during my lifespan. Oh my! Many dreams always end up blissful, as the love stories you see on the screen, but this never happens in real life. Maybe it's normal, as a woman, to be a dreamer and want the world to be a better, more romantic place. This is especially true during stages of my life where one crisis piles on top of the next and I wish the fantasy would come true. I'm a living example of a daydreamer, of happiness, love, and a perfect life with my man, my children, and our dogs. I delusion of having a house close to the Caribbean Sea and enjoying life, but of course, it's not realistic. When I love someone, I love with my all-embracing heart and soul, and I love them forever. Even as I write this, I still love Paul, despite what has happened to us. I will always fight like the wildest cat for what belongs to me—my family and my marriage, and this means a lot to me as a Catholic and as a loving, caring woman. However, this time, it's not realistic, and someone might say it's selfish when you struggle and fight to keep your husband, who wants to be free. I can't see there is anything wrong with my attempt to keep the entire family together, no matter what. What do you think? I have no doubt! It's not selfish. It's your right!

Yet my inner self is giving up on these many unachievable struggles. I begin to think, *let him go to this other woman if that's what he wants. And if it makes him content.* At the same time, it worries and pains me, pondering, *what does she have that I don't have?*

It is a wonderful day, and today marks the start of a fresh day and my third appointment at the clinic. I slip into a pair of shorts and a t-shirt, then eat my yoghurt, and swallow my coffee and pulse my first cigarette, and lastly, I'm ready to walk with Spotty. Peculiarly, I'm looking forward to going back to the clinic and have high hopes of Drake helping me, because something is changing for me, even he is oddly curious, with his questions about my life with my husband. I see him as a nice elderly gentleman with whom I feel quite comfortable, but why is my mania with him so different from so many other things? I can't understand it. Maybe it's the hope of help and his understanding of my total frustration? Then, he gives me plenty of attention, and the way he presents himself, gives me such amazing self-confidence. Certainly, there is something different and indescribably strange about his presence when I'm nearby him.

After I step out of the shower, I once again face the dilemma of what clothes I will wear. Nothing too bizarre or business-like—no dresses or high heels—so it will be my best casual summery clothes. I believe this is a common frustration among many women. I fancy to dress myself up in expensive brands—business outfits with tight dresses, blazers, and high heels, mostly black leather pumps and a matching Prada bag or something similar. I have my favourite black Prada shoes with the red soles, though, I must admit, this is not the most proper outfit for treatment at the clinic. So, I dress my tanned bare body in a delicious white La Perla lace bra and a matching thong. Paul buys most of my lingerie, because he loves it, especially when he invites me out for shopping, and we spend hours in the shop. Sometimes we are erotic and naughty in the changing room, and as Paul pressed himself closer against me, I felt a certain stiffness near his trouser pocket.

'Is that what I think it is?' I asked breathlessly while standing half naked in the changing room at the store.

'Yes, he replied,' and smiled while he next opened my bra.

I turned around, unzipped his trouser and gave him a blowjob.

Paul loves when the lingerie doesn't leave anything to his imagination about the beauty that lies underneath the pretty lace. My drawers are mostly black or white La Perla, Mary Jo, or PrimaDonna. Ick, my style is not grandma panties, sports bras, and other cheap products.

As I come back from my stroll with the dog, I slip my long, slender legs into my tight bright fancy jeans, which gets my bumps to give the expression as two lovely round little Parisian balconies. I also choose a wonderful sleeveless pink top, which brings out my firm, vast bosom, then slip my feet, into some matching sandals to complete the casual outfit. I gather my hair into a light, loose braid, and my makeup is the same as it did the other day, not to fancy and not too many colours. A shiny twist of cherry-coloured lipstick perfects the appearance, and I'm ready to leave my home after I spray a great deal of Chanel No 5 over my body and hair.

As I arrive at the clinic, Kate and Drake has not arrived. Odd. Ding-dong, I ring the doorbell repeatedly, and no one answers, so I'm upset. My irritation abruptly stops when a jingling sound pops up on my phone along with a message.

'Hey, we're a little late. Stuck in a traffic jam.'

I reply, 'OK.' Swoosh, so everything is forgiven.

Jingle-jangle, another one pops up. 'We are coming in fifteen minutes, Kate.' Then I turn around and sit on a chair at the café below the clinic.

'*Un café con leche, por favour,*' I request when the waiter comes. Seemingly a split second later, the coffee, with too much milk, lands on my table, cling, clang. I wrinkle my nose, stare at the coffee, bleh, gross, then realise how hopeless and awful it tastes. They can't produce proper and decent tasty coffee like I'm used to in Copenhagen. Sitting here, I gawk after Kate and Drake, hoping I do not have to wait too long, that I'm not fond of when people come late for an appointment. But it's typical in Spain because life is so tranquil, and this is how it goes here, so I'm mindful of the crazy traffic.

Fifteen minutes pass before I finally see them on the horizon, and I'm extremely curious whether they are holding hands. I understand this may seem petty, but I love studying people everywhere. Kate stomps directly towards me, as an angry bull who wants to chase me around the arena. I imagine her two angry horns piercing through my pink top and puncturing my lungs, or my big boobs. Instead of chasing her target, she passes by me coldly as the Snow Queen from the fairy-tale by Hans Christian Andersen, centring on the struggle between good and evil. She does not glance at me for one second even when I look up to see her eyes. Hers are fiery with rage. Oh my. How is this day going to end up? I muse: What is going on between them? Why is she so mad? Drake, however, seems much calmer and friendlier as he slides towards my table, then appears kindly and flirtatiously at me and speaks with an easy-going, apologetic voice.

'I'm so sorry for the delay. The traffic is horrible in the city.'

'No problem. I grabbed a cup of coffee while I am waiting for your arrival.'

I sweetly smile, while he is waiting for me to pay the waiter. Then he stares at me with predatory eyes, studying me from head to toe. Finally, he turns around, indicating we must leave now.

'Well, let's go. Such a beautiful woman deserves to be well treated. I must help you.' He smiles and points in the direction to the clinic with a friendly gesture. Together, we enter the building and wow, what is happening with him? Unexpectedly, he lays his hand gently on my lower back, as if he is guiding my first step up the stairs. I shiver strangely inside my body when he gently touches my back, as we go up the stairs to the second floor. It feels he wants to get in closer and initiate more intimate contact. When we stand in front of the clinic entrance, he opens it with a quick, elegant push and guides me to the waiting room. Again, he plants his hand on my back, and millions of goosebumps run down my neck and spine.

'Please, sit down. Wait here while I prepare my equipment,' as he slides his soft hand firmly across my shoulder and glides it down my back, letting go millimetres before he reaches the belt on my jeans. How abnormal of him!

'Kate will call you when I'm ready.' He beams gorgeously. I stare at the ugly sofa and at him while he continues talking kindly and smirking victoriously.

'It will only take a moment,' he slickly excuses and goes into the treatment room, telling Kate, I'm waiting outside. I slap my bum into the horrible, worn-out brown leather sofa, which they have positioned up against the wall. In front of it, stands some ugly old brown armchairs on each side of the table and in the rest of the room, a few ordinary brown chairs. *Yuck! Real Spanish style,* I muse, and suddenly I discover that the clinic is also being used by other doctors. Interesting! The chap said it was his, but this clinic doesn't even belong to Drake. Why is he lying about that? I get up from the sofa and browse the waiting room.

Perhaps I can discover further secrets he is keeping from me, then I grab some water from the dispenser in the corner. At the same time, I hear Kate open the door and hear her stomping footsteps on the dull grey linoleum floor, walking towards me.

'You're welcome. Yes, grab some water. He is ready now,' she says ironically with a fake smile, pointing at the treatment room. I am not in the mood for her intimidating manners today, so I falsely smile at her.

'Thank you! It was nice and cold,' I answer, equally ironically, though politely. *Ice cold as you are.*

I twirl on my heels with a nice smile and go into the room, where I see Drake standing casually in the opening, watching me as I'm a queen he is waiting for, beaming with his gorgeous, warm grin that spreads wildly over his handsome face. His dark almond-shaped brown eyes, whose irises shine as sparkling stars, glisten as the Caribbean Sea.

'Congratulation on your birthday,' I immediately and gladly peep, so at least that part is not forgotten. I have no intention to ask his age, and nor do I have any idea how old he is. Wham, whoa, he looks great, with astonishing charm and a fantastic personality, which Paul doesn't possess. Drake has so far given me some great feelings about myself, and somehow, he has managed to convince me to think twice about my future. Not that he knows anything about it, but it's what he does to my thoughts. Oh God! Those 'not so good' plans I have in my mind.

'Oh, many thanks. I'm surprised. It's very kind of you to remember my birthday.' He smiles, and Christ, oh, dear, phew, I am about to faint. Whoa, he absolutely looks smashing. Damn, and the way he answers, with such a flirtatious smile that I almost want to jump into his arms and hug him. Holy cow, what's wrong with this guy? Normal people don't do what he does.

Of course, I control my manners. Hmm, is Drake a normal person? I can't figure it out, but in my opinion, normal people usually give ordinary smiles, *but not him*. Geez, when he smiles at me, there is something magical and breath-taking about it. Something grandiose and flirtatious! Man, when I catch his eyes, they seem so playful, and when he blinks his eyelashes with calm movements, they remind me of

Bambi on ice. I love this animated movie. It's so cute, oh gosh, and now Drake is cute.

Silly me. Don't even think about it, Mary, I deliberate, angry with myself. I have no idea what is happening to me when he does what he does, and I'm not aware of any agenda he is plotting. I try my best not to let him distress me, while I know I'm wiser, a faithful wife and a decent woman. Besides, I only know his birthday, otherwise I know virtually nothing about the man except for what my fantasy tells me.

Oh dear! He will certainly mean trouble over time.

But what do I mean by 'trouble', and in what way? I must come back to this later. Sorry, folks, for not revealing the plot beforehand, but then the rest of the story would be boring. Somehow, I feel the troubles began from this day forward.

No man has ever skimmed at me the way Drake does, at least not that I can remember the past twenty years. Normal men don't send such loving, greedy, wet, sparkling glances to me if they aren't up to something. Not to brag, but I'm quite used to it, other men eyeing intensely after me. But the way Drake glimpses at me is completely different, intense and with a mind-blowing passion. My intellect begins to react to his manipulative flirtations, and my goodness gracious, he comes into my miserable life as a luminous star. But it never occurs to me—and cross my fingers to my heart, it's far from my normal thinking—that I ever have it in mind to think on an affair with him. Nor do I never consider Googling him or investigating the facts to see what kind of a guy he truly is. Why do so? *But maybe I should!* Rubbish, I fully trust him. *Which I perhaps shouldn't!* So, does he have something up in his sleeve that I absolutely can't see through his handsome, shady, dark disguise?

'Well, Mary, how has it been with you the last two days?' Gosh, then he reaches out for my hand again to say hello, and I shiver.

'Hmm, oh, yea, well, thanks. It's been okay.' I pause deeply with a yawning sigh.

'I am glad to hear. Then my treatment works.'

'Hmm ... I've had more pain in my neck. Gosh, and on the left side of my buttocks.

Well, also down at the same side of my leg,' I complain, bewildered. 'Oh! Okay. Don't worry!'

'Hmm… it's somehow foggy to me. I was somewhat worn out. Yea, and a little dizzy over the past days.'

'It's normal to get dizzy. Did you remember to drink plenty of water?' he says, not even commenting on any of the other information.

'What do you think?' *Come on dude, I muse*. 'Hey, haven't you noticed the heat?' *Litres of waters ran down my throat.* I muse this with annoyance as I glare at his pretty face.

'Good. Take off your jeans. Get down on your stomach,' he commands strictly. In my mind, I assume he is going to treat only my foot, so this jeans thing knocks me completely off.

'My jeans? Why take off my jeans?' I mumble, as my mind is spinning with panic. 'And I must lay on my stomach?'

You gotta be kidding! Help! This is not what I expect at all. The anxious thoughts glide speedily through my brain. Yes, dear reader, you're right in your observation, if you remember my morning ritual. I'm wearing sexy lingerie, including a *tremendously* tiny thong! Shit! And now I must take off my pants? Show him my Parisian balconies? Oh my, that drops as a bombshell, and I become sudden embarrassed at his sneaky attack. Few seconds, I feel my jaw drop to the ground, crash, bang, and I'm speechless. My feelings those microseconds swirl around as a German cuckoo clock, cuckoo, cuckoo, while it's spinning wacko out of control. How embarrassing an idea, placing my bare ass straight up into his gorgeous face. No! I cannot grasp this, and my imagination cannot fathom how uncomfortable it will be. Letting him see my butt and foxy thong like that, because fashion dictates that we women must wear such things. What shall I do? He has not asked me before to do anything like this, so I must find a solution to resolve this awkwardness.

'Oh… um… are you sure this is necessary?' I ask gently.

'Yes, it is! I'm not able to treat your sweet *buttock hills*. Nor your legs. And feet when you wear such tight jeans.' came his prompt and extremely self-assured answer.

'Buttock hills?' What kind of self-made word is that? English? Not Danish! Is it Swedish? No, it can't be! I've never heard it before. 'What do you mean by this strange phrase?' It is now even more dreadful that I must take off my pants in front of him.

'Surprise! Ha-ha. It's a self-made word.' He smirks. Yikes, I certainly dislike surprises, but I might as well surrender and torment myself to answer him.

'OK, if I have to. I'm not pleased about it.'

I turn my eyes downwards out of pure shyness, staring at the ugly grey linoleum floor. I want to dig myself under the floor, and best if I can crawl into the nearest mouse hole, if that's an option. *Harry Potter save me with your magic wand. Turn me into a mouse*, I beg in my imagination.

I stare at Kate, who don't notice my shyness but stares angrily at Drake. My half-naked body is on the treatment table, and I glance suspiciously at him.

'Don't worry. There's nothing to be shy about,' tweets from his calm, crispy voice, and his gorgeous smile pops up again. 'I'm used to it. Every woman takes off her clothes for me.' He beams. *Good for you, chap. You must indeed be a fortunate man since women voluntarily take of their clothes for you*, I muse, 'Ha-ha, ha-ha,' laughing at me, which is sending cold chills down my spine.

Prick! *I'm not every woman, dude!* Such a self-assured dandy, I reflect silently. A son of something abnormal. Immediately I lose all respect and admiration for this self-possessed, blasted, lofty jerk. The next moment, he interrupts my inner negative judgements about him.

'Trust me. Given the many years I've treated women, I've seen a little of everything. Nicely shaped breasts. Ha-ha, and hanging breasts. Bare butts. Ha-ha, yea even full naked bodies.'

My jaw drops to the floor—*crash!*

'So, you don't have to react like that. Man, you certainly don't need to worry about anything.' *Easy for him to say all this BS.* 'Definitely not with these nice long tanned legs you have. Man, Look at yourself. Don't be shy, Mary.'

'Thanks for the compliment.' Pondering, *such an overheated, overconfident asshole*, then I glare at him, and he giggles. Next I gaze at Kate, who is about to explode with anger.

'Sorry to say. But I'm not used to taking off my clothes for Mister Anyone!' I answer ironically. *You piece of shit of a sickly bragging fella*, I muse. I'm appalled, and Kate is boiling in her tiny miserable corner. Honestly, who does he think he is? Casanova? I'm incredibly disappointed.

For a long time, I've considered the source of my negativity towards men. Perhaps it's frigidity, or maybe it's because of the betrayal by Paul. This situation with Drake is an abomination, because his flirting is deeply unethical. I pick up he apparently needs to be in the centre of everything and possesses a huge need for self-attention and need to control his surroundings. He suddenly changes for the worse, so I feel he has no respect or understanding of Kate's feelings. He seems to forget that I'm *his patient!* Constantly! He even has the audacity to do it in the presence of Kate, which is far beyond my understanding. He certainly has nerve, but I resolve to ignore his intimate comments about my body.

'You must be a sought-after woman. Every man's dream,' he almost whispers so Kate can't hear it. At the same time, he glimpses eagerly and greedily at my big breasts. This is followed by many tactless questions about my private life and economic situation. I do everything in my power to ignore the flashing of his Bambi eyes, even though he is presenting a nice opportunity to say yes to him. Christ, things like that never happen with Paul.

These are not normal thoughts for me, though I am about to enter the timeworn age, where hormones play a strange negative game within me. Am I panicking over my age? I'm not sure if I'm afraid of never being able to get a new man again if I ever get divorced. And yet here is this fascinating handsome smiling chap in front of me, who is trying desperately to lure me. Okay, he is charming, but he is far from the perfect man I have in my mind, and apart from that, he is too old for me. At the same time, the thought runs through my mind how easy it always is for men to snatch a much younger woman. No one ever considers about how difficult it is for the woman to get a much younger man. Oh, surely, if she is so lucky, yea, then people will gossip badly about it. *Not fair!* But one thing is for sure: weird things are happening to my body, and I don't know what. Am I getting antiquated? The thought frightens me shitless! I suddenly feel as a wrinkled old witch, though I'm not! When I look inside myself, and at the mirror, I'm still young in my heart, body, soul, and mind.

While I'm on the table, my butt is straight into Drake's face, and I turn my head every time he talks to me, while I at the same time also glimpse at Kate to see if she sees me turning my head. I finally give up out of awkwardness and speak a few quiet words.

'Uh… hmm… sorry, I wonder if you can give me a towel. Or something else to put over my botty?'

'Kate, grab a towel for Mary's butt,' he strictly commands, and with a violent, annoyed gesture, she grabs a towel off the shelf. Harshly she throws it over Drake's head, so it strikes his hair and lands right on the middle of my back. Blimey, her irritation doesn't end as she addresses me directly.

'There you go! Now you can cover your bare ass.'

'Whoa, thanks.' *What a bitch!* I muse, wondering whether she treats other patients the same way.

After this, she sits back in her chair and begins typing furiously on her computer. I am shaken. I notice his bewilderment as he rolls his eyes at her manner and continues to treat me. Gently, he strikes my calf muscle with his left warm palm as he moves the machine's treatment head in a similar rhythmic direction, up and down the muscle. It doesn't hurt, and I can only sense small clicks. It's comparable to the rhythm of my own heartbeat, and occasionally, it feels as tiny elastic snaps when he approaches areas close to a bone or tendon. At one point, he ends up inappropriately close to my butt. I sense a peculiarly manner of petting in this area when he touches me, blasting those energies into what he calls *buttock hills!*

'Why do you call them *buttocks hills?* Aren't you a doctor?' I ask him. 'Doctors don't use terms like *that.*'

'Yes, I'm a doctor. Ha-ha, but most of all, I'm a funny doctor. I love to play games with words.' He laughs.

'Oh! Funny! I must admit, I have a hard time understanding how your electric waves of my body will help,' I question, next pondering, *playing with words? You are flirting and playing with me, dude!*

Gently he moves the device to my ankle, and with tenderness, he holds the ankle in his hand and blasts some energies into that area as well. I feel great discomfort and lots of hard, smashing elastic strokes, so it's quite painful.

'Sadist!' I shout. But sad to say, a charming one. Hereafter, he works his way down to the underside of my foot, telling me he is spotting something great.

'Ha-ha, it's such an amazing technology,' he erupts with excitement. 'Wow, I can actually see and feel that your toes are spreading a lot more. Even more than the other day,' he adds, but jeez, I don't notice any change, and sense it is nonsense he's trying to convince me of. Nor do I feel comfortable about his unusual gentle, almost coquettish touching of my body parts. It makes me irritated when he also keeps on pressing the painful area under the foot. Does the sadist enjoy seeing me in pain? I feel somewhat humiliated and have no idea of how to deal with this weird situation. Yet I somehow feel attracted to his flirting.

There is suddenly an odd, deep silence around us, and the only thing I can hear is the little clicks from the machine and from Kate's keyboard. I can sense his sparkling aura sending sentinel signals through his fingertips and up through my legs, along my spine, and enter my brain. I instinctively recall an old episode I experienced six years earlier—a creepy encounter with a guy who was a healer. He used his magic eyes and soft touching techniques to enchant and seduce women, and eventually he ended up having sex with them at his clinic. Ugh! I got so scared after my six healing sessions with that creepy guy. During the last session, he tried to hypnotise me, making a hot connection with intensive eye therapy. Luckily for me, I started laughing during our intense eye session, and he interrupted me and tried to continue. *Not successful!* He was a gorgeous, tall, slender man, same age as me, and his eyes shone as an amazing blue ocean, then he had a stunning trim body. But I was done with this sleazebag, so I cancelled the rest of the appointed seduction sessions. Scary—he knew

I was married, and so was he. I had to stop before he succeeded in either raping me or seducing me with his hypnosis. Wow! That was surely a spine-chilling experience. Worst of all, he was a good friend of the family, I was best friends with his wife, and the boys went to school with their child.

I'm having the same feelings with Drake, that he tries to hypnotise me with his stunning, glittering brown eyes, and I'm sure he wants Kate out of the room. In his dreams, I bet he wants to be alone with me. Thought runs cold down my spine, and I glare several times over my left shoulder just to be sure Kate is still there, even if she is angry at me. Each time I turn my head, he *instantly* answers me back with a slight tilting of his head, then smiles sweetly and puts on his Bambi glare with his courting brown eyes. Gosh! He is flirting, no doubt about that. My goodness, he resembles Sean Connery or Michael Douglas when he does that. Oh, my what a handsome guy Sean is! Oh, Sean, come and borrow some sugar from me and stay with me. Wow, I adore this stunningly foxy actor. *Is Drake also foxy?* I speculate, and quickly, I peek the other way again. I feel this weird magical power, as he is trying to get over me, and repeatedly, I try to drift away from this strange performance and erase everything from my feelings.

Drake breaks the silence.

'When are you going back to Denmark?' he asks.

'Uhm… eh… I haven't decided yet. I don't know.' With his calm, rasping chat, he takes the conversation in an entirely different direction from what I expect.

'It must be so nice—and expensive—to have a great home right in the best part of Copenhagen.' I turn my head and can see he is eyeing intensely at me, while I wait for him to bring up the next curious question. 'Your husband obviously earns a bunch of dough' is his next surprising conclusion, and he stares at me with an easily squeezed, cunning smile. What the fuck is this guy doing? The thought grabs my mind. Constantly he is talking about wealth and expensive housing. Naive as I'm, I stupidly answer him.

'Well … I don't know. We manage well. Hmm, I suppose. I'm not complaining.'

'What kind of cars do have?' Blimey, he continues with more questions about us, what other assets, and so on. The thought strikes me again: *What is this bastard up to with all these questions?* Within seconds, he interrupts me again, then tilting his head slightly and blinks las a lovely deer. Oh… my… it looks so cute.

'I must say, it's not anyone who can afford a penthouse here on the Spanish coast. Then you also have a great apartment in the heart of Copenhagen,' he repeats himself.

'What? Huh?' The stunning rasping voice I don't mind listening to, but those many questions are odd, especially when accompanied by his cunning smile. His voice is indeed alluring, and his eyes and smile are incredibly beautiful, and that is what makes him so charming and attractive. But it's not an excuse to flirt with patients in this inappropriate manner. He has been flirting hardcore since day one, and I begin to speculate if he has Googled us. How does he know so much about us when I haven't mentioned anything to him? Kate got my addresses during the first phone call—that's it. Not that I mind anyone Googling us, but I do mind if he's using that information to create a special agenda with me. That's not OK.

Well, enough of that. I don't want to think any more about such craziness, nor do I want to talk any more about Paul and wealth. To me, it's insignificant, and in the end, I believe such bragging is usually about making small talk. Perhaps he's such a person, who asks about anything to keep a conversation going. Who knows?

I give in to his small talk and try to slide around it when he brings up Paul or finance. Later, we fall into some decent conversation about him and his achievements.

'I give many lectures abroad. Only I possess a breadth of such knowledge and skills.' He brags. 'I've done loads of extensive medical research of stem cells. Isn't it true, Kate? And much more exciting medical research.' Wow, he seems extremely educated and clever. 'Am I not right Kate?' he repeats at least ten times.

I want to puke! She seems clearly annoyed by his many cunning questions and his bragging. I peek at Kate, who still sits silent in her dark, angry little corner. Occasionally, she twists some grim words at us when Drake asks her about something. Mostly, he wants her to confirm some of the things he is telling me about.

'Isn't it true, Kate? Wasn't it so, Kate?' It seems somehow odd to me, as he is an insecure child. *What is his real agenda?*

'What are you going to do on your birthday today? The weather looks amazing for some outdoor activities,' I interrupt, trying to turn the conversation to something else. Kate abruptly stares at me and him and is curious of what his answer will be.

'Oh... ah... Kate has some surprise for me... Hmmm... ay... she has invited me out on a boat trip. Hmmm ... I think it's for lunch. Isn't it correct, Kate? Also fishing for the rest of the day. Isn't it so, Kate?' he stammers.' His voice is less nice to her than it is to me, then he seems indifferent to her feelings and even whether he wants to go on this trip with her.

'Lucky chap. Good for you,' I comment happily. Damn, I forgot to ask if they are married. I'm quite convinced that she wants to beat him unconscious with a baseball bat. Her anger is easy to see when he tells me what plans they have. Grumpy, she mumbles something indecipherable while Drake speaks to me at the same time.

'What are you going to do for the rest of the day?' He smirks.

'Hmmm... I haven't considered that yet. For sure, swimming my daily rounds in the pool. Then some fitness.' In the same moment, he glances resolutely at my body from top to toe, as a greedy predator.

'Well, I must admit, your muscle mass is well-trained. Wow, not a gram of fat out of place.' He smirks, and I am happily surprised at his nice compliment while he continues chanting.

'Yes, no doubt about that. I can easily tell that you are incredibly fit.' Then he gently squeezes my calf muscle. Next, he softly strokes along my leg until he ends up with his finger on my buttock, pressing it mildly. I can glimpse from my eye corner Kate is getting angry at him, and she is sending me murderous stares.

'What kind of exercise do you do?' he asks.

Is he trying to make her jealous? I ponder.

'I swim a lot. Bicycling. Ha-ha, and of course several hours daily walking with the dogs,' I proudly tell him.

'Sounds great,' he comments, and I notice that he, for certain, doesn't do much exercise himself.

'I believe it's important to take care of the body. Best so it doesn't fall apart. In my younger days, I did a lot of horseback riding. Some extreme sports. Loads of cycling. Jeez, often between forty and fifty kilometres several times a week. I also do Pilates. Something new I started last year is Gyrotonic.'

Chuckling, he interrupts me, 'Gyro… what-is-it-for-a-thing?'

'It provides nice agility. It helped me keep back problems away after the surgery. During my rehab, I was using it a lot. Faster than I expected, I was able to bicycle again. Best was my daily dog walking.'

'But what's gyro… tonic? Sounds like gin and tonic.' He laughs at himself, as if it's funny, which he obviously assumes he is. When he stops grinning, I explain what the *gin and tonic* concept is about.

'I practice the exercises on special benches. A reformer among or on the floor. It's with specially designed tools. A Pilates ball as well… blah, blah, blah,' I am chattering, trying to explain.

The time passes like a whirlwind, and we are almost done with the treatment of leg, buttocks, thighs, and foot.

'Okidoki, I'm done "electrifying" you. Ha-ha, as you call it. Go to the chair,' he commands, and performs his usual *clunk* and *crack* of my neck. Why? I still don't get it! Again, clunks and crashes arise, simultaneously triggering one of the nerves in my neck. The same awful electrical feeling runs rapidly from my shoulder, down my arm, and to my fingers. The left side begins to buzz strangely and becomes numb. Unpleasant!

'Shit it's buzzing … and feels numb through my neck and arm again. Is it normal?' I stutter, afraid.

'No worries. It's quite normal. Just calm down. It's because I've done it correctly.

Ha-ha, and perfectly,' he brags while his hands still are resting behind my neck and he squeezes it softly. He massages my shoulder with gentle movements and finishes with a firm soft squeeze around my neck again. It gets my neck hair to rise and this time it's trillions of goosebumps, which runs down along my spine to my arms and legs, and my nipples becomes hard. His touches are not quite normal; however, they are soft and insinuating in a gentle way. So, honestly, what has happened today? I have no clue, but it worries me, and on top of it, I'm not sure if I trust him regarding the nerve pain.

When I try to get up, I get a little dizzy and must sit down again: however, this time, I feel a less reluctant feeling of the neck and can turn it from side to side, and afterwards, I feel slight relief.

Finally, he shows me to another treatment device, standing in the nearest left side corner, which he calls a knee chest.

'A *knee chest!* What in the name of heaven do I have to do on that *thing?* It looks like a Catholic prayer stool.' I gawk at this awful implement of punishment and want in the same split second to deny this nasty creature. 'Honestly, I'm not her for absolution.' The frightening thought flickers maniacally around in my head, then Drake interrupts my desperate mood.

'Come on. What's taking you so long? Chop, chop and hop up. You must lean your upper body forwards. Ha-ha, yes on this monster here,' he instructs me. My panicking awareness screams, *What! No! No!*

'You can't mean that?' I scowl at him suspiciously, and my eyes stares frightening back at this horrifying mahogany hulk of a stool. Oh gosh! It's upholstered with ugly fake red leather. Anyhow I reluctantly agree to kneel on this disgusting apocalyptic bench. *Hold to your hat and belt!* In an awful compromising positioning, my body is situated on this monstrous thing, me down on my knees, pondering terrified, *is it time to pray now?*

'Man, this looks like something from a torture chamber.' In a split second, my thoughts flash back to the many punishments at the orphanage and the many beatings from my parents.

Clearly, in this odd position, my ass is in even greater view for his gaze than before. Even, my butt will also be extended in a position straight up to his well-proportioned nose. As all this is happening, I have no chance at all to cover myself, and the tiny thong covers my female parts only a bit. Imagine this sexy horrifying picture, can you? It situates as a female person sitting in the ultimate naughty and under the circumstances most inappropriate position: doggy style. Then he is ready to penetrate me from behind, as if this is a fresh chapter for *Fifty Shades of Grey*.

I'm *horrified*! Most of all, I want to *run*! I am so embarrassed, traumatised and frozen as a plastic doll. I don't move as much as an inch, lest I give him any feeling of what is going through my shame-filled mind during the seconds he is palpating my loins. In the same moment, he puts his warm, soft hand in an advantageous position, as it's a bestial play. A naughty thought goes through my mind, and I meditate of the times when Paul bangs me from behind. Next, Drake firmly pushes my lower skeleton. *Klonk! Crash!* And he is convinced he has positioned the loins in the right and proper place. What do I know about that? I trust his professional skills to the utmost and have no idea what he is doing to my corpus. I hear a crunchy sound and notice how the skeleton gets another, perhaps better movement, but that's it. Not the least, I feel the awkwardness of the situation—outrageous, appalling—because of my tiny thong, because I haven't even have had the brains to consider grabbing the towel from the table and putting it over my lovely bare round balconies of an ass. The moment the treatment is over, I'm allowed to raise myself up, and I blush in embarrassment when I glare at him.

'All done for this time,' he smirks with his self-assured sly smile.

I scowl at him, pondering, *Well, did you see what you wanted to see?'*

I spot small fine lines around his face when he grins at me.

Hmmm… nice and charming! Hmmm, yeah… nice! Oh… yes! Wow! it makes him look much younger than he is.

In my uncomfortable rush to snatch my jeans, I stumble across the chair in front of me as a storm-tossed clown. Hastily, I put on my tight jeans, zip the zipper up in a firm grip, and fumble to snap my belt into hole number tree. All the time, I notice how he curiously stands there and watches all my movements, and that makes me much more nervous.

'Can you come again in a few days?' he asks sweetly and smilingly, though I hesitate a few seconds. I don't know if I want to come back. Everything seems so odd, and my feelings are so confused—first thinking of him as a charming man, then losing total respect for him, and finally get the impression I'm a character in a porn movie with him. Then he is sexy and charming and resembles Sean Connery and Michael Douglas and speaks like Clint Eastwood.

Oh, my stars, I'm speculating: *Did Doctor Drake get hard?*

CHAPTER 9

HER ANGRY BODY LANGUAGE

The narcissist when you are in need.

When the chips are down, a person who genuinely cares for you, wants to be there for you because you need it. A narcissist, however, will only be there for you, because they need it. For the drama. To promote their fake persona. To build your debt of obligation to them. In none of these scenarios are your needs involved. You are an opportunity to be capitalized on. Your misfortune. Is their fortune.

—Narcwise.com

Drake asks me to come back in two days, and after a slight hesitation, I answer agreeably.

'Fine, no problem. What time? Which day?' I ask nervously as my stomach tries to overrule me. Perhaps, it's best *not* to come back anymore, because he is troubled, and I'm uneasy of getting into a problem with him, though for some strange reason, I'm becoming addicted to him and his treatments. Worst, I am fascinated by his charm and weight over me, that I feel a certain obligation to continue.

'Kate, check out the schedule. See if there is space for Mary Liz to come in two days.' he rudely asks, and she turns over the pages in the diary, then stares angrily at me.

'Can you come in the morning?' she asks, irritable and heated.

'Yes, sure. I've nothing else planned. What time is best?' I kindly request.

'Come at ten o'clock,' her sour crooked mummified face mumbles. (Just to let the reader know, this is Drake's expression when he's negative and angry with her.) The air is awfully hot in the room as she hands me the bill for one hundred and ten euros. From my first visit, I know I can only pay in cool cash, so I had withdrawn currency from the ATM to be sure I would have for the sour dough payment.

'Here you go. Cool cash.' Wham, bam, and slam, I smack the sour dough into her furious hand. I notice that she writes down the amount in a small brownish notebook and packs it into her bag, along with the computer, and then stares suspiciously at me. *Strange, dark money?* I muse, but I don't bother my head more about it and gesture a farewell to her. No response! Instead, I stretch out my hand to Drake, swiftly he grabs it intensely, with pleasure, using both hands, while twisting it gently and puts the other hand on top of it as he drags me closer to him, as if he wants to hug me. It feels as though he's extremely controlling me, but also sweetly and gently.

'Bye-bye for now, Mary Liz. I'm looking *very much* forward to seeing you again,' he beams with his crisp, sexy voice. I nod affirmatively, pondering his words. 'Looking *very much* forward to seeing me again'? Okay, wow! Big words to use, and once again, I confirm my farewell to both. Kate doesn't squawk a single sound. Nor does she say goodbye. I can see how her sour muzzle hangs right down to the bottom of her chin and that she is extremely annoyed by the situation and me. Not that she is a particularly mind-blowingly good-looking woman, appearing with an ordinary pretty look, worn out, with short highlighted hair. I guess she is probably close to her sixties. Her eyes are blue-grey, and she certainly doesn't know how-to put-on makeup very well. She is slim, with a shapeless figure and a pear-shaped butt, and her thighs are plagued with cellulite. I pity her. Today, she is wearing shorts (that's why I can see it), and her clothing borders on absurd tastelessness, but the colours are nice and correctly put together. She seems anxious about something, so maybe Drake isn't so nice and loving to her? I can't help noticing it because several times he was so rude and unkind to her that I almost felt sad for her. No woman, nor any employee, should be treated the way he treats her. Not that I have anything against her figure or her personality; in fact, the first time on the phone and at the clinic, she was extremely sweet and helpful. Something must have changed her attitude towards me since the first visit, which has made my attitude towards her afterwards slightly negative.

What also bothers me is that since my first visit, she began to treat me rudely as a patient. I'm not aware of what tricked her regarding my presence, or whether their acquaintance more akin to a marriage or a business relationship. Maybe she is jealous of me? *Oh my!* That would be imprudent and inappropriate of her—actually, both. Yet I forgive her, because there must be a reason for her unprofessional behaviour.

Frankly, what does it matter to me?

The thought buzzes around in my head, and I realise, *I certainly am not interested in any affair with the doctor; nor do I want to involve myself in adultery*. I have more than enough of such things in my own private life, having to deal with Paul's mistresses.

Gosh! It's so good to be down on the street again, that I instantly gasp deeply a few extra times and exhale again in relief, relieved to be away from his craziness. I simply need to do several of these breathing exercises so I can philosophise a little over today's mysterious and unpleasant experience. I gaze up at the building towards the window where I know the treatment room is, on the second floor. Holy cow! Calmly, I ponder this madness. *Shut off. What a strange day. What a crazy performance from both.* At the same moment, I'm thinking of a quote that fits so well with Kate: 'People who say mean things to you are just jealous of your awesomeness.'

Having that in mind, I consider whether I should continue with the next treatment or cancel the appointment and never come back. *I should have quit!* But if that were the case, the story would end right now, and I'm sure you would be disappointed with me. So instead, let's continue!

While standing on the street goggling, I once again breathe deeply and turn my head to see if there is a café close by. I'm hungry, so I want to have a quick snack and something to drink before returning home to my Spotty. Oh, my furry sugar baby dog! I've had dogs most of my adult life, and I love and adore my dogs. The two I have now, are beagle-terrier hybrids, not big dogs, around ten kilos each, named, Lady and Spotty, mother and son. Many years ago, she did a naughty 'Lady in the Park' thing with the neighbour's fox terrier. Sneaky little girl she is, all while I was talking to John, the owner of the other mutt. Okay, we know each other well, so perhaps both of us did turn our heads away when we looked at them and saw what was going on with our two horny mongrels. At that time, I desperately wished for some puppies, so sneakily, I met with John to have an excuse if Paul asked how this happened.

'Damn, Paul, it was 'a dogs' crosswalk accident'. Jeez, none of us saw it,' so, I lied to him but later, my bad conscience admitted it. Lady became pregnant and had two cute puppy boys, one white with several brown spots, Spotty and the brother chocolate brown, Choco. So adorable and so difficult to choose which one to keep, but we ended up with Spotty, while Choco was adopted by another loving mature woman.

Well, I hurry up and find the café so I can get home to Spotty. The Lady mama is back home in Denmark with Paul and the boys, after they recently left Spain. Spotty is still young and such a fun, lively, clever pooch, but he still needs a lot of dog training. He's a rascal, but I gladly keep him with me so I've some good company in my lonely time. He's also a lovely comfort to me in the despair of my marriage and keeps me away from my bad intentions. With him, there is daily opportunity to go on long walks in hilly areas, and often, we meet other dog owners and chitchat with them. I've loved all the dogs I have had, and they have gradually become a big part of my life. Giving them all the love, I have means so much to me, in addition to what I give to my children and Paul.

On the opposite side of the road, I spot a café, then I stroll over there and order some water and snacks. From where I sit, I can see the clinic, and whoops, suddenly, Kate comes stomping out the door. Alone! Raging! Uh oh! I'm glad I'm not in his black shoes, because her body language clearly shows anger. *She must be fed up with him*, I muse, watching her in a raging march, while she strides towards her old grey Peugeot, parked on the same side as the clinic. In a fury, she rips open the door, jumps in, and sits down, apparently waiting for Drake.

Shortly after, he comes out of the building, appearing energised and vibrant, with his head high and proud as he walks to the car. Has he won some big prize or what? Amused, he gets into the car and closes the door as if nothing is unusual, and none of them sees me watching the farce curiously from the opposite side of the street. I can almost feel the hurricane of negative impact, of bad smoking dark aura, hitting the other side of the street. She revs the engine and swings sharply out of the parking spot, then accelerating rapidly, as she drives off down the street and disappears hastily out into thin air, so I can no longer see them. Wow! Such a drama queen! I speculate, *what happened after I left the clinic? Did they have a fight or some crazy argument? Trouble in paradise!*

In the meantime, I have eaten my snacks and emptied my water bottle, so I wave at the waiter to pay my bill and consider what to do for the rest of my day. Almost dead beat I drag my sore treated body to my car and, bewildered, I notice it has been parked next to Kate's. Great—at least she didn't know it was mine. I figured she would have scratched it with her car keys or bumped her door into mine. And nor did I know it was hers upon my arrival.

Christ, it's hot in here.

I start the engine, roll down the windows and the hardtop, and as I'm driving, the warm wind sways my braided hair, and it's all loosened up before I arrive at my home. The ugly green garage door opens after I push on my fob, and I park the Mercedes in our underground garage. Determined, I take the stairs up to the apartment, lock myself into my cooled home, then being greeted by a sweet, enthusiastic mutt. My God, he's so loveable, wagging his eager tail as a crazy nut. Immediately, I squat down and begin petting him behind his ears, thinking he must have missed my company, wagging his tail around as a whisk in the wind. Oh, my, the pooch is highly motivated for a nice long walk.

'Sorry, buddy, but it's too hot,' I insist, because the Sun shines in a cloudless blue sky, with a temperature over thirty-five degrees with no fresh breeze. However, I decide on a small stroll so he can do what he needs to do, despite the Sun is unbearable, and I'm feeling the sweat begin to drift down from my face and body. Not precisely ladylike or sexy.

'You, poor dog. Jeez, you're wearing a fur all year round,' I pity him, and I notice he probably feels the heat is unbearable. His tongue hangs far out of his mouth, so we quickly turn around in the direction of our cooled home. Luckily, he manages to pee a few times and do his bigger business card on the roadside, which I with a plastic bag, pick up his droppings and go straight to the space where all the smelly bins are located.

Oh boy! I loathe that stinky space, especially on a hot day like this, when the stink is unbearable in there. I'm about to suffocate from the odour when I open the green metal door, so I squeeze my nose with my fingers and at the same time quickly toss the dog's shit into one of the many containers. Luckily, I score perfectly in the first container. Yuck! I simply can't stand the idea of bending down to pick up the shit bag if I miss the first throw. Disgusting! On our way up to the flat, we briefly greet some of my good German friends, Peter and Claudia who are splashing around in the pool, which is next to the road and just below my home.

'Looks heavenly!' I shout in German. It's so close, so it's easy to get a quick cool dip when the heat is as it is today. Phew, what a wonderful liberation it is when we finally enter our fabulous cooled-down flat.

The area of the apartment is located about thirty kilometres away from the nearest airport, Malaga, and not so far from the nearest town, Fuengirola, shopping centres, and the beach. Puebla Aida is a nice upscale region with lots of golfing opportunities and several golf courses close by, but to get to the zone, one must drive through a stunning golf course connected to our site. You can also drive a different route, which I often do, for not always to drive the same way home. The complete complex, with fewer than 180 properties, took about twenty years to build, and the stunning site beautifies itself, with many unique buildings consisting of a mix of villas and apartments. It's all designed according to the great historic Andalusian style, where the homes slip through one exciting little alley after the other, with many kinds of fountains. None of the residences is built in the same way, and many have a wonderful view over either the twin golf course, the sea, or the mountains. Our apartment is blessed with a stunningly beautiful sunset every night. We have several vast swimming pools in the many beautiful green gardens and are blessed with large lovely sun decks and palm trees in many different spices, providing adequate shades. The many amazing gardens are adorned with all sorts of exotic flowers, blooming all year round, which inspires my idea to live here all year round, in a colourful, warm, and peaceful zone, because the atmosphere fulfils my craving to have a lovely, striking life in Spain. Everything, from buildings to botanical gardens, is put together in a stunning Andalusian fashion, to the utmost detail. Imagine, dear reader, a magical scene from the Arabian adventure *One Thousand and One Nights*. I simply love this magical part and can't get enough of it.

CHAPTER 10

TIME IS JUST AN ILLUSION

> Reality is just an illusion, though a very persistent one.
> —Albert Einstein

Kate meets me at the reception area for my fourth treatment and she seems unpleased with my visit while she shows incredible anger at me. Why? Drake's warm, sensitive handshake again sends strange magical vibrations through my body when he greets me. Self-important, he glances compassionately at me, as if he is signalling, he wants more of me than merely being his patient. Arrogantly, I pretend I need nothing further fussiness, and that Kate's feelings about me are a crazy misunderstanding. What is it with her strange behaviour? I don't understand it.

'Please take off your clothes.

'What?'

'Yea, T-shirt, and jeans. Then get up on your stomach,' he says, smiling. As last time, I jump embarrassed up on the table, only wearing a bra and a thong, and he begins to examine my back, sensing his hands in a soft sliding movement down my back, across my buttocks and the backs of my thighs, until he finishes by palpitating my calf muscle and finally my foot.

'Oh, Mary, I can feel it's much better,' he marvels.

'Huh? I can't feel any changes. The pain is the same as always.'

He continues the same treatment, and I sense his calming movements as he touches me, as well as using the device. Up and down with his finger, sliding soft insinuating caresses along my leg.

'Your foot is so soft. Hmmm, so tiny, and sweet,' he again dares to say slickly to me when he takes it in his hand. I'm wondering if he has foot fetish, because he seems to be immensely in love and obsessed with my feet. When he speaks to me, it's with the same loving, flashing, flirtatious eyes he sends to me every time when I turn my head around. Again, he tilts his head at that cute angle, as if he wants to be extra charming to me, and somehow, he succeeds, although I feel it's intimidating, and I muse, *What's he up to, with his strange slick and kind performance?* I try to ignore it all. While he treats the backside of my body, I see Kate typing hard and angrily on her computer and doesn't want to speak with him or me.

'Today, I'll treat one of the nerves. This here running along the side of your shinbone,' he proclaims and points with a gentle sliding finger.

'What? I have no idea what the relation is between the feet and shinbone.' Somehow, and most of the time, there is dead silence between all of us, and his flirting consists of unspoken gestures. Cheerfully, he directs me over to the famous prayer chair.

'Shit, not again,' and I again become extremely embarrassed with this awkward position. This time, I remember the towel to cover myself.

'No, no. You must leave the towel on the table. Otherwise, I'm not able to see what I'm doing.' He laughs mockingly. *He sure has nerve. What is it he wants to see besides my bare ass?* I muse. Humiliated, I crawl on my knees into an awkward doggy-style position, ready for the sadist to beat me up. It reminds me of the orphanage, when I received punishment upon my bare butt, hanging either over the nun's or priest's knee or half-bent over the table. Then the stroke from the bamboo stick or the wooden ruler came. Well, I hope this is not what Drake is going to do standing behind me. Swiftly, he plants his hands on my lower back and, without no warning, pushes it downwards, crunch, clonk, and it produces crunching noises and scares me.

'Well, now it's the neck. Sit on the chair. I will check it out.' While I sit there, he hums, 'Hmmm... yes, okay,' and continues, 'It looks good.

It seems your neck is much better now. Maybe don't use a bikini with the strap going around your neck,' he explains.

'How did you know I do that?' No answer and he make his adjustment in the upper and lower neck with a fast twist and without no warning. Crunch! Crack! Clunk! Fuck! And I hear fierce crunching sounds in my head. My head feels totally wacko, as if it's completely out of joint as I'm a character in the horror movie *The Exorcist*. A new star is born for the next *Exorcist* movie—that's how I feel, with my head sitting on wrong. I'm horrified, and I'm not sure what he is doing.

'Shut off! It's painful. Is it proper to trigger the same nerve again? It feels as 280 volts running like lightning all the way down to my fingertips,' I tell him, irritated.'

'I must tell you; I'm considered one of the best in the world.'

'I'm not sure if you are Doctor Frankenstein instead of Doctor Bates.'

'Don't question my special techniques.' He growls.

'But, it feels as if I'm being electrocuted.'

'I know exactly what I'm doing.' He raises his voice unpleasantly and stares at me with annoyance.

'Okay, but I feel like Frankenstein's dead corpse. Jeez, I feel more dead than alive,' I complain. Whoa, this makes him somewhat angry at me.

'Don't question my work. You are in safe hands.'

'Gosh, I must sit a minute with my head between my knees. I need to get back the blood and oxygen to my head.' I'm close to enter a panic attack.

'There is nothing to fear. What I do gets your blood to flow automatically up to your head again.'

'Are you sure this is normal? I don't feel it's normal. I feel extremely dizzy.'

'Yes, yes. Oh boy, everything is quite normal.'

'Ick, I want to puke.' I glare at him worried and scared.

'Listen, Mary. What I'm doing is only an adjustment. I'm much more careful than others.' He changes his mood from angry to caring, squeezing my neck and shoulders. Every time he does that, it does not feel as a normal squeeze; it's with passion, love, and tenderness, sending mystical signals through my body, up to my brain. Maybe he is sure of his tactic, using it to open his way to me. He tries to give me the impression that things are other than they seem.

'Apart from that, how's your tiredness?' he tries to talk around the subject, to confuse me.

'Yes, well … I'm constantly tired. Much more than usual.'

'It's normal with these kinds of reactions. *I promise* you, it's a good sign. It tells that the treatment works well for you. Have faith in me.'

'I'm often dizzy. As I walk beside my body,' I say worriedly.

'Don't be sad. *I promise* it will be good. Wow, and such a beautiful woman as you, we need to get you back on track, as a fresh person.' He grins, and I stare at him, nod, and smile. I must trust in him and that everything he does is *normal*. Somehow, he captivates me more today than the other day. Is it because of his sudden extra attentive care?

The treatment takes about forty-five minutes, then I get dressed again, and Kate gives me the invoice in anger. One hundred and forty-five *dirty* dark euros for the *laundry*. I hand her the cash (I wonder if they wash them before use?).

CHAPTER 11

THE EXOTIC DREAM

> Every morning you have two options: Turn around to continue to dream or stand up to realize one's dreams.
> —Visdom.dk

Last night, I dreamt someone loved me! It's the same fantasy that has haunted me several times, since shortly before I met Drake and Kate. I gradually get the impression that it's more a premonition, something I may experience as a reality, so I have no idea of what makes me have this strange sense that somewhat mysterious is going on. It's not unusual when I wake up to remember most of it, and often I write the crazy, funny, or realistic fantasies down to remember them. It's said, 'You should follow your dream and live it out, but you also must listen to the danger and signs associated with the dreams.' Shall I do so, or is it some trivial nonsense that I should overlook?

Disagreement 2: Dreams

Freud's position: Freud believes that we can learn much about an individual through the interpretation of dreams. Freud argued that when we are awake, our deepest desires are not acted upon the considerations of reality (the ego) and morality (the superego). But during sleep, these restraining forces are weakened, and we may experience our desires through our dreams.

Jung's position: Jung believes that dream analysis allows for a window into the unconscious mind. But unlike Freud, Jung did *not* believe that the content of all dreams is necessarily sexual in nature or that they disguise their true meaning. Instead, Jung's depiction of dreams concentrates more on symbolic imagery. He believes dreams can have many different meanings, according to the dreamer's associations.

Are dreams only illusions? I'm confused by their observations, because my dreams are more related to reality. Freud and Young believe that dreams are an expression of what moves us in our unconscious. Perhaps dreams are a signal of my struggles, an increased self-awareness or further elaboration of the things that fill me in my awakening life. My dreams are about things relevant or important to me, perhaps offering a suitable solution to my struggles—past, present, or future. It's said you normally can't remember your dreams, but I remember quite a few of them. Are the studies correct that our dreams reflect thoughts and experiences? That they are a means of coming to terms with what we experience in our waking life? I'm discovering, engaging in the intensive process with this book, that as I rewrite each chapter countless times, I dream about the content of the chapters. Next morning, when I wake up, I'm able to make changes or additions to it because I have forgotten some important parts in it. Later, I think about; what in my dreams have not yet been experienced in real life? Is my dream a premonition? That we will discover as my story unfolds, so I will try to reverse the odd dream-movie from before I met Drake.

The orchid field, the exotic life, and the man appear, and it seems odd and true-to-life, as if I have experienced it before. Is it real or not, or is it an experience, a new-fangled adventure, or a warning, or can it be an opening of a window to realise what is going on? I'm resting in my chilly bedroom, reading a book before I tuck myself comfortably under the duvet. The dog is in his basket next to me and has already fallen into his mutt dreams, snoring loudly with pleasure, resting on his back with all four paws slightly cracking downwards, pointing in a relaxed position up to the ceiling.

'Night, doggy boy,' I whisper and lay on my left side. I want to pick him up and let him sleep in my bed because he is so cute, with his white paws bent like that. I toss around endlessly, before the dream sneaks and twists in my inner thoughts mysteriously. At times, I'm so confused with the feelings of inner electrical impulses, flying around as wildly ionised particles in the sky. Millions of flashing stars confuse my brain and seem messy, in many tiny flashes of romance.

Exotic areas, flowers, and butterflies appear in beautiful colours, surrounded by the blue water and the fine sandy beach. It's such a perfect dream, happening in the middle of the 1800s, and is so mysterious, magical, and fascinating, with confusing structures and calmness. It's the year the author Emily Brontë published her book *Wuthering Heights*, about Heathcliff and Catherine's stormy love affair. What is it with this specific number: 1847? However, the timeframe does not fit correctly because some of the events are from the twenty-first century. The number pops up several times in my dream and in my waking hours. Something doesn't add up! Shall I or shall I not search for the dream ghost again? I live in a new night world of astronomical illusion, of unexplored events and warnings. It begins beautifully, full of warmth, tenderness, and love, and I'm curious to know about this cryptic person. My eyes are flickering wildly, possibly it's the REM sleep. My body becomes relaxed, and I travel into the fable of a paradise. I don't know the exact country, the main character, but I know I'm one of them. (The dream is an important plot which will hold powerful meaning later in the storyline.)

The exotic country, at a white sandy beach, close to the beautiful turquoise blue sea, where I want to live with the man of my life, begins, as an illusionistic and romanticised saga! Will it come true?

Along the seaside, the woman sees swaying palms, spreading their roots to many more palm trees, and waving their long green leaves, hanging down from the crown swinging in the light breeze with a slight rustling sound. Swoosh, swoosh, and the waves splash gently and faintly hitting the shoreline. She walks slowly along the edge of the shore and sees many beautiful white and pink seashells, coming up one by one, noticing some of them are lightly covered with sand which is remaining in there. Others withdraw again when the water hits the shore and splash back again. Close to the beach, there are a small white wooden house, with its many carvings, window frames, and shutters, painted in soft pastel blue and rose colours. They have decorated the white columns with small light blue and rose rings reinforcing the stability of the house. White eaves along the roof edge resemble small flower ornaments, all painted light blue, while the terrace and stairs are kept in the proper position and go all the way down to the soft, finely cut green lawn. On the terrace stands a small glass table in the middle, decorated with a vase full of orchids and next to the table stands two white Adirondack chairs (also called the Westport chair, and sometimes the Muskoka chair).

The sharp edges of the white fence reveal the plot size of the property, adorned with a white hammock in the lovely garden, with gorgeous handmade old fashion wooden furniture, in a Caribbean style. In the corner of the garden is a romantic white pergola with amazing deep red flowers clinging around the columns as well as there are many pots with roses and orchids. Inside the old-fashioned house, stands beige and white furniture, then vases full of roses and orchids, standing on tables and in various locations on each floor area. The frosted white glass door is adorned with a grey nameplate that reads, 'M. M.'

The woman is ecstatic about her dream house, the turquoise Caribbean Sea and the beach, that shows its beautiful and exotic aspects to her eyes every day. Elegantly, almost floating, she strolls every day to the beach and enjoys the whitewashed powdery soft sand, on her way to the orchid farm. She buys lots of multi-coloured orchids to sweetening her life, such as; pink and white, some with pink stripes, or yellow ones with red stripes or violet ones with white edges, and in all sorts of colours and sizes, throughout this wonderful field. Has happiness finally reached her path of life? She dances joyfully in the flower field with her chic ballerina steps while listening to Enigma, 'Return to Innocence'. (So, you see, that's odd because, it's from the twentieth century,) and the song turns recalls of her wonderful experiences with her husband. Her light, soft milky-coloured silk dress perfectly matches the colours of the flowers, and swings chicly between her tanned legs while it gently touches her hands when she turns herself around. Her favourite white sandals cause the dust to swirl up in the air in a light cloud. The stunning woman's soft Scandinavian hair hangs loosely over her tanned shoulders and spreads in small curly locks, swaying gentle in the breeze when she swings back and forth around herself.

She gets terribly frightened when a strange, mysterious man appears on the horizon, then her heart jumps faster, and she gasps and snatches after her breath. *Never seen him before. Who is this mystical person?* She ponders and feels cosmically drawn to him. As he passes the butterfly bush and with one hand strikes it, and it creates a mess, when all the resting butterflies swirl up then appear in many different species and colours and all become one with the colourful orchid field. Wow, such a beautiful sight, as this silky bush resembles the tap-dancing confusion of Polka-dancing butterflies on their way up to the light blue sky. They flutter around confused, with their delicate light wings going first one way and then turning around the next. The confusion of his touch quickly stops when they continue a calm delicate dance in beautiful soft jumps, bounding from one flower to the next. Few lands softly on the woman's shiny hair and play a lovely game with her, then suddenly a big black and blue one sits on her finger when she reaches out for it. Aww, so pretty, then, it flies off again.

She follows their gentle wing strokes and curiously glares at the shadowy man, in bright canvas pants, light blue polo shirt, and canvas shoes. His strong, muscular arms, chest, and abdomen give the impression that he is in good shape, and from the corner of her eye, she peeks at him, while she can sense many singing birds sitting in the trees. Swooshing waves hit the soft white sand as the mysterious man approaches her at an elegant pace. Though she is afraid, she notices he is smiling at her; she smiles cautiously back, then her cheeks flare up to an embarrassing red blush. His walk is fascinating, when he watchful and calm, sets one foot in front of the other without harming any orchids. Then he picks one of the big ones and lays it delicate in his left hand, resembling a magnificent sleeping flower, and gazes at her with a gentle, loving smile and comes closer. She spots his stunning red lips and senses a cosmic aura rising around him, with magical glittering sparks that look like wild luminescent ions shining up against the luminous Moon in the darkness of the night. He appears as Jesus, with an amazing bright glow around him, while it all shifts between the sunny day and the shiny moonlit night. His dark grey hair looks silky, as soft mink fur, and his brown eyes shine as the clearest blinking stars in the night when he unexpectedly stands in front of her. Suddenly, his head is slightly tilted to one side, then he grabs her hands and pulls her close to him, but she gets scared and wants to scream, however inside her head, there is silence. She freezes as a statue in fear, while he intensely, stares into her eyes and swiftly gives her a surprising kiss. Mwah! Smack! Five fingers plant themselves readily against his cheek, and next she wants to kick him hard in his balls, but instead, she falls on her butt. The embarrassment sight of her clumsy fall makes him laugh at her.

'Ha-ha, ha-ha. Oh my… oh my… how clumsy you are,' he pranks with a gorgeous, crispy, old-fashion British voice, then reaches out his hand to help her up while he continues talking. 'Wow, such beautiful eyes. You are disturbingly stunning.' He smiles.

What? Run! Poppycock! What the hell is that about? Such a fishy old chap. Is he flirting?

He continues being a smart ass as she sits in the dust. 'No way! Go!' Curses run through her mind. Then he suddenly begins speaking with an American accent.

'Why are you so furious? It is only a bloody good kiss. I'm a damn good kisser. And a hot damn lover,' he brags. Prick! Self-satisfied creep! He continues talking with his crispy voice, sounding as he is eating a bowl of corn flakes. Oh my! What's wrong with this dodgy fella, because he is switching between soft, educated, gentlemanly English and rude American dialect. Confusing!

(Not that I'm saying every American speaks rudely, but *he* does! My sincere apologies to my American readers if you think I consider every American speaks rudely. That's not the case, and this is only a dream.)

'Ha-ha. It will be better if you don't make such a fool out of yourself. It seems to you don't like unfair treatment!' he barks in his American slang. 'Right? Ha-ha, so great!'

Not nice when a stranger rudely analyses and judges her, and the language confusion makes it difficult for her to comprehend. The thought runs through her head: *OK! Got it! Why are we playing this guess-and-grimace game? Is the cat after the mouse?*

'Yes, maybe you are right! I dislike injustice. Lies! Deception!' She answers, frustrated, and the matter is settled. She accepts his hand, then he helps her up as a true handsome British prince, and she is ashamed of her angry answer. With the other hand, she brushes off the dusty soil and glances at him, pondering he resembles Sean Connery, so is it him? No, it's more like Michael Douglas. Dear God! He still squeezes her one hand in his as he presents himself.

'By the way, my name is …'

The words disappear into thin air, and she doesn't get a single word of what he mumbles, except for, 'What is your name?' She stares questioningly at him and is lost for words.

'Hmmm… oh… eh…' she stammers and gawks at his fine laugh lines and dimples. His mild, not-to-young face looks great with the sophisticated tiny lines around his mildly brown eyes, giving him an intense expression of depth, and his crispy voice sounds like that of Clint Eastwood.

Suddenly, in my sleep I get some mysterious glimpses and a strange structure in the dream scenario, which comes and goes with blinking confusing warning signals. As if it's uncontrollable lightning, firework and screaming voices: 'Beware! Deceiver! Charlatan! Fraudster! Watch out! Run now!' Then the voices disappear into nothingness.

The woman in my dream runs as fast as she can. But she can't get away from the man, and she falls into a deep black hole, which captures her as a fly in a sticky spider web. Terrified she struggles but gets nowhere, then discovers that she is being misused by this human animal, who lures her and steals everything from her. Despite he is charming in the beginning, of a promised blissful life with him in an exotic country, she twists herself like crazy to get out, but the web glues her more and more firmly to it. She can't get free again, and she eventually gives up the fight, then the predator comes back, steals her soul, and eats her—first the heart, then her skin and organs, and lets the sad remains fall to the bottom of the dark, shady hole.

Sudden unrest in my body begins, while I sleep more nervously in my awakening phase, tossing and turning, pondering who this mysterious and dangerous man is. Swiftly, the mysterious 1847 pops up again, so is this a serious warning signal, or will this be a fresh part of my life? My heart pumps rapidly, and I feel my blood pressure is enormously high, I'm sweating anxiously, then I wake up from my nightmare and stare at my alarm clock. Ugh, it's almost five in the morning, yet I'm feeling that I'm still running from the unknown, the black hole and the danger in the dream. Who is this man in my fantasy world? Did he manipulate her, exploit her emotionally, and destroyed her financially? Is it me? That's the big question, and maybe we will get an answer to it later! I don't understand the context and don't comprehend what is happening to me, but there must be something wrong with this illusory dream-man. Half-awake I calm down again from my panicked state and fall asleep again, and the dream continues, ending up again in the middle of the beautiful orchid field. I'm not able to fantasise more of the horrible part of the dream, and everything seems to have been a terrible nightmare. What a weird dream, but *important*!

Noises from the road, of fast-moving roaring trucks, enter my room, because the balcony door is slightly open, and I sense in my awakening glimpses that the Sun has risen, and the alarm clock now shows almost eighth in the morning. The dream disappears into nothingness, although I have not forgotten it, and I let it remain a mystery in my memory. The noisy rubbish carts vanish again, and it all becomes peaceful outside, and while I'm still resting in my bed, rubbing my eyes, I twist and stretch myself as a cat.

'Time and dreams are just an illusion.' Whispering while I glare at the resting snoring pooch in his basket, with four paws pointing up against the ceiling. I jump out of bed, and Spotty wakes up from the bustle and goes downstairs together with me. Grabbing a pen and a

piece of paper, I sit down and write down the number 1847, then the most vital things from the dream, and snatch my dream book and search for the most important words.

> **Flowers:** Connect with feelings of joy and beauty. Something new is emerging. The rose indicates love, while the orchid represents beauty, love, thoughtfulness, and deep sensitivity, or maybe something you regret. The pink orchid brings grace and joy into your life.

> **The House:** Refers to the soul. The way of arranging life. If the house is not empty, this indicates an aspect that I must consider. The facade of the house represents one's own façade. And it strikes my mind, the house looks clean and bright, so it must be because I have a clean and honest conscience. A small house. You seek security without obligations. Hmmm! Exactly what I want in my life.

> **Warnings:** Emphasize one's ability to discover difficulties or danger. Receiving such a warning indicates one should be aware of something—that requires *attention*. The circumstances of the dream will clarify in which way I will put myself at risk, so will I pay attention to those warnings?

> **The Unknown Man:** Can be a part of my own personality.

> **Falling into the Hole:** Acknowledgement of a bottomless depth or void in yourself and the fear of losing control or your identity or that you're not good enough. Or you're taking a risk, without having the certainty of the result and exceeding your own limits or current base of experience. Is this what we will experience during the reading?

Instead of *not* taking any of these signs into decent consideration, of what is happening, I blame it all on Paul, because I see him as the person to fault and whom these warnings are so crucially about. But am I wrong, or are they all warnings about Drake? It might be it's all an illusion, the hopeless dream of finding the ultimate love in my life.

CHAPTER 12

A WORLD FULL OF TWO-FACED PEOPLE

> Behold a universe so immense that I am lost in it. I no longer know where I am. I am just nothing at all. Our world is terrifying in its insignificance.
> —Bernard Le Bovier de Fontenelle (1657–1757)

Spotty sits next to me by the table and glares at me with his mildly brown eyes, amused, while I'm trying to figure out my dream-mess as he begs for a walk and wags his tail joyfully.

'No, not now Spotty. Wait! There is I no time for you now!' I feel sorry for him and bad for my selfishness. He is the most wonderful and funny pooch I ever have owned, and possesses such a special loving and warm character, so he is my cuddle dog.

Outside, the temperature begins to rise, so it will not be too pleasant for a long walk, so I grab a quick coffee and smoke my first morning cigarette.

'Okay, come on, you little Scooby Doo, and let's go for a long one before it gets too hot.' The mutt wags his tail enthusiastically.

'Finally! What's wrong with her? Why doesn't she walk me right away? Humans!' he seems to be musing about me. Fast, I jump into a pair of shorts, pull a sleeveless white T-shirt on, and slip my feet into my trainers, so the bathing must wait until we are back. After a few seconds, he urinates several litres. Oh my God! Shame on me, the poor thing was in such desperate need, and I feel bad again. He is still on the leash as we walk up the steep road, but when we reach the hilly area, I let go of him, while I stroll in the dry shrubbery landscape, which no longer is green because of the dry spell. The south coast of Spain has more than three hundred days of sunshine a year, so it's extremely dry at this time of year. Spotty keeps watching at me with a playful attitude and wants me to throw the tennis ball, I give in and toss it into the wilderness. Running with the agility of a born sprinter, he chases the ball, and during his search, the dust swirls up as a wild cloudburst around his funny kangaroo jumps, so I begin to laugh. Quickly, he comes back and wants another toss, and the game goes on again, until I hide the slimy, dirty ball in my pocket to distract his mind from it. Dog training is on the program every day, and he is very obedient, funny and such a grateful creature, so I reward him with some goodies when he does good.

While we take a break, I drink half of the bottle of water and give Spotty the rest when I pour it into my slightly cupped hands. 'Good boy. You are so thirsty,' I praise him, next we continue to a big roundabout, planted with a lot of greenery and some African daisies, in pink and white. Close by is a huge white compound and another big roundabout planted with a tall palm in the middle and plenty of purple Cape marguerites. After one hour, the heat has overtaken the previously chill morning air, and finally, we arrive at our chilly home.

I prepare the breakfast, with a bowl of yoghurt and sprinkle some granola, fresh strawberries, and Canadian maple syrup on top of it. Yummy! Spotty is having his crunchy dog food and fresh chill water, then I grab my bowl and freshly brewed coffee with me out on the balcony. The stunning view of the mountains gets my thoughts running through my head about my next appointment, at two o'clock. How should I handle Kate and her negativity, her angriness, her fierce throwing of towels? Oh, it so depressing, and the ugly considerations are a stupid reminder, so if it happens again, I will stop.

I take a steamy shower, and as the warm water sprinkles over my long blonde hair, face, and tanned body, a smirky smile appears on my face. The night's fantasy and the enigmatic man gets recalled in small flashes, because I'm a philosopher, a dreamer who thinks too deeply over life. My idols are Plato and Socrates, two great Athenian philosophers during the Classical period in Ancient Greece, as are the poets Homer and Ovid. Instead of thinking of the complexity of these great men's histories, my head is filled with thousands of peculiar thoughts, feelings, with anxiety about loneliness, and I dislike loneliness; it scares me immensely. Death and fear spread as lunacy in my mind, from the crucial cold Friday night in Denmark in 2004, when the police arrived at our doorstep with a horrible message. The fear of losing a family member becomes a reality, when our son was torn away from us, and losing a child breaks my heart into millions of pieces. Terror and psychological shock hit the entire family, and my trauma wants me dead too. I can no longer handle ill-fated life during the past many years. Being doomed, and having a huge crisis with daily battles, with fight-or-flight situations, the thought constantly goes through my head: 'We must survive, we must survive,' and struggles of rescuing the entire family begin.

'It's the worst and the wrong order, taking away children from their parents.' It cannot happen. I lost my last bit of faith in God, Jesus, and the Virgin Mary, and I'm about to lose my own mind to craziness. And six years later, I'm about to lose my marriage. What more does God want to take away from me? Am I born to be beaten by sadists, to be ill-used, to be the old in loneliness? So, why all this fighting only to survive the burning inferno? I lost it all! My life's terminology is not right. I have feared death since my childhood, since the horrifying chapter in my life as a small child, nearly drowning in a bathtub. I must survive all my fears! There are too many of them. That's why I begin my journey again, embark on a religious path the year before I suddenly meet my fresh saviour of a 'dark angel' practically standing unexpected on my doorstep in Spain in 2010.

Spotty is happily waiting in front of the shower, wagging his tail, when I step out.

'More walking?'

Ha-ha, ha-ha, his excitement shows. Tossing around the towel in my hair and grabbing the big towel to dry my body, I glimpse sweetly at him. 'Maybe I will be a horse or a dog when I die. Hmmm ... reincarnation?' Such stupid nonsense, so I laugh instead. 'Ha, ha, ha.' He glares so cute as he begs for one more walk. 'Yes, yes, yes ... you are so lovely. Oh, my, and beautiful. I love you. Mwah.' He tilts his head at a skewed angle, bends his ears in half, and gazes begging me at me, with lovely pleading brown eyes. Oh dear! You will not believe it! I received a massive revelation! It's as observing Drake, when he gazes at me at that same skewed angle. Drake resembles a *begging basset hound*! But not as handsome, loyal, and lovely as Spotty, I muse. The similarity is stunning, and I can't stop laughing while petting and chit-chatting with Spotty. 'Ha-ha, ha-ha, and I love to take good care of you. Mwah! My little wild chap,' Foolishly I imagine he understands it all.

I put on my amazing light blue lace bra and thong, my white jeans, and a white T-shirt. Argh, I deny the pressure to wear grandma underwear and to be a suppressed object by Kate. Is she wearing unexciting Sloggi panties and bra? Don't misunderstand me, but I'm blessed with nice, sexy lingerie, and it looks good on me, then I begin to muse, *Will I be a part of the natural circle I love so much? Is my life about to begin. Hmm, despite years of sorrow hiding in my backpack. Is that what my dream is about?*

Eyeing at Spotty and thinking of my kids gives me the joy I need. Betrayal by others makes me wish I could leave life and follow my late son. My anxiety, grief, and insecurity sometimes pop up from half-forgotten memories and make it difficult to get the skewed puzzle to fit together. I want to gather the thousands of chaotic thoughts into an organised unit, but why is it so difficult? Hereafter, I must confront the trees of common sense, which will blossom, first with buds, to flourish, until it ends up with millions of great sensing insanity-flowers of happiness, which I will share with the man I love. But Paul has never time for such nonsensical poetic shit.

'Forget about it. Move on with your life. You're too emotional. Too sensitive. A daydreamer. It makes no sense,' he often tells me, so he never got to know everything about my life. He is a stubborn and private person who doesn't take the time to listen or understand my inner thoughts. He is impossible to talk to and has only work, work, and women in his head. It's sad when he has such a pretty, devoted wife. The art of loving and being understood is important to me. Drake understands me, and I am attracted to the shady mystery side of him. But I must restrain myself and not fall into his act of seduction. He gives me something to think about, the perspective to figure out how to put the puzzle pieces together. Well, get going, Mary. Don't think more about this rubbish, I ponder, and I smilingly glance at Spotty. 'Oh, my baby dog. I love you so much. Ha-ha, you spotted little devil,' and I begin to do my daily chores, answering emails and phone calls, making the bed, cleaning, and finally taking the dog again for a quick walk before I leave home for my fifth appointment.

On Calle Jesús Santos, I park the car in front of the clinic, get out, pay for parking, and then ding, ding, ring the doorbell. The same humming sound unlocks the door, then I walk up the stairs and into the waiting room and flop my butt into the ugly brown leather sofa. Strange! Kate is not welcoming me, so I patiently wait for her. The door to the treatment room opens, and Doctor Drake comes into the waiting area.

'Hi, Mary. It's so nice to see you again. I've been looking forward to this day. Oh, boy, *so much*,' he utters with a happy smile. *This day? So much?* I puzzle. Gently, he takes my hand and strikes my palm tenderly, then let's go of the grip. I shiver! What's he doing? Outraged! I enter the room. Kate is not there. Why? Basically, I don't mind. I am thrilled about her absence and that I won't have to hear her grotesque remarks.

'Wow … where is Kate?' I try to sound as if I'm surprised as he gazes jubilant and smiles, satisfied.

'She is not coming today,' he answers, appearing incredibly content.

'Huh? Well, why not?' I asked, sensing something is wrong between them.

'Don't you worry your pretty little head over her absence. I'm sure this is the best way—only you and me.' He chuckles boldly and is ecstatic to have me by himself.

'Hmmm ... I'm not quite sure what you mean.' I gaze at him, confused.

'After last time, I told her, "What the hell is wrong with you? Why can't you do things as I say? You can't treat patients in such a rude manner as have with Mary. I tell you, if you cross me, there will be consequences", whoa, man then she was so pissed at me and threw a mug at me. It nearly hit me in my face. Phew, but I'm so quick in my manoeuvring that I avoided it.' I sense how angry he is when I glare at him, surprised, then I feel sorry for him.

'Oh, my goodness. I hope you are okay. Well, maybe she didn't mean it in such a bad way.'

Suddenly, I am defending her. But he is wrathful at her, so my defence doesn't help.

'No matter what, this is not the way to behave. Argh, if she can't use her damn silly head, she must stay away. I mean, from all future treatments, which concern *only* you.' His voice changes from anger to the calmest, crispiest Clint Eastwood singing, underlining the words *concerns only you*. Amazing how he can swing from one pitch to another and how it immediately glides through my mind. *Only me?* What does he mean? However, somehow, I'm relieved by the thought of not seeing this fuzzy woman again. It's a little too much for me. The atmosphere changes between him and me, and he is more relaxed, and I'm more concerned about being alone with him.

'Okay ... I hope it's not my fault?'

'No, no, you did nothing wrong. She did. It is unprofessional. Don't you worry. She is never grateful for anything I do for her. She never believes in me. Argh, such a bitch. Always complaining. Jeez, and whining.' Again, the angry man disappears, replaced by the smiling chap. 'But let's begin! Take off your clothes. Jump up on the table.' He smirks and stares intensely at me while I'm taking off my T-shirt.

'Do you also want me to take off my pants again today?' I asked, embarrassed.

'Yes, of course. Take it all off.' He smirks and stares more intensely at me 'Ha-ha, ha-ha,' and bursts out in a funny, contented laugh.

'Take it all off?' Idiotically I ask.

I worry and become nervous about him, because he seems more intense and weirder in his behaviour, as if there are more scary strategies. It concerns me when I glare at him and see his satisfied smile, me standing in front of him almost naked. Being alone with him makes me more anxious than before.

'Sorry, of course. You may keep your sexy lingerie on. It's no problem. I will open your bra when you're lying on your stomach.'

To calm my anxiousness, I try to reply cheerfully.

'Wow … how wonderful! At least I can keep something on. Please toss me a towel,' I joke, and he bursts out in a massive laugh.

'Ha, ha, ha! That is a good one. Are you always so quick with your answers?' At this point, his mood is bizarrely high.

'Well … I suppose I am,' I hint, then he laughs at my comment and bats his eyelashes flirtatiously. He's a master at pulling his invisible puppet strings, and once again, he manages to take down all my defences, so I'm more relaxed and feel comfortable in his presence. Incredible how he's able to do this, and I begin to fancy him much more. Not that I'm in love with him, but I see him as a terrific person to talk to, pleasant and funny. Okay, he is also incredibly charismatic, and yet he also scares me somehow, which makes him even more mysterious. He changes something in my self-doubt and makes me talk about things I would rather not talk about to others, pondering; *what does he do to me?* Mysteriously, his physical presence overwhelms me, and he emits something powerful with his untamed charisma. And then those magic eyes! *Ay caramba!* I'm sure he knows the powerful effect these eyes have on a woman—and on me. Despite his shadowy behaviour, I feel some more friendly openness from him today, and he affects me positively in my way of thinking about him. I try to be more accommodating and open to his kindness and want to be friends with him. I feel transfixed by all the mystery goings-on in his presence, but I don't see that *we are living in a world full of two-faced people* who are loyal only to themselves. But it's even worse when they give you the impression that they are your loyal friend or are supposed to be your family.

CHAPTER 13

A Seductive Sneaky Hour, and the Tattoo

> Pay attention… Sometimes it's the person giving you the medicine who's making you sick.
> —Steve Maraboli

It's funny how people try to be sneaky, but the only ones they are fooling are themselves. I don't want to be intimidated by his Bambi eyes, so the sudden silence becomes somewhat weird. In my trance of the morning's previous thoughts, I'm missing Paul, and we must solve our problems. Agitated, Drake suddenly interrupts my thinking while I wait on the table for him to start.

'How are you today?' he grumbles, stressed and slick.

'Well, I suppose I'm okay. A strange morning, though.' I stare glumly at him.

'Odd? How? Well, well. I take it everything is going well with you?' he growls. 'Get on your stomach. I'll begin with your back,' harshly he commands, so I turn around then he abruptly appears to be in astonishment.

'What? Something wrong?' pondering his behaviour. My tattoo? No, why did he react like that? He has seen it before!

'Oh boy! That's something!' Shouting in surprise.

What? Huh? Do I have a rash? Or a big cancer mole?' I can't see it myself, so I get nervous and scared of his reaction. He puts his warm magical hand on my right shoulder and almost stops breathing. Resolute and surprising, his hand moves along my back.

'Oh, no. Wow, what a big tattoo!' He astonishingly and slyly starts to comment on my tattoo, as if it's the first time he has seen it.

'Ooh-la-la. Oh, my ... how amazing! Wow! Beautiful!' So, what is he up to now? In his attempt to make conversation with me, is he abruptly commenting on this crazy artwork on my back. Why?

'Thanks a lot,' I reply uncomfortably.

'Wow, I've never seen such a big—no, huge—artwork on such an incredibly slim female body before.' I determine he is lying, so what is his purpose?

'What does all this mean?' surprisingly he asks, then I turn my head and glare at him astonished. 'Hopefully, it's okay I'm asking?' He glances at me and caresses it slowly with his soft feather finger several times up and down my bare back. Well, I never! God damn it! He ends at my right gluteus and presses his finger inappropriate on my butt.

'What does this sign on your firm glute I mean?' he presses hard on my glute, the pauses. 'Is it Chinese?' he questions curiously. *As if he knows the Chinese alphabet* goes rapidly through my mind. *Well, better answer the clever chap*, I muse, so I give him an explanation.

'Yay, it's Chinese. It means "dog". It's my Chinese astrology sign.'

'Wow sounds interesting. Why have you chosen that?' *Blimey! Listen, buddy boy, I just told you! Are you deaf, or don't you hear my words?* But I can't give him such a rude answer, so I try to behave politely. Occasionally you must play the clown when dealing with a fool.

'I'm merely interested in Chinese astrology. The way they use the twelve animal signs. It tells much about the person, depending on which animal year they are born in.'

'Hmmm ... exciting!'

'Yay. Our zodiac astrology has a monthly aspect. There you can analyse our strengths and weaknesses from the position of the planets. Okay, I mean the milky Moon and the shiny Sun. The Chinese have their yearly twelve different animals—dog, rooster, monkey, ox, and so on.'

'Hmm, interesting. How did you find out what animal you are? Which is the first?'

'Hmm, let me see. Oh, if I remember correctly, the rat started to gather all the other animals. It's fascinating. We always see the rat as something disgusting. Though, the rat is clever. The dog, for instance, which I am, means strong, loyal, and patient. It's number eleven. The last one is the pig.'

'Did you get it done in China?' he seems to ponder something.

'Where did you get such a crazy idea from?'

'I'm curious of which Chinese animal sign I'm born in?' he appears questioning and of course, I don't know. He is probably a *pig!* Not the perfect match for the dog. Casually and quickly, he fires a ton of questions eagerly around the room. He is as a crazy running waterfall, with words running out of his mouth. Then he pauses and peeks at me with his blinking brown eyes.

'Maybe we are a good match? Can you find out one day? I want to know it.' But I'm totally ignoring his stupid comment. I know it will not be easy for me, because I only know his day of birth. Asking for his birth year, I don't dare.

'Ha, ha, ha, if you are a tiger, we will be a good match.' I laugh mockingly while his face suddenly turns the other way in disappointment at my sarcastic answer. Silence in the room. Paul is a tiger!

'It must have hurt like crazy. Wow, and taken many hours!' while he is suddenly breaking the silence in the room.

'Oh yes! Believe me. Damn, it's a mixed experience of painfulness. I'm sure my tattoo artist would not be pleased with me if I had kicked him in his balls when he put the needle on my back. Many times, I have had the urge to do so. It took more than thirty hours, and lots of—'

The assmonkey rudely interrupts me.

'What! At one time? Oh my God!' he yells strangely in a brassy explosion, and I get a massive shock.

'Oh, my goodness. Jeez, you gave me a huge chock. Don't scare me like that!' I shake, afraid, and continue. 'No, no, that's impossible. Are you crazy? Such artwork takes time. Lots of pain as well. I had to come back many times.' *Christ! What is he thinking? How can he ask something so stupid?* I ponder. Maybe his IQ is not so high, though he gives the impression him being smart and brags of his high IQ. It becomes clear to me he doesn't know fiddly squat about human body parts, as well as many other things. But he knows how to wildly flirt with me. He doesn't know how painful the process is to create such stunning art, but the monkey is excused. How can he know everything? *Strange, why hasn't he commented on it before, when Kate was in the clinic? Can it be he doesn't want to say more about my body parts?* I muse. Of course! It's because Kate did go mental over his ridiculous *cute little foot* comment the first day. Such craziness! Understandably, she is miffed.

'What about all those flowers? Is it a tree? What kind of wood is it?' the fast chit-chatting parrot curiously questions. *Well, well, mate, your imagination and creativity are not that high, I can hear. Is the tattoo done so badly, or is it that difficult to see its flowers on a tree? Well, I better complain to the artist,* I muse.

'It's a Japanese cherry blossom tree.' I beam friendly, but in my mind, I am irritated.

'Oh, why something Japanese? Have you ever visited Japan, since you have such a tree?' he stupidly comments. China and Japan? Blah, blah, blah. Oh dear, why does he think you have to do it there? I'm about to get more irritated, but I react nicely.

'No, not yet. It's a great dream I have. Most of all, I would love to travel in springtime. Wow, when all the cherry blossom trees go into full bloom. It's the most beautiful tree I've have seen. Can you imagine all—'

I'm barely done talking when the turd once again interrupts me. How rude!

'It's not that long ago since I was in Tokyo. I held a big seminar for many hundreds of people,' he boasts. *Well good for you, chap.* He continues, 'I have a good friend over there. Over the past few years he has invited me several times.'

'Lucky guy you are.'.

'Yep, I once experienced a fantastic huge fish market in the middle of Tokyo.' It's all about him, him, and him!

'You did? Oh my, it must smell fishy all over the city,' I said, surprised.

'You will not believe it before you try it. When you are walking around at the fish market in this overheated city, you will at least expect it to smell awful. Right?' he cutely tilts his head and glances flirtatiously at me. Oh, my, he's cute.

'Well, didn't it?' I question, 'I have never been to a fish market in Tokyo.'

'No, no, not at all. That's why it's not to understand. It's super clean.' His eyes are as big as teacups in astonishment, and he smiles so cutely. I can hardly believe the story of a non-smelling fish market in a gigantic city.

'You were perhaps alone in Japan?' I question curiously, as a sneaky female, and he glances at me deviously and stares downwards, then I turn my head the other way.

'Yeah! Who should travel with me? I don't understand your question. Of course, I always travel alone. I was meeting with Mr Minitzu. The guy I was doing a seminar for.'

'Hmm, exciting.'

'Yep, it was a wonderful experience. You must go there one day,' he justifies, and in his excitement, he opens my bra without asking for my permission and begins palpating my back. I sense his teasing tender fingers sliding with sensitive movements with his tender fingertips and sometimes with his warm, soft palm. Up and down my spine and along the side, until his fingertips touch the sides of my breasts when he spreads his fingers as widely as he can. It sends shivers up my spine as well as trillions of nicely chilling goosebumps all over my body.

'Are you freezing? Is it cold in the room?' he smirkingly jokes and he knows quite well it's not cold in the room. I glance at him and hold in my stare. He is doing everything he can to touch my erogenous zones so that I get the chills, and every time he smiles at me.

'No, no, I don't know where the chills come from,' *but I'm pretty sure you know why!* I muse and continue, 'Maybe my guardian angel is passing by. Hehe, and trying to deliver a message for me. It often happens to me. Oops, then I feel a sudden chill passing through my body in seconds,' I lie because I don't want to give him the satisfaction that the goosebumps are because of his tender sneaky touch.

'You are something special. Wow, so beautiful you are. We must get such a lovely girl like you well.' I freeze to an ice statue, and do not reply to his comment. A sudden silence comes over the atmosphere, and he doesn't say anything to my previous comment. The silence gives me time to think about my dream, where certain features fit so well into the picture of Drake. He gives me a few minutes to ponder before he interrupts me again.

'Okay, there are some more issues. I'll fix them now.' He places his palms on my upper back, turns them slightly, and gives me a proper push so my big boobs almost fall out of my open bra. I gasp in a panic to get my breath back while his inappropriate, devious hands creep softly up to my shoulder blades, then gives that body part the same kind of push, and my boobs are squeezed flat, as pancakes, nearly hopping up to my throat. Grasping for my breath, I get my irritation out of my mouth.

'Ouch, it's damn painful to get my tits squeezed like that,' I growl in frustration. 'It's almost like in the mammographic X-ray. Christ! Ow, they squeeze my tits so much until there is no more tissue left,' I whine.

'Come on. You can't call them *tits*. Jeez, not with such great round breasts you have. Only animals have tits. Yours are gorgeous—nice, round, and big,' he almost drools over my boobs. 'I know it's a problem to treat women with big breasts. They always get squeezed like that. I feel sorry for you.'

'Okay, no problem.'

'I'm developing a new treatment table. Specially designed for women's big *babes*. Like your breasts,' he arrogantly boasts.'

'What? Eh, babes?' Apparently *babes* are breasts in his terminology. I'm about to fall off the table at his unusual comment. Holy cow! Good, I'm not falling. Otherwise, I will lose my bra as well, splattering out on the floor wearing only a tiny thong and some flat pancakes in front of my chest. Similarities between Mr Gyro Gearloose and Drake flutter in my head, and his character changes from being a decent practitioner to a self-satisfied smutty guy. My goodness, his inappropriate flirtations, his nasty comments, and his touching make me creep. I no longer think he's nice. He's a womaniser and a revolting guy. Am I deaf or blind since I don't do anything about it? Strangely, he manages to get away with his odd comments. Is he like that to everyone or only to me? He continues his light touch over my back, and once again, I shiver as it is angels' feathers creating the goosebumps. His fingertips stop millimetres under the edge of my thong, then fear runs speedily through my panicking mind. *Damn it! Now he will tear off my thong and rape me*, but I try to ignore the fear.

'Okay, turn around on your right side. Then I can treat your pelvic floor,' he commands, taking his hand off the edge of my thong. While I turn, I notice he has not closed my bra, so it's almost falling off, then I hurry to close it. Resting on my side, he comments again on my breasts.

'Are they yours by nature?' *What?* I muse and with a fierce stare, I irritated ignore his rude, intimidating question. Then he points his finger at my lower tummy.

'Why do you have a rose there? Can I see all of it? Also, what's under the thong?' he dares freshly to ask, while he is licking his lips, hoping I will take down my thong. Imbecile! Such a basket case! His Chinese sign for sure *must* be *pig*.

'No, you may not. That's private,' I snap crossly. Instead, he puts his hand on my hip and indicates that I must get closer to him. Oh my God! I'm scared shitless, when he grabs my half-naked body and pushes it out to the edge of the table, so I almost fall to the floor. I'm shivering from fear and suddenly sense my body cold and clammy. It's awkward, and I'm petrified that he will abuse me. No one knows I'm here alone with him, so I can't get any help if I need it. I muse; *how many women he does this sneaky conduct with.*

'Are you okay? Suddenly you seem so gloomy and sweaty?' He grins. Damn you!

'Why do you think so?' Though, I'm scared like hell. He comes closer to the edge of the table and supports my body in an extremely intimate manner with his own corpus.

'Don't you worry your pretty little head.'

'Yes, yes ... I think so. It might be because I don't feel so comfortable in this position.' Shaky and afraid, I lie that I'm okay.

No worries. I have a perfect hold on your beautiful body.' He laughs and grabs my arms, placing them across each other, as if I'm about to hug myself. My lower leg is stretched, and the other one is bent as I'm resting in the left lateral recumbent position. I'm resting in this most peculiar sideways position right out to the edge of the table. My body is extremely close to his, and while he holds me firmly, he squeezes my upper knee straight into his scrotum, holding it with his inner thighs. *Eww... aw... Ouch!* I muse. Then he plunks his one hand behind my back and the other one on my hip so it's impossible to get out of his sadistic locked-in position. I feel totally helpless and trapped in his grip and can't move one inch. I'm so terrified that my mind is screaming, *How the hell can I get out of this situation if he sexual assaults me? Horror!*

'Are you okay?' he calmly tests. 'I have such a perfect hold on you. Hehe, you are totally in my power now.' He laughs.

'Seriously, man?' Oh boy. I become even more frightened, when he leans his body over me so there is complete intimate contact between him and my almost naked body. This is beyond my normal limits and the most outrageous, awkward, intimidating contact I have ever experienced. He enjoys it tremendously, and I can feel it, because he has such huge power over me.

'Okay, here we go. Are you ready?' he jokes.

'What the hell to be ready for? I don't even know what you are doing.' I wanted to ignore him but couldn't. It's virtually impossible for me to get out of his strange power hold, as it's difficult for him to get the adjustment set as he wishes, while he is moaning like crazy, as a horny bull liberated by an orgasm. I'm breathless and can hardly get any oxygen into my lungs, while he pushes his ninety kilos over me, with his one leg holding my upper leg firmly so my knee goes further into his precious duffle bag. Well, imagine this picture, which must be seen in real life, though I can't imagine it myself. What a crazy, sadistic bondage position I'm in, and it's not nice. I imagine myself being strapped in his voluptuous rope bondage, but the red and black riggings are missing. I'm hoping he is done, but suddenly, he prepares the same position once more.

'Holy crap! Do you never stop?' *Does the freak have a hidden camera for his next porn movie? So, go my nervous thoughts.*

'I'll try one more time. It will not move down there. I will not give up yet,' he insists, and he tries several times to loosen the damn pelvis and lower back without any luck. He must have forgotten that I have this metal implant, I worry, but assume he knows what he is doing. In good faith, I let him continue, even though I don't have any severe back problems. But for certain, I'll probably get a lot more back pain after his adjustments. I must admit—and believe me, women also have many naughty thoughts in their mind—many such thoughts were running through my brain. Especially, when I'm lying in this unwilling hot embrace with him, holding me so tight to his spicy body. I don't peep one word, but I moan in chorus along with his sensual moan, because he absolutely takes all breath out of me. I realise he is amazingly strong, with some nice, well-trained arms, very masculine and nice. Sexy! *Maybe he can give me a good ride? So, go my naughty thoughts.* However, he fails in getting it done, so he stops.

'Okay, turn around. Let's try the other side as well.' Arrogant he pretends it's all a piece of cake, when he has tumbled around my fifty-eight kilos several times now. Once again, my arms are crossed, the lower leg is stretched and the other bent, directly between his body and his nutsack. Naughty Mary, my eyes are fixed on his golden kangaroo purse, with nuts, and his danger noddle pecker. His body is resting in a hugging position on top of me, and he is preparing for the next big push. Gosh! *I wonder if I can ever get used to it.* I mean, the way he is hugging me, and his hot body is resting on top of mine. I'm quite embarrassed at the naughty position, having my knee touching his golden purse with seeds and a Swedish rotator stick. This time, it's obviously easier for him, and immediately I hear a *clunk* and a *crunch* as the joints fall into the position as he intended.

'Yes! Perfect. That's a good one. I'm sure your back and loins are good again.' He happily smiles and continues talking as a cheerful parrot. 'Let me just treat your leg while you still are on the table. Turn around on your stomach again.' Aw, how sweet, when Bambi blinks attentively and more sensually than before. Adorable! Christ, he is cute, and he does it in a completely different way today. His eyes are much more flirtatious, wet and shiny glaring. Yes, it's as if everything is a lot different, powerful and with many dirty tricks in his mind. I can't figure out what he is thinking.

'Why are you so quiet today? Are you all right?' he asks, worried, and continues his gentle, flirtatious touches under my foot, softly pressing the painful area. 'Oh … your little calcification is still here. I can feel it.'

'Strange! Now it's suddenly a calcification and not a nerve knot. What's the difference?' I upsettingly question then become worried about his gentle treatment, because it's as if he is having a hot love affair with my foot. Next, he caringly palpates my calf and strikes his hands tenderly up along the back of my thigh.

'Did the shock waves help you?' I turn my head over my left shoulder, eyeing at him. Damn! That smile and those eyes. What is he doing? His touches and his eyes somehow begin to affect me too much.

'I certainly don't think there have been any improvements,' I react, disappointed.

'Don't you worry. It may take some time before it works. You need many more treatments.' He smirks.

'But after the first time you told me it was much better' So, I don't understand his inconsistency, and it concerns me.

'Let's see how it's going to work after today.' He starts shooting the impulses through my thigh, then a scary silence settles in the clinic, and I can hear only the pulsating clicks from the rhythmic treatment head and his shockwave machine. I feel his warm, tender hand sliding up and down the leg, while he continues his caressing movements until he ends down at my *cute little foot*.

His crispy voice breaks the silence when he suddenly grins. 'Aw, such wonderfully soft skin you have. Are you using any special cream? It's so nice and smooth touching it.'

'What? No!'

'It's amazing how firm your skin is. What do you do to keep it like that?'

'Huh? Oh, thanks.' I begin to tremble. What kind of questions is that?

'You have some well-trained muscles.' To my astonishment, when I turn my head, jeez, then he does his Bambi eye trick.

I humbly answer. 'Hmmm … maybe …'

'I love to see the female anatomy when it's as fit and beautiful as yours. You are obviously keeping it healthy. Nice!' My head turns around once more. Christ! The same thing happens again, while he is flirting like crazy. Shy I turn my head the other way so he can't intimidate me.

'You are so beautiful. Wow, and sexy.' I'm surprised but also flattered, then I turn my head again, and he glimpses intensely into my eyes.

'Huh? Okay, Well thanks.'

'You have some amazing beautiful green eyes—do you know that? Very foxy and sparkling,' he marvels, and I turn my head the other way so he can't see I'm blushing. Seconds after I turn my head towards him again and can see he's doing his Bambi trick. Holy mother! He glances happily as if he has won this game of making me turn around all the time.

'How about getting a cup of coffee together? I mean, when we are done? Okay only if you want to, he-he,' he cheerful tosses out the invitation and laughs.

'What? Have coffee with you?' Oh my! His smile is so gorgeous, and on top of it, he is shooting as a wild, uncontrolled hurricane with all his fancy compliments, flying through my mind. Again, he sets his head in a tilting position and blinks as the cute *Bambi on ice*. Oh, my Goodness, how do I answer? I don't want to appear as a prudish woman. He compliments me so kindly, which I am not used to from

Paul, even though I'm sure Paul is thrilled with my appearance. I have always been a trusting person when it comes to authorities and to superior people as Drake. On the other hand, I feel he is different and more outspoken than other practitioners, who are prudish and self-obsessed. But there is something different about him, which I find casual and exciting. If the reader is sincere and true to themselves, imagine, if you are able, as a woman resisting as much charm and compliments from a man as Drake. Can you resist such charm? It is damn hard.

'Sounds nice. Good idea ... I would love to ... but unfortunately, I have another appointment afterwards,' I politely lie. Quite frankly, I've *never* experienced a practitioner inviting a patient for coffee after a treatment session, and did *not* expect such surprising comments from him, so I'm in distress. *He is a doctor! Damn it! I'm his patient!* He is violating all ethical rules, and I believe this is damn abnormal, inviting his patients out. Next, it's shopping. Then dinner at his home. Christ and then ending up in the sack with him. I bet that's his plan. It's unprofessional and awfully offensive. Does he like that with other female patients?

'Okay. What a shame. It would have been lovely enjoying some free time with you. But it's okay. We can do it another time. I will truly like that. Call me if you regret it. I'm almost done with the treatment for today.' Disappointed, he continues without us saying any more to each other. I consider that he is weird, with dangerous, sneaky behaviour. The silence mysteriously settles, and I'm nervous whether he is angry or insulted. I don't like when people get angry at me, because I always try to be decent and polite to everyone—a skill I learned during my childhood, with the heated nuns and the crazy, sadistic priest. Always be a nice, sweet girl, and do whatever they tell you, or you will feel the pain on your tiny body with the bamboo stick, the wooden ruler or the wooden ladle.

'Okay, I only need to adjust your neck. Sit on the chair.' He points strictly at it.

'Oh no. Not my neck again.' I slap my butt unwillingly on the cold upholstered plastic chair. It takes him only seconds to do the movements of checking the head, and in a clever manoeuvre, he holds my head and tilts it from side to side. He sets his fingers in the correct positions, and with a quick set, he clunks the neck. Clunk! Crunch! The loud clunky sound in my head goes along with the electrical feeling all the way down to my fingertips.

'It can't be normal!' I shout, even he says so! I become petrified and scream inside. With his hands on my shoulder, he tenderly massages them for the next five minutes, which he has not done that before. Why now?

'Well, all good for today, precious, sweet Mary. It's such a pleasure to see you again. It's so nice to be alone with you.' His one hand rests on my shoulder, and the other one gives me a lovely tender squeeze on the back of my neck. Goosebumps turns up. Jeez, with all these geese today, I can fabricate several duvets and pillows.

'It's indeed a fantastic *breath of fresh air* to see you today.' Then he lets go with his hands and turns himself in front of me. *What is it with him?* Again, he tilts his handsome head and sends me a charismatic dazzle with his gorgeous eyes. I quickly jump into my jeans and put on my T-shirt and sandals while he is writing a bill. He writes his cash notes into the brownish little book and sticks it into his computer bag, which Kate normally brings. When I grab the bill and look at it, hmm, strangely, it's cheaper than usual. Only 80 euros. Why? Anyway, I give him the dark cash, which he sticks in his pocket. I can hardly get out of the clinic fast enough, then I want to give him my hand to say bye, and at the same moment, I see a wet spot on his beige canvas pants. Holy crap! I'm terrified! What happened? Has he been *horny* while I rested on the table, so much so that his cum is dripping in his pants? I'm absolutely bewildered. Ick, it's disgusting! And it runs cold down my spine. He is creepy and fucked up in his mind. During the entire treatment session, he aggressively commented on my body and sent inappropriate glances at me. He must have planned his *alone* treatment carefully to flirt with me.

'Do you mind waiting for a moment?' he asks eagerly before I can run out of the clinic. He goes to the bathroom, and I hear he is peeing. He washes his hands and comes out while he is drying them in a towel.

'Just give me a second while I shut down the equipment. Then we can walk together to our cars.' He smiles and tosses the towel into the laundry basket, then presses several buttons on the machinery, wipes off the gel, and shuts it down. Curiously, I follow all his movements, and it's difficult for me to get over the knowledge of his nasty *wet spot* on his pants. Puah, it's located centrally in the front and close to the zipper, and his one-eyed-yoghurt slinger. Okay, I admit, I don't know on which side it normally rests in his pants. Yikes! Hideous! He obviously hasn't discovered it himself, or he might have pretended as if nothing happened. Eww! Did he have a hard-on while treating me? Anyhow, I don't want to say anything about it, but I'm losing a lot of respect for him in this very instant and want only to get out. Down the street, he suddenly gives me a tender farewell hug and kisses me intensely on the cheek.

'Are you sure you don't have time for coffee? I want to get to know you a little better,' he pleads.

'No, thank you,' I fume, then turn around, and we go in each direction. In the same flash, he calls my name, and I turn my head, eyeing he walks towards me.

'We forgot to make a new appointment. I'm suggesting in two days. Let's say at 10 a.m., okay? Let's arrange a double session. Then we will have more time to talk. Okay?' Unwillingly I nod, and he walks away, because there is no option for me to protest his self-assured appointment, and I'm taken by surprise that I accept the time I don't want. His cheerful spontaneity makes me curious and takes my breath away, as his magic seizes me.

Can I not say no to his power?

I continue down the street to my car, which is parked not so far from his. He doesn't know which car I'm driving, and at the same moment, I see him passing me, driving fast in the same direction I'm going. As a spy behind him, I keep some distance between us so he will not have the impression I am following him, and the hardtop is up so that he can't see me. We turn right at the junction and drive through the first roundabout, which is adorned with a beautiful horse fountain. We continue straight ahead and drive through several other roundabouts until we reach the highway. The old grey Peugeot drives fast, and I'm sure it's Kate's car. I lose the sight of him, until I suddenly can see his car again on the horizon, while following him as a Russian spy in a fresh James Bond movie. Well I never! This is odd. His tour is the same way as mine, so I become more curious which way he is heading. He slows down at the end of his journey and swings the car into a private garage facility at some white blocks of flats. It goes into a spasm in my head, grasping he lives close to my home, only one kilometre away. Shut up! This is too much, because we are close neighbours! How strange is that, reflecting that I every day walk the dog here. Even this morning, I walked here, and I've never noticed Drake before. Unbelievable, since I often speak with people during my walks, and yet I did not realise there were any other Scandinavians in the neighbourhood. Does he live here with Kate? My imagination tells me he does, and he is also driving the same car as hers. *What a farce.*

CHAPTER 14

REVEALING THE LETTERS

> It is better to conquer yourself than to win a thousand battles. Then the victory is yours. It cannot be taken from you, not by angels or by demons, heaven or hell.
>
> —Buddha

The happiest day of my life is the day I got married, and I wanted it to last for eternity, but the wish is not a reality, and the man is a temporary loan. The baggage, with all its history, gives me certain problems, so it's also going to be tough, even though we love each other much. Is our love enough? No! Paul is unfaithful again, though he is a sweet and loving husband, and our children mean everything to us, but do I mean everything to him? The good life I search for is a non-existent path, so what I believe is perfect is no longer perfect.

In the afternoon, the day before my next appointment at the clinic, I'm immensely downhearted and consider cancelling it, but I don't, since I'm much too drawn to the mystery.

This morning, I'm exhausted and want to stay in bed, because I hardly slept at night. I worry about Paul, and simultaneously I'm at unease of my appointment with Drake. I must stop the treatment, but he is my last hope, and I feel obliged to show up at the clinic. Drake is welcoming me with a delightful smile, and it's placing some positivity in my mind, which I find amazing. He always smiles so mind-blowing, which makes me sparkle, and I'm certain his attractive smile makes every woman's heart bleed. Entering the room, I slap my butt on the table, and silently, I robotically perform the same routine as the other times: clothes off, lie on the table.

'Oh boy. What's going on with you today?' he questions, concerned.

'I can't take it anymore. It's too much. I want to leave this crazy perverted world,' I whimper.

'Come on, Mary. Take it easy. There is no reason to leave the world. Where do you want to go? Are you talking about travelling to the Moon? Ha-ha, or something more drastic?' He grins and gawks at me. I'm sure he can guess my stupid answer, since my depressing face tells more than enough.

'Oh my God! Never have such nonsense thoughts. What's happening? We have plenty of time today to talk,' he beams appearing satisfied.

Oh dear, at that instant, he is so nice and understanding that I want to hug him. His mood feels great, and I am glad that he cares about my sadness. Desperate, I crave to tell him; mostly, I want to scream and cry, but can't. The tears are stuck in my rough inner dark ocean of misery and hopelessness, so I surrender and talk to him about the sadness and the secrets of my marriage.

Now, you will maybe think, *this is the worst thing she can do. Show weaknesses to a man who is trying to lure her?*

You're right, how stupid of me, but the strong bond between doctor and patient has already been established. He already knows some of my secrets, so I continue with more complaints of misery, babbling nonstop as Niagara Falls.

'Paul has an affair! Damn, since spring. People talk about it. I have seen what there is to see. My heart can't cope anymore. I'm stressed. So anxious.'

'Wow! I'm sad to hear.'

'I'm falling into thousands of pieces. The last drop is flowing over in this huge cup of betrayal.' I sniffle, despairing, and repeat myself several times. 'I should put an end to it!' He stares desperately at me and tries to calm me down with a sympathetic smile and a tender hand on my shoulder.

'Don't think like that. Why are you suicidal?'

'The confidence and love are gone. Jeez, I feel hateful towards men.'

'Why?'

'Maybe I'm suicidal. Yesterday, I was driving up in the mountains.'

'Mary, come on. You're such a wonderful woman.'

'Gosh, I had the urge to drive fast over the cliff.' I'm choking on my own words now, then I pause a second, and cry inside my soul trying desperately to get the tears out. It's awful! I can't get those damn millions of tears out, since they are so stuck, as the burning fire of hell, of dry tears.

'I've never before met a woman so sweet and beautiful as you,' he interrupts, lays his head sweet askew, and smiles. I'm *trapped*! His answer is genuine, and he seems serious. I'm flattered and express how I try to fight for my marriage and my inner struggles.

'I've been writing so many desperate letters to Paul—how I felt on the cloud nine with him. Especially when we first met. I want to be peaceful with him. Oh, my goodness, he ignores me. He doesn't answer,' I moan in despair.

'Oh my! That is awful! What did you write to him?' He glares at me while his soft, sensitive feather strokes are treating me. It begins to touch my emotions, which I certainly don't want. Drake has never told me so much about himself, but he fills the room in such a bold way. I feel as I'm the only important person in his life, and regularly he tells me sweet things and gives me many compliments. His gentle touches excite my mind-set too much, though I try to ignore it. He makes me feel good in his closeness, but there are also things I don't fancy about him, but I feel great talking to him. Over the last six treatment, I've been feeling emotionally better than I have in a long time in his presence. *But what is it? Why does he have so much focus on me?* I ruminate.

'Oh, it's a lot of rubbish I write. I can't remember it all in my head.' I sigh in misery.

'Will you share with me?'

'Hmmm ... maybe.'

'Do you have them with you?' he smirks curious.

'They are in my bag. Why? Do you want to know?'

'Yes, of course I want to. That's why I ask.'

'Oh, it's not so interesting. But okay.' I stupidly answer. *I am so dumb. Why can't I keep my mouth shut?* I muse.

He lays down his treatment hand piece, grabs the bag, and hands it over to me. I toss around in the bag to find the damn phone, which is hidden in the bottom.

'Oh gosh!' I reflect.

What?? Can't you find it?'

'Jeez, why are women's bags always such a mess?'

'Ha-ha, ha-ha.'

'Yeah, it's impossible to find anything.' I get irritated then I find the phone, and search through my mail to find the wedding letter.

I start reading it out loud:

Dear Paul,

The real beginning of my new life started when I met you. We went through the universe without any distance or unpleasant feelings of mistrust between us. You were the calm and well-thought-out guy, while I was the funkier, perhaps a little wild, funny troublemaker, who jazzed it up with a little more than salt and pepper. Was I perhaps too wild and crazy? We couldn't avoid being exposed to the true bombardment of attacks by others, who tried to split us apart. I've no emptiness and feel a strong connection to you when we are together. Back then, you wanted the wedding in a church, and *I wanted only you!* So, I became your picturesque bride, and you made me feel as a queen for a day. Your eyes shone as blue sapphires when we confirmed our *yes*. This was a moment nobody ever can take away from me. A common dream with love, faithfulness, and happiness till death do us part. Where did it all go? The stars are fading, and I miss you dearly.

Love and kizzez from your Mary

'Wow, what an incredible declaration of love. You must love him deeply. I admire you for what you write.' Drake seems astonished while I glance at him feeling proud, but I remain humble.

'No, it's too much for you to say. I'm not a good writer. Sorry, I've only been reading fragments of the letter. Most of it is private. I don't feel you should hear it all,' I add.

'Do you know what, Mary? I believe the reason why he doesn't answer you is that he is a fool. Out of words. He must have a bad conscience about everything he has done to you. You should write a book! You write incredibly well. You must become a writer.'

'Nah, no one has told me such nice things before,' so this becomes the beginning of a book. 'I'm only used to criticism. I often lose faith in my writing.'

'Many can benefit from your deep emotions. It's fascinating. You are truly a genius with words. Use this unique talent.'

'Nah, besides Paul and the kids always complain. Okay, they support me and are proud of mom going to school again. Then it's easier for me to help them with their schoolwork.' My old education needed an update, so I'm a hardworking housewife and a student. It's not so easy to study and take care of the family. It's a fulltime job, but I like it. When the kids grew older, I began to learn new subjects, like Danish literature. Oh, my goodness! The teacher is a nightmare and complains about my assignments and often tells me, 'It's some horrible crap you deliver,' and she bullies me. I almost wanted to give up the damn shit, and then I began to concentrate instead on math, rhetoric, religion, Latin, and ancient Greek history. Suddenly, I decided to begin Spanish and English, so I'm extremely busy with school. So, wow, the acknowledgement from Drake feels nice and gives me great satisfaction.

'So, what are your plans?' he questions curiously.

'Honestly, I don't know. We have been married for over twenty years. I think the stars are falling from the sky. Shit, they are no longer shining.'

'You sound so poetic. Such a sensitive woman. Wow, with a huge heart for others.'

'Well, the sunrays can no longer penetrate through the heavy dark clouds that hang over us. Oh, my, then the house tumbles from its solid foundation,' I blabber in my half-sobbing state and pause a few seconds. Smilingly, he glimpses at me and blinks sweetly.

'Funny, so many metaphors you use. He-he, clever and adorable.' He giggles.

'Hmm, well, I'm waiting in the hope that we can be happy again. So far, it's only loneliness. Pooh, frustration. And tears in my saddened core and torn up soul,' I linger with my splashing wild waterfall of words.

'If you were my wife, I'd *never* let you down. You are too lovely to leave in the gutter.' He glows as a magic star. Holy mackerel, and *bullseye*! He goes straight into my emotional core of feelings and pierces my wounded heart with a flaming arrow. He shows me loving kindness, and that is what I'm missing and craving for.

'Oh, so sweet of you. Yea, I wonder, hmmm …' and lay my hand on my broken heart and speak to my inner soul. *Is this the life I want? Is this the dream I have about Paul and me? Will I live in loneliness with my dry tears? No*, not this nightmare anymore.

'What do you decide to do then? I don't get it. Why are you not leaving him? There are many lovely men out there. Ha-ha, like me.' He grins, and damn, again, the overheated flaming arrow hits my core. 'You have to believe in yourself. Man! Peek into the mirror. Holy smokes, you are such an eye-catching woman.' He pauses and glances at me with his Bambi expression. *Boom, boom*, the flatter goes straight to my ripped up, distressed heart.

'I have never deceived my wife. I'm not like that.' He smiles convincingly. Good Lord! I'm about to fall for his many sweet tricks as he continues, 'But, sadly, you are not my woman.' He pauses with a deep sigh, then licks his lips so they shine, sexy and inviting.

'Hmmm, hmmm,' I hum as a bumblebee, and he glances intensely at me.

'My offer is still open. Day or night. If you need a comforting person, I'm there for you. *Trust me*, I'll help you. Sweet Mary, no matter what. I couldn't bear it if anything bad happened to such a gorgeous person. Don't stand alone with so much trouble in life,' he insists and puts his comforting warm magical hand on me. I shiver and feel the angels' white gentle feathers striking behind my neck, and the nice goose pimples pop up, so I believe in him.

'I appreciate your many wonderful compliments.' Perhaps I haven't seen what Drake is up to, but geez, I can imagine him as my man. Will he then be as he tells me? A great soulmate? My heart is touched, but I will not make the same mistake twice. 'The wise one does not encounter the same stone twice' the Russian proverb says. I can feel something good within myself when he admires me so much, so I must watch out. It's, of course, great for my self-esteem, and I embrace his amazing warmth, but I can't figure out how to handle all his flattery.

'Maybe it will be an idea divorcing,' I jabber, then I sense I'm no longer miserable, while feeling great talking to him.

'Then do it. I will gladly help you. *Get rid of him! ASAP!* You must be a wildly desired woman. You are absolutely an impressive, classy lady,' he eagerly flatters.

'Maybe? Yes! Might be you are right.'

'Your story of life is an incredible account of dedication. Such truthfulness on your part. Oh, boy, and a huge shame on him. He doesn't have the guts to give you answers.'

'Best to get a divorce. I'm tired of fighting and done with other women in our life.'

'Mary, he is pissing on you. I'm not a psychologist, but it doesn't take much human knowledge to see the picture here. My heart is crying for you. It's said, "There is not much distance between love to hate." You show it's not true. You don't hate the bloke!'

'It's frustrating! I'm about to give everything up. I want not to bother with Paul's baloney anymore.'

'Oh, my goodness. You carry a heavy bag of crap. You need to throw it in a box. Toss it on the fire,' he urges in keen English, despite the fact we speak mostly in Scandinavian. It makes him seem very smart and clever, and I sense he has a lot of knowledge from his time living in the States. My English is far from his level. It's horrible. I have not the slightest suspicion that he is searching for something different from me, with his pressure to get a divorce. Danger! Unnoticed red flags! Pling,

pling, beware! The railroad crossing is not guarded, and I will be run over by his train.

'Damn, what are other women giving him that I can't give him? Spicy excitement? Stronger than salt and pepper?' I babble, which leads to sorrowful, agitated thinking, and for several minutes it's quiet in the room, then Drake scowls at me.

'What are you thinking?' he asks.

'Salt and pepper!' It flies out of my mouth. 'No, I don't know. Being alone, maybe. I'm afraid of that. I'm scared being alone with the kids. I don't know how to handle a divorce,' I mumble and muse, *nothing will happen in my life unless I try something different.*

'Don't you worry. I can help you.' He smiles enthusiastic..

'Hmmm … I'm not sure … hmmm … well, I did write something else to Paul. I need him to understand my destiny.' I suddenly sniffle, and I take my hand to my nose as I want to dry away the snot.

'What is it? Tell me,' he eagerly asks, and I'm not sure if I want to and peek at him.

'Nahhhh … maybe it's best not to tell anymore,' I squeak, having already said too much.

'No, no. Come on, Mary. You can't stop in the middle of a sentence. I want you to tell me everything. Just get it all out of your conscience. Get rid of the problems that weigh on your shoulder. It's as you are having a lot of devilish demons you need to get rid of.' I get somewhat suspicious and feel he is only interested that I reveal all my secret.

'I'm here for the same reason. *Trust me Mary*. I sincerely want to know everything about you,' he cheerful begs, powerfully and enthusiastically.

My gut tells me not to tell any more, but my unwise chicken brain wants to blabber.

I'm not sure why this feeling runs through my mind, and I'm confused. What is his purpose with the information? Use it against me? I'm naive, blind, and ethical—too trusting—but he makes me feel a great sense of trust and care for me. Red flag! Imagine yourself in this situation, how confusing this is.

Perhaps he is not that bad. He might be a wonderful, empathic man. *Perhaps he talks to everyone about everything, and maybe I am mistaking his good intension*, I consider. His conduct of self-esteem fascinates me, and he is a perfect listener, so I stupidly surrender and find the other letter.

> Dear Paul,
>
> I'm waiting alone with my emptiness. My gloomy tears are sitting deep in my heart and try to run down my cheeks. Both of us show parts of us we probably don't like or want. You are the only one who can fill my heart, delete the emptiness, and remove the fateful tears from my cheek. What do you want me to do for you? Do you want to give it all up, then be lonely with your memories and thoughts, or even be with another woman? Maybe there is no more love for us. Am I wrong? I sit with my guardian angel, and it tries to fight together with me so I can find you again. The angel tells me how our lives are, in both good and bad. Together with it, I continue fighting for our love and will never give up. There is only one thing the angel never tells me—if I fight in vain. Do I? Love you deeply.
>
> Love and kizzez, Mary

'Mamma mia, it's incredible. Gee, you fight some unachievable battles. It's malicious to leave you in such a lurch. I would never do this to you.'

'Hmmm,' why does he say that?

'Sounds as you've had a rough time. I pity you. You don't deserve such crap, Mary. You are too sweet to be treated in such a bad way.' He smirks and gives me several comforting hugs during the treatment and his comforting words.

'Gosh, yea, I have had my share of ups and downs. My trust in Paul is wavering vastly, but I remain his faithful wife.'

'When he has these women, do you still have sex?' He asks. I pause some moments because the question is somehow embarrassing and private, but I give in to his curiosity.

'No, not for a long time. I try to fulfil his wishes. Gosh, as well as the more advanced dreams of his,' I say shamefully.

'Okay, that sounds bizarre to me. You're sure his Barbie doll. Then he uses you in the most despicable way for his own pleasure and satisfaction. Oh lord, it's insane! Or is it simply he who's crazy?' He expresses strongly.

'What holds everything together with us is our children. I want to give him all the sex and love that he seeks in others. But it's a challenge because he is never home.'

'Okay, you got the point there. That's, of course, somehow difficult.'

'Then he complains about missing sex.'

'But sex is also an important part of life.'

'How do you then keep the erotic moments alive when he's never home?' I question, since it's difficult for me to understand.

'I don't get it. You are such a striking woman who must have a great life. Oh man, look at your body. Geez, with such great soft skin you have. One's can only enjoy touching it. Wow, and have intense intimacy with you. Can't he see that? He is crazy!' He beams excitingly and sweetly then gives me the elevator glare and licks his stunning red lips, so they are wet and shiny. Christ, I want to touch them. Oh, dear me! Okay, it's sweet but also a little above my comprehension what he rejoices in, so I slip, easy and elegant, over these obnoxious remarks.

'Of course, sex is important. But for him, materialistic goods and money seem more important than me. I stay solely for the sake of the children, though I love him,'

'Do you have more on your phone? Read it, if you want to,' he requests wishfully.

'Nah, I'm not sure. I've read more than enough,' I'm twisting myself in thought.

'Oh, no, come on. It can't be that bad. Can it?' He grins.

'Okay then, but this will be the last one. It's quite private what I share with you. Please keep it confidential. Promise me? I will only read some of it.' Drake stares intensely and affectionately at me with big eyes.

> Dear Paul,
>
> We are waiting on a battlefield in a modern age, and at the same time, we live in another universe. We live in a war zone that doesn't even belong in a modern world, nor in Denmark. We live under the same broken roof in our collapsed house. We desperately and barely are alive and survive as half—and not as whole—people. Maybe we imagine our own dramatic, unimaginative thoughts and ideas about each other. I'm not sure if it is so. I try to remember what we once had together, where the truth, the imagination, and the human emotions once were solid. It's there we will call it *love*, but we park our love and turn away from each other. As I know you well, I'm sure you still have a lot of feelings and love hidden inside you. This can be my destiny to find you again. Carpe diem! If our ways must separate, we must separate here, if none of us dares to grab after the last straw of love.
>
> Hugz and kizzez, Mary

'Fine, this is the last one. I don't want to read any more. Maybe my possession in need for Paul is linked to some of my trauma in my childhood. But which trauma is it? Hmmm, if any at all?' and I end up hoping Drake will *not* ask for more questions, because he shall not know it all.

'What kind of trauma are you talking about. Is it from your childhood? You must tell me about it one day. Still and all, my offer is open for a cup of coffee. Or a beer.' He appears cheerfully.

'Thank you so much. Maybe one day. Let me think about it. I normally don't go out with strangers. Hehe, even though you are no longer a stranger to me.'

'Let's meet for the next treatment in a few days.'

I'm trapped in what I believe is genuine kindness, and yet there are probably many *red flags* I don't see. He has arms that's made of solid rough steel which are impossible to escape from, and I'm not sure if everything is too good to be true. Despite my tiny awareness and warnings from others, I want to believe the best in him because he has some good parts as well.

CHAPTER 15

Hidden Shades of Doctor Bates

Do not overrate what you have received, nor envy others. He who envies others does not obtain peace of mind.

—Buddha

Two days have passed and today, I have already been at the clinic for an hour, so it feels as if the sessions are getting longer and longer every time. I'd hoped the treatment would be over by now, but Drake is so curious about everything, including my childhood trauma, and it's pressing me he is taking so much of my time, because I wanted to get home to my dog.

'Tell me more about Paul.'

'Why do you want to know?'

'But what does he do in the company? He must apparently earn very well?'

'I thought we were almost done. I assume there is no more time to talk,' I answer.

'Don't worry. We have plenty of time. I have no patients after you. We can chat longer today.'

'Nah. Okeydokey, I can speak a little about Paul. Only until you're finished with the treatment,'

'I have an idea. Let's grab some tapas and continue your story.' He joyfully beams.

'Nah, I don't think I have time afterwards. I'm not hungry. The dog. He needs me.' I reply and pause for a few seconds.

'Ah, come on. It is so interesting. How is Paul?'

'I enjoy watching him in the morning. Sometimes he leaves early. Before the kids and I get up. I don't like that. I imagine I'll never see him again.'

'Oh! How does he dress for work?'

'He is a typical suit guy. Black leather shoes and a black attaché bag. Often, I laugh at him because he is such a car geek. I speculate how many cars he has bought during our lifespan. Lucky me, because he has bought me two convertibles.'

'Wow, he must earn a lot. Does he own the company?'

'Ha, ha, one for Spain and one for Denmark. I feel as I'm on *The Bold and the Beautiful*.'

'Ha, it's always the rich and bold who can afford all this.' Drake laughs enviously.

'Oh no. It's not that bad. He doesn't buy the cheapest models. I never protest.'

'No, you can't allow yourself to complain. Not with two convertibles.' He asks me more questions before I can answer the previous ones. 'How does your home look in Copenhagen? Is it huge?'

'Hmm… I guess it's among the better ones. I've everything my heart desires. Paul loves expensive design. Wine and liquor. Oh, my, we have a lot in the wine cellar.'

'Ha, ha, let's go to your flat and have a party! But only if you have Hendrick's gin. Or maybe the original Gentleman Jack. Hi, hi, for a real gentleman like me.'

'We have that gin. No problem. Also, the rare Tennessee whiskey.' I wonder, *who is this gentleman, named Jack?* 'Ha, ha, we can provide those brands,' I brag and laugh.

'No, no, no, I don't believe that. They're expensive. No one normally has it,' he answers arrogantly. Such a *bigmouth*!

'I love whiskey! So, I know we have it. I only drink Jack Daniels,' I assure him. Amazed, he nearly drops the machine's handheld treatment device and his jaw on the floor. Ha-ha! I got you! Dumb bragging maniac!

'Having cars, kids, dogs, a boat, and our holiday home, is perfect. With that, people look at us with great respect.'

'I lived in the most expensive area of California. We had a gigantic house with an enormous swimming pool. I had many big, expensive cars. There is nothing wrong with materialistic goods.'

'Well, I'm not missing anything. Hmmm, except for mutual love. And respect.'

Drake then blabber as a chatterbox about his life. That's the first time he tells me this much about his life, and I'm flabbergasted at his blabbering.

'It's always nice to have many things.'

'I don't care about all this materialistic shit. I believe it's important for Paul.'

'During my time in Sweden, my clinic was the largest one in the world. Thirty-thousand square feet in the heart of Stockholm. I built the biggest swimming pool. Yeah, it was Olympic-sized. There was a patient hotel, rehabilitation centre, restaurants, and lots of staff. No one had the success I had. Everyone back then was talking about me worldwide.'

'Wow, that's massive.'

'Oh, boy, I was so busy with thousands of patients who took all my energy. Over 45.000. I was always there for them. Oh, dear, as I'm with you now. I must have done something perfectly. Everyone talked about how fantastic my treatment protocol was.'

'Geez, that a lot of patients. How could you manage that?'

'Yea, damn! It was exhausting. Shit, then I had to pay 68 percent in TAX to the government. Imagine for being allowed to work 17 hours a day. Gee, such tax mafia. It was not a life. I am perceived of being a perfectionist. I'm a very hard worker who demands much of my co-workers. I felt abused and worn out.'

'Sounds awful.'

'Man, when I needed help, there was nobody to give me a hand. I became more and more isolated and alone. Maybe others did not think that I needed any help.'

'Why not?'

'I projected so much self-confidence. So much that other people have sucked up to me to be part of such confidence. Holy Jesus, I gave people self-confidence. Even my wife didn't care.' His blabbering continues constantly, and I ponder, Wauw, *Paul has no such megalomania as Drake*.

'I don't understand?'

'Patients came from all over the world. It was a golden goose laying plenty of golden eggs. Oh, my goodness, I was earning so much money. Millions. Then the greedy tax mafia took their massive cut. It angered me so much, so I sold it all.'

'Oh, so you don't have it anymore?'

'No, no, it's sold. On that sale, I earned millions. Puff, then I left Sweden. First, I began some business in Caribbean.'

'Sounds exotic.'

'It was. When there was no more work there then the USA represented a significant chance for me. I looked at my masterpiece of a clinic and realized the mistake I made when I let it go. Then the family moved to another World for a better life. *To a better life?*'

'What do you mean?'

'Yea, wow, even I thought it. So, I made what I thought were superb choices given the circumstances. Quickly, I established a giant clinic there. Shortly after, several clinics at different regions in the United States. It was over thirty years ago—ha, ha—when I still was young, handsome, and full of energy. This event in the USA was a huge mistake.'

'What happened?'

'Jeez, to think it was a country of fairness. Jesus Christ, reason and positive thinking—ha, ha! A land of opportunities. Shit, it was not. Damn! Several times people defrauded me. They stole all the money that I had entrusted them.' He smirks.

'I'm dumbfounded. Wow, out of words,' thinking, *Yeah, right! Keep it up. You're a winner! It's always others fault. To me, it sounds like a* competition to see who has the biggest one-eyed monster. Him or Paul! Goodness gracious me! His self-important story continues.

'How could I even think I would have a chance in that country? I have always differed from most people.'

'What do you mean about being differed?'

'After many years in the States, I sold the clinics to my partners. Holy cow, I was so tired of the US system. I thought USA represented the best in people. And for people. Oh, boy, damn, I was wrong. Like Sweden is permeated by jealous people. They think more about themselves than others. I left because it frustrated me over our failed life. I sought a better on if I could find it.'

'What do you mean about a better life? How come you talk about you failed?'

'I am too much of an idealist. Throughout history, idealists are the ones that get executed for their convictions.'

'Executed? Sounds dangerous. Who got executed?'

'Beforehand a Norwegian bloke swindled me. I had witnessed against him in a fraud case a Danish investor had brought against him. He had taken more than $2 million from him.'

'Sounds crazy.'

'It was. He was to invest money for him concerning some of my business in USA. That was a lie. They never made such investment. The guy got away with stealing all the money that they entrusted him by this foolish man.' I feel anger in his voice when he feels defeated.

'What about you? Did you also lose a lot?'

'The fact is that I had made lots of money throughout my career. Mary, believe me, also in my many recent ideas and ventures. I took the money and began all over in Spain. This time with a lot more knowledge. No one has as much knowledge about this treatment as I do. So, Mary, trust me when I tell you—you have come to the most experienced man in the world.'

'Wow, good for you. I'm glad you are doing so well.'

'*Trust me!* I'll do everything for my precious lady. You deserve the best treatment.'

'Oh, thanks. So sweet of you.'

Mr Bigmouth has finally stopped bragging. Gee! Give me a cheer, man! The dude is successful! So, dear reader, be aware when a man is bragging so much and says, 'Trust me.' In that case, *don't*! Red flags!

'Were you married? Did you have kids? Or perhaps you don't have time for kids and a wife?' I ask nicely with a lovely smile.

'Married? Oh yes! I got divorced for many years ago.' He is silent for a minute while he stares downwards. Is he thinking of something or of what he wants to say? The answer comes with a strange change in his speech when he glares at me again.

'Ohhh… hmmm… well, my wife did not want to go with me. She stayed in the USA with the kids. I paid her out with a vast amount. Then gave her the house and cars.' He rolls his eyes to the left and stares down again. He is silent for a minute and glares to the right with his eyes turning upwards and then talks again. It reminds me of when Paul lies to me.

'Oh, so nice of you. Then she can manage for the rest of her life?' I ask, curious.

'Oh… yes… my goodness, she got a great lump of money. She will not suffer any distress. When she is in need, I still send her money to cover her expenses. God Almighty, she spends a lot of money. Shit, then I have to pay for it,' he complains arrogantly, and I trust it all. Wow! *What a glorious man he is, still helping his ex with money*, I muse, and I believe he is amazing.

'Oh gosh! So nice of you. What a genuine gentleman. How gallant you are.' I get the impression he is wealthy. 'Why did you divorce her?'

'Oh, she is so dense. Oh, boy, then she was having an affair with someone from the clinic. I can't take such betrayal. I do everything for her. Shit, then she can only complain. I got tired of her untidiness; jeez, the home was never in proper order or clean. All her stupid boxes.'

'Strange. Ha, ha, perhaps she likes boxes.'

'Damn, all over in our house. Hmmm, what was she hiding in them?' He seems pissed off at her.

'Are you and Kate married?' I ask sneakily.

'Yuck! No way! She is not my type. She is only my part-time secretary,' he snaps nastily, turning his head away, staring down to the left, and then continuing to focus on the area he treated on me.

'Oh… I got the impression that you were married to her.'

'No, we are *not* married. Nor lovers. Are you crazy? She is not my type.'

'I watched you driving off with her the other day,' I say, bluffing.

'Yikes, she is only working for me. I only like classically educated women. Hmmm, like you.'

'Well, I was sure you lived together.'

'Oh, no! I've briefly rented a room at her flat. I'm soon leaving for the Far East, as you know,' he grunts, content, and turns his eyes left and down again. Now I know he is living in this building close by me.

'Hmmm, one day, both of you were driving in the same car. I could see that from the café when I was having my lunch.' I turn my head over my left shoulder to see his reaction, and he stares at me suspiciously, and seems irritated. Could it be because I have seen them together, and I have hit a soft spot? I can't figure out if he is lying or not.

'I'm sure it was not us. What car was it then? You have not given me the answer.'

'It's was grey Peugeot,'

'Right! Not us.' and his reply is rapid. 'Everybody drives an old grey Peugeot, so it's not us!' And now I'm more certain he is lying.

'Old? Did I say that?'

'And to make it clear, I'm not married to anyone! I have told you so before.' He seems extremely agitated. Well! Then, that's clear, I ponder, but my gut tells me something else, and it doesn't match with what he tells me. Have I been driving him around as a dancing bear in the circus? He goes dead silent, as if he is afraid, I've found out something I shouldn't have.

'Might have been some others. Let's not talk more about me. Tell me more about you.' He smirks.

'Oh, my, everyone believes our marriage is perfect. Apparently we appear as the happiest family. Well, no one believes me when I tell them the opposite. Are we behaving as a blissful couple, on the top of the world?' I alleged.

'Have you never been happy with Paul?' he tested me.

'Of course! I got a perfect husband. My dream came true around the time I turned 30,' I answer cheerfully.

'Oh, that is late in life. So, do you have children with him?'

'Yes. Having them within the marriage was important for me.' I smile.

'Why within a marriage?'

'Hmmm, sounds old-fashioned. The dream of the good, old-fashioned, idyllic family. Ha, ha, with the house, kids, and doggies. What more can I ask for in a man? I guess it's because of my Catholic faith. Perhaps my personality.'

'Oh, I didn't know you are Catholic. I'm an atheist. I don't believe in any religions. Nor gods. He-he, only in myself.' He smirks, and he seems self-satisfied, with a tremendous amount of self-importance.

'I suppose it's not crucial. For me, warmth and love are more important. I will not fly on my soft pink cloud any longer. Where has it all gone? They are only empty dreams. Oh, my, like those you see in the movies.' I peek at him sadly.

'Yes, I suppose it's so. I wasn't pleased in my marriage either. I wish I had met you back then.' He grins in his usual sweet foxy way and blinks with his great Bambi eyes.

'You must show your priest and your lawyer your letters.'

'Why show them to the priest and a lawyer? I don't have a lawyer. I'm not that far in my consideration. I'm not sure what to do!' I then sob.

'Get out of the closet. Get it all out for the first time. Get some space in your soul. Seek for forgiveness and peace,' he responds, forgetting that I have already sought for absolution on his damn *Fifty Shades of a Prayer Stool*, the red torture knee chest.

'What do you mean *get out of the closet*? I'm not a lesbian!' I grunt and believe in my vivid imagination that my life will be well again with Paul.

'Have you ever tried a proper man? I was hoping you could get rid of this self-important bloke. I mean that.'

'What? I want a peaceful and good life that I can embrace with my soul.'

'Paul is not worth your love. He is a self-absorbed fucking twat… and… and…' he stutters angrily. I'm waiting for the next blow of his words, but nothing happens.

'I will do whatever it takes to keep the family together. I suppose there isn't anything wrong with that?' but Drake can't come up with any answer to my question. 'I've had many wonderful moments of happiness and love. Hmm, as being in heaven. I love to glance deep into Paul's amazing blue gaze. It makes me dizzy with love. Just holding his hands. Then I feel close to him. But we never do that anymore.'

'So, what do you want to do?'

'I have no idea. I'm crawling like a zombie on the dirty floor. I have no more power left for impossible struggles. I'm torn into thousands of pieces. I don't know how to end it. I'm afraid of losing Paul.' I panic, and my anxiety is spreading to my nerves and bones so I can hardly breathe. 'Imagine the feeling when your life has been a randomly sown field. Can you see the picture in front of you when it's harvested?'

'No! I don't know this feeling. I can't imagine it.'

'One got used and discarded! What happens then to that little seed? The beautiful imaginary picture of something is about to grow. Poof, everything fades in the glum space.'

'You're such a wonderful woman. You deserve and need my help.' He blinks.

'I might as well disappear into the darkness of space,' I'm almost bawling.

'It doesn't help to escape the battle with suicide. Let me help you.' He gently touches my skin as with soft feather strokes with his fingertips.

'To love and be loved is possible. Only if both are ready. And under equal conditions. Otherwise, I have no more to give.'

'Mary listen, Kate is going on vacation. Then we can meet in private.' He flashes at me convincingly and is sure of the abilities of his magnificent powers with his eyes.

'I'm not sure it's a good idea. Let me think about it,' but he keeps on pushing me.

'Perhaps tomorrow. After I have treated you,' his eyes sparkle, as if it's obvious I will show up tomorrow. I don't want to be unfaithful, but I'm in desperate need of somebody to hold in my embrace and to love. Do I want to end the marriage? There is no longer any solid foundation in my life. Several years ago, Paul had an affair that shattered my life, causing a deep depression. I've been spying on them and got all the evidence. But he kept on denying the betrayal. I forgave him from the deepest part of my wounded heart. *What God has put together, let no man or woman separate.* After a year, things turned in a positive direction. I'm happy again and trust him fully—until it all begins over again.

So again, I spied on his next chapter of betrayal and hired a private detective, who gave me all the evidence. The grieving has been cruel. I was weak, and it's still difficult to handle the battles in my life. The house of cards has fallen apart, and I am in a new deep black hole of depression. I want to get out of this damn horrifying quicksand, but I can't. It drags us deeper into a hell of scorching, sucking sand. Now psychological collapse stands in front of me again. I imagine that I'm more than done, like an over-grilled chicken, who is severely boiling back to hell. Then the weirdest suicide solutions pop up. I imagine dangling from the rooftop. Cutting myself into pieces with a razor blade, squashed in a pool of several litres of blood. Drowning myself in the ocean in the grim night, having a chain and a massive lump of led tied to my legs, that's dragging me further at the bottom of the sea. Or driving at full blast my car over the cliff in the amazing mountains of Spain, then it will explode, and I will burn in hell.

I don't dare execute any of these macabre solutions. Such messy, bloody macabre solutions, and so much bloody shit. Paul's betrayal is torture and drives me mad, as an angry grizzly bear who has lost its cubs, falling over the cliff and died instantly. The feeling of powerlessness is unbearable. Humans are so egocentric, and everything is only about themselves or to get sex with their neighbour or secretary. The grass is always greener on the other side! Is genuine love a marvellous creation? Is it my punishment for being a loving wife and mother, or do I love them too much? I have lost all faith, joy, and quality of life. Emotionally, I'm in a dying process in the abyss of severe blazing darkness.

Suddenly! Poof! Out of the amazing blue sky, Drake pops up on a soft white floating cloud as an angel and tries to convince me of his fantastic abilities to heal me. He has a superb way of getting close to me with his eager, hot charisma and the electricity he emitted from his fingertips, sending hot, ecstatic quivers through my lost body. And then he has those eyes! *Boom!* The bomb is heavily dropping to the floor, and I'm blasted into total blindness.

'Okeydokey, we are almost finished,' he burst out as he is interrupting my thoughts. 'Only your back and neck need to go. You have much more movement in your spine. Can you feel the difference?' he smiles so sweetly and touches me softly and chillingly with a finger running along the spine.

'Might be? Hmmm… I'm not sure,' I answer, and honestly, I can't feel shit except for more pain.

'I'd like to hear more of the story. Come again tomorrow at 10 p.m. We'll grab some coffee afterwards when I'm back from the airport.' He grins boldly and blinks with those amazing shiny eyes. Geez, he knows exactly what effect those eyes have on me and plays them on purpose. 'Sit on the chair,' as he commands me to sit on the ugly cold blue PVC upholstered plastic chair. And I'm shaking. Nervously, I wait for him to put his warm hands around my neck and do his crazy crunchy thing I fear so much, and suddenly, without warning, *Crack! Crunch!* Done! I grab his hand slightly, and he turns it around, giving me a lovely squeeze, and holds it tight. A strange, passionate feeling goes through my body, and I don't want him to let go of my hand.

'Let's meet tomorrow. Kate will be gone. She will first be back before I leave for Asia,' he utters softly, still holding my hand, and seems delighted to get rid of her.

'Fine, I'll think about it.' I glance at him differently than I usually do. Oh, my, he is so nice, and I fancy him somewhat differently. 'Where is Kate going? With you to Asia?' I ask stupidly, somehow jealously.

'No, no, she is visiting family in Denmark,'

'Oh, I see. Your family?' I try to test him slyly.

'No, not at all. *Her* family. *Not* mine. I have nothing to do with them. My family lives in Sweden,' he seems annoyed.

'Okay! Are you going to Denmark or Sweden?' I'm confused, and I wonder if I'm too nosy.

'Yes, in two days. To help her family. Then to Stockholm,' he adds, and I notice the inconsistency.

'Where in Denmark are you staying? I'm also leaving in a few days.'

'Nearby Copenhagen. We can meet and get some coffee!' he eagerly smiles. I muse, *well, I'll be very black in my stomach, with all the coffee he's inviting me to.*

'You can give a guided tour,' he replies happily, and now it's *coffee and a tour guide*. I smile.

'Sounds exciting. Which hotel do you want me to pick you up at?' Am I too tricky? 'Ha, ha.' At first, he glares confused, like a dancing bear in the circus, and then he gets angry.

'Argh! No, no! Don't you understand anything? I'm not staying at any hotel! Christ! I'm staying with Kate and her family. We have a family thing this weekend,' he angers.

'Oh, I'm lost. Confused!' I don't understand diddly squat of what this goofy dude is going on about. Is it him or me suffering from dementia? Why is he going to stay with her? Family thing? Something doesn't add up with my math. Oh, my!! Liar! Perhaps he has never learned math?

'I'll give you my Swedish phone number. Then you can call and tell me where we can meet. I've yours,'

'Clever guy!' He has a superb way of saying things, so I can hardly get out of his invitation. He is steadfast in his approach to meet up. I let him finish his treatment in peace.

I still must kneel on my damn *Fifty Shades of Drake* prayer stool, and he gives me a commanding stare.

'Kneel! Lean forward!' the controlling master orders, and clonk, he has set the back. 'We are all done now!' and he gently lays his palms on my shoulders and massages them with gentle caressing movements. As I stand only in my thong and a bra, he gives me a tender hug and a tender squeeze with his one hand behind my neck. It feels somehow nice, in such a bold way, and the feeling shudders through my bones when he draws my half-naked body close to him. Compassionately! Oh, yes indeed! He's able to emit his feelings from his stomach to mine and up to my brain, or is it my feelings that radiate to him? At first, it feels weird, and then it's calm and nice, embracing him. I get dressed while he writes my bill for 120 euros, then he closes his machinery and cleans it, next, tossing the towels in the basket.

'What are you going to do in Asia?' I glimpse at him curiously.

'Clinics and a hospital on a golf course. Together with some business partners in Macau. Later, we are expanding to China and Japan. It will be a massive success. Many investors,' he beams happily.

'Wow! But why leave Europe? Why so far away?' I'm stunned.

'I've had enough of Spain. The system is stupid. I have no friends. They are all Kate's friends. Yikes, dirty old mountain goats! Stinky local mountain monkeys from smelly Pueblo pups. That's not for me. I like classier people, like you.' He smirks at his insults of the Spanish people. How rude of him! (I'm so sorry! Apologies to the readers from those countries he talks nasty about. These words are not in my normal vocabulary, only in Drake's, so I allowed myself to borrow them for the book.) 'In Sweden, they rip you off with their wild tax system. I'm sure it's the same in Denmark. I have no intention of going back to the States. I might as well travel to Asia.' He seems furious as he expresses his anger at others, so I have the impression that he hasn't found the right clues of his life, neither professionally nor personally. But I can be mistaken in my observations.

'Well, what do I know about that?' Then I stare at him to see if he had finished his cleaning.

'It sounds exciting. I've never been to Asia. Hopefully, I will visit one day.'

He smilingly replies while he moves closer to me, 'Oh my goodness. Of course, you must come and visit me there. Yes, it will be good. I also have lectures. I will educate doctors and alternative practitioners.' How arrogant he is.

'Shut up. Give me five. What a unique person you are.' Expressing it ironically.

'I want my fantastic knowledge moved to many others in the world. Best before I die!' he boasts. Wow! Outstanding talent, and he states so naturally that he is the world's best, most clever doctor. My jaw drops to the floor.

'Wow! So wonderful for you. Wish you all the best,' I cheer loudly, unable to hold back my full-blown outburst. Next, I'm thinking strategically. Strange. If he is so unique, why does no one else in the world possess this education? Why didn't he start that program a long time ago? I haven't heard about him before. In my imagination, it all sounds too good to be true! Blink! Blink! You are crossing the red light! Watch out, he doesn't run you over with a self-important runaway train! I can't see through his grandiose statements. *Amazing! The man is an educated and exciting person with expert knowledge and experience in life.* I look up to him even more because he seems so confident and empathetic. I had not invented the red flags in my small world! Now, dear friends, this is probably where everybody must *run, run, run,* even faster and preferably as far away as possible. But promise me not to run after him to Asia.

As we come down to our parked cars in front of the clinic, he hugs me tenderly, and we say goodbye after a nice, though confusing and meaningful day. Then he gets into his car, waves contently at me, and drives off.

At home, I'm feeling such an enigmatic sensation, though there are things that aren't fitting together properly. Shall I meet with him or not? The coffee invitation is open. Gosh! It's getting on my nerves, but I'm also curious about his fantastic adventure to Asia. My common sense tells me *not* to meet him, but he has been so sweet, listening and flirting with me. I don't ponder too much about it, because it's not unusual for men to get lost and twisted in their heads from my beauty, so I have often experienced their flirtatious gazes and their interest. Stupid men! Their eyeballs always fall out of their silly heads.

CHAPTER 16

Chiringuito and Gentleman Jack

An old Cherokee is teaching his grandson about life. "A fight is going on inside me," he said to the boy.

"It is a terrible fight and it is between two wolves. One is evil—he is anger, envy, sorrow, regret, greed, arrogance, self-pity, guilt, resentment, inferiority, lies, false pride, superiority, and ego."

He continued, "The other is good—he is joy, peace, love, hope, serenity, humility, kindness, benevolence, empathy, generosity, truth, compassion, and faith. The same fight is going on inside you—and inside every other person, too."

The grandson thought about it for a minute and then asked his grandfather, "Which wolf will win?"

The old Cherokee simply replied, "The one you feed."
—Author Unknown

The earliest known version is a story told by the Reverend Billy Graham 1978 The Holy Spirit: Activating God's Power in Your Life. Two Wolves
–Wikipedia, the free encyclopaedia.

This Cherokee story tells us about the continuous battle between the two forces within us. The conflict between our grim side, the feeling of inferiority, and the ego. The other bright part is our more noble and peaceful side and told as a certain life lesson from an old man to his grandson, explaining that we should not deplete the animal, which is as dark as the night. The Cherokee Indians are one of the so-called *five civilised tribes*, known for their cultural wealth, language, and traditions, according to Professor Panther-Yates in The Cherokee Clans.

Since my childhood, I have been fascinated by the Indians and legends of their many battles during their time for survival. I adore wolves, because it's such a clever and beautiful animal. The stunning horses, the mysterious wolves, and the way they the native dresses, and the men's and women's proudness and beauty, with long, shiny black smoother hair. It makes me a little envious and captivates me at the same time. The quote feels true and spiritual to me, and I sense the two wolfs, as the fate of my upside-down rollercoaster. One moment, I feel immensely joyful, and the next, I experience adversity, sorrow, anger, and despair as the two wolves' battles take place inside me.

Hallelujah! Here he is! Drake, the old man, telling me the fairytale, I shall no longer fight for my husband. But who is the wise one? None of us are! I can no longer control the chaos in my head and am becoming weaker! Unwillingly, I feed the black wolf with stories and choose his shady side. Patiently, the gobble has been sitting in the corner, waiting to see when I become weaker and unprepared for him to strike. Drake has many pleasant qualities, but does he know how to use them properly? His determination, persistence, courage, and strategic thinking might lack in the white wolf, so he might use them for evil, and I ponder, is he the black wolf? What a shame if he misuses excellent skills. As the white wolf, I should be able to recognise and transform my anger, grudge, or grief in a better way. Will I learn a moral lesson and use both parts of the white and black wolf and not end up in a mess with Drake?

After my last treatment and my blabbering, I went out like a light, though he has that day persuaded me to come again today. At the appointment I notice he has changed the treatment plan to nerves on both my tibias, groin, butt, lower back, and again on my neck. Oh no! It has again sent Doctor Frankenstein's thunderbolt through my entire left side. Suddenly it seems it's my complete body Drake wants to treat, although I have only come for treatment of my foot. He seems grouchy and stressed, so we hardly speak with each other. But there is one thing he hasn't forgotten, sending me his massive magic energy with his flirting glances.

'We must meet before I travel to Denmark. Promise me that?' He grins and shuts down the equipment when I have paid my bill. Before we part ways, he embraces me.

'Call or write to me. I'll be waiting,' he insists, and after that, I drive home. His words run through my mind repeatedly, then I regret telling him so much and keep thinking, *it will be better not to tell him anymore.* I'm too open and have told him too much, though I'm pleased about his many compliments and that he wants to help me. As a female lion, I run distressed in my cage and don't know if I want to meet with him. Geez, he is so cool, handsome, and understanding, and wow, then there are those eyes and his gorgeous smile. Fine, it's only a coffee, nothing else, not a date! Yes, no, yes, no, send the damn message! The evil devil pokes at me. Don't do it! The protecting angel whispers in my ear. Call him. Don't call him! It goes through my brain several times, back and forth in a fight with the devil and the angel. If I do it, will it then be a betrayal to Paul? No, Drake is only a dear friend, the devil shouts, and what's wrong with that? It's a betrayal to Paul, the angel whispers. The panic runs through my head. What if Kate sees the message? My gut tells me they might be a couple, but it doesn't fit into the narrative Drake has told me.

In the afternoon, I take the devilish chance, and grab my mobile and write him a message in Spanish, hoping he understands it. If not, I can always excuse myself, saying, 'It's for my Spanish friend.' Holy moly, how difficult can this be?

'*Holà*, I hope this finds you well. I'm back in Spain. Shall we meet if you have time? Let's meet downtown over a cup of coffee. See you. Greetings, Mary.'

Bewildered, I stare at the damn phone, then place it back on the table and next I feverish snatch it again. Shall I press *send* or delete it? Shit, shit, shit. If I push send, there is no going back. Oh no! Wrongly, my finger slips and presses send. Eeek, my body goes into an uncontrolled anxiety attack. I get hot and cold flashes because of my stupid action and immediately regret sending the text. Duh, it's heedless, and my guilty conscience plagues me, because I have broken my own ethical rules. Who will see the message? Is Kate already on the aeroplane yet or not? What if he doesn't understand Spanish? Jingle, jingle, and to my surprise, my mobile rings hours later. Damn, it's Drake on the line, on his way back from the airport.

'Hey, it's Drake.' he seems joyfully.

Oh… my goodness. My speech freezes, my body shakes, and chills run down my spine. It takes a long time before I'm calm again.

'Well … hmmm … oh, hey … hmmm … it's you… why are you calling me?'

'Did you send me a text in Spanish?'

'Huh? What do you mean about a text?' I stutter clumsily.

'Yes, somebody has sent me a text. Isn't it from you?'

'Nah … hmm … I don't think so, I … I … no … I have sent no text.'

'It's in Spanish. You speak Spanish, don't you?' he questions.

'Why would I send a Spanish text to you?' I stammer and lie. If he could see me, he'd know I am lying. I'm a horrible liar, and everyone can see if I lie. I'm as an open book and will never be a talented poker player.

'Come on! Can't you see it on your phone if it's you?'

'Honestly, no! How can I peek at my phone if I'm speaking with you?'

'It looks like your number. I know it so well.'

'It's impossible. I'm sure you're mistaken. It's not from me,' I lie and tease.

'Well … I don't think that's correct. Please, are you sure it's not from you?' Suddenly, he seems disappointed that it's not from me. 'Kate grabbed the phone out of my hand before I got the chance to read the text,' he grunts, annoyed.

'Wow! Sounds brutal.' I panic, then get nervous and sweaty that she has seen the text. 'Did she read it?' I'm scared.

'Oh, dear me. What do you think? Yes, she did. The situation got so uncomfortable, so I tried to pretend there was nothing and asked her, "What does it say? I don't understand Spanish."'

'Wow … that's not good.' I worry and feel awful.

'Okay, so tell me, is it you?' he snaps at me. 'The only thing I understand is something about coffee. Kate is so angry, raging as a fireball! She asked, "Are you going to meet with Mary when I'm gone?" Stupid cow.' He laughs. I am trembling.

'Well … what happened?' I respond nervously.

'She went total nutcase in her stupid head. Quite frankly, I don't give a damn about it. She is crazy.' He laughs louder than before. 'So, tell me *now*! Is it you? Or did she get crazy in vain?' he pleads as an upset kitten. It occurs to me, why would she get mad if they aren't in a relationship? My belly feels this is a correct observation. Has he lied to me?

'What do you want me to say?' I answer teasingly. 'Do you want the truth or an untruth?'

'Well, I actually prefer the truth.'

'Hmm …' Damn, that's not the best question I have asked.

'Come on. Chop, chop. I don't have all day. What is your answer? The truth or what?' he orders.

'No, no, no … I don't think it was from me,' I lie, playing cat and mouse.

'Right? Come on, I know it's your number. Why are you lying? Tell me!' he demands heatedly.

'Okey! It's me. We might as well get that coffee deal you have been asking for.'

'About time. I'd love to meet with you. Sounds great! Had you not written; I had called you anyway today to invite you out.' Then he pauses, and I can hear his deep breathing. 'But obviously, you got the jump on me with this lovely text. I'm delighted.'

'Oh … hmm … maybe it's not such a good idea anyway,' I mumble anxiously, and he gets disappointed.

'Of course, it's a great idea. I have been thinking so much about you lately. I was only waiting for the opportunity to be alone with you. I want to know you much better,' he marvels, and uneasily I muse, *Alone with me?*

'But you are alone with me at the clinic.'

'I want to see you again in a slightly more private way. Let's meet at seven tonight. For dinner instead of coffee,' he joys with a nice and crispy speech, so I hardly dare to say no. I'm not prepared for a dinner date. Coffee is one thing, but dinner is as an actual date. I've no idea of what I shall say, but it's my fault because I sent this stupid text.

'Honestly, I will feel better if we only grab a coffee below the clinic—in half an hour?' I respond hesitantly. Damn, how do I get out of it?

'No, it doesn't suit me so well now. I've promised Kate to fix some things in the apartment. Painting some walls and some repairs. We can meet later for dinner. Are you cool with that?' Again, he mentions something about Kate. It seems mysterious to me, but perhaps he is just a helpful guy. So, I overrule the red flag!

'Okay, it's a deal. Are you picking me up? Or do we meet downtown?'

'No, it's not so good. The car doesn't belong to me. What about you picking me up further down the road? At the white buildings?'

'Which white buildings?'

'Do you know where Calle Del Palma is?'

'Sure! I think I know where it is.'

'I'll wait for you there. At seven. What car are you driving?' he appears cheerful.

'Seven, okeydokey. I'm driving a Mercedes convertible.'

'Super! I'm so looking forward to see you.' He's ecstatic, then he hangs up, and I regret the action, because my inner voice tells me it's my biggest mistake of them all. I'm playing with a dangerous fire which I can no longer extinguish. The forbidden fiery flame of an uncontrollable bonfire is burning on my way to hell. I excuse my action, thinking he has given me so many invitations, so it's him flirting with me and not the reverse. Christ! Listen to yourself, Mary. A sick and lame excuse! I run from my own responsibilities, hiding as a coward and exploring the forbidden game. And that's more than a little unhealthy for me.

The hours go by slowly, and I have walked the dog, then taken a shower and am now preparing myself. Perfect makeup, hair hanging loose. Then I slip into a pair of tight white jeans, a striped short-sleeved Hilfiger shirt, and a pair of Swarovski sandals. While I drive off, ready to pick him up, my body is shaking as a leaf on a tree. I don't know what to say to him, and it all seems different from the first time until the last treatment today. The reality goes through my head: it's a date, but it isn't the kind of a date I want. I only want to meet him as a friend.

For some mysterious reason, I have passed him or not seen him, because he wasn't there. Is he avoiding me, resembling a cowardly dog with his tail between the legs? I turn the car, then want to drive home and forget about the meeting. Gosh! Unexpectedly, there he is at the roadside. The evening is wonderfully warm, and I'm listening to a tune about being hit in the night. I have an indescribable feeling about love, and it tingles deep inside me with excitement. It becomes a total turning point for my life when I see him on the unlit road, waiting for me. My hands become clammy on the wheel, and my heart beats in uncontrollable rhythms, identical to a little schoolgirl on her first date.

My feet have difficulty controlling the pedals when I stop in front of him, then he opens the door and slides into the passenger seat elegantly. Wow. He flashes intensely at me, as if I am a precious angel sent down from heaven to him. Am I supposed to be the angel? Or have the stars sent him to me? Hmm … nice! He has the wildest trophy eyes and the biggest smile on his lips. The effect is unexpected, because he looks stunning, smiling with his gorgeous, amazing smile. Ay Caramba! And then those expectant, glittering eyes. He's ecstatic and smells great, of a delicious lemony men's perfume, and he looks so different from usual, yea, wow, gorgeous. His casual bohemian pants and light blue polo shirt are sending a scorching quake through my mind. It's as if I'm sent right back to my previous Caribbean dream. You gotta be kidding me! His entire face smiles, and I glare at his shinning brown eyes, resembling thousands of blinking stars. I fall in love with them right away, when

I see two gentle and naughty eyes, and immediately, I make love with them and will never forget them. I see a pair of glowing hottie eyes, and maybe I'll burn my heart dreadfully on them. Wow—he takes my hand and squeezes it gently, realising his hands are magic to me.

'Hi … it's so nice that you want to meet with me. I've been looking forward to seeing you. So, this is the famous convertible?' He smiles, and I stare at his lovely red lips. My heart and mind immediately dream about making love with them when I see his soft, wet, beautiful full lips, then my imaginary mind wants to kiss them. I sense his lips in the air, kissing mine when he leans forward to me and gives me a loving hug and a kiss on my cheek. I become feverish and do not understand what to do with myself.

'Oh … hi there. Likewise. Where do you want to go?' I ask, confused, and tremble with nervousness.

'I don't know any good cafes. Don't you know a snack bar?' he beams sweetly.

'Well, hmmm … let me think! I know a great restaurant in the mountains. They make great steaks. Do you like steaks?' I ask and fumble stupidly with my manual gearshift to put the car into reverse.

'Yes, sounds great. I love a good steak. And some excellent red wine.'

Finally, the car is in reverse, so I make a U-turn but have problems getting it into drive. I mess up everything and turn the steering wheel the wrong way. I have no idea which way to drive and block the road for others by standing on both sides. Total nut-head! Embarrassing. It must look heedless, as if have I recently received my driver's license, but we are finally heading to the mountain. Or at least I think we are. It's dark, and my sense of direction falls apart.

'Do you know which direction to drive?' he tests with a mocking grin.

'Hmmm … yep. I guess so.' I try to be smart with my driving, pretending I know the back roads.

'It doesn't seem you know the direction! It looks as we are driving in circles,' he mocks, and he is right. I'm lost with my orientation in those many narrow alleys, which I usually know well, and I've no idea where I'm driving. I'm so nervous about having Drake sitting next to me in an unfamiliar situation than I'm used to, but finally, we arrive. Damn! It's closed, and I need to think fast.

'What if we drive to the beach area downtown? I know a great fish restaurant there.'

'Whatever you like, Mary.'

'Oh, my goodness. It's too much! It's also closed. A million dollars for some expert advice!' Then we drive along the beach from one end to the other.

At the end of the road is a *Chiringuito*, (it's a small establishment.) Most of those found on the beaches are ranging from seasonally open huts serving drinks to year-round buildings with full restaurant facilities.

'Do you want to go in there? I don't have the faintest idea if it's good. Do you like fish? We can take a chance if you like?' I suggest.

'Alright, let's go in there.' He agrees, and we park the car close by.

'It seems cosy except for the white plastic chairs.'

The waiter comes to our table and asks, 'What do you want to drink,' then hands over the menu cards.

'I'm snatching a beer and a Gentleman Jack.'

'Sparkling water, please.' I need to have control over myself, and I know I'm the one who needs to drive back again. With my today's crazy driving, wine is not the best idea, and it strikes me, I must have looked ridiculous and resembled a new driver. A nutcase who doesn't know the way my car works. I'm normally an excellent driver and have been for over thirty years. Most import for me, I have a zero-tolerance policy about drinking and driving.

I stare fixated at the menu, figuring out what I want to eat. Out of my eye corner, I notice he is gazing at me, so I glance back, and he bursts out, 'Goodness gracious, you look like a goddess. Oh, boy, so beautiful you are.' I flare up in a colour like that of an overripe tomato, peeking away from him, embarrassed.

'Hmmm … oh … do … do … you think so?' I stammer, resembling a silly goose.

'Sincerely! Yes, I do. You are such a stunning woman. You look like a million-dollar model taken out of one of the best American beauty magazines.' He states eagerly, and I stare nervously at the menu card.

'I'll have a meat dish. Yea, this steak looks great. I take one more beer. And a Gentleman Jack,' which he is calling a set.

'Red snapper is my choice. And more water.'

'Well, Mary, let me hear about your childhood. Tell me about which traumas you have had,' and I ponder if I want to talk about it. Is he suddenly my private pocket shrink?

'Hmm ... No, it's boring.'

'I'm so glad you *trust me* with your life story. Tell me, where do you come from? I want to know everything about you. And your childhood.' I glimpse around the restaurant, embarrassed, and turn my eyes to the blue Spanish sea, which now appears black.

'Oh gosh! Why do you want to know?' I question. Then I glance at him and, silly me, in good faith, I open on page one in the dusky book of my childhood. He stares at me with his controlling and calming Bambi glance. It's not an ordinary glare, but a flash that glows playfully and questioningly. I love Bambi with Thumper on the Ice, though Drake gawks greedily up and down my body and fixated he can't take away his gaze of my large breasts. His scowl suggests he wishes to put his entire mouth on them, as a baby suckling from his mother's breast. I've never seen such greediness in his eyes before, so I get distracted and wonder, *what's going through his brain?* As I tell the story of the darkest time from my childhood, told in another book of this path of my burning desire for life.

CHAPTER 17

WHERE DO YOU COME FROM?

> Trust, love, what we call sexy, who we trust in a business situation, are all based on how open we are. Openness is bodily openness, muscular relaxation, heart openness as opposed to hiding behind some emotional wall, and spiritual openness, which is actually feeling so fully into the moment that there's no separation between you and the entire moment.
>
> —David Deida

Damn it! He is so cute, and I believe he is an appropriate, trustworthy, and pleasant man. So now we sit on our first date at this cosy *Chiringuito* right on the beach and enjoy a lovely dinner together. Trusting him, I tell him where I was born, on a frosty winter morning. The confidentiality between him and me has gradually become close, and I'm as an open book to him. It's not the first time I have exchanged several private things with him, thoughts and feelings I never have shared with others before. Why? I don't know, but he seems so trustworthy and charming.

'Well, Mary, let me hear a little about your childhood while we wait for the food to come.'

'I was born on a snowy winter morning many years ago, in Germany. There was still snow and frost in the air. It was a bitter time, when people only dream that spring soon will come because winter has lasted too long. My mother is a miss. Gee, a confusing prima donna. She's so angry that she blames and curses the unborn child in her belly. As if it's my fault,' I say ironically. 'The nurses and the midwife swarm in a slightly confusing way around her, preparing everything for my "beautiful, brave unknown world"! The father isn't a part of the fresh family life.'

'Wow sounds bad.'

'She is annoyed by this unforgivable situation she has put herself into. Shameful! As a result, she is all alone in this motherly hell with me. What a grim world to be born in to,' Glaring sadly at him.

'You went through purgatory from the day you were born. Then you stepped onto a hard path to survive, finding me.' *What does he mean by that?* I continue my story.

'My skin is pale. My body is delicate, and I've a head round like a ball. On my bald head, you can see some bright, thin hairs. Soft as goose down. The nurse tucks me into my mother's warm embrace. And what happens? She is not the slightest bit amazed by this little unknown creature, who stops crying.'

'Aww, well, here I am to help you. To support you. Isn't it amazing?' He marvels.

'She stares at the tiny new-born wretch. And puts me back into the cradle. A girl! That morning is to be my first delighted day of life. But I'm the German cuckoo wretch who arrives into a relentless raw world.' I hesitate and peek down in shame.

'I must say, it was easier in the desert. When Jesus and Mary were walking there. Or was it not? No doubt that mankind has not changed.' He knows I'm a Catholic.

Drake wants to know more. 'Okay, continue. I'm listening.' He smirks.

'Her name is Karla. Twenty-four years old, with short cut dark, soft, undulating hair. A beautiful and sporting woman with a well-trained body. An independent woman. A sole master of her own. My father has left her and me. Phew, it's a tough thing for me to swallow.'

'It seems we still must fight against injustice. And selfishness.'

'My father is a womaniser. He has many affairs. And possess ultimate power over the women.'

'I can't imagine a father leaving his child. It must have made you hopeless. Broken-hearted.' Drake trembles synthetically. And I must admit, I found it glum that my father left my mother all alone with their firstborn child.

'I managed. Well, did they use condoms. *No*, such a selfish bastard. That could have saved my being born into a tough world. Damn, into which I was not welcome. Truly, I have not asked for this ticket to be born into this living hell,' I rant.

Déjà vu pops up in my mind again! Have I met my actual father before, even though I don't know him at all? He suddenly reminds me of Drake.

'I have no loving breast to tuck myself into. Nor do I get the warmth and tenderness from her. Nor her family, friends, sisters, or brothers.'

'I can see it must have made you desperate and unfortunate.'

'Karla rests in her bed next to my crib. Exhausted. She stares annoyed at this tiny teasing thing in the crib. She wants it gone. Best to another planet.'

'It was selfish of your mother to behave like that. I do wonder why you don't get a little tenderness from her. Poor you,' he responds with pity.

'My grandfather Brams Adolph, arrives a few days after Karla gives birth. Furious, he stands there. Christ, acting as an imprudent angry wild boar. Copper-red in his face. "Sign now! The kid is going away," Adolph screams at her. Awful hair day! Fucking country!'

'How cruel it must have been for you?'

'Her stubbornness of not signing will rob me the option to get a chance for a caring and loving life with another family. So, I end up in a cruel orphanage for unwanted children.'

'Wow … I'm glad you told me. It's good that we have each other to share everything with.

'Crazy madam she is. Insane is the heated bloke! I have not asked to be conceived and be born. Then orphaned and abandoned in a tiny baby prison. Imagine a life in a white prison baby bed. No one to care for you,' I almost sob.

'I have noticed you can sometimes be sharp—maybe a little hot-headed. But I'll be there for you. You will, in time, find your inner peace with my help.' So, what does he mean with this comment? I hardly know him.

'Being where you are today must have been a part of your survival. You must find ways to explain your situation. Not least of which to yourself! Well, I'm sure you have much more to tell.' I'm content that he has been listening intensely to my story. I try not to show him how much I, deep inside myself, cry during the telling of the broken child with no parents to love her. I've never understood why it's turning out for me like that. The best thing about it all is that I survived!

'My ears are yours if you want to continue. Please do. It's exciting to listen to,' he glows, and I'm considering if I want to tell more. I take a pause and sip some of my water, while I shyly turn my head away from him. I stare out of the restaurant's windows, searching for the warmth and the brightly shining Sun. But it has already set long ago, so instead, I find the powerful light from a lamp on the beach and stare at it. Then, I peek at the shining Moon, which lights up the sand, as if it's the purest gold. Waves are splashing in and out in slight movements, and the enthralling Moon makes a streak of mystical light in the black water. It grabs my close attention, and I am close to flight mode, ready to jump into the sea and I will drown myself.

Then I think about my dream, with the turquoise sea and the many beautiful seashells on the beach in the Caribbean. It blurs out of my mind, so instead, I turn my head again to him. He glares at me, and I glance deep into his magical eyes and fall in love with them. Bambi! Oh my God! He is so cute. Suddenly, I once again get the urge to continue the story about my childhood, because he touches something inside my inner struggles with his many sweet comments. So, I blabber with the story of what happened to this innocent little child.

'I know Karla is the third child out of six siblings. All were born in the years before the outbreak of the Second World War in Europe. Her mother Angela died at a young age during the war. I don't know so much about my grandparents, except for my grandmother was angelic. The kids received a militaristic and sadistic upbringing. Maybe that's the reason she is so violent towards me.'

'Oh… she must have been a temperamental woman?' he comments, and yes, Drake's observation is correct. 'A temper such as hers must confuse anyone. And make everyone miserable. The adrenaline gets up. Then you become aggressive. Are you also aggressive?' he asks strangely and gazes deeply and intensely at me, with a gentle smile.

'I'm sure I'm not like my mother. I am more frustrated over other people's strange behaviour. And hers,' I answer firmly and continue. 'I grew up in this dreadful orphanage. Jeez, it's strict run by Catholic nuns. And a devilish Redemptorist Priest. I'm obedient. Always loyal. I'm doing whatever I am told. Sometimes the consequences hit me when the nuns are in their headless minds.'

'What do you mean?'

'Yea, when they think I'm disobedient. Aw, Ohhh, the damn punishment often takes place on parts of my tiny body. Where they can find areas where it will hurt the most.'

'How can it be possible to beat up small children?'

'Hmm, I have no teddy bear to embrace. No pacifier. When boredom and the crying from loneliness become too difficult for me, I suck my thumb. Ha-ha, or both. As a pacifier in my mouth. Carefully, I learn to manage my tears. I keep them hidden inside my soul, and heart.'

'Oh, it sounds so mournful. The noradrenaline in your system must have taken over. Got you exhausted. And shy when your tears ran like a battle. Oh, my, then fell down your cheeks—or where they just dry tears that ran inside your mind? This makes one gloomy. At the same time determined that it not will ruin one's life.'

'Huh? What? To be honest, I don't understand a bit of what you are talking about.' Is he trying to be a smart ass on my behalf?

'It sounds as you stand up and fight for your fate, Mary.'

'Hmm …' I nod one's head, feeling my inner tears wanting to burst out. But I pretend as if it means nothing to me.

'You then do whatever you can to escape from your miserable destiny,' he is glaring at me with sad eyes, as if he feels pity for me. But

I don't need any pity from him or anyone else. I only want to tell the child's story of my real cruel world.

'Worst of all, I have many times asked my mother about my father. I don't understand why she keeps on lying. Even hiding the truth.'

'Oh, I can hear it in your voice. Your anger is rising. I understand you so well.'

'Damn! She was robbing me from my actual dad. Liar! I'm disappointed!'

'You owe those who were right next to you during the time of these experiences to let them be knocked hard in their head.'

'Well, now it's too late. Alex was already dead at the time when I found the papers about him. She has never had respect. No understanding. Or even an inch of empathy for my feelings.'

'This is not nice what they have done to you! I she still alive?'

'Yeah. The only thing she has is an interest in herself.' I feel like crying.

'I can feel your adrenalin is pushing into your system. It must be because you're going through this phase of your fateful state again. Fight yourself out of it.'

I'm content to let him listen to my story, but I'm not sure if I'm ready to understand his strange comments.

At the restaurant, the food is finally arriving, and I pause in the telling of my story.

I stare at my plate, pick up my knife and fork, and sit still, without moving them closer to the plate.

'Are you not hungry?' He tucks into his own food as if nothing about my story matters. I put back the utensils, sip the rest of my water, and order another water.

'I don't even know if I'm hungry.' He stares oddly at me.

'Eat your food. Or you might as well just continue your story,' he orders me, and I know I can't eat. 'Keep on talking. Come on. You know I want to know everything about you,' he commands as he continues shovelling his food into his mouth.

Shortly after, he finished eating he sits quietly for hours, listening to my grim telling, then I ponder it might be better if I don't tell him anymore. It's pitch-black outside, and the lights on the beach are turned off, and the dark clouds cover the Moon. We are the last couple, except for one more pair in the restaurant, and it appears as if the staff wants to toss us out so they can go home. I feel that I have opened too much of Pandora's box, and I have not once asked questions about him and his life. That is not nice of me. My food is still untouched on the plate, and I move it around with my fork from one side to the other and drink the rest of my water. Drake has drunken several beers and two whiskey, along with some wine standing on our table.

'Maybe it's best I stop telling any more about this miserable life. It's not so interesting. It's depressing. Besides, the staff is staring at us as they want to go home,' and he glares weirdly at me.

'No, no, don't stop. It's fascinating. Please continue. I want to know more. The staff can wait until we are done. How do you cope with all this?' he asks and glares at me.

'Are you sure? Maybe it's too much' I mumble,

'You're such an amazing woman. A stunning woman like you should not have experienced such tragic things. When did you move to Denmark?'

On his loving request, I continue to tell more. 'When I'm eight, Karla gets divorced. She finds herself a new man from Denmark. That's why we moved. I'm disappointed and angry at both. The first year is a nightmare for me. I'm teased at the school. And called the world's foulest words by the other kids.'

'Oh, why?'

'Destructive things happen between Karla and my stepfather; he is constantly unfaithful to her. Damn Norman Cock. Their problems accumulate to unbearable heights.

Again, another womaniser!' I complain. *What is it with men?* I can't figure it out during my writing. It seems to be so normal, as if all men are all like that. 'Constantly, I'm yellow, green, and blue on my arms. My back, or legs because of their beating. I believe and trust I will have a blissful life in Denmark. Christ, in the beginning, it feels so blissful. Something goes wrong. More unpleasant things happen in theirs and my life.'

'I'm deeply shocked. It's immense for you.'

'The children's consultants find out about the child abuse. Finally, I'm removed from my family. With force, by the child's authorities. Again, I end up in an orphanage. Life changes. I become a diligent student. Am taking part in various works at the orphanage. There I ride horseback. But don't think it's a dance on happy pink clouds. It's not. Life is a hell. But the end of the story is that, as a teenager, I end up in foster care. That's it! I don't want to talk more about it.'

I stop talking, then glance at him and then stare on my plate. I still haven't touched my food throughout the blabbering, while he has eaten, drunken, and listened intently to me. I notice he is shaken by the story, so basically, I'm a little uncertain if it's a good idea to tell him so much. Now that he knows about some of my deep-rooted secrets, will he take advantage of it? I notice that he somehow feels something for me, as if his thoughts feel real pity for me.

'Oh… my goodness, little darling girl,' he shouts, distressed.

When I had stopped jabbering, he suddenly grasps my cheeks and kisses me passionately for the first time. Wow! What's happening in this magical moment? I blush out of embarrassment. *Dear me!* I muse, nearly in a state of tremor. 'Is the story that bad?' I regret telling him so much.

'Wow, it's deeply traumatic. A terrible experience. I feel sorry for you.' He gently takes my hand and squeezes it lovingly, holding it tight to his heart. Next he hugs me.

'Nah, I've survived. Promise me that you'll keep it confidential. I've never told the whole story to anyone,' Raising my head proudly, I gaze at those striking brown eyes.

'I promise you. I'll never do so. Oh, boy, it's awful.'

Can I trust him? I expect his discretion as a doctor to his patients. He seemed as a good pocket psychologist, and I was so naive and talkative, as I always have been by nature. I'm always talking like Niagara Falls, without stopping.

'Well, it's the slight bumps along the road the world sometimes gives you.' I smile.

CHAPTER 18

VIAGRA, SEX, AND THE MAGIC WAND

> You gotta be cool when you're macho man, cuz you can't be sensitive and care about someone having a good time in bed, cuz that's too scary ... When you don't use sensitivity when you're having sex, or share some of your soul, noting gonna happen, because men really get afraid. Men really get scared in bed.
>
> —Richard Pryor

It's surreal to talk so confidentially about my worst experiences; even Paul doesn't know as much as Drake knows. The fear of Paul's or other people's negative reactions scares me—I worry whether they will judge me as a terrible person. I'm sensitive, but Drake's presence makes me safe, in a pleasantly way, and I have dared to open the scary book to him. It's as if I have known him for years, but I can't figure out why I experienced such déjà vu when I first heard his crispy voice. The eighteen-hundred number I use as a password long before my dream, and before I know about Drake, is a mystery. We are also mentally closer, although I have trouble seeing through him and his intentions.

So far, he's been a perfect puppet master and can twist many things out of me. Many times, I've tried to slip around the questions and his flirting, but oddly, he has softened me up again. He talks about himself and his years in the States, his time in Sweden, then of his many travels in Asia and Europe, and boasts a lot about his medical research, lectures, and seminars around the world. He is an exciting and well-educated elderly gentleman with vast life experience; as I swallow everything, unsweetened, and I feel him as trustworthy, though he is an exquisite puppet master whom guides me by the strings. He makes me talk, talk, and talk too much about myself, telling me he wants only the best for me in my life, and does something mystic to me and calms me, so it stops my anger and sadness. The friendship quickly becomes one of dependence, then I become addicted to him and blinded by his charm, intellectuality, and warmth, so I overrule the most important warning signs. He knows about the love letters to Paul and his betrayal, our wealth, and too much about my childhood. Drake wants to know about *everything!* Help me, God. I really feel the need to tell him about the years I suppressed in my life. Warning!

Life is not about being rich, popular, educated, or perfect. It's about being real, humble, and kind—and that's what I am, though, I'm not perfect. Perhaps I'm too talkative, like a chit-chatting parrot, blabbering with no pauses until I'm done. Before he kissed me intensely, it struck me that he called me his *precious little darling*. Not that I mind it. It was sweet. Time and cosmos disappeared when he kissed me, and I forgot all about the danger if anyone caught us while he melted his hot lips to mine, and the moment tear away all my defences into millions of pieces. My fish was cold on the plate, my glass was empty, and I didn't care about anything else than his tender lips close to mine.

As the restaurant is closing, I glare at him waiting for him as a gentleman to pay the bill, and fumbles desperately in his trousers back pocket to grab the wallet.

'Oh, boy ... I forgot my wallet,' he burst as he seems shocked and scowls convincing at me. 'What do I do? Can you pay? I give you the money later,' so I grab my purse and pay the bill, and then we go for a walk on the beach. During the stroll, he smoothly takes my hand and locks it safely around mine as if it's the most natural thing for him to do, as he lovingly takes me out of my darkness when he clinches my hand, and my heart pounds faster and faster. The heated love starts boiling my blood in me, and paces wild through all my veins, in my entire body. It's comparable to magic, though I let go of his soft embracing hand, when he suddenly stops and glimmers intensely at me.

'Let's sit here for a moment and enjoy the sounds of the splashing waves,' then, we sit in the warm sand. Gently, he takes a steady hold of me and lays me down in the warm golden sand, and with passion, he kisses me as no one has kissed me before. His embrace emerges from me so close into his warm, soft body, as no man ever has embraced me before. I'm melting as butter, while his kisses will never end in his marvellous cuddle of passion, as I glide into the heat of his tender embrace. I can't get myself out of this burning situation. It feels as if two people are merging into one soul, then I imagine it's identical to *Wuthering Heights*; he is my Heathcliff, and I'm his Catherine. You probably remember the story about the poor boy and the high-society, English girl. A fabulous love story, where it all evolves into a passionate relationship, lots of drama, erotic moments, and not least with stormy consequences between them. Is there any resemblance between Wuthering Heights and the story I'm about to enter with him and me?

Is that my déjà vu? I'm in seventh heaven, when his sweltering hurricane drags me into his mesh of heated, tender kisses on my lips, neck, and shoulders. His warm hugs comfort me, and his one soft and warm hand holds me behind my neck in a secure grip. Trillions of uncontrolled goose bumps appear on my body, as I never want the moment to end, because I have never felt such intensity from any man before. Imagine you of being in a fairy tale of compassionate love, where he radiates the wildest colourful electricity through your entire body, sitting in the enchanted moonlight while the stars glitter from the magical universe.

I must be dreaming!

The tenderness can only be a fictional story, as we see in happy movies. Over one hour we rest in the warm sand, gazing intensely at the universe of the dark shiny bright night. He has taken me out of my gloomy mind and healed my damaged soul as we watch the glowing half-moon and the many shooting stars. Only one thing is missing on the golden Moon, and that's the man with his fishing pole, trying to catch me into his web. Drake has caught me on the beach and not on the Moon, as only the body language and our hands are talking between us. He often turns around and kisses me with gigantic passion, so I feel this is the genuine love of the centre of my universe. My life suddenly changes, as we have forgotten time and space while we silently lie on the enchanting beach. It's dreamlike, and I have never thought I would become so consumed by another man again. Motionless in my cosmos, I have not given a thought to what I'm doing with him on the beach, as he became the nectar for the starving hummingbird—what I needed to survive.

That's the shattering year when Drake has entered the depths of my emotions and the most depressing part of my life. As the saving enlightened angel, I have waited for, and there he is, interrupting in my life. It is the year when his first little seed is sown on the farmer's field where he steals my heart. It is the year when the dangerous black wolf blows on Paul's and my established little home, and it ends in a chaotic, disorganised mess. So, both Paul and I have thrown ourselves into the claws of the forbidden love game and let the big, nasty wolf in sheepskin destroy our life. Will Paul and I ever rebuild our love life again? It's a massive avalanche that's hitting and burying us in sucking dangerous quicksand, dragging the entire family into the chaotic mess of our selfishness, which can end up in a massive fall.

Is it a double moral that I give it the last punch by falling into Drake's enchanting embraces and feverish kisses? I do not understand why I do so, and with my lack of knowledge, he is close to dragging me into his impulsive, dangerous spider trap. Is Drake diligently using his power of smoothness, compliments, and his stunning charm to catch me in his snare? What are his actual intentions with me? I still don't know! I'm close to fall in love, and I'm overjoyed for his breath-taking kisses and for being so blissful on this sparkling night with him. Whew! My body becomes hot and ecstatic when his tender red lips touch mine, so the wonderful feeling he gives me in my heart and soul fulfil me. I surrender in blindness for him while we lie on the warm, sandy golden beach, because no one else can knock me off the bench while I'm in his embrace. People can see me. I don't care if they see what I'm doing in his fervent embrace, lovingly floating in his breathtaking brown eyes and drifting on a mellow cloud in the sky with his divine sweet smile. We are alone on the beach; the hour has become late, the cool breeze hits us, and I freeze. He gives me a caring hug and strokes my hair while he holds me tightly to his warm body. His arms are strong while his closeness holds onto me and he tries to keep me warm. This heated summer night; I'm struck in my heart with the dangerous flaming arrow under the beautiful light of the gleaming Moon and the many sparkling bright stars in the middle of a passionate summer kiss on the beach.

'Oh, my precious little girl, let's head home.'

'Yah, it's late. It's better I drive you home.'

'Let's enjoy some wine or something stronger at your apartment,' he says sweetly.

'Hmm, or we can have the drink at your flat,' I whisper because it will be wrong of me to take him to my place.

'If you think so. Hmmm… but it's not so good at my flat. It's not my place. What about one last drink at your home? As a blissful ending to a wonderful evening. And night.' he smilingly pleads, and wields enormous power over me, taking my defences down.

We drive to my home, drink several glasses of Gentleman Jack, so before I know it, I'm more than half drunk and can't drive him back.

'I'm so tired. Phew, I've also had too much to drink. Do you mind walking home yourself? I can't drive.' He glares, disappointed over my question.

'Oh boy, I can't. I'm also too drunk. Can't I stay?' he smirks.

'You can stay in my guest room.' I kindly offer.

'Thank you so much. I'll happily take your offer. Come, let's have a shower,' He surprises me and grabs my hand and asks if I have two bathrooms.

'Yes, sure. But, I first need to go for a quick walk with Spotty. Please go with me. It scares me when it's so late now. I'm not so fond of walking alone. Not in the dark,' then we stroll for a brief walk with Spotty.

'You can take this bath. Here is the guest room.' I show him as we get back home. 'It's already prepared with clean bedding.'

'Oh ... Nice. Thanks. So great.' He smiles satisfied.

'You can find towels in the bathroom. I'll bring you a fresh toothbrush.'

'Oh! Are you always so prepared for strangers?' He questions.

'Huh? Strangers? No, I've always extras of them. I'll be in there,' as I point at my door, and we each go to our separate rooms. I take a quick shower and jump naked into bed. Strange! He is not done yet; I can hear the water is still running. He has stayed there for quite a while, and I speculate why he spent so long in there, then I turn off my light so only the brightness from the calm Moon and the streetlights illuminate the room. The balcony door is slightly open for the fresh breeze to enter, and Spotty is resting next to me, with his four paws pointing up to the ceiling. I hear Drake open the bathroom door, and within seconds, he stands in front of my bedroom, then leans against the door frame and stares intensely at me. Damn, he is wearing only a pair of boxer shorts and showing off his bare, sturdy upper body. With grand surprise, I can't help noticing his upright, stiff cock in his boxers, while he talks to me. I'm about to suffocate in my own saliva, so it takes a few more seconds before it sinks in. Oh no! How to deal with this unexpected situation.

'Wow, you're the most wonderful woman I've ever met,' he smirks and greedily licks his lips.

'Are you not tired? Sleep well.'

'No, I'm not. I want to make love to you.'

'Eh? What?'

'Yea, I want to touch your entire body. I must feel your soft skin against mine.' Suddenly, he sits on the edge of my bed, and I feel unmoving, as a frozen Lolita doll. He gently moves my blanket down a little so he can see my bare breasts, and his intense greedy stare gazes at them. Next, he slides his soft finger around my nipple, and sexual chills arouse my body, as the nipples get hard with excitement, and he turns me on slightly. Carefully, he fondles my breast with his finger, one than the other, so I feel the warmth down to my stomach and get exciting pleasures running to my private parts, so I get lustful. Gently he caresses my breasts with both palms, slides one hand up towards my neck, and then holds it tenderly around my neck.

'Such firm babes you have. So soft your skin is,' he whispers, calm and sexy, then licks his lips. I get so hot and wet that millions of goosebumps run uncontrolled down my entire body, as his warm lips end up close to mine, while he kisses me with intense passion. Unexpectedly, he stops kissing me.

'Come on. How is it you are kissing?' he snaps, irritated at me. 'Yea, it's as your tongue in my mouth is driving around as a whisk in the wind.'

'Oh ... my... what?' Imagine yourself in such a heated, sexy tenderness with a man, and wow... holy moly ... it turns me off when he is criticising me.

'Look at me,' he dictates, 'and learn. Do the same thing as I do.'

'I have never heard before that my kisses are bad.' I excuse myself and get miffed.

'Now I will teach you how to kiss a proper tongue kiss with passion.' Wow! He is licking my tongue as a kitten licks its milk. Soft and slow he moves his tongue around, and I ponder, *why has he not complained about the kisses before, on the beach. Maybe they were not so intense?* It must be because the man on the magical Moon has caught me on his fishing hook, so now he can allow himself to complain. *Or is it because I drank too much whiskey?* Undeniable, because the bed and my head are spinning around, and my senses are not in full control. *It might be I'm sloppy with my kissing. Hmmm… or is it that the kiss of his is not that great? Or that I'm not ready for sex and feverish kisses.*

Visualise yourself taken part in a party with your firm and then you get drunk. In Denmark, we have a traditional Christmas party for most of December, and they often end up wild, and people get drunk. Someone has *an eye* for a colleague, someone they have long had sexual dreams about. In that weak, magical, intoxicated moment, you fall in love, or perhaps you only want to have quick rough sex for a night. Infidelity is the next move. Twenty-three percent of men and fourteen percent of women have been unfaithful to their partner at least once, shows a new Danish report in 2019. That's a high number of adultery incidences, measured amongst sixty-two-thousand people. The same thing is happening to me tonight of blissful, intoxicated moments, where all my defences are down, being plastered, and in bed with another man.

Shame on me! I'm a dead drunken fish on his hook! In my half-drunk condition, I've left my brain in the last glass of whisky. Oops! I know I must say no, but I'm only human and have desires! So, I'm about to fall right into his cunning, sexy plan to seduce me, as his gentle caresses and while he speaks sensitive words in my ears. It makes me move on with the forbidden game of heated, compassionate sex, as he takes off his boxer shorts. Oh… I admit it! Yes, it stands upright as a *petty* God Adonis. Not with the greatest and utmost splendour, though, that's for sure! My husband is a lot more endowed than Drake is, so I glimpse at it disappointed. The paltry excuse down there for a pink torpedo is ready for its lovemaking with the goddess resting naked in the bed, with a wet, horny pussy. Although Adonis is the mortal lover of the goddess Aphrodite in Greek mythology, so I ponder, *It's not always the size it depends on*, but, but, genuinely I'm sorry, I have to acknowledge my disappointment in the size of his baby anaconda, however, he knows how to make me feel as a real woman in a man's cuddle.

Bang!

I slightly enjoy his lovemaking in the disastrous night of my weak moment and, *wow*; he ends up as a wild bull, as he has strongly prepared himself to conquer his prey, so he can't control his purple headed soldier man filed up with Viagra. At the same moment, he collapses with an orgasm on top of me, whispering to himself, 'Oh… Mom.'

'Eh? Huh? What?' I'm outraged!

I go fairly into a spasm in my thought: *What the fuck is that about?* I ponder, *Wow! The dude he doesn't even have something to brag about with his man-size*. I can barely feel his wee-wee inside my inner walls, though I know I'm strong inside my secret private wet hole. Besides, he has problems with the rest of the sex act, and utterly, it annoys him not to succeed, to get me up to the pleasure of the height of orgasm. Dead drunken meat? Or am I not into a one-night stand. Or is it the lecture about the *ill kiss*? Or is it the baby anaconda that is turning me off?

'This has never happened to me before.'

'What?' I ask stupidly.

'Geez, that I can't bring a woman to climax.'

'Perhaps I'm too tanked-up with whiskey.' I counteract.

'All women have always praised me I'm a fantastic lover. And great kisser,' he brags, which is a vast surprise for me. I suppose he assumes he's some amazing Adonis. Because, no doubt about it, he has superb control of how to rotate his golden tool inside my vagina, but the wiener cannot fill me out. Although some sex act is an enjoyable feeling, except for my missing orgasm. I'm musing, *has he emptied an entire pack of Viagra before we had sex* (I'm very sure he has), because at no time, the pink gizmo is down in a relaxed position.

Please, guys, help me out here. I know it normally gets relaxed after a man's coming, right? I'm sure Drake could have humped me as Thumper the Rabbit the entire night. So, if he's that good at giving a woman a great climax, I give him another chance. I stick my hand in the drawer of my night table and hand him over my lovely magic wand. He goes into a spastic paralysed coma when he sees this purple vibrating thing.

'What is that?' He stares horrified at the dildo.

'A vibrator.' I say seriously and smile.

'How do you want me to use that monster on you?' he complains, denying taking it in his hand.

'Turn it on there. You can choose the speed there.' Sorry, folks, I must show the dude how to turn it on and demonstrate how it works.

'You can't use a thing like that on your little pearl.' He protests.

'Why not?'

'This is not good for your sensation down there.'

'Oh ... but it's soooo ... nice.' I love my purple wand.

'Jeez, your little Minnie will hide away,' he whines, then I realise that he baptises my pussy Minnie.

'Huh? Minnie?' Well, how sweet, and I muse it's funny. How did he come up with such a name? I'm never asking him and put no more into it.

'She gets scared like hell!'

'Scared? Why?' And I'm close to lose the moment for an orgasm with him.

'Like I get scared of such a horrible vibrating thing.' He smirks.

'Listen, don't use it on you! Use it on me!' I smirk, and gaze dumbly at him as I wait for my grand finale of an orgasm.

'I will, in time, teach you how to get a good climax.'

'How?' And my pussy is close to get very dry of this heedless discussion.

'Yea, when my spunk torpedo and my fingers are playing with your tiny little Minnie pearl.'

'Oh ... Then let's start now.' And I sense my vagina is about to moisten again.

'You will get on the high mountain. Yeeha! Full of pleasure,' he whispers, and I'm ready for the massive joy for my grand finale. At least he tries to work with the vibrator, fumbles around with it as a moron, so sadly, it's a total fiasco, no matter how much I fight for the famous plateau of my grand orgasm he has promised me. It is absent, and the poor scared Minnie Pearl is hiding from the devious devil in the dry Arabian desert. Instead, we rest in each other's arms and fall asleep. His performance is okeydokey but not *that good*, as I grasp he is *not the God Adonis*.

CHAPTER 19

THE ANGRY BIRD'S FIRST MORNING SONG

> *Judge Peckinpah:* There seems to be a recurring issue here, anger.
>
> *Red:* I don't have an anger issue; I think you got an anger issue. Are you aware that robe you are wearing isn't fooling anyone?
>
> —The Angry Birds Movie

For heaven's sake! I'm so plagued by yesterday's tipsiness as I feel tremendous guilt and bad conscience over my one-night stand with Drake. Worst of all, I wake up with another man in my bed, and that's bad.

Before I wake up, I sense in my awakening time, that Drake is penetrating me from behind, and his sudden unpleasant way of sex scares me. His sleazy back attack gives him bad points of behaviour, so I'm disappointed with him.

'Good morning, little girl. Oh… you are so soft.'

'Hmmm … hmmm …'

'I wanted to feel you again this morning,' he whispers in my ear. *Does his ding-a-ling never relax?* I consider, as he keeps talking.

'You were so wonderful last night.'

'Hmmm …' I grumble.

'I like to make love to my women early in the morning. It's the time the lovemaking is best. I will give you great pleasure this morning.'

'Hmmm … ehhhh …'

'Without the dildo. Now that you have slept. And are more relaxed in the morning hours,' he sings resembling a sexy spinning bird-of-paradise. *What is he, a premium bull?* as I tried to rouse myself awaken from sleep and grumble, annoyed at him.

'Hmmm … Ohhh … hmmm …' Most of all, I want him to *stop*.

'I don't like sex in the morning.' I grumble as I'm *not* a morning person. What is it with men's bacon bazooka and their big macho way of behaviour? So, he screws me from behind, which gives me bad, ugly flashbacks of my stepfather in action. In fact, I don't feel it's nice what Drake does, but quickly the randy bull gets his orgasm and empty his fuckjuice as he groans the same words as yesterday. 'Oh … mom … ahh …' It must be his Oedipus Complex. Sigmund Freud was the first to recognize this sexual dynamic in humans and theorised that every male has this fixation, but few ever act on it.

Resembling a scared rabbit, I wake up with a start and jump out of bed, then run to the bathroom, sit down on the potty, and empty his man milk out of my vagina. Irritated, I jump into the shower and scrub my entire body, and when I come into the room again, he's not there, but hear the other shower is drizzling, in the other bathroom. Hastily I get dressed, go to the kitchen and prepare breakfast. Freshly bathed, he hugs and kisses me again as if the morning ritual is the most natural thing for him to do. Does he consider us as a couple in a new-fangled sexual relationship? For me, it's an unforgivable one-night stand that I regret deeply, including the many glasses of whiskey I drank yesterday. Oh … my… I've a terrible banging head, filled with an irritating hangover. It frustrates me, I've not kicked the old timer out, but I do my best to stay calm so he can't see my frustration.

'Are you okay?' he asks curiously.

'Yea … hmmm, but I have a terrible headache.'

'Do you need an adjustment?'

'No … no … But I don't feel good about your surprising stunt yesterday. Grr, and the sudden attack you did this morning.'

'What??? Jeez, what the heck are you accusing me of?'

'I'm not ready for such surprises. If you understand?' I complain, slightly upset.

'Bloody hell. It's not an attack,' he yells angrily and keeps on blabbering. So, the singing affectionate "bird-of-paradise" becomes "Angry Bird Judge Peckinpah". Yee-haw! Judge power!

'Honestly! I don't feel it's nice.'

'Mornings are always the best.'

'Eh? What? Why?'

'Yea, the most relaxed way of having sex' is his arrogant answer, Christ, in my head, it swirls around confusingly.

'Perhaps it's not an attack for you. But it is for me!'

'Stop! What are you bloody hell talking about?'

'During your act, I thought of something gruesome from my childhood.'

'What? It can't be that bad. Can it?'

'Remember, I related to the story yesterday. You must have forgotten that part. Or did you not hear it?' I stare at him, hoping for an understanding response.

'Christ! I have no clue what you are talking about.' He angers.

'Well, anyhow! Let's get some breakfast. Then we must talk about yesterday. And this morning,' I seem to be firm and turn my back on him.

I have cooked the soft-boiled eggs and squeezed the last orange in the juicer. I have prepared the toasted bread and the yoghurt with fresh strawberries and blueberries, so only the granola and maple syrup need to go on top of it. Then I pour the freshly brewed coffee into two mugs, put in on my tray table and bring it all out to the balcony. In silence, Drake takes his coffee and slurps from the mug while he sour glares at me. I ignore him and enjoy my meal while viewing the mountains. Mostly, I only want my coffee and my morning ciggy—and the dawg out of the apartment, but instead, I let go of the cravings and eat my yoghurt. For a long time, I haven't eaten properly, living only on toast, cancer sticks, water, and coffee. I know it's a filthy habit, and it's not healthy for me.

'Wow! Do you always prepare such a nice breakfast in the morning?'

'Hmm. Spotty needs a walk afterwards. When we have finished, I can walk with you some way on your way back home,' I kindly tell him.

'Yummy, this is delightful. Such wonderful service. Delicious, fresh-pressed orange juice. Every day?' He smiles contentedly.

'Yes, every day.' I peek down at myself and hope he can't see I'm being dishonest.

'Wow sounds good. Something I can get used to easily.' He can't hide his smirky smile, hoping I'll do this for him every morning. I muse, *please fly back to your other nests,* as his comment scares me. I wish there is a delete button to erase this meeting and my sleeping with him. What have I done to my marriage? I have not respected my promise never to be unfaithful to Paul. By now, it's sadly too late, and I have been as bad as Paul. There are things you can't predict, and it's impossible to erase the act. I can't pick the feathers off the bird sitting in front of me and afterwards throw him over the balcony and forget what has happened the first night with Drake. Unwillingly, I allowed him to make love with me when he made his sneaky move and jumped into my bed, and I took part in a mistaken one-night stand. I feel he used my weakness, with his damn manoeuvring, to fuck with me, and I realise I have fallen for his dazzling love tricks. He let me fall into his dark, shady predatory trap and misused my excessive intake of liquor to his advantage. Damn. Then I no longer controlled myself. A genuine gentleman would never do so. But it's not an excuse, because he's also nice and loving, so I'm in a shitty struggle with myself, as I fancy him. Sitting on the balcony, having our first morning meal, I must tell him what's going on in my mind.

'We need to talk about this. I'm not sure this is right, what we did,' I mumble.

'What? Mary, you're so wonderful. It was so great.'

'I know it was a special moment yesterday. I enjoyed everything on the beach.'

'I took myself away from your glorious beauty. You must understand this is what you are… and you're so divine.' He caringly smiles. Oh… he looks so cute when he speaks so. Again, I fall for his brilliant charm.

'Damn it, we got drunk. Darn, and we went further. Phew, more than I expected. I love Paul.'

'Little darling girl, understand, he doesn't want to bother with you.'

'I want to find my way into his heart again,' I remorse.

'Little girl, I like you! Maybe I'm a little too old for you.'

'Did you sincerely play the old dude card trick? Honestly!'

'Ha-ha, I don't feel old when I'm with you. You make me handsome. And loveable inside my myself again.'

'To be frank with you—which you also should be to yourself—what is the chance for us to build a relationship?'

'Having spent this magical night with you makes me feel young again.'

'Honestly? You are on your way to Asia.'

'You are a gorgeous woman. I have never felt so comfortable with anyone before.'

'Huh? Don't you think it's a little silly for us to get involved?'

'Oh … No, no … I'm in love with you. I want more of you.' He smirks.

'You are a great and handsome man. Gee, Drake, I'm married. It will be easier if I weren't. What do you mean, being in love with me?'

'It has been so since the first day I met you,' he marvels convincingly.

'Oh! Our night must stay what it was. A one-night stand!'

'You have changed something about my life and feelings since I met you.'

'I know it can feel fantastic if you haven't had a woman for a long time.'

'Yes, it's true.'

'Suddenly I come into your life as a breath of fresh air.'

'Oh… my… and the first day when I saw your cute little foot. Phew, I melted. I wanted to know you more,' he speaks passionately, and I'm stunned.

'We must stop here,' I say in shame. 'It was a cosy dinner on the beach.'

'I like you with such a passion.'

'Well, your first kiss took me by surprise. I have a hard time with surprises.'

'God created you for me. He made us for each other.' And he keeps on trying to convince me otherwise.

'You sweetly charmed me. It blew me away. To be direct, it's best not to meet again.'

'Does that mean we will never meet again? At least you can continue your treatment until I leave.' He gazes at me, displeased with my decision.

'Don't you worry. I'll continue my treatment. I hope we can meet as best friends. Do you understand what I mean?' I question.

'To be true with you, Mary? No! I don't. Why did you then send me the text?'

'What's wrong with having a cup of coffee? You have asked so many times.'

'You even went out on a date with me. Why? I went home with you.' The anger and disappointment in his voice are rising to a level that makes me uncomfortable.

'Finally, I give in to your invitation. Wow, it ends up with a cosy dinner. Ouch, and night. I truly liked it.'

'Oh… I see, *cosy*? That means it wasn't specifically for my sake that you took this so-called cup of coffee with me.'

'That doesn't mean we have to continue our relationship further. Does it?'

'What the heck? It's not for me you ended up going out with me? And we made love?'

'Besides, I don't know so many Scandinavians in this area. It was cosy to meet with you,' I defend myself.

'Cosy, cosy. Ha! Do my kisses even mean anything to you?'

'Yesterday was nice. I wanted to make friends with you.'

'Friends? Bloody hell!'

'It wasn't my plan to have sex with you. All was like a bombshell. Too fast.'

'Honestly, were you only using me? And why?' His frustration and rage remind me of Angry Bomb.

'I'm not glad that you feel I have ill-used you. I'm thrilled with all the lovely things you have commented about me lately. Though I feel it's wrong of you to flirt with me as your patient,' I try to be polite.

'What! Attack you? Flirting with you?' He blows up as a detonated bomb and defends himself, as his eyes resemble thunder and lightning. 'What kind of bullshit is that? You sure have the nerve. How can you say such nonsense?'

'I'm sensitive. You know, I'm in a genuinely awful situation now.' He scares me.

'Jeez, you must stop with such accusations. My clinic is as *white as snow*.'

'Drake, you're sweet. A listening person—that means a lot to me— but that does not mean that we are lovers. Does it? You flirted with me since day one.'

'I have at no time flirted with you! *You* flirted with me! That's a fact! I will never do such things with a patient.' He's fuming, so I get scared and feel he's lying right to my face. Appalling!

'Please, let's act as friends. I like you. You make me feel good.'

'Well ... sounds good. But only like me? Hmmm ...'

'Please sit down again. Let's talk as adults,' I beg.

'I suppose you don't want to take the next step yet?' he calms.

'No, I don't think so. Let's see what happens.'

'So… hmmm. You only need to get to know me better.'

'Please, Drake, let's see how our friendship grows. Let's stay in touch. I mean it.'

'Ask me what you want to know about me. I'll tell you everything. What do you want to know?' he asks, jumpy.

'I like you much. But give me some time.'

'Okeydokey, we can agree that.' he positively nods. 'But mark my words. You will *never* win the fight against your husband. He is only interested in this other woman.'

'I must find out what to do with my marriage.'

'Trust me. He has no interest at all in you anymore. He has a taste for younger women. You are *nothing* to him *anymore*.' He ends his speech, and we talk no more about it, then we quickly walk Spotty, before I drive Drake back home.

CHAPTER 20

SECRETS AND LIES

> I don't know what disappoints me the most ... When a person tries to hide something from me and tells me a lie ... or that he thinks I'm so stupid, that I know nothing at all.
> —Visdom.dk

Being born and becoming a mature adult woman, I'm still learning a lot from the hard school of life. Sometimes, I wonder if I have learned everything from what life has given me. Obviously, I have not! I make incorrect decisions and sometimes go in a fatal wrong direction. After I have driven Drake back to his home, both of us have a flight to Denmark the following day; he in the morning and I in the afternoon. Thursday afternoon a taxi picks me up, and after forty-five minutes, I'm at Malaga airport, checking in and ready to enter the security area when strange things are happening to my body, and I feel suddenly unwell. Sweating, shaking, clammy, and feeling cold. Oh, dear, I want to get back to my apartment, pondering; is it the flu? Okay, well, then it's not so bad, so I continue my trip.

Inside the terminal, I buy a bottle of water, pace to the announced gate, and try to get hold of myself, though millions of nervous speculations about Drake and Paul speeds wildly through my mind. The flight staff is boarding us, and it's outrageously hot in the aircraft. I'm browsing to find my seat, then sit down, take my tiny travel pillow, and want to sleep my nervousness away. No success, because I'm repenting like crazy over my inappropriate one-night stand. I don't know if it's bad conscience, the flu, being worried, or too many treatments that makes me sick. It's a nightmare of millions of distinct considerations, and out of the blue, I become nauseated after take-off.

What's happening to me? My stomach growls wildly, then nausea and dizziness grip my system, and I'm about to faint. My body literally walks, well, rather sits beside me, and I frequently run to the toilet, and by me having the window seat on row 6 becomes a great nuisance to the two guys next to me. Maddeningly, they send me several sour faces, even though I'm apologetic for disturbing them during their napping, when I must go.

'Are you alright?' The flight attendant asks me, 'Do you need any help?' when she notices my sweating and pale face. My head keeps on telling me it's the fault of the treatment, so I get even more scared and can't find rest. Beforehand, Drake gave me his phone number for an emergency, so I'm in this moment glad that he gave it to me. After four hours in the air, the flight prepares its landing gear and sits its wheels smoothly on the ground. While they taxi the plane into the parking area, I turn on my phone and search for Drake's number, and finally, we get to the gate. It takes ages before they open the cabin, and people keeps on pushing and stepping over my toes. It's scorching, and people's sweaty smell as a heavy perfume a woman has doused herself with enters my nostrils, so I want most of all to puke. With my fast-beating heart, I'm close to getting a panic attack, as I can hardly breathe, while the blood is boiling, and my brain is screaming to get out of this crowded, humid, stinking plane.

The two men next to me keep on pushing me, in revenge for disturbing them during the flight. Everyone is inappropriately rude and pushy, grabbing selfishly for their luggage in the overhead compartments, because they want to get out fast, and best first. I have got my backpack down and put it on my back, sit down on my seat until they finally allow us to get out. They have parked the plane far away from all the other normal terminals, so oh my gosh, it's a lengthy walk before I reach the baggage area. Ugh! Eww, the first thing I can smell is the typical Danish hotdog stand, yuck, so disgusting, because I can't stand any more abominable odours. I desperately need some fresh air, not the smell from ketchup and Danish red sausages. While I'm sitting a little away from the transport belt number 10, I wait in quietness for fifteen minutes for my luggage; I grab my phone and dial Drake's number before I can pick up the dog in another area.

'Hi, it's me. Am I disturbing you? Is it too late?'

'Hi, Mary. What a surprise you're calling me! I knew you would need the number. Wow, and here you are on the phone. I'm delighted. Do you miss me?'

'I'm in a panic. The flight was a nightmare. I'm scared over my health condition.'

'What's going on? Why are you in panic?' He seems calm.

'I'm worried if it's because of too many treatments. Can you help me?' I beg him.

'It's not so good for me to talk right now. Can you call me later?' he jabbers quickly, and I feel he is letting me down.

'No. I have to talk to you now. I'm not feeling well.' I complain in frustration.

'Fine, hold on for a second. I need to find a quiet spot so no one can hear me.' And I notice there is a lot of noise in the background.

'It's been a terrible trip! Shortness of breath. Heart palpitations. Dizziness, and I'm about to faint. My body is shaking. I'm freezing like crazy.'

'Oh dear! Sounds awful! Are you catching the flu?'

'I'm hot and sweating. Geez, I have lots of pain in my neck. Several times I wanted to vomit. Oh, dear, I can't. Yuck, I loathe vomiting,' I sob while my body shakes even more when I speak with him.

'Oh, boy! It might be something with your kidneys. Oh, maybe your gallbladder!' He sounds so different and it scares me when he mentions something about kidney and gallbladder problems. What is that suddenly?

'No, I don't think it has anything to do with the flu. Why kidney? Gallbladder? I'm more worried that it has something to do with too many treatments.'

'Come on. It can't be that bad.'

'Oh, my goodness, it's all these many adjustments.'

'There is nothing wrong with my treatments.' He snarls angry.

'Damn, it's that powerful energy equipment you use,' I mumble, even more gripped by fear that something worse might happen. The worst-case scenarios go through my head. Am I about to die? I feel lost.

'Don't be nervous. There is plenty of evidence that it is not harmful to the body.'

'Are you sure it has nothing to do with your machine? It might be dangerous.'

'Your symptoms tell me the treatment works. I know what I'm doing. *Trust me.*'

'Shit, perhaps it's harmful to the body.' I babble worriedly.

'I will do nothing bad to my little girl. Don't you *trust me?* Let's see how it goes after a good night's sleep.' he returns in a sugary pitch, and his reassuring and competent comments calm me slightly down.

'I'm scared. It feels as I'm on a rocking boat. I'm seasick constantly.'

'Are you still stressed? Nervous about getting home to Paul? I'll call you tomorrow, Mary. Then we can meet. I miss you so much. I want to see you tomorrow. Sleep well, little girl. Don't worry.' He ends the conversation without saying good night, so I feel alone and abandoned by him.

Well, not much help from him, I muse. And the comment, 'I miss you so much.'—

For that, I'm not prepared, and makes me even more nervous. Which part about 'I want to save my marriage' does he not understand?

I grab the suitcase and run to the pickup zone where Spotty waits for me and is excited to get out of the cage. After passing the customs area, we finally get out in the fresh air, spotting hundreds of black taxis parked outside waiting for customers. I snatch one and after fifteen minutes' drive on the highway and twenty minutes in the inner city, I finally arrive at our home in Copenhagen.

'Hello, I'm home,' And place my luggage in the bedroom.

Paul is not there, and the boys are busy in their rooms, playing wild, noisy games on their PlayStation. Spotty goes mental as he gets reunited with his mother, then speeds around and hunts Lady's ears and legs in happiness. She gets annoyed at him and growls, but he doesn't calm down, so the wild chase continues in and out of the living room, hallway, and kitchen. Ha-ha, funny dogs, and Lady only wants to say hello to me.

Shortly after a brief snooze, I go for a walk with the dogs, because I need some fresh air to see if I can get better, but it's with no success. It's spinning even more around in my head, so I call Drake again, even though it's late now.

'Hey, it's me again. I'm so worried.'

'Oh boy... don't be! I'm sure there is nothing wrong with you.'

'I don't know what's going on with me. I'm so sick,' I complain.

'It's stress! You are nervous about being home again,' he answers arrogantly.

'Well, I worry. I'm scared. You must help me.'

'Come on. What do you want me to do? I can't run from here just because you called me. Try to be calm. I'll think of you.'

'But ... but ... okay ... yes, you might be right.'

'Baby, we have something very special together. Something I have never felt before with others. You are so lovely and unique.'

'Hmmm ... Perhaps I'm stressed. Or afraid of everything with Paul. What do I know?' I moan.

'Let's meet tomorrow. Somewhere nearby you. Don't let your husband influence you too much. He doesn't care a shit about you. Go home. Get some sleep. I'll call you. Good night.' He giggles sweetly and convincingly.

'What do you mean he doesn't care?' I question, curious.

'Sweet little girl, have you not noticed he has no interest in you? He only uses you.

As his little status symbol for his many powerful, stupid, horny business plans.'

'Yep, you could be right,' I peep, trusting his promises.

'He is a sick bastard. He wants to show you off. Put you on a pedestal as his beautiful, stupid little goose. That's what he sees in you. You know I'm not like that. I see you as a clever person. A striking woman.'

'Aww, thanks. Do you mean that?'

'We will find a solution so we can be together. I promise you. I'm crazier about you than he ever has been. Or will be with you. Forget him! Get rid of him!'

'What are you doing right now? There is so much noise in the background.'

'Oh… eh… hmmm… yes, you see. I arrived at Kate's house for a brief time ago. I'm together with her family. I can't talk with you every time you call me…' he growls, upset.

I ponder, *but he left Spain early this morning.*

'What more are you going to do while you are here?'

'I'm leaving for Stockholm. Don't call me anymore. I'll call you. It's best so.'

'Oh! When are you leaving for Stockholm?' I notice his voice becomes insecure, and his answer is hesitant.

'Soon. Now, I'm taking part in some event with Kate. It sucks. Argh, I don't want to be with her horrible family.'

'Hmm, eh, why are you then with Kate if you don't want to be there?'

'They only want free treatments from me. Grr, they are so ungrateful all the time,' he crossly complains. How am I going to handle such a message from him? Then I realise the same pattern and similarities in Drake's answers as when Paul lies to me.

'You told me before you have nothing to do with her. Nor the family. Something is not right!' Irritated, I grumble. At this instant, he becomes more irritated at me.

'Don't you understand anything? There is nothing wrong with me staying with her.

She is only my secretary. While I'm here, I'll help her and the family. What part of it don't you understand?'

'Well… oh… fine.'

'I'm only in your corner. Baby, I'll always be there for you. And care for you. I'm only thinking of you,' he seems offended, and within the last sentence, he changes from angry to sweet.

'It sounds as you are more with her privately than just friends.' Though, I want to believe his explanation, as it swirls stupidly in my brain: *Am I jealous or in love with him?*

'You must be calm now. I want nothing to do with that woman. She is not my type as a woman. She is disgusting. I've told you so before.' Then he pauses so I can hear several deep breaths, as something irritates him.

'Fine ... fine ... I get it.'

'Go home. I'll call you. Kate is approaching me now. Can't talk anymore with you. Don't worry!' Then he hangs up, and I'm so upset while I march home with the dogs.

Paul is home and sits in the living room with an attitude as cold as a polar bear and stares angry at me. No hello, no nothing. I approach him and want to give him a hug, then sitting next to him on the sofa and trying to talk with him. It's impossible to get a conversation rolling when I talk about how merciless the flight has been and how awful I feel about our problems in paradise. His coldness feels as the worst frosty Antarctica and makes me even more dejected, so I jump to bed.

The following day, Drake calls me.

'Hello, how are you? I have figured out when we can meet today. This afternoon.'

'Sounds great. I'm feeling better today.'

'I'm glad to hear you're doing better. I told you so. Nothing to worry about.'

'Well, I'm still dizzy. Yuck and have nausea.'

'I'm the best guy in the world at what I'm doing. I will never harm you; you know that! Trust me. Where can we meet?' He seems overjoyed and content.

'Let's meet in the park near my space. There is a lovely little café. Yummy, they make a good café latte.' And I give him the time and address.

'I still think you should get a scan of your kidneys. And gallbladder. Problems may be there. Think about it.'

'Today I've the appointment with my doctor.' Though he finds nothing wrong with me. No flu and no problems with my inner organs, so a scan isn't necessary. 'I ponder if I should travel back to Spain. Get it done there at a private hospital.'

'Yea! Well, see you soon. Miss you, my darling little girl,' he laughs and hangs up.

The following afternoon, I meet with Drake, who is in an ecstatic mood as he strolls towards me. Sweet Jesus, the way he walks; it's such a dream of sexy elegance. He gives me heartfelt hugs and kisses, and I melt in his embrace when he takes my hand before we enter the café.

'How wonderful to see you again. I've missed you madly. It's almost impossible for me to get away from Kate. Gosh, and her horrible family.' He smiles boldly, and I clench his hand in mine.

'Why do you then stay there, if you don't want to be there? Stay at a hotel nearby me,' I question curiously.

'Oh, you know, I'm such a helpful man.' He smirks. 'Kate has asked for a long time ago. So, I've promised to help her family before I leave for Asia. I always help my secretary.' But I can't find out if it's true or not, and he continues chatting constantly.

'The most awful thing is they keep on complaining. Fuck, Kate is impossible.'

'Impossible? How?'

'Oh, boy, she is constantly yakking at me. She says I'm on the phone all the time.'

'With whom?'

'She accuses me for it's with you. Argh, such a stupid woman! She has not realised you are ill.' He pauses, takes a deep breath and glares at me, while he continues yakking.

'I'm so sick and tired of them. It's too much. They don't pay.'

'Pay? What do you mean?'

'Everybody always wants my expertise for free. What's wrong with people?' he grumbles.

'Wow… sounds awful.' I worry about this, because I've still not comprehended the connection with him and her family. Something does not add up, and I believe he's lying.

On this gorgeous sultry summer afternoon, after we have finished the coffee at the café, Drake and I stroll in the park, then find a nice green spot and sit down on the soft grass. I pick a few of the millions of tiny Bellises in the grass, and it reminds me of my time as a child. Oh… I love these tiny white flowers, with their buttery yellow spot in the middle, so I make a little garland.

'I have booked a flight back to Spain next week. Also, an appointment for a scan at the private hospital.' Swiftly I say, fixing my garland in my hands.

'What a superb idea.' He beams.

'When the event with Paul is over, I'll leave again. I can't stand it here anymore.' I glance expectantly at Drake while sitting with my many Bellises in hand.

'If he asks why you are leaving again, you tell him you are looking for peace of mind. And forgiveness to get on with your life. Because you feel he has abused you,' he sweetly dictates and smiles happily.

'What do you mean "forgiveness? Peace in my mind"? Do you mean I should forgive him?' I query foolishly.

'No, no, your silly cuckoo. That's not what I mean. Get on with this stupid divorce.'

'Why such a hurry?'

'You must use this as an excuse to go back to Spain. Remember, always have some suitable excuse. Ha-ha, even if it's a lie.'

'I don't lie.' For sure, lies are not the best performance I can project.

'Baby, I've promised to help you.' He smiles.

'Well, it's not been easy for me since I came home. Paul doesn't want to talk about his unfaithfulness.'

'As soon you are back in Spain, and before I leave for good, we'll start *project divorce*. The rest we can do over Skype. Or by mail.'

'Paul is playing the freezing-cold-ice card. Instead, he accuses me of being the culprit of unfaithfulness.'

'Oh yah, that was a magnificent night! Ha-ha, we must do it again.'

'Oh, no, it's not with you. But I got rapidly nervous if he had discovered about us. But how can he know?'

'What? Oh ... baby, I want to touch your soft skin. Kiss your neck. Have my hands all over your body again.'

'No, it's with one of our friends a long time ago. But that's not true.'

'Oh, I see. I need to teach you to have multiple orgasms. *Trust me*, they are fantastic. With the help of my soft fingers on your little pearl. Minnie will grow bigger and bigger with pleasure. Yeeha, until you come explosively in tremendous orgasms. One by one.'

'Okay, Drake. Please, let's not talk about it.'

'Why not? Oh, boy, my girlfriend in the US loved it. Hmmm… it's nice thinking of it. Gee, I can feel Willy moving down there.'

'Gee, stop it.'

'He wants to get inside your warm, tight Minnie again.' He smirks, pleased, and tilts his head, sending me those loving Bambi eyes. For heaven's sake, those eyes. I can't resist them. I don't know what to do with myself, but I get excited about what he tells me, and suddenly I miss him a lot.

'Please, you promised. And you know I've to save my marriage,' I beg.

'Argh! Whatever! But you started this conversation,' he nags.

'Paul's phone rings all the time. Then he walks away. He never does that. Damn, only when he has something going one.'

'Paul is angry at you. Kate is furious at me. So, what do we do?' he concerns thoughtfully.

'Honestly? I don't know! I'm confused!'

'I'm sure Paul will accuse you of having sex affairs with others all the time.'

'He keeps on cancelling all kinds of arrangements. It would not surprise me if he cancelled the next event next week.'

'What event?'

'With the board of directors. He uses stupid, lame excuses, as "a sudden meeting" or he has "overtime" or whatever? It doesn't fit together! He lies faster than a horse can run. He can't remember one lie from the other. Then the next comes. Christ, it's unbearable!' I complain.

'From his point of view, you're a wild and demanding sex-hungry woman. One who can't get enough sex with him.' Aggravated Drake mocks me.

'I don't get it. Why do you think so?'

'I'm sure that's his way of thinking.'

'It's not how it is. I'm not like that.'

'Babe, he will turn everything upside-down in case of a divorce. He will say that it's *you* who wants *bizarre sex*. Then he will appear as the respectful *guy*.'

'Do you think I'm like that?' I'm desperate and confused.

'No, silly head. It's him who believes you are like that He will try to stand out as if he is the one who must suffer from your wild sex-hunger. That's why he believes you are the unfaithful person. Don't you get it? He will use it in court. Use it as an excuse.'

'He's not like that. It sounds too scary to me.' Drake is scaring me.

'He will throw you on the street without a dime. Afterwards, you must defend yourself. Tell them in court it's not you who call all those skunks who have enjoyed themselves on your body.'

'Wow... hold on, Drake. You overdramatise this. I don't think Paul ever will come up with such stories.'

'But it's Paul who calls them. He forces you to do *his* desires. Even you don't want to.'

'Jeez! We are not talking about how it's in the US. Over there, everybody can sue everyone. They have different rules. It doesn't work like that in Danish law—and not with such crazy scenarios.'

'Remember, it's him who sold his wife with sexy pictures online. Never forget that!' Drake's claim is persuasive. Oh my! I am horrified by his outburst.

'Stop! Oh, my goodness. I'm sure the guy has never sold pictures of me. All our pictures are private. He will not do so.' Somehow, the thought scares me.

'No, don't you get it? People look so normal on the outside.'

'No, I don't get. it'

'I did something like that to my first wife. She cheated on me. Bitch! She ran off with another dickhead. On the inside, they are all maggots. As Paul is. I got off the hook.'

'What hook?'

'I did not pay a dime to her when I got rid of her. She was a disgusting worm,' he gloats.'

'Hmmm… did you not tell me you paid her off?' What does not add up?

'Mary, *trust me*, you will end up in court with Paul. He will interpret his words as if it's all your idea to visit other men. He will appear as a poor thing who must sit and watch what *you* want.'

'Come on. Stop. Paul will never do so.'

'Believe me. I bet on it. He will say *it turns you on* to see him get horny without him taking part in the sex act. Do you understand what I mean? You must prepare yourself.

Get a suitable explanation of what he can do with such comments. He will use them against you.'

'He is *not* like that,' I defend Paul, and I must refuse to believe in such nonsense.

'Legal interpretations' are not fair or correct. You must be in front of him. Tell your lawyer how he is. You need to be fully aware of his dirty accusations.'

'What accusations? There are none.'

'He might even call you a prostitute to win this round. You can argue against this and say, "If I'm a prostitute, I'd probably get good pay for it." And then tell him, "But you'll only get money from him when you come crawling and humbly beg him to buy new clothes." Yea, even food, or other things.'

'Truly, Paul has never called me a prostitute.'

'Mary, he is the one who sells you. He makes a big profit out of it. He gets all that black money. In the end, he's the *pimp* and lives like one.' At Drake's frightening dramatization of the entire scenario, I drop my jaw on the floor. Scandalous! I can't believe these appalling words coming out of his imagination. Where the hell does he get such ideas from? Which fantasy world does he belong to? We have never talked about such awful things before.

'I don't get it, Drake. Paul has never sold me. Never earned shadowy money on my account. How can you come up with such scary scenarios?' Though I recall that Paul once accused me of having an affair with one of our friends.

This dear friend is not even my type of man and he is married. I would never interfere, even if I liked him. I got furious at Paul back then, and he threatens me, I'd not get a dime if I ran off with this friend. But it's not even in my farthest imagination to run off with this bloke, so I asked Paul back then, 'So, what if I do so? And you do not want to pay for a settlement? Do I then have to earn my money on the street?' Paul never offered an answer. Drake knows that story, and now he is mixing it all up.

'Oh cripes! Gosh! You have scared me shitless, Drake.' Is that how he does it with his women? Or is it his own bad conscience. His foolish imagination which makes up such daunting stories?

'Baby, I've to go now. Kate doesn't know where I am. She thinks I'm out shopping for things which I need for my Stockholm trip.'

'Hmm ...'

'I also must treat one of the *rotten*, screaming, spoiled kids of the family.' He hugs me passionately and kisses me.

'Ta-ta, sweet little girl.' I'm gloomy and watch him disappear over the horizon with his elegant, hasty steps. Alone and abandoned, I stand with lots of whopping question marks on my forehead from today's many pieces of advice from him. *What's all this about? These scary scenarios of his?* I ponder and cannot see through all his peculiar secrets, scams, and lies. But once again, I believe in him and act.

Essentially, I'm stupid, or I'm fallen in love with him and can't reflect proper from the scary image of him, and don't see it is multiple red flags! My common sense has disappeared, and instead, I get more fascinated by him, pondering, *it's only nice of him to help me and prepare me for a decent divorce.* Drake wins, and Paul has lost. Paul's fixation with a woman from work makes me want to puke when he tells me constantly how clever and smart she is. So, I'm certain she is the 'mysterious woman' in his secret life. Shocking, because this summer, he has even had the audacity to tell me she will also have her vacation close by us, so he picks her up at Malaga airport. He guides tours for her and meets her by the pool every day. Wow! Brilliant and helpful of him, and he has no time for us. I get suspicious and traumatised over their behaviour, and as I think back to it, Drake's creepy stories sound reasonable to me. Then Drake also tells me it's natural to help his secretary, and that makes my brain spin around irrationally, knowing two men have the same point of secretary view. I'm terrified and about to become a total crackpot who can't think straight. It's as two men are fighting over who has the biggest pink tally whacker and most wealth. Oh, yea, I've seen and heard it all. Which one of them thinks I'm *that stupid?* Or a wacko? Which of them is lying? Or maybe both are! It's been a horrifying, stressful drama this summer, so no wonder I want to kill myself because I have had enough.

I must tell the reader and be honest with you, because fast I figure out it's *not* the secretary, but another trull Paul has an affair with. So, I have wrongly accused a person for his betrayal. But we are all human and make mistakes, except for those who do it all as some crooked strategy, to get you into their nasty spider web.

> *2018: Study reveals that husbands stress women twice as much as children do.*
>
> Given the fact that children have needs which require constant tending and attention, people often think that the greatest source of stress in a family are the children. However, a recent study conducted by 'Today' shows otherwise. With more than 7,000 mothers from United States participating in a recent survey and an interview conducted by 'Today', the result shows that majority of mothers rated their stress levels at unsurprising 8.5 out of 10. What makes the study surprising though is, that about half of the mothers who participated in the survey and interview told that more than the children, the husbands were noted to be a greater source of stress. Apparently, women can cope with depression and stress a lot easier than

when their husband is still with them. One in every five mothers told that a major source of daily stress was a lack of help from their significant other.[4]

Raising and keeping a family together is not a simple task to achieve, and I feel hopeless in my fights, so it must end. Drake has a powerful influence on me, especially during the last month, so the problems between Paul and me are unbearable. The quarrels have risen to heights of nightmares, though both of us have our faults, and in our modern society, everyone screws around. It's selfish, and it's all about our self! I'm sure many have tried—or are going through—the unfaithful path in their life, so it's not only in our home that it happens. Do you ever think about it? How horrible it is, what the betrayed person experiences, and the nightmares? It's traumatic! It's shattering! It's a living hell and impossible to fight against! It's your partner who lets you down, as Paul shatters my entire dream. I have given up, and the marriage is one enormous failure, so the bimbo can have him, and I can choose Drake.

---

[4] Aye Duran, mypositiveoutlooks.com.

CHAPTER 21

I Do Nothing Wrong. You Do!

There's a snake hidden in the grass.
—Virgil, *Ecologues*

The week in Copenhagen was awful. So, I travel back to Spain, alone! Finally, my life can end up great—I believe it, and my plan is to figure out whether to divorce. It's now three weeks since I met Doctor Bates for the first time in his clinic, though today is a specific day when the scariest thing happens and the day I fear the most. Humbly, I had during my first visits, told him about my suicide plan, because I could not cope with my life anymore, and I was depressed and weak. As I have finished the MRI scan I meet with Drake at his clinic, and everything ends up in a total disaster instead of something great. It's traumatic!

The foul snake in the grass is rattling at me, rather than me finding many stunning Bellis. As he has ripped off my thong and raped me, I realise he is a poisonous snake. I've not agreed for him to act so outrageously, so as a powerless plastic doll, I lay on his damn treatment table, and don't dare to move my body an inch. (See 3.) Next, I become angry and ashamed. As I lie there terrified and disabled, many creepy thoughts run through my mind—what the sneaky bastard has done and why. It's absurd to understand, and I try to reflect on what has happened during the last weeks of treatments. I conclude that he is eager in his flirting tactics, and I'm sure I have control of his flattery. It's not meant to be for us, but he doesn't understand that I want to save my marriage, thus, he tries to convince me of the opposite. Okay, I have a one-night stand in my baggage, which is not so good. But that he has so little respect for me, I cannot comprehend, and I cannot believe what the snake has done in my vulnerable moment today.

I lose all respect for him and his fake kindness, so in my mind, he instantly suffers a tremendous crash. He's supposed to be a good, loving guy, but his wicked rapist behaviour is too much for me, so I want him out of my life. When he lets me go to the bathroom, I'm shaking as a leaf and muse, *I need to get home now! Get my body cleaned from his touch.* Christ! I want to cry, to scream and jump out of the window but can't. He apologises seconds after his orgasm, sexually exhausted and relaxing flat on my body, as a dried, wrinkled, disgusting lizard.

'Oh my God! I'm so sorry. I have done nothing like this before. Can you forgive me?' He's begging.

'Huh?' Ugh! I only stare fossilized at him, while my mind ponders: *What do you think?*

Next, he has the audacity to command me something weird. 'Ahem, do not to say anything to anyone.' *Holy crap! What's that about?* 'Not even to your husband.' I'm devastated and confused.

'Eh? A-ha. Ohhh.' I stare speechless at him and can't find any words for his selfish act. I'm dumbstruck. Stupid, bogus, plastic American! And he pulls up his boxer shorts as if it didn't disturb him a diddly squat. *Arrogant bastard!*

'Oh, no… no… I've an idea,' the foul snake in the grass shouts at me and asks me, 'Let's get some food. Have a beer at the tapas bar.' What a creep! How tasteless of him! I have the angry urge to slam him with a scorching hot frying pan in his handsome face, so he bleeds to death, but I have none.

'No!' I scream angrily at him, to the invitation, stalk out of the clinic and drive home as a terrified dead, abused plastic doll.

Imagine how I now must deal with the trauma of his rape. As I enter my flat, I furiously tear off all my clothes, throw them in the washer, and have a long steamy shower. Shameful and depressed, I sit in the corner and want to scream and weep, but I'm speechless, and my tears are dry inside me. My stomach and heart crumble into shards of glass, tearing my insides apart as someone was cutting me with a lethal sharp razor blade. I'm reaching out for my nail brush, then scrub myself as a shattered woman, until I bleed. I don't dare to call anyone, either the police, or Lucy, Kate or Paul. I'm mentally shut down and go depressed and petrified to bed in my own living hell. Some hours after, he calls me many times, but I refuse to answer the phone, however ultimately, I surrender and pick up the damn phone, and its Drake.

'Why aren't you answering the phone? I've called you many times!'
'Huh? And?'
What the hell is wrong with you? Have I done something wrong to you?' he yells as if nothing has happened today. I want to throw the phone out of the window, but I don't, so, grudgingly, I answer his stupid question.

'Honestly? What you did to me is beyond my understanding,' I whimper.

'I've apologised, haven't I?' is his grouchy cold polar bear answer.
'Excuse me!'
'You lay there and looked so gorgeous. Oh, God, and so attractive.' He grins, and I get miffed and angry. *Shut up!* I could have smashed him solidly with a baseball bat, first in his head and next in his stupid balls, until his pink rape tool ended up being minced meat, over his egoistic nature.

'Perhaps you think an apology is enough. I'm shattered by your action.' Within seconds comes a lame excuse.

'I have always kept a complete distance to my patients.'
'Oh ... so, you have never done so before?' I' asking ironically.
'I've never done such things before.' I'm sure it's a lie, and I ponder, *What? Does he seriously believe that himself?* The thought swirls confusingly around in my head.

'Fuck, what's then the difference between me and your other patients?'

'My clinics have *always*—and I tell you *always*—been an exceptionally important priority to me. They are *always crystal clear. White as snow.*' He shouts.

'Do you think it's okay?' What part does he not understand? Mostly I get angry at myself. Why have I allowed myself to pick up the damn phone and continue this rape conversation, where he tries to assure me he speaks the truth? I should hang up, but I don't.

'I harmed none of my patients. Even many of them have flirted with me,' he proudly and firmly attempts to convince me.

'This is fucked up, Drake.'

'Believe me, I've had hundreds of options of temptations from women who wanted to get in the sack with me. I've always rejected them!'

'Good for you. Wow! You are a hero!'

'I'm sorry if I've offended you,' and he blabbers and blabbers, blah, blah, blah.

'You have!'

'But you are something very special. I know you like me too.'

'I do, but not with what you did.'

'I have done nothing wrong. You have! You didn't even resist.'

'Baloney. That's the stupidest thing I've ever heard.'

'In good faith, I believed it was okay. That you liked it.'

'Gah, this is hopeless. I don't think we have anything to talk about.' Once more, I want to knock him down with a baseball bat and muse, *such a self-confident Doctor Dickhead* while he continues as a fast-running waterfall.

'Listen, what happened today was innocent.'

'Gah, I give up.'

'Come on, Mary. We had had sex before we went to Denmark. I can't see what the problem is. You wanted it for yourself as well. Right?' he self-assuredly claims. I'm deeply upset by his self-possessed comment.

'Geez, do you sincerely have the nerve to believe that? Wow.'

'Come on, Mary. Let's forget about it. Let's move on. It's not something to make so much fuss about.

'Fuss about? Booh, come on, man!'

'Get ongoing with your life. I like you. I want you. We are meant to be.'

'Ha! In my terminology, it's rape! You can't just take what you want because you suddenly have sexual desire for a patient. Damn, and who is lying on your treatment table.' He knows I'm not ready to commit to him.

'I'm sorry about today. I promise you on my children's lives that I'm usually not like that. I'm a clear-cut decent person,' he tries to reassure me. I lay motionless in my bed and stare at all my scratches from the scrubbing, which he can't see.

'That one-night stand was a gigantic mistake. We did it in our drunkenness. Oh gosh! You smashed me out with too much whiskey. You took advantage of the situation.'

Then he continues as if it's he who is the victim. 'Mary, please, you are such a lovely woman. Come again. Let's continue the treatments. Let's make a new appointment. Then we can talk.' His cynical coolness shudders through my body, and I hang up without saying goodbye. Many times, during the next days, he tries to reach me, and finally, I unwisely answer him once more.

'I don't understand why you keep on ignoring me. We must meet and talk!' he nervously demands.

'Hmm, well, I don't know. Yet, I want to tell you a distressing story! It's from my time as a teenager. Then you might understand me better. And why it was not okay what you did,' I insist, but truthfully, I doubt whether I should tell him. In his excitement, it seems not to affect him.

'Well, let me hear what you have to say. Tell me how you looked like as a teenager,' he answers selfishly. Wham bam! Smack right into my head; his stupid comment twists my conversation into something other than what I have in mind.

'Huh? What? Hmmm… how I looked? Why do you want to know? It's not exactly the thing about my story. But okay.' I scratch my neck and he interrupt me once again.

'Yeah! How tall were you?'

'What? Eh? Well, it was many years ago. I was not as tall as now.'

'How developed were you bodily?' he asks gladly. I'm getting annoyed at him as he constantly interrupts me and asks curious, imprudent questions. He has got it all turned in the wrong direction. I wish I could get it onto the track where I want it, but somehow, it seems as if he is trying to make me the culprit of destructive behaviour. Tricky dude!

'Body shape? Hmm, though, not developed with my female form. I believe I was late getting my breasts and so on.' I sound embarrassed. Does he think he can slip away from talking about his beastly action?

'Did you have short or long hair? Have you always been blonde?' he eagerly asks and has an impressive ability and an instinctive way of turning the conversation completely in the opposite direction. So, instead of me not disconnecting him on the phone and never talking to him again, I describe myself. How the hell does he manipulate me like this? Again, I'm impressed with his fantastic gift of speech.

'Eh, yea, I had long blonde hair. Why?'

'When did you have your first sexual experience?' Bingo! Yeeeaah, that's exactly the track I want to get on, so I tell him about the ghastly experience I had as a teenager.

'When I was young, I worked as a waitress. On weekends, I had to work extra behind the bar at the disco. It was normally open until five o'clock in the morning—'

He interrupts me again.

'Oh my God! Did you work until five?' He seems surprised.

'No, no, not always. But, I was there until three or four. I could not serve drinks to the guests, and—'

To my irritation, he interrupts me again.

'Please. Doh! Nah… it must have been because you are a girl. Or not old enough, I assume.' Smart ass!

'I don't know. I was behind the bar. Cutting lemons, oranges, and cleaning glasses. Putting beer and soft drinks in the cooling stand, and so on.' I sigh for a moment and need to get some breath into my lungs.

'Come on, what's more? That's it? Tell more! Chop, chop, hurry. I don't have all day. I'm curious,' he dictates impatiently. Mostly, I want to stop the conversation.

'Well, that night, there were two actors in the bar. One was a well-known dude. Good looking. Nice fella. He seemed normal. The other one was not so famous. He looked nasty. Yikes, a gross fatty brute. I'm sure he weighed 350 pounds.'

'Oh boy, who is it? Anyone I know?' He sounds almost ecstatic, as he expects a sexual conclusion to the story.

'I don't know. Maybe you do. Do you know these mild funny erotic movies?'

'Oh, those from the late seventies. Or was it the early eighties? Never seen them!' So, either he is pretending to be stupid, or he has full knowledge of those movies. Everybody knows them, and they are funny, but I can't see if he is lying.

'Yes, it's them. But not real porn.' At the same moment, my stomach turns upside down, when I get this disgusting vomiting feeling just thinking about telling this nasty story. 'Anyhow, Soren Bergstrom was the most famous—I even think he's the guy who owned the disco, Beidershall. The brute was Malvin Linneberg. He was not so famous. I think he was also a singer. They kept complimenting me. Idiotically commenting on my clothes. Daftly telling me how "incredibly" beautiful I was. Absurdly asking, "Do you want to be an actress in one of our movies?" Psycho!'

'Yuck, such creeps.'

'In fact, I was certain they were already very drunk. Those half-wits seemed to be in a euphoric mood. I rejected the weirdos offer. "No way! Stupid idiots!" I shouted. Then I went down to the basement. I'd done it so many times before. Oh my! I was there alone. There was a small table for the bottles. As I was taking beer out of old wooden bear crates.'

'Oh, yea, I remember those.'

'Well, I had my butt pointed up at the ceiling. I got scared when I heard some male voices at the stairs. They came into that dimly lit nasty room,' I stutter.

'Oh boy. What happened? Did you get scared? And why were there suddenly two men in the room?' he asks, surprised and outraged.

'Well, this is the tough part to tell about. But yes, I was scared shitless. What the hell do you think? Only God knows why they were suddenly down there. When I wanted to turn around, I could see the fat ugly guy and his friend. I was not able to turn myself around and get up before the fat, slimy bloke grabbed my tiny arms. Soren grabbed my legs. The maniacs throw me on this table. Goddam, all the bottles were tumbling around on the floor. Something more for my book I'll publish someday.'

While I'm half-sobbing, I tell him the rest of the story.

'Holy crap. That sounds terrible!' And he seems actual genuinely outraged. 'Did you not scream for help?'

'How could I? It was impossible. They totally gagged me,' I say with a shaky voice as I retell this story, which I'm trying to forget about.

'Have you never spoken to anyone about it?'

'I don't want to talk more about it.'

'Surely, you must have told your husband. I'm sure he has used it against you by misleading you with all his bullshit?' I am flabbergasted over his outlandish comment.

'No, I've told no one about it. Only my psychologist back some years ago. But only in small fragments. Paul can't have used it against me. Heck, no, I've never told him,' And I know Paul will never use such a tragic thing against me.

'Oh… my goodness, my darling little girl. Jeez, you have been married to him for over twenty years. Hideously, you have never told him. Get rid of this scumbag. He is not worthy of you.' I want to weep when he shows me all this passion and feels pity for me. I've no idea where that suddenly comes from.

'To be honest with you, I told you the story, so you know how it feels being raped by a man. Goddamn, it's not nice when men do something sexual that a woman has not agreed to.' I don't know whether I should stop the conversation immediately or keep on talking to him. Next, it becomes silent over the phone, until he unleashes another outburst.

'Bloody Mary. What the hell is that kind of rubbish to accuse me of?'

'The message is simple. Men cannot rudely grab what they like because of their power. And because they are horny. Shit, just because a delicious little *steak* lays gorgeously on your table.'

'Hogwash! You have no rights to accuse me of raping you. I did *not rape* you. I don't do such things!' Surely, I want to punch him solidly in his balls with a sledgehammer. I can't believe that he is angry and insulted *at me*, and now he tries to blame *me* for it all? 'Bullshit! You have some damn nasty nerve! Maybe you can ask first. You are poisoning me with your devious snakebite. Prick!' I snap.

'Such stupid nonsense to say. I've apologised. Isn't that good enough? The snakebite is yours!'

'You're such a fuck-stick. You seem not to have understood my message at all. You pretend as nothing has happened. Shit, then you are angry at me. Next time jerk it of yourself.'

'Jesus Christ! Then you tell me this depressing story. Kiss my ass. It must feel good for you to get rid of that demon,' he quarrels. I have the feeling that he seems not to even care.

'Well, I don't know. But it's good for me to tell the story. You speak of my demon?'

'Mary, it's not my fault!' So, according to him, it's only my fault?

'Anyhow, those guys are not the only ones. It's not the first time I had an experience of such nasty, selfish wrongdoers.' I immediately regret saying so.

'Oh… you have more? Tell me.'

'But I'm not prepared to talk about it.'

'I want to know. I'm listening.' So, I tell him, however, despite the stupid comments that occasionally come out of his filthy mouth. I play the jukebox once more and begin with the next record. Damn! I chatter too much. Why can't I keep my mouth shut?

'It's the same year. It might have been half a year before? A person exposed me to something nasty at my other workplace. Not so bad. But unpleasant. It was my employer. A janitor at a school.' I must swallow the story if I want to tell it to the end. I briefly pause and can hear his deep breathing on the phone, then I imagine his nostrils moving up and down when he takes his deep breath and exhales.

'Yes! I'm sure now! It's the same summer I got this job at the discotheque. During the daytime, I worked at a second restaurant. It was only open in the summer. Shut up! When I think about it! Yikes, it had been a horrible year,' I stutter the last word out of fury.

'Oh, my goodness! You have been a diligent workaholic,' he comments.

'Well? Hmm. Might be. Yea, you can call it that. It's better to work than to steal from others. Don't you think?' My comment comes as a self-assured statement. 'Anyhow! At my young age, I saw the janitor Magnusson as an old duffer. Christ! Geez, he was an Old Norse from Methusalem—ha-ha—but in the beginning, I believe he was super nice. The old methuselah asked me to come down to his wretched, mouldy office in the basement. There was only a small table. Two wooden chairs and an old desk. Yuck! It stank awfully of mould in there.' In the same moment, it strikes me that the oldster Magnusson reminds me of Drake. Brown eyes and grey hair.

'Odd name. It sounds as another exciting story you're about to tell. What happens?

Does the pop also rape you?' he interrupts with his annoying question.

'Come on! You must stop interrupting me all the time. I'll come to the point soon,' I say with a grumpy sneer.

'The old duffer wanted to give me some extra work. Yeeeaah, I was glad. I was saving money for my education as an architect. Also, for a driver's license,' I say proudly. 'But the old geezer wanted something in return. "Get over here," he told me. I glare at him and said, "What? Something in return?" *Nasty parasite!* In good faith, I went towards him...'

I shudder in my bones as I finish the story to Drake.

'Well, this is also one of the horrifying chapters for my upcoming book.' It's horrible for me, bringing these stories up to the surface again, yet I can feel Drake has somehow some sympathy for me.

'Such a disgusting pig he is! What did you then do?'

'Kapow! Slam! I whacked the old methuselah a hard punch on his ugly face. Next, I slipped away. To protect myself, I pretended it never happened. I did everything in my power to forget this perpetrator. Shit, it still plagues my life.'

'Did you never tell it to anyone?' He asks.

'At my foster parents' home, I told them I got sacked. There was no more work for me. So that was why I afterwards work at the restaurant.' Damn! What a shitty year! Christ! It has saddened me I've experienced such disgusting sex offenders. Yuck! Then it runs through my mind what Drake the sex maniac has done to me. Good Lord! Am I only born to be misused. Sexually abused? It freaks me out.

'But this incident with Magnusson—I have *never* told it to anyone. No one knows.'

'Wow! How terrible, darling little girl. I will tell no one. You can fully *trust me*. I promise you! I swear!'

'I mean it. *No one knows*, except for you,' I yell.

'You know I have patient confidentiality. What you tell me is between us.'

'Thanks for not telling anyone. And we can have this confidentiality between us.'

'Little girl, I'll always listen to you. Be there for you if you need it. I promise I will take worthy care of you. Gee so, traumatised you are with such horrible experiences? I feel so sorry for you.' I am so close to a breakdown, so I'm only content he can't see my face.

'Thanks! I'm pleased to hear.' I genuinely feel that he has a lot of understanding and sudden respect for my feelings about my ugly experiences.

'Okay, then! I don't want to talk more about this. Nor about what you've done to me. Despite how bad it was. Not nice!' I mumble.

'Stop! Stop talking about what occurred up there.' He screams, furious. 'Instead, let's agree that we'll meet at the clinic again. So, I can continue treating you. For free!'

'We can make a new appointment.'

'Do you promise me we will forget what happened? Also, you won't say anything to anyone. Not even your husband. Promise!' he begs, and he's as a pendulum; suddenly his voice becomes calm, indulgent, so he almost seems slick.

'Fine! Yes, yes... I promise you.'

'I'm so sorry! *Trust me*! I will do whatever you want. You need not to pay. Let's make a new appointment! Now!' he continues and pleads. I'm speechless about his sudden offer of free treatments.

'It's fine. But not for free. I want to pay what it costs.' I end the conversation, and the incident never comes to the surface again, because for me, it's best to forget about it. I feel it will at no time bear any fruit if I report him to the police or tell my husband about it. Besides, the greybeard bird will soon fly away. So, in good faith, I continue with the rest of the treatments, until the chap leaves for Asia.

Was that wise? 'This is too crazy. Why doesn't she stop such a thing? Why doesn't she reports it to the police. Or the health authorities?' you're possibly thinking! You are right! I should have. But I didn't. Other victims will do it. Or will they? I'm not even sure. For some of these questions, I will get back to it later. So, why do I not report it? Mostly, I have *no trust* in the police, nor in any other authorities. Why? As a child, I feared them in my life at the orphanage. What's the worst, or best? I am too prone to see the best in all people.

Damn, why do I like him so much? Drake has massive power over me and has convinced me he has an empathetic side to him. At least that's what I want to believe. So, I take the blame and imagine it's me who wanted him and not the other way around. So, is it the snake or the forbidden bite from the poisoned able which is to blame? Whatever he tells me, I believe in it, and he can always turn everything upside-down and twist it against me. The puppet master has found me and has put his invisible strings on me. I've thought what he has done was just a clumsy way to show his passion, so I chose not to see him as the monster. I've noticed a different side to him, when he becomes understanding, sweet, and nice to me—that's why I forgive him. I'm not capable of hating people, because I only want love. I'm wiser today, and can see what has happened, realising it's absolutely a gigantic wrongdoing on his part.

CHAPTER 22

Trust, Scams, and Women

It's not that he wants to be a liar; It's just that he doesn't know the truth.
—Warsan Shire

A week goes by, and it's a beautiful sunny morning while I sit on the balcony, drinking my coffee and having a smoke. I've not seen Drake the last week when he suddenly calls me in panic.

'Hi, beautiful sweet Mary Liz. It's Drake. I've a massive problem. You need to help me. The stupid bitch has kicked me out with no notice.'

'Huh? What? Kate?'

'Yea all my stuff, she threw it outside the door. I don't know what to do.'

'Oh, that's awful!' I am pitying him

'I've only a few weeks left before I'm leaving. So, I have no place to stay.' I can only ponder, *Well, get a hotel dude!* Instead of hanging up, unwisely, I answer him.

'How so? I assumed you would stay there. No? Until you were leaving.'

'I've no idea of what's going on with Kate.'

'What's going on?' I muse next, *this is strange!*

'Since this stupid witch came back from vacation, she has screaming at me like a lunatic.' he says with anger and frustration. 'I've done nothing wrong! She has! I've spent days helping her with the damn apartment. Painting walls and other things.'

'So, how do I get into the picture here?'

'What? Goddam it. I worked like crazy for her while she is away. Scratch-cat. And this is how she thanks me?' he screams, and I remove the phone from my ears.

'Worked. You were together with her in Denmark.'

'Huh? Damn, she is only using me! From the beginning of our relationship. I should have recognized the dangers. Slut!'

'Relationship? Using you?'

'Even our first night got off to a rocky start by her screaming at me during a dinner.'

'Eh? First night? She is only your secretary. No?'

'What? Eh? Shit, it could have been a sign I should have listened to. Nasty bitch!' he growls, and then his voice becomes calmer. 'What about your husband?'

'What about him? How does he get into the picture here?'

'Can he help me? You've one more apartment, correct?'

'Correct. It belongs to the company.'

'Can I stay there for a few weeks?' he pleads, and now he takes it for granted that I will help him. I can hear his deep breathing and picture his angry nostrils moving up and down as a fuming Spanish bull, chasing the *torero* (matador) in the arena.

'I suppose I can't stay with you until then? Can I?'

'No, you can't. Putting me in such an awkward situation is embarrassing for me. Gosh, I can't ask Paul for help.' Holy smokes, he doesn't even know what Drake has done to me, and I regret I've not told Paul. Now I don't dare!

'Please ask him. Do it for us.' His eagerness is not to be mistaken, and I don't feel comfortable letting Drake staying at my apartment, although I want to help him.

'Us? I must think about it. I don't know how to deal with it,' I answer indiscreetly, but my guts tell me I don't want to help.

'You must do it today. She wants my belongings gone before the end of tomorrow.'

'Wow! That doesn't sound good.' I try to stay calm with my answer.

'Otherwise, she will throw them out. Jeez, she thundered in her insane outburst of rage.' He's desperate and pressing in his commands.

'Let me talk to Paul later. I can't promise you anything. I'll call you back.' and hang up the phone.

Oh my! It turns the entire situation upside-down, from him helping me, then raping me, and now I must help him in his emergency. If I do so, I feel he will have total control over me. Still, I feel sorry for him, but truthfully, I don't owe him a damn shit. Yet, I'm always caring to others, so my good heart convinces me to help. It's my biggest weakness of all, always aiding others without thinking of myself. Often my generosity gets punished, and I get repeatedly disappointed over people's fake behaviour. However, I feel trapped in his controlling web and help him. Why can't I say *no*?

'Hi, Paul. Are you okay? Are you busy? Do you recall the doctor who treats me?'

I briefly tell him about Drake's horrible situation with Kate. 'He needs a space to stay for a few weeks before he leaves for Asia.'

'Right, I understand. It's not good for him.'

'Eh, phew, hmm, can he rent the other apartment for two or three weeks?' I mumble, pleading and shaking as a leaf, as I feel bad.

'Sure, no problem. I'll find out if it's available. I'll call you back,' Paul understandingly replies. He is such a helping guy, and from left to right, he helps everybody in need. I love him for that, even though it's hard to get out of my mind that I allowed myself to ask of this favour.

It is a two-bedroom west-facing apartment with a stunning view of the mountains and a magnificent sunset. I can't see it from our home, but there are only a few hundred metres between them, and I walk over there to see if anyone is staying there now. Holy mackerel. When I come back to my flat again, I can see Drake has called me many times. He calls again and again, and we speak many times over the next few hours, as he's so impatient and keeps pushing for answers. Damn! It's awful.

'It's me again. Have you spoken to him yet? I need some answers *now*!'

'Paul will call back ASAP. Then I'll call you,' I grunt, and fifteen minutes later, he calls again.

'Kate is mental over our conversations. Stupid bitch!'

'Be calm now, Drake. *Wait!* Please.'

'Blimey, she never understood me. That's why we could never communicate about anything. Bloody hell, and now this,' he desperately roars rude, which I don't like.

'I've spoken with Paul several times. I told you he will call back. He is busy at work. He can't throw everything overboard only for you.' I snap, irritated, and wonder if he even understands the message.

'Okeydokey, I'll call you again in one hour,' snarling and ending the phone call. Shortly after, Paul calls. Oh… my… goodness. I'm about to go nuts over these many calls.

'Hi, I've looked at the vacation schedule. It's fine. He can borrow it,' Paul agrees.

'Oh, gosh, thanks a bunch. How much shall he pay?'

'Don't you worry. If he keeps on helping you with the treatment, then I'm pleased,' and he ends the phone call. Oh, my. I feel so embarrassed but also glad for the help. The hour has passed, and Drake rings right on the spot.

'Any news? Can I rent the apartment or not?' he asks. Most of all, I want to lie.

'No, you can't.' At this point in my life, I should have refused! No, no, no, no!

'Damn. Bullshit. What the heck do I do?'

'Booh! Ha-ha. Yes, I spoke with him. It's okay.' So, am I relieved or not? At least I will be free of the burden of his rude behaviour. Perhaps this is the biggest mistake I make by saying *yes*! Red flag!

'Great. How much do I have to pay?'

'He wants a thousand euros for the month,' I'm lying to test him.

'Shucks! Frankly, I don't have that much money. I need it in Asia. I've also paid for the month at Kate's flat.'

'Well, that's not so good.'

'This reckless woman will not give me my money back,' he shouts, so it's clear he's extremely angry and upset, and I'm sure she can hear his roaring voice.

'What do you want to do?'

'Come on, seriously? I don't have that kind of money. I thought I could get it cheaper. Maybe for free,' he grunts and gets disappointed.

'Hmmm, sorry, then I can't help you,' I tease, and he gets pissed at me.

'Can I stay at your place?' he begs as a little schoolboy. I try not to fall into his trap.

'No, you cannot! But don't worry. You can have the apartment for free.'

'Wonderful!' he rejoices, as if it has all been a matter of course.

'Paul expects you will finish my treatments before your departure.' My voice seems fresh and optimistic, and I expect him to interpret treatments as "free treatments". But that he has already promised me, which Paul doesn't know about.

'Later, I'll be there with all my things. See you,' and he hangs up. Later in the afternoon, he calls again.

'Can you pick me up? She won't let me borrow the car. Such a cow!' is his rude, pissed-off comment.

'So now I'm also your local taxi company? You gotta be kidding me! Geez, okay, where?' and overrule my irritation.

'Where we met the first time,' he freshly replies. I grab my keys, lock the front door and drive off. Copper-red with anger in his face, he jumps into the car.

'I'm pissed at her. Damn cow! She describes me as an angry person who is unstable. As a ticking bomb that could go off at any time.' I glare, shakenly at him.

'Where is all your stuff?'

'She defines me as being a lying irritable old grouch. And would get angry at anyone who would oppose me. What kind of rubbish is that?' he angers.

'Aren't you supposed to move it all by now?'

'I need your car to move my things. Can I borrow it?' he hastily reacts. *Shut up! I don't know what I've messed myself into.*

'What? Rental company! Taxi driver! Removal company! Oh gosh, this is so complicated.'

'Such a bitch! A ridiculous burdensome shrimp she is. I don't know why the hell she threw me out. Christ! A ticking bomb? I am not sure I can recognize it.' Angry, he's sitting in the passenger seat and criticise and yell about Kate. 'People who know me well, could never see or had experienced that aspect of me or somewhere in me.' He seems surprised by her action, and bad-mannered and negative, he keeps on blabbering in a way I don't like at all. 'I'm perceived of being a perfectionist. Bloody hell, not angry. When it comes to incompetence, I was not afraid to tell her as it was.' He is transforming into a chameleon that's nice to me and explosively dramatic towards Kate. I say nothing.

'She is too much. No woman has ever treated me like that before. I've never even liked her. Or her family.' I don't comment on any. I'm all ears to his rage. 'Such a creep she is with her cellulite legs. Yikes, and nauseating smell from her crotch.' He's so pissed off, so I'm utterly speechless at his heated offensive words. I hope he will never talk to me like that or speak so revoltingly about me.

'She should hang upside down. With her head downwards.' His temper continues all the way home to my flat. Wow, he has changed his behaviour gravely. 'Hell, yeah, drying on a clothesline. Such an old smelly and wrinkled cunt,' he bursts furiously. Sweet Jesus and Virgin Mary! His rage won't stop, and I become more and more flummoxed at his evil, dreadful language. But I don't know what has happened before this incident. So, I trust what he tells me, and try to urge him to calm down, while I choose not to comment on his wild explosions.

'Well, at least we can be together without her interference. Let's cook some delicious food together.' He's satisfied with his own obviousness. It's taken less than ten minutes before we arrive at my apartment, and he has blabbered *so much*. I glance confusingly at him, as he's taken me by surprise with his barrage of fast and self-assured grim words.

'Fine, we can do that. But let me show you the apartment first. When you pick up your things, we can start cooking,' I shockingly answer him, and he gets the car key and disappears as a whirlwind on the horizon. I'm extremely confused, and shortly after, he's back. He glares relieved, smiling when he sees me again, as if has he conquered the enormous battle or won the million-dollar lottery. He empties all his stuff on my table, and next we walk over to the other apartment.

'I'm pleased. Thanks.' He smiles, having the key in his hand, while we stroll back to my home. Next, he loads few of his stuff into my car and moves it to the other flat.

While I'm resting on the sofa, I ponder over Paul's generosity to help Drake, which I feel works out admirably, as one hand helps the other, and I get my treatments for free. But now the many *buts*, *why's*, and *what's* appears. I'm sure you will think it's all a cunning plan of his, and perhaps you are right. He contacts me daily and influences me severely day and night, when he comes for visits! I get in his pocket with free treatments, sweetness, and his help with my many matrimonial problems! We talk, talk, talk for hours, and by now he knows too much about me. So yes, you are right, as I blindfolded, plunged right into his cunning seduction plan. He has no more patients, I'm the only one left, as the business is officially closed, and he has plenty of time to influence and sugar me. Proudly, he shows me the notice for the local news magazine, about his next move. Dear reader, please carefully read the first lines of the text, because they will have an important meaning when the story is developing. Try not to forget these first lines:

> Everything has a beginning and a natural ending. The ending can often be the beginning of something new and exciting.
>
> For a few years, I've been here in Spain, and got to know many people and patients as different individuals. I had the ambition to establish education for those who would like to learn from my knowledge so I could establish this amazing therapy in Europe. I found out Spain do not make the special business condition here for the benefit of

forward-looking and energetic people as me. It soon became clear to me that meeting my goals and desires in a term of education and multi-clinic would be very difficult here.

Interesting! Many will believe these first lines are poetic and fine words. I commit them to memory, and as I read the same sentence again, and then the word *patients* strike my mind! This must be the way he catches his female audience, and that must be how he charms himself into the women's hearts. Women in a weak, desperate, and devastating situation, as me. Female patients that fit right into his calculating play and gets captured into his maze.

As I read about his desirable future business, I question, 'Is it the country or the person who has failed the project?' Perhaps we will find the answer further down.

> Many times, Asia had invited me to hold seminars, and it led to a partnership in Asia. It gave me the opportunity to further develop special treatments at hospitals and universities within teaching, research, and controlled clinical studies. I could not say no to that. So, I'll concentrate my work on this fresh and exciting continent for me. I thank my many friends here.
>
> I'm about to create my new website and blog. Please keep up with my work in the new-fangled world. The best greetings to everyone.
>
> Doctor Drake, Lucifer Bates.

For that, I'll return when 'Travels around the World' begins. Reading the word *friends*, I thought that was strange, since he told me they were only Kate's friends. The *mountain goats* from the lousy local bars. Oh yes, not to forget; 'All of them thought only about themselves.' Is this two-faced? Then the las comment!

Wow... I'm impressed and thrilled on his behalf. I wish him all the best with grand success. So, I'm looking forward to following his website and his blog, and as I did, you might think, 'This man is brilliant and an adventurous entrepreneur. Dazzling and creative in his mindset.' Yes, he is! For that, I will get back when he begins his many plans for me. Then you will figure out that everything it's not entirely related to *The Red Thread* as described by him. I deliberate, where do I go wrong?

As a tropical storm, Drake diligently continues his tricky flirting plan with me, and courts me with oceans and twisters of love, by bombarding my fragile personality. His performance is changing, while he's more than charming and gorgeous towards me, when he's helping me with everything, goes grocery shopping, invites me for romantic dinners and does many other mesmerising things for me. It's as if something is happening all the time for him, and his charisma becomes even more seductive than before. We meet daily and go to restaurants, eat tapas at lunch, or steaks for dinner, or go to cafés and drink coffee or go to bars to get wine or beers. Then we dance salsa on the and sometimes he stays with me overnight, then have breakfast together, and fast he even gets the spare key to my flat. We laugh as lunatics, because he's hilarious and loving and joke about how he has smashed two flies at one time, by getting the heavy burden of Kate off his shoulders and catching me in his mesh. It becomes an unconditional, wonderful friendship between him and me, and my perception of him changes when he turns 180 degrees to the better. He speaks about his plans in Asia, he has prepared to the utmost detail, and proudly shows me his many PowerPoint for future seminars, about lectures and teachings. Interesting and creative, and as a storm-tossed clown I get fascinated when I see his grandiose business plans with his new-fangled partners. His forthcoming looks fruitful. His stormy, wild, charming approach knocks me out, and I feel more for him. Yeah, I fall in love with him! Gently and steadily, he drags me into his shadowy hanging spider web and places me exactly where he wants me to hang in his corner. I become the boiling frog put in tepid water, then brought to boil slowly, where I will not perceive the danger before he will cook me to death. With these love declarations, the little mouse gets trapped in the sly maze, because of my refusal to be aware or to react of this ominous threat that arises gradually on my way to the slippery slope. However, I still haven't gleaned the sinister intent behind his plan.

'Can't you see how great my plan is? I will earn millions of dollars. Oh, darling girl, you must come with me. Be a part of it.'

'No, I'm not going to Asia. I understand not such things,' I stare shocked at him.

'Of course, you have. You are a super smart woman. You have street smarts. I'll teach you the treatment protocol. You have an amazing talent.' He acts as if he has taken ecstasy or cocaine. 'A great financial background. Invest in this project. Cash is king! You have cash. I'm the king with knowledge.' He laughs and is going on as a runaway train. 'I can see how interested you are!' The fast-running jerk smirks so I can't keep up with him.

'When I'm ready in Macau, you must come. Visit me. See how it goes. It will thrill me for your visit. I will love it!' And Bambi's glint does all to convince me to invest.

'Sounds as a marvellous idea. I've never been to Asia before.' I'm about to swallow the complete concept, when he carefully sows seeds of doubt in me, by making me question my perception, whether it's okay I travel to Asia with him. Next, we go through all his boxes, and there he finds a phone.

'We can use this phone when I've left. You can call me without Paul knowing. Never use your own phone!' He hands it over to me.

'Clever guy! Ha-ha, a secret between us.'

'Mary, get rid of Paul. Do the divorce. He doesn't care about you. Paul cheats on you in such an unworthy way. He is a lying and cheating bastard.'

'I know!' I hardly comment on any of his jabbering.

'You are too lovely. I'm crazy about you. I'll help with the divorce plan.'

'I'm scared.' Then I stare dazed at him as he continues blabbering.

'Forget his existence. We will get it so great together. I'll take care of you.'

'I don't know. I must be completely out of my sense of normality.'

'I'll be there for you. All the time. I promise! You can *trust me*. I've never deceived or lied to anyone before. Not as Paul does.' So, once again, I swallow the wonderful, sugary promises of his gaslighting and don't consider the red flags: 'Trust me' or 'I don't lie'. Can I trust him? Or do his lies run faster than a racehorse can run?

Why do I forgive him then help him and allow him into my life? Is that perhaps also your impression? Am I right? Perhaps I don't see what he is doing. But! But! But! Have you ever been in the claws of a charming manipulator? Maybe not, but some of you have, I'm certain of it. I'm not the only one who gets trapped in such a snare, and remember, never underestimate people as Drake. His high IQ and weight of power over me dazzles me and makes me deaf and blind. I *don't* use my common sense and fall in love with him, and within a short time, he raises above the stage of Paul. Drake knows I'm weak, and he knows which buttons he shall push in his psychological game of manipulation. To be honest with you, I'm not trying to run from the responsibility of my own deceptive actions. As they say, it takes two to tango. My upbringing has never taught me to take care of manipulative people, because I have only learned to do what people told me to do. Strict obedience!

We keep the plans in secret. Family or friends knows nothing, except from Lacy who knows a little about it, but I don't listen to her advice. Insane and heedless of me, so I have nowhere to go to get proper advice, but it's always easiest to be wise after the event.

By not being wise, it gets much better—or rather, more appalling. Ha, ha, ha, I must laugh at my foolishness, when his famous plan gets solidly printed in my head. Drake is a romantic getaway from my marriage, and with him in my backhand, I find the perfect opportunity to escape. I'm hooked, and everything goes fast between us. I overrule all the warning signs, and walk blindfolded, and in confidence into his plans for us. Oh my gosh, I wish so much for a stronger and better love life. Drake has his previous faults, so do I, but it's all forgotten, while he shoots straight to my overheated, boiling heart. As the boiling frog, I'm subconsciously waiting for him to cook me, while he gives me love and caring in massive amounts, which I don't get at home. He creates understanding, trust, and closeness, and gives me the entire package of love, served on a grand gold platter. What more can I dream of; the guy is every women's dream? It's amazing how love blinds you! We go through my entire finances I have with Paul to see what I can get out of it with a divorce. A great settlement—the pension fund and a sizeable amount up front.

'I don't think it's possible. I need a talented lawyer.' I peep in despair.

'That's why I must help you, sweet little girl.'

'A lawyer is expensive. But I have saved thirty thousand dollars in cash. Paul doesn't know about it.' I tell him, and his eyes go as big as teacups.

'Oh boy, where do you have the money? You can't have such a large amount sitting around in cash. What if he finds it? He will take it away from you.' He grins.

'No, no, he will not. It's hidden away. No, he won't find them.' I scowl strangely and questioningly at him.

'You must deposit it in the bank. In your account, where Paul has no access,' he quickly responds.

'But that's impossible. We have a shared account.' I get nervous at this point.

'*Trust me*. It's bad if he finds the dough. Bloody hell! He will demand at least half of it. I can help you.' I scowl curiously at him.

'How? What do you have in mind?' I'm speculating what his next idea is.

'Listen! It's easy. I have a non-disclosed account. Tax authorities can't get insight on it. Put the money in there until you need it. I never use it. It will only be your money in there. A piece of cake!' He glances at me with a slick smile.

'Fine, I'll think about it. I get back to you. When I'm back from Israel,' Naïve as I am, I believe he speaks the truth, so I take the bait on his great idea and think, *Brilliant!* But perhaps it's not! Have I become a heedless, dumb fool?

Don't Laugh!

Though, I wish I could hear the many readers screaming at me now, 'Stop! You didn't?' Why not? I trust him. He promises me I will get it back. Will I do it? Wow! He even gives me all the bank information before he travels to Asia.

Ladies and gentlemen, please hold a firm grip to the belts and bridles. Buckle up, because I assure you will burst out loud in a choir. Honest! Yes, it sounds as the worst and oldest Nigeria scam. You are entirely right. The only thing is I have never heard about such scams before, nor email scams or others of such a kind. I'm a loving and trusting housewife, taking care of my family, and have not learned about scamming people. I go to school for adults in my spare time, so I use my computer only for school assignments. I'm not a big consumer of emails or Facebook, and that year of 2010 Instagram got launched. I don't know of Twitter, and I don't read online news or warnings about scammers. (Today I'm totally up to date with these many warnings about fraud). I mostly used my phone; therefore, knowledge of scammers was an unknown factor to me. So, what does the trusting housewife do? No offences to housewives—it's a hard job.

You will probably think, 'No! Impossible! There can't be any more. Does she never stop?' Oh no! I haven't started yet, because from now on, all the exciting things begin, when I get snatched into the spider's web, while I'm in my romantic corner. If you want to join me on a trip around the world, then you will find out much more about the affection I have for Doctor Drake Lucifer Bates.

CHAPTER 23

THE KING OF ISRAEL—
THE CHOSEN ONE

> You must remember that no one lives a life free from pain and suffering.
>
> —Sophocles

Drake has moved to Asia by now, and I'm waiting at the airport in Copenhagen for my unique journey to Israel. In good faith and hope, I wish I can find my inner spirit there and answers to my chaotic life, musing deeply about Drake and hurry to write a letter to him, because I miss him massively.

Darling Drake my Angel Lucifer,

I'm listening to some casual music and can't help having you rushing around in my mind. I hope you had a pleasant flight, though you are still in the air on your way to China. Your departure was the worst of it all; my tears came easily, and I couldn't get enough of you before you turned your back on me as you walked through the security area to catch your plane. I felt the urge to write to you when I found your T-shirt before my journey. I hug it and kiss your picture standing on my table, then glance at your amazing sparkling smiling eyes and cry, because you make me cry.

Why? I have never done so before. Think about that next time you touch some water, because it's all the thousands of tears I'm crying since I miss you so much. I've sent them through the universe of life as tiny glittering crystallised particles, becoming to stars, so I'm wishing you will never forget me. The time with you in Spain was breath-taking, despite the heated situations that ravaged you violently when I saw you again in the evening. But still we spent some magnificent quality time together when we were finally alone, even though you got fatigued by the day's work. I enjoy glancing at our pictures and think about the gorgeous moments we had together. You go so fully under my skin that I forget about the universe. I have eyes only for you and the love you fill me with, something I never imagined I would ever experience. The next day will be super difficult to get through before I'll travel on my unique journey to Israel. What do you do to me? My mind is running confused in my head, and the emptiness is indescribable, so I can't understand it. One moment, you are so close to me, and the next moment, you are on the other side of the world. Philosophising about that makes me sad because you are not here to comfort me, which makes life difficult to live. It takes only a short time before I get hit so hard in my soul that it feels as I'm being consumed, and everything feels as inscrutable chaos. It subjects a terror to both of us and a pressure that hangs over our shoulders. But I know I've to be strong, because I so much believe I deserve the happiness both of us are dreaming about. I'll kiss my Madonna, who will pass the kisses on to you, and I'll send glittering stars through the universe to you. I'll think of the day when both of us can walk the Milky Way, which is the bond between us, in the light of the amazing cosmos. I'll create a symbol of stars around the Sun, which will be my soul, and surround all the love I have for you. I'll wait until the day when I can sit on the edge of the glowing Moon with you. When we finally sit on the Moon ablaze, we can look at the happiness we have achieved in our life. With all these symbols, you know that my divine spirit will always be there for you. As a hurricane, you have taken my love to you, and I have never felt such a blistering storm in my heart before. Darling, keep in mind, the next cheek your lips touch, pretend they are my lips, and then send the kisses back to me with all your love. Keep in mind next time you hold somebody's hand, consider it as if it's my hand you are holding. When you have all that deep in your awareness, you will then know what to do. Send all those blissful kisses, tears, and touches back to me in the same condition as I've sent the happiness to you. My soul is now your soul, and it creates trust and consciousness, which makes lovers one united part.

Love you forever,

Mary Liz

Shortly before I board the flight, he calls me via Skype.

'My sweet, precious darling. This is the most touching and loving letter I have ever received. How can I not do other than to love you so much?'

'We have only a short time to talk. We will board soon.'

'Baby, it's so lovely to hear your voice. I'll go to sleep and think of you and Minnie.'

'Ha-ha. Yea, it must be late by you now.'

'You will not believe it. There must be something wrong with me. When I read your mail, I went afterwards out to pee. Oh, boy! Willy is totally wet with tears.'

'What? Did you get horny?'

'There must be something wrong with me when he cries thinking of you.'

'I must go now. Bye. Love you.'

'Bye, I love you too.'

Yuck, I ponder, and, yes, something is wrong. What's happening to him and his Willy? His heat-seeking-moisture missile is always in tears! Why is he so fixated on this all the time? So, I shut down the phone by putting it on airplane mode. A long time ago, I took part in this long-desired pilgrimage, with a group from the Catholic church, and now I'm on my way to the Holy Land. It's great to see all the other pilgrims and the priest Jonas when we meet at the airport. In the late evening hours, we land in Jerusalem, the capital of Israel. It's magic; the luminous full Moon casts a bright and clear light over the city, while Venus and the stars glow as the clearest and most beautiful polished diamonds. That specific year in late September is special, while Venus stands at its peak and shines powerfully over the clear sky of Jerusalem's night. It all begins here, and it also ends here with Jesus, and in the same way, I sense it with Drake and me. He's the Chosen One, and here it all begins for us, but it also ends for Paul and me. Drake comes into my life as the enlightened cloudless morning and evening star and promises to polish the rough, gloomy diamond, though my senses tell me it's not right what I'm doing to Paul. Confusingly, my heart tells me I must let Drake into my life and love him instead of Paul. Drake promises me a painless and worthy life and has enchanted me greatly before he left for Macau and me to Israel. I can't discern the difference between right and wrong. Thus, I need this pilgrimage to find forgiveness for my sins and get control of my inner chaos, with the blessing from my priest, Jonas.

In 2009 I achieved a renewed confirmation of my faith, and I took part in a retreat weekend in Our Lady's Monastery of the Benedictine Nuns. It took place in incredible silence, which is a must for us to achieve a spiritual structure, so for us to get admitted to the church, we all did our preparation for baptism and confirmation. Ass teenager, during my time at the orphanage, they denied me the completion of this holy ritual. I've been therefore only a half-Christian all these years, so time is now for me to fulfil the last part. It's important for me to get a closed circle about my religious life so I can be a whole person again. The time finishes the last part of it, for me to be all-embracing, as all of us wish to get the blessing of forgiveness for our sins.

I'm captivated by the Benedictine Sisters Monastery and the surroundings, so in the misty early morning hours, I walk to their graveyards. The mist and the blue light make it picturesque, as a spellbinding Claude Monet painting, in the natural surroundings. Beautifully is the garden, fields, and forest covered with new-fallen sparkling snow. While walking, I perceive the sound of lovely birdsongs from many species, and the twittering from the blackbirds makes me feel calm and enchanted. The mist disappears, and I sense how the weather becomes colder and brighter, after the Sun has risen with a clear light on this amazing Saturday morning when I reach all the impressive graves. In a good way, it has with passion pleased my soul as the angels strike their tender wings over my hair and a nice chill runs through my body. Watching at the many stunning tombstones and the various names, my heart craves for red roses, while it paces with faster rhythms as I want to put a deep red rose on each of the graves. It's as I have known all the nuns from a previous lifetime, so is this my déjà vu? I want to run to the city and buy as many flowers as possible and lay them in honour and respect for each of the nuns resting peacefully on this amazing spot.

The Sun shines on the snow that lies on the stones and glitters as millions of diamonds, and the fresh garden air reaches my nostrils as a fresh flowering mix of citrus and lavender perfume. But there is neither time nor opportunity to reach my goal for the roses, so I turn around and see that my footsteps have ruined the dazzling snow. I carefully stroll back in my previous footprints, so I do not spoil more of the new-fallen powdery white snow. As I arrive at the monastery, I'm ready to take part in the retreat, and I muse, *one day, I'll come back and show my respect for the nuns, and I will place my deep red roses, which I didn't lay on that snowy bright and magnificent sunny winter morning.*

Thus, I'm born into Catholicism, I still must join these many events. So, I've spent one year to prepare the entire Christian ritual, which was a great eye-opener during my distressing matrimonial time. Some months before we left for Israel, at Eastertime, I fulfil the spectacular holy rituals in the church and become almost complete with my soul. Next, I'm ready for my pilgrimage, but only one thing is missing. Often, I speak with pastor Jonas about my relationship and the enormous questions of life and marriage. Did I ever get the blessing from the Catholic Church or not? That's the million-dollar question for me, and in his opinion, I have not fulfilled it in the eyes of God, the Son, and the Holy Spirit.

'The Catholic Church has never blessed it,' Jonas say.

'Why?' I ask.

'Because you married in the Protestant Church.' With this knowledge, Jonas releases me from the Holy promise so I can continue my life as an unmarried Catholic.

By now I'm on my way to Israel, and with Jonas' words in my mind, it should be a simple task for me. On the contrary! They make it more difficult, while the completion of my marriage all these years never was as I wanted it to be. Therefore, I hope the trip to the Holy Land will give me some decent answers. I'm confused and don't know if I want to leave the married life, because I still love Paul, but I'm also deeply in love with Drake. Did I let Drake come into my life too early? He promises me it will be an amazing, liberating for me to make this holy journey and I will find all my answers to my many questions there. But what does he know about God, Jesus, and the Virgin Mary? He's not even a believer in God! Yet he speaks with two tongues.

'It's a perfect way for both of us to go back. We, and especially you, sweet Mary, will relive the desert hike you have done with your Jesus before. I'm the Chosen One. The king of Israel!' Drake gladly praises himself, observing symbolically at the cross of Jesus when we once visited a Catholic church in Spain. So, what did he mean by that? Before I left for the trip to Israel, we spoke a lot about my religion. He believes he is Eesa (Jesus) and I'm his Mary Magdalene. So, I consider, did he use my faith to get to me? True, he sincerely believes of the marriage of those two persons and they have two kids, meaning his kids he had with another woman are now his and mine.

'Babe, you know Mary and Jesus have a boy and a daughter. We made them out of great divine love to each other,' he praises. Well, now we know that, according to him, but how is that possible? He spent so much time and effort during my time of bewilderment convincing me that this is the truth. But why? *He's a nonbeliever!* What's his game? He loves it when I call him Eesa, after I told him this is another name for Jesus. To be honest though, calling him Jesus is grotesque blasphemy for me. Let's get to the point. Drake believes he's the resurrection of this Holy Icon, and I hardly dare to write this because I feel its sacrilege. Is this a massive red flag I don't see? He has many sweet short names for me, as MM (Mary Magdalene), baby and babe. At Eastertime, I receive a sweet religious e-card greeting from him.

> My darling MM, I wish you the happiest of all Easter, and remember what happened for real with us. You saved a precious life and gave it to the world when he resurrected. Bless you.
>
> Yours forever,
>
> J

Am I that sightless, or can't I read? Well, to be honest, this e-card comes the following Easter, after I have been in Israel. But that makes it even worse, because he believes he walked the old-time desert hike with me and our children. Then, there is the J! Does it stand for Jesus? Or can it be John, Jacob, or Johann? Did I save Jesus from the cross? Was that what he has written? But I swallow it all unsweetened, because he's an expert at getting my faith in him and removing my trust further away from my family and friends. Remember, Jesus and the Virgin Mary are my icons and Drake is my new enlightened star and Angel. Sounds crazy? Indeed! Where do I go wrong? Humans become crazy when they are madly in love, blindfolded and trusting the other person. The worst thing happens for me, as I become more irrational in my perplexed mind, and end up in his massive power of affection, that he convinces me to change my name and passport after I came back from Israel. That's gigantic power he has over me. I don't even dare to write the name here. But I'm sure you can guess it, but it's the worst sacrilege I ever have done. Don't worry. It's all changed back again to my actual name, but it took a long time to get it changed, while Denmark can't change it, because I was not living there. How ridiculous can a person in love be? I'm ashamed, so I hope you will forgive me for my gigantic mistakes. I still believe it's important to tell how my foolishness allows him to screw me around in his sick, perverted game.

Jerusalem is a noisy, compact, populated district with a long history of many sacred houses, while the group walks the cobblestoned zigzagging narrow streets among so many other believers through the streets of Via Dolorosa. That's the Path of Pain, where the bleeding and bruised Jesus Christ walked with his burden of the big heavy cross. When he reached the top of Golgotha, he received his divine destiny. Our group takes the same hike together with Jonas and our guide Ellen, and its magic, as being sent back in time. Daily, I speak with Drake over Skype and tell him about our trip and when we will do it. I also write prayers in emails or messages to him every day, so he knows all the tours and every holy step I take in this amazing paradise. Today, I've been terribly distressed and need his understanding and support.

> Darling Drake, my loving Angel,
>
> I wish to return in the stage I had with you in the past, present, and in the future I will have with you. You need to polish the diamond and care for it so it will shine on your path. In its glory, you and Venus have decided it's the diamond in the Holy Land. Once we have stored the fruit of our love here, under my unreasonable past, it's supposed to return and be cared for. Then we can once again feel our love and tenderness for the rest of our lives. Venus got her name after the Greek-Roman love goddess, and I believe that she is on our way for us to succeed, as she has spent a long time circling our past lives and helps us once again to reunite as you have told me we will. For a fact, I know that since a long time ago, Venus has been very close to earth, and that's why you can see her so clear and bright in the night sky. Her journey has taken 225 days as the Sun circles the earth. We have known Venus as one of the five classic planets since ancient times, and she has played a role several times in the history of science. The first time was in antiquity, when they named her as the "morning star" and the "evening star". So, your name should have been "Lucifer Morningstar" (the Light-bringer) and not "Bates". Later, they discovered that it's the same planet, just as, to me, you are my morning and evening star, and you are my solid planet.

Sadly, they associated Lucifer to stories of a fall from heaven to end up as Satan.

But, my darling love, I don't care on this breath-taking night, while I glance intently at the clear atmospheres of the night and at Venus, the divine Moon and the sparkling Stars. You are my special Angel, and I have deep thoughts of you, so I finally have sent the letter to the lawyer. Thanks for your amazing help with it. The request for separation and divorce is a fact. The priest Jonas has released me from the bond of marriage and confirmed that I have not yet accepted my yes to Paul in front of God. So, the marriage is not valid for me as a Catholic. I hope you someday will gaze deep at Venus, the distant Moon and the glistening Stars, with me and then tell me you also love me forever. I love you forever, with no strings through the entire universe, while thinking of you on this bright night. I only need to finish by saying, Amen!

I attach the last document to the lawyer. Look at it and give me your last comments. I have made the final decision.

Yours forever,

Mary Liz

I'm vastly fixated with the glorious Moon, the Stars, Venus and Drake, so at the same time I push send, I get scared and relieved at the same time. Have I made the right decision for my life? I was not sure whether my experience in Israel would be the answer to my previous déjà vu, so I must find out. None of us have so far figured out the mystery of where in the past we know each other—or is my déjà vu from the nun's graveyard? Drake's empathetic and magical behaviour works on me, so I assure myself I will find the answers of "the reunion" he has promised me, and it will be in magical Israel.

I wonder if this is terrible religious blasphemy and superstitious nonsense. Today, I will answer *yes*! But back then it was a *no*, in this important phase of my perplexed religious life, as I have no sensation of upside-down. The depression has taken hold of me, and I only sought spiritual guidance, and not least in my infatuation with Drake, who is by my side all the time. He's *so* noble at helping and being persuasive. Countless times, he tells me how important this pilgrimage is for *our future*. He often tells me his patients see him as the "resurrected Jesus" and that is why he heals so many suffering people. Yet he's still a nonbeliever!

'Mary, you will relive our common walk with our two children,' he tells me. Wow! What a whopping surprise to me, that he believes in it, that he's the only Christ. I suppose we all know that Jesus was not Christian but born as a Jew, meaning Christianity comes in the footsteps after the Jews. Walking the desert hike with his children is a little beyond my ability.

'Darling, I don't even know of the marriage between Jesus and Mary Magdalene. Nor if they had children.'

Drake suddenly reads books about my Holy Icon, Mary Magdalene.

'Do you get all your inspiration from there?' I ask when I notice him reading the book by Kathleen McGowan, The book of Love and The Expected One, among other ones.

Gullible as I am, I involve myself in his grandiose stories, although it's difficult! Most of the time, I try to talk about something else when he brings the subject to the surface. I must ask my pastor about it, but I never dare to do it, so should I believe in Drake's crap. It never comes to the surface that *my* four children are a part of the total adventure, because he hates them, so he isolates me more and more from them.

'Baby, your kids have no interest in you. You might as well forget about them.' Stubborn as he is, he claims. Let's continue where I'm walking on the important adventure to find His Holiness.

'When you find him, you have found the answer of your déjà vu,' Drake claims. So why not trust him? So many other fools believe in his words and the powers of his magic healing! Okay, I'm not the last idiot in the world, believing in his profanity. Though I must be a complete cheering halfwit to believe in everything he puts in my head. Had I told it to Jonas during our Israel adventure, I am certain he would have thrown me out of the church for sacrilege. Perhaps he would have hospitalised me at the nearest mental hospital. In my overheated passion for Drake, I continue my new-fangled beliefs.

Oh, my goodness! Everyone must believe I'm stubborn and blind, that I can't see the woods for the trees or the water in the oceans are factual. In my not so clever light of knowledge, I realise I'm only surrounded by Drake, Via Dolorosa, and the famed desert hike. All that he tells me is the truth, right? My insane imagination of this fantasy of a magical life-walk must be right! I feel as high as a junkie who takes her latest fix, thinking about the Venus event of the night and the affection of love. It's painted in my foggy brain as a floating, colourful, spinning LSD trip, and Drake fills me completely with joy. When I read his many devoted letters, or when I talk to him, I'm conquered in my thoughts by a sweltering love-fire of blazing desire. It has more control over me than my common sense, that I'm so addicted to those many fire-spitting dragon fixes, and my body is a burning desire for him. I become a mentally cracked junkie to the immense charm and amour he radiates over me when he fills me with everything I want to hear and feel. Soft down and tender angel feathers strike my body, and the intoxication from his magical poison mesmerises me, making me see bright flickering images, as you see in a kaleidoscope. With all the other warning signs blinking as crazy firecrackers, I overlook everything, when he bombards me with a veritable storm of compliments and tender affection. So, I need the daily adrenaline shots when I open my computer to see what he writes every day or wait for his call over Skype. There are so many letters, geez, I can write ten books. Oh my, I'm blind and deaf to the outside world and *can't* resist his temptation at all. However, I also regret taking this forbidden and dangerous drug.

As Adam and Eve in the garden of paradise, I eat of the prohibited fruit the devious snake brings to me, and in my intoxication, I feel Drake walks by my side everywhere I step in Israel. As the snake, Drake follows me from tree to tree and provides me with a new poisoned apple every day. Yee-haw ... I'm in the seventh heaven with the illuminated Moon and the shiny Stars, with Drake rocking the deadly cradle.

After a long day of excursions, we have time for ourselves, so I open my computer and shortly after he calls me.

'My baby love, have you seen the picture of me? You might like it.'

'No, I have not read my mails.'

'All I can say is "you surely said it all" in your letter. It makes me feel as the luckiest man, in the universe to say you are *my baby.*'

'Ha-ha, yea, we are as two newly unreachable teens in love.'

'Never have I felt such love before. And affection. Being so heartfelt. It's so blunt, and so beautifully expressed. You have an amazing gift of expressing yourself—in such perfect terms. With such grace. With beauty. It makes me tear up.' He is so ecstatic that I can taste the cocaine lying on his table.

'I'm glad you liked it.' And I'm eager to get my next fix.

'Baby, we will prevail together. We are so meant to be together. We are made for each other. Never forget. I will be by your side always.' As his cocaine trip continues.

'I must leave now. Talk to you later. Love you so much.'

'I've prepared a letter for you. Read it later. Bye, my everlasting love.'

After our draining excursion, I get back to my room and take the time to read his letter. All the tension in my body has relaxed while I sit on the chair, ready to read it. It's long, so I grab a pillow to support my body and lean comfortably back into the chair, because the mail requires my full attention. I can hear some cracking or shooting noises from the street which scares me and makes my eyes open wide even though they can almost no longer stay open. I wonder if there is a minor war going on, so I go to the window to see what is happening, but I can't see anything going on, so I return to my letter and begin to read in part:

Dear Babe,

My corrections are a guideline that you, of course, must edit. Keep in mind what the purpose of the trip is, which you have told Paul, that you "seek the peace of mind and forgiveness to move forward" since he has abused you and you "don't want him to expose you again". So that's why you want to divorce, which is the only way forward for you. We

> also discussed you want to write a book about the torture he put you through. I'm sure it will be a bestseller. You can consider giving me all the rights so I can help you get it released and filmed. Paul does not want it to happen, so he will have to buy your silence. For that, you must at least have two to three million dollars from him. The amount you need must be what you can profit from publishing a bestselling book on the subject. Since you must keep up with his sexual escapades and his sick behaviour, he must pay. It can easily be a further two or three million dollars or more. We will talk about it and get your lawyer to talk to a publisher about it. Besides, you can sell the story to the daily and weekly magazines for a generous amount. It's hot for a well-known person as him. He may avoid this by paying to ensure it does not happen …

What! I nearly tumble off the chair, and my eyes become wide open with distress. *Abuse* and *torture?* Next, I don't understand why it's so important to get the rights to my book. Is it that important to him? Although, because of my confidence in him, I don't question it, and besides, I've not decided yet if I want to finish the book. It scares me he's writing so much about wealth, of how much I can get and what he will earn on me. Then there are the rights to the book. How should I handle this process? His offer of copyrights seems to come too quick, and I feel there's a strange fixation on capital in his behaviour.

Outside, the noise grows louder, until I feel I must get up from the chair and see what is happening. I can't see anything, so I let go of my worries and continue (in part) to read:

> So, besides sharing in the value, you can get it in cash. Paul can keep the one apartment in Spain and sell the other one. The value of your current apartment is the same as when you bought it when it comes to the math of the split. He does not get credit for the purchase value, and you don't take over the debt in it but must have it free, without debt. Otherwise, he can keep it, and you must then have the value in cash. This is half the investment that you made,

and you don't take the loss on it. Such is legal justice when negotiating. To the lawyer, you write that you should have refused to agree to what he arranged only to please himself. Otherwise, he will beat you or subject you to mental torture …

Eh? Huh? What? Mental torture? An icy shiver shot through my spine. What the hell? Does he believe Paul abuses, beats, and tortures me? Drake must confuse me with this other abused woman which he once lived together with. But that's a different story, so I can't understand why he writes such nonsense. He lost me there. I'm totally frustrated and have a massive question mark standing in front of me. I don't understand shit of what he is writing. Drake knows Paul and I have made no decision to buy the apartment next door. There is no meaning in a purchase if I divorce Paul, so how do I relate to that in writing? Next, my husband is famous? Hogwash! He's not! But a successful businessman! Upset, I continue reading, although I want to show my half-sleeping roommate Susan what's in it. She has several times warned me against him and asked many times, 'Are you sure what you are doing with him?' because she has discovered what his game is about.

'He gives me a peaceful feeling in my soul. Nothing can hurt me. He's there for me as my enlightened angel and shining Star,' I tell Susan, and she shakes her head at my ignorance because I don't listen to her advice. Damn! Should I have paid attention to her?

I continue (in part) reading:

> But as a people pleaser, you close your eyes and ears, and your feelings, just to get through with life. In fact, you have satisfied the person you love and will not divorce. Remember, I told you Paul might call you a prostitute to win the round. Also, that he sells you and earns money on you. He's a *pimp*! You lost confidence in him little by little, which enters full bloom as he also is unfaithful to you …

Correct, I have lost confidence, but being a prostitute and Paul a *pimp*? That's a horrifying accusation and is not a fact. Being a people pleaser, I can recognise, because I'm the most helpful person who can't say *no* to anyone, and they can always count on me. I always do my job and even help others with their work. Then I do all the planning, and I am always there for family and friends. Well, it sounds so good, but it can unfortunately also be a harmful pattern of behaviour, as I act around people the way they want me to. That's exactly what I do with Drake. Normal people bring other sides of their personality into their lives, but a *pleaser* often sabotages their own goals. Studies have, in fact, shown that such people engage in self-destructive behaviour if they believe that a pleaser will help others feel more comfortable in each situation. Is that the case for me?

I continue to read (in part) the heavy letter.

> You don't want to see that Paul is with other women and men during the sex assault.
>
> I believe he is gay and enjoys watching men. But you allow it to go beyond your body while he's able to get his orgasm when he gazes at the scenery. I'm sure he even does so when he stares through the keyhole, seeing his dad do the same with "Flopper's" mum...

Gosh Almighty! Horror and more disgust run through my body and make my neck hair rise. Drake renames Paul to "Flopper", (I'll continue to use it for the rest of my telling) a name Drake fancies to use. I must ponder these sentences carefully, so I disconnect the laptop from the wall socket, grab my jacket and my ciggy, and go outside. My body is quivering, so I need the fag to calm me down.

The *keyhole* concept in Drake's scary story makes me wonder what it's about, so I develop a thesis about it, though I'm not sure if it's correctly interpreted.

I consider if Drake, as a child, might have seen his father grab his mother. So now he does the same to his women, because he can't help it. Why does he put everything in the context of my husband? He doesn't know much about our sex life, and the idea that Paul is gay is out of my reach. However, I often speculated whether Drake is gay, because of his quick lack of interest in sex with women. He also loves to imitate gay people, which makes me more certain he's not honest with his own sexuality. He is not out of the closet. I've several homosexual friends and have nothing against them, because there is room for all of us, and I love them very much. But something doesn't add up with Drake's behaviour. Hmmm ... is it him who is gazing through the keyhole? Has he seen what his own father has done to his mother? He might have hated his father for doing so and might not have been able to stop the assault. It might be him who has totally lost confidence in adults and feels abandoned and alone, something he knows so well, but he can't tell others. This might also be a reason a man hates and abuses women in a psychological, tyrannical way, to establish themselves as a macho man. Perhaps they can't help it! Hence why they treat women in the same cruel, ugly, narcissistic way. Has Drake experienced it himself? Being dominated so much by his mother it can be the reason, and perhaps therefore he says, "Oh, Mom" when he gets his liberating bliss in bed? I can be wrong in my thesis! This is only my speculation and not an accusation. Yet it's abnormal to read him accusing Paul of such cruelty. I dig further (in part) into the letter:

> About your savings, don't be afraid to cash in. For the pension savings, it's best that you get at least half paid in cash, and Flopper can keep the rest for himself until he retires. You must have half of what they are worth at retirement age, and he can pay monthly the amount that it will be at that time. Next, you can invest them abroad, where you must have accounts in the country you move to. With the alimony, it must relate to what you have lost by not having union support. That amount he must add to the wage part, which must last for at least ten years. I'm sure you can get more now, since he has destroyed your back because of his unreasonable demands on you. You argue that it's what put your back out, by his use of force. That's why you must have your back operated on. Divorce is a rough business, and there is no need to be nice to him. You must be tough, for that's what he will be, because he will use all the tricks to get

> you down with the neck. You must be at the forefront of the case and in the attack position …

Gasp! Is it now all suddenly a matter of course to him because I've opened for my feelings and decided on a divorce? Next, he expects me to move over to him! I can't comprehend what he has in the melting pot for me, and I'm speechless and don't understand his context. Drake knows about the surgery and my improvement after the rehabilitation, so it's not Paul's fault. The weirdest thing is I've experienced more back pain after Drake's many treatments. So, there's a bit of confusion which of those two guys ruined my back? Mostly, I want to give up the entire divorce project; it all sounds like it will be a tough battle for me. However, I'm glad about the advice he gives me, I'm also utterly bewildered as an unwise woman. Is this good for me? Despite I'm so tired, I keep on (in part) reading the letter:

> I have lived by a principle, a boxer taught me to punch first and hard, and then you can negotiate the further options. When the other is down to counting, then you must knock him one more, as soon as he comes stumbling on his crooked legs! Or will you give him a chance to swing his thin arms a little in the air before bobbing him one more hook or uppercut? Baby don't give a millimetre, because Flopper will take it as weakness and take ten metres away from you. You must be tough because that's all Flopper can relate to. He has always done so, and the weak ones, he is always used to squeeze …

Holy moly! I laugh so much that I almost can't stop. Yes, Paul has crooked Charlie Chaplin legs and thin arms, and Drake and I laugh often about it. Hmmm … reading between the lines, it's Drake who wants to "knock" Paul with an uppercut. Yeah, and best when Drake gives Paul a chance to swing his thin arms in the air, then he "bobs him an uppercut or hook more". Whether I find it funny or scary, I can't agree with myself, so I exhale, sink the lump in my throat, and snatch another cigarette. I know Paul is a tough businessman, but I can't relate to the idea that he will squeeze me. Maybe Drake is right in his opinions, but I muse, is it Drake who gets the millimetre and then takes ten metres from me. Is he the one who squeezes me? Perhaps the entire description fits Drake perfectly, because I have noticed he is tough. I'm sure he can squeeze the weak person while he has massive weight and the vast power over others. So, perhaps he has transferred all his theories to my husband and not to himself! I finish the last part of the heavy letter:

> Baby, my precious MM. This is what you are up against and what you need to do to survive this. Are you ready for it? Trust me, we will see each other soon, one of these days, but you will not know it when I'm walking beside you on your desert hike. Neither will you know the day I walk besides you on our important hike on Via Dolorosa, on my devastating way through Jerusalem's old town, before I'm brutally crucified.
>
> Your very best friend,
>
> Eesa

I tremble into spasm and understand nothing except that the entire concept seems dreadfully dramatic. It's chilly outside, so I close the laptop and go back to my room, and on my way back, I'm pondering about the mafia methods Drake comes up with. Oh, and now he's only my *very best friend*? That disappoints me, but as a pleaser, I take the guidance and declare war between Paul and me. I'm certain I can handle it with General Drake beside me, with him planning all the strategies, as I am fighting the last battle between good and evil on the Armageddon. Practically I flee as Bonnie with my Clyde still wearing my wedding ring, while Clyde is robbing everything from Paul!

CHAPTER 24

IT'S SHEER MAGIC IN ISRAEL

> I have always been delighted at the prospect of a new day, a fresh try, one more start, with perhaps a bit of magic waiting somewhere behind the morning.
>
> —J. B. Priestley

It's late at night, and my brain is snapping with wild ions, so I can't fall asleep. It's boiling in the room, with no air conditioning or fan, so I'm sweating like hell, even the window is open. Susan snores as a wacko gismo, and I toss restlessly around in my awful hard bed, kicking off the blanket several times, then drag it over my body again. The pillow is as hard as stone, so I can't form it as I want to get good comfort for my head. I give up sleeping and get up again, sneak out the door, and go up on the rooftop to puff a cigarette. It's a beautiful night, with millions of Stars and a bright Moon. The cool breeze ripples through my loose bright hair and strikes my skin softly, cooling me down. To let go of my worries and psychical tension, I allow myself a slow, transient inhale to exhale ten times. I imagine that I sense my body sinking into the deep golden sand from the Spanish beach with Drake, then I feel calm in the memories. I sit for almost one hour, philosophising, before I go back to my room again. Quietly I open the door, so I don't wake Susan, who sleeps as a baby and is no longer snoring. My bottle of water stands on my night table, so I slurp some of it and lay myself down on the bed again and grab the picture of Drake standing on the table and glare at it while the streetlights and the bright Moon shine through the window. I can only see his lovely face slightly, then I miss him desperately and ponder of the many heavenly hours we have had so far. Finally, my eyes get so tired that I fall asleep with the picture in my hands.

In the morning, the sunlight is catching my eyes after a peaceful night's rest. I sit up in my bed and glance at Susan sitting in the corner, slurping from her mug.

'Good morning, Mary. I'll make you a coffee, and we can have a smoke.' She smiles, and I go first to the bathroom and brush my teeth, then grab the mug standing on the table and snatch my fags, and we go outside.

'I'm a little worried. Hmm, but also pleased with Drake's eagerness to help. He wrote a massive letter to me, so I don't know what to do.' I light my cigarette and puff out the light grey smoke in the air. 'With joy, I do everything to immerse myself. Jeez, I'm trying to get into his existing life. Hoping we can create a fresh life together.' Glaring at her while I inhale the smoke.

'Watch out with him. He has too much power over you.' She sighs.

'Thinking of him gives me good chills to my bones,' I blabber, and we discuss the rest of the letter. 'I have no opinion of my own. I don't go against him. I trust that what he believes is the right thing to do. In time, when he tells something I do is wrong, I apologise. No matter what is in my mind-set.' I slurp my coffee and stare sadly at Susan.

'There is nothing wrong with an apology. But why do it for what's in your mind?' she questions while sweeping her hair away from her face.

'He's irresistible. I don't want to hurt his opinions. It makes me feel worse if I don't follow his advice.'

'What does he say to your decision? Isn't he happy?' Susan glares at me and lights another cigarette.

'He's delighted at the news. Shining as a superstar. As he is enlightening the entire universe. I bet his triumphing flirtatious battle to get me makes him glad. Now he has me completely.' While I puff the smoke out into the air, I gaze worriedly at her. 'I do everything the way he wants. Geez, even avoiding questions and conflicts with what he writes.' My low self-esteem allows Drake to make such bombastic and dramatic descriptions of my life with Paul.

'Let's talk more about it later. We have to go now.' She puts out her ciggy and walks away.

'Is it stupid of me I take all Drake's sweet angels' music into my mind? I feel somewhat bad about it.' I blabber while I'm running behind her on our way to our gathering with the others. She is so sweet in supporting me.

The morning is amazing, and it's already hot while the Sun shines from a clear blue sky. Today our visit goes to the River of Jordan, where John the Baptist baptised Jesus. It is therefore a central site for many Christians. I'm enjoying this amazing green spot with the river running as far as the eye can reach, and I dip my feet in the brown river, as the water is washing over my feet and dragging muddy sand over them while the water cools my feet. The Jordan River cuts down through the Middle Eastern landscape, dividing the land between Israel, Jordan, and Palestine. The peace between Jordan and Israel has lasted over three decades, so it's easy to travel between these two countries, and while we are passing the Green Line, we drive into the West Bank, where Ellen tells us of the region. It's an unforgettable experience, thinking how Jesus crossed the river here.

Similarly, the river stretches through the history of religion and sets the stage for several important events in Judaism, Christianity, and Islam. It's also the site where the Jews of their time crossed over to reach the Promised Land. Thus, it has the potential to be sacred to more than half of earth's population. This conflict-filled area that the river runs through has degraded over the years and decayed so that today, you can compare the Jordan River to a gutter, because the water is so polluted. What a shame, because a few decades ago, the Jordan River was an enormous rushing river of fresh water. Every year, the site has about half a million visitors, who come to get baptised in their white pilgrim dresses. Jonas performs a delightful ritual, as we get our first baptism in the still brownish river. It's piercing deeply into my heart and soul, while I mentally and spiritually transform myself into a better person. The gentle glow of the Sun hits the brownish river in a sparkling strike, and we leave the locality in peace after the baptising ritual.

As we are walking the amazing long hike in the Judean desert, we meet many other pilgrims from many countries, and pass many natural caves, and ancient monasteries for monks and hermits in this captivating holy landscape. It cleans my soul and is also confusing me with thoughts swirling around in my head. The area around us beautifies itself with beige-coloured stones, sand, and caves, and I can see the mountains in the desert with no signs of trees or greens. It is so breathtaking.

The next day, we take part in the famous walking of Via Dolorosa with its nine out of fourteen crossroads; the remaining five are inside the Church of the Holy Crypts, built on Golgotha, where they crucified Jesus. It's mysterious, and I want to investigate my Christian faith furthermore, and feel the soulful journey with Drake. It is incredible to walkin in the many small cobblestoned narrow streets, full of many stony stairs and lots of tiny shops, with loads of interesting things. It's a vast bazar zone of various narrow streets, where you easily can get lost, so I cling tightly to the group. The countless exotic smells of oils and spices sneak up to my nostrils, and my eyes take all the magic in. It's so captivating with the countless colours and selections of fresh fruits, cheeses, and other foods to buy from these many small exotic stores. Plenty of delicious southern and Asian scents bring my imagination back to the time of Jesus Christ, as everything in this exotic, busy part is so different from the technical and well-developed modern world of the twenty-first century. The delightful scent of the sizzling shawarma gets my stomach to crave for some food. My gaze fixes on the colourful bazaar shops, and I stop at most of them or pass them with an intensely curious stare. The countless striking fresh fruits lies in baskets around the shops, taking me into a different time of age. At every corner, I see the biggest red pomegranates I have ever seen, and some shops offer to press their juice. I buy a refreshing pomegranate juice and enjoy the magnificent taste; the clear deep red colour, which sparkles when the sunbeams hit the plastic glass.

In every corner, I hear men shouting in Arabic or Hebrew, 'Come and buy' or 'I have an excellent offer for you'. Leather, clothes, food, fruit, nuts, yes, whatever the heart desires, is for sale. It's sheer magic, and I wish I can devote myself to the faith of Jesus Christ and hope of the healing power will come over me, to help me in my tough time to think about something else. During my breath-taking week, we live at a local monastery with its own little church, where we have our daily prayers. Every night, when we come back from our trips, I either sent emails or talk to Drake to describe our many amazing tours; as I'm telling him of the fascinating bazar and the desert hike. Most important is to tell him about Via Dolorosa.

'Isn't it great to have a long-distance relationship in the twenty-first century? A gift that's not common to others for generations before the seventies.'

'Oh, my beloved MM. You are the most amazing woman I have ever known. I'm so euphoric you are mine. I knew from the start that you were something very special. You are the only woman in my life.'

'While sitting in the most sacred country, I put my heart and soul in your hands.'

'Baby, the day I ventured to give you the first crusher in the clinic, a fire of dimensions I have not felt before was lit.'

'Oh, so sweet. Give me more of those, darling.'

'Yea! Finally, I had the courage to call you. Remember, I had to see you? Feel your closeness again. There was a magical shiver going through me. The rest is history.'

'Huh? History? I'm hoping we can keep the love we have built in such a short time.'

'Sure! When I gave you the first brief kiss at the beach restaurant, I felt the power of your soft lips. I was totally sold! No turning back. We fused in love. An affection beyond belief.'

'Phew! It's so though with over nine thousand kilometres between us.' I peep.

'My lovely baby. You must not wonder that we are far apart. I'm sure we will be together again. In the present and in the future.'

'Well, let me tell you more about today. We first walked—' he interrupts me.

'Things evolved for us. It seemed as if the world came to a halt. With us at the centre. Nothing or nobody can take it away from us.'

'No, you're right. Well, we first walked to Herod's Gate on the northern wall of the Old City, and—' he interrupts me again.

'How can it be that I have been so lucky to find the best love ever?' He smiles sweetly and I get mesmerised by his glare.

'Both of us have, darling. Mwah! Well, then to the Lion's Gate. This is the beginning of the traditional Christian observance of the last walk of Jesus, going from prison to crucifixion—the Via Dolorosa. Hmmm ... sadly, I didn't see you.'

'Maybe you aren't strong enough in the faith.' He smirks.

'Maybe, because I could not feel you in the desert. You promised me.'

'My sweet, MM. We are still within each other. That makes us feel the love we share—even at this long distance. Mwah! You are magical. We get more and more absorbed in our merging. In total love. In affection. Baby, we fuse together.' He must have taken his daily doses of his LSD fix.

'But ... honestly ... I could not feel you on Via Dolorosa. I'm deeply disappointed.'

'Baby, there is nothing that will, or can, take what we have away from us. No one person. No distance. No circumstance. We are so much meant to be together, always!'

'But you were not there to follow me. I'm distressed about it.' I keep on japing.

'I was part of your desert walk. Also, as you all went along Via Dolorosa. That is the closest I can get to my darling right now. But that will change! Now we must manage our love through the difficulties that lie ahead.'

'Hmm, maybe I will never see you again.'

'Why not? We will grow stronger. With each other. And within each other.'

'Because now that you will live for good in Asia.'

'Baby, we will support each other. Make each day count, as if it's the last one in life. Let us never speak or feel one negative thought about each other.'

'Negative thoughts?'

'Yea, we must be truthful with each other. As we will be true to each other.'

'It warms my heart what you say. But, what's the point of a divorce, if you think I speak negative about you?'

'My precious MM, the love of my life. When two people meet where everything fits as perfectly as it does for us, then we must stick together. We will create total happiness together. And for each other.' The sweet little hummingbird swallows all his sweet nectar.

'Mwah, mwah! Okay, nice, but let me tell you about today, as we were passing the Pool of Bethesda in the Muslim Quarter. It's known from the New Testament story of "healing the paralytic at Bethesda". Found in the gospel of John. People came here to fetch water. Did you know, it healed the first person from sickness whom collected water here? I mean; when the water moved.'

'Wow! My wonderful MM, I love your fantastic, adventurous telling.' He beams.

'We ha one-hour visit at The Order of the White Monks and Nuns. A branch from the Benedictines. A peaceful spiritual rest came over me when I could hear them singing. Jeez, honey, it was so mesmerising as stunning angels sent from heaven. Later we spoke with them of Saint Anne. She who could not have a child. An angel blessed her when it heard her praying and told her that God granted her a baby. She had promised God to bring the baby up to minister to God in holy things for each day of her life. She then gets blessed as Virgin Mary.'

'Wow, it's the most amazing interpretation of the thoughts about us.'

'Eh? What? Hmm, well, after attending church, our ending task was what we have waited for with excitement. Via Dolorosa!'

'It's also about our love for each other. About the fact that we are meant to be.'

'What? Yea, maybe. Well, thousands of Pilgrims walked together with us in a slow pace. All walking from the Stations of the Cross devotions, and fourteen stations along the path of suffering. At each station we sang Adoramus te, Christe, a rendition of Dubois.'

'Oh, beautiful. The day they betrayed Eesa (Jesus), he knew it only because he and MM had such powerful senses of it. The same power as we have. He listened. He had to make a clean table with his disciples. Those who didn't trust him, he knew, will hurt him.'

'Yea, it's gruesome. Imagine the city is teeming with crying, singing and praying pilgrims. Also, many ordinary tourists glaring at the attractions.'

'Baby, it's so sad. They did not accept that one who they thought was one of theirs had special abilities to heal. He had heavenly contact.'

'Yea, he is special.'

'MM didn't let him suffer a grim death on the cross. He had to endure the torture.'

'Yea, so grim, grim and horrible. Today it was rising hot. Geez, and cramped in the many narrow cobblestoned streets—' then he interrupts me.

'Baby, it's of tragic. I got my hands and feet brutally mutilated. Not just being hung on the cross with ropes as they usually did. Grr, the Romans nailed me through my feet. Damn, and my healing hands.' Drake is so obsessed with his own tragic story.

'Yea, I know. Tragic. Anyhow, at each station, Jonas reads from the Bible. We kneel, humbly praying the Lord's Prayer. It's magical. Though a sorrowful experience—' and he interrupts me again.

'Eesa made the less gifted see that they should look to God for salvation—instead of seeing to the Romans for short-term relief. They had nothing else to offer. Only to take people's money and valuables. They have always seen it as destroying people's relationships and good intentions. Many wanted to be worthy.'

'Hmm ...' *How much pot has he smoked?*

'None couldn't find their better self. Or because of mere greed and selfishness. Eesa told them of goodness—a truth the Romans could not tolerate.' I give him the time he needs to tell me about Jesus, something which I didn't know of, so he continues.

'The rulers lost control of their subjects. Never have people realised that they can look beyond this horrible way of behaving.'

'Hmm ... Wow! Really?'

'They always think at their own well-being. And push everyone else aside.'

'Yea, true.'

'Eesa taught them the simplicity of showing consideration. Loving one's neighbour—with an honest, kind heart.'

'Wow! I did not know of it. At noon we had lunch at Muristand square in The Old City. There—' He interrupts me again.

'Jesus had to prove that man couldn't understand. So, he sacrificed himself.'

'Tragic. Hmm ... well, there was a tall beige flowing beautiful fountain. Stunningly surrounded with two square decorated blocks. And two round decorated columns and—' it seems to I'm not allowed to tell my story.

'Jesus wanted to show them that love, and humanity were greater than selfishness. And greed.' As a good Christian and in my actual weak state of my Christianity, I believe in every word Drake preaches.

'Wow, Amazing. How do you know all this if you are an atheist?'

'Ha-ha, because I'm very clever and knew MM had a plan. She performed it perfectly. She couldn't, under any conditions, allow them to sacrifice Jesus. They should allow him to continue delivering his message—*as I do*—to humankind forever.'

'What do you mean?'

'Babe, it was a dangerous plan for us. It could fast have gone wrong. But *you* got *your Eesa* down from the cross.'

'Huh? I didn't take anyone down from a cross.'

'You did. *You* tucked *me* into our cave. Tended for *me*. Nurtured me back to life.'

'Ah, come on. It must come from "The Book of Love" you are reading.'

'No, no. I know this from our past. Only behind the hidden scenes could we now complete our future for humankind. However, they didn't know that the so-called priests possessed an even more significant threat to the truth.' He shuts up, and I ponder, is this my Déjà Vu? Next, I can continue with the rest of my story.

'Wow! Amazing. Anyhow, the afternoon got cloudy and colder with a nice fresh breeze. We continued through the Jewish Quarter. Oh ... my ... It was a mindboggling change. From smutty to a total cleanliness and structure.'

'Oh, I love you with my entire heart, my beloved Mary Magdalene. I'll be yours forever.'

'I'm glad. Nice. Just remember to take me with you if you ever dream of vanishing from the surface. Let's sit on the beach again. Listening to the waves break, in crystallised sways. Smelling the sharp taste of the sea salt. When the mist from the waves ends up on my lips before you kiss them again.' I get poetic when I miss him.

'Oh, yea, baby. We went through our first hot infatuation. We could have found that it was a wonderful experience.'

'Darling, we will sit with our hands clutching in the hot golden sand again. Then glimpsing in each other's eyes with great love.'.

'Hmm. But perhaps everyday life will come, Baby. Maybe the Star will fade. I hope it doesn't happen to us. On the contrary.'

'Without me, your life is meaningless. Without you, my life is empty.'

'Oh ... my baby, sweetheart, our love will grow. Every day we are not together hurts deep inside my soul.'

'Oh, thanks. It hurts me too. Remember, it when we one day elope together. Take me with you to the promised land of love.' I pause for a second. 'While strolling around in the neighbourhood, several of us got abruptly blessed with positive Jewish manners. Ha-ha, not to forget how they begged us for money for the blessings. They gave us a red ribbon on our wrist.' I show it to him. 'Shit, then they trapped us.'

'Trapped you? How? Be careful, my precious MM.'

'Oh, my goodness! Begging for money. In a hurry, we arrived by the Western Wall. I wrote a poem to you. Do you want to hear it?'

'Yes, I must know what you wrote to your Eesa. What was it?' He asks eagerly.

'Hang on. I must find the picture I took,' and search swiftly in my camera.

'Have you found it?'

'Oh, yea, here it is. I will read it for you:'

'Thank you for what makes my life precious. You are my inspiration. You make it enjoyable, with every blink of The Stars, The Moon's light, and for the birds singing in every bush and tree. Together with you, I've much that makes my life rich, bold, but complicated, thus, I chose not to complain of the grief that weighs on me now. I'm glad that I hopefully can trust your faithfulness and your understanding. Together we will help each other and to greet the people we walk among, and live every day, hour, and second with open eyes. I wish you would let me live in the happiness and love I have for you.'

'Oh, my, that reminds me suddenly of the first night we made love.'

'Huh? What do you mean?'

'It was more than special to me. It was sheer magic! The intensity of the moment was so strong that I found it hard to control myself.'

'Oh, good for you, it was "sheer magic". Darling, we were drunk. I disappointed you that night!' I'm astonished and put my hand to my head. Hmmm... which part of the description is then "sheer magic"? But it's genuine love from him today, so I don't want to interpret it as negative. My heart is flaming for him, because I'm so attracted to him, as I've never been to a man. I allow myself to let go of any negative thoughts and treasure the beauty of the present moment of the experience I have with him.

'My eternal love. It is so wonderful written. I hope it will stay there forever. Could you see my tears ran along my cheeks, while you were reading it?' he peeps sorrowful.

'Yea, okay. Anyhow, I reached the highest corner, standing on my toes, and placed it in a slight crack in the wall. Do you like it?' I smile.

'Oh ... my little girl, you are mine forever. It's powerful, what we have together.' Mwah, and he smiles so lovingly that I melt I melt as butter in the heat.

'Darling, there are so many things I'd like to say to you. Most of all, you are all I see. All I can feel in this world. Okay, let me tell you the last part of the trip.'

'Nothing and nobody can take that away from us, little girl. Nor come between us. We are for us. And together from now on.'

'So nice. I hope so, darling. It gives me so much strength to know I can run off with you when I'm back from this trip.'

'Baby, I also have so much more to tell you. I'll take it little by little.'

'While we are in the underground part of the wall, Uganda's prime minister showed up and talked to us. Of the sudden the trip ended at the first gate to Via Dolorosa.'

'But let there be no doubt that I love you with all my heart and soul.'

'I love you too, darling. You're all I want in my life. You are so stuck in my heart and head. I can't resist you. You are my only precious man.'

'I want to be your only one. The one who will be by your side. Protect you, my precious MM.'

'You are. At the monastery and after dinner, Jonas blesses our bought holy things.

We also got our pilgrim certificates. Last, we enjoy beer and wine in the backyard.'

'I'm the one you can always turn to for advice. Help and total unconditional love.'

'I can hardly help it. I'll send you two small video clips. My darling love, sit down and listen to Hurts, Wonderful Life. I'm imagining it can be the two of us who can have such a wonderful life. She has also met the man of her dream, as I have met you. I miss you more and more. Everything is as torture without you by my side. My heart beats only for you. Darlin, I need you so much.'

'Baby, you are so blessed by the experiences you are now going through in Israel. You are cleaning your soul from the wrongs of the past. This is a fresh beginning.'

'I know. There are many blissful things in the air for us. I won't let go of you. I will never give up having the vital blissful dream with you.'

'Whoever believes that life starts at fifty is right.'

'I love you more and more. Above what you can imagine.' I sigh.

'The experiences of our past will strengthen us. We will not carry it with us as a burden. It's gone now, baby. Let our fresh life begin, my sweetheart.'

'Yea, I so much look forward to seeing you again. I'm dreaming about a breathtaking life with you. Now, it's difficult for me to fall asleep without you. I'm constantly thinking of you.'

'It's important you get your beauty sleep. Otherwise you will fade. Get ugly.'

'I love you more today than yesterday and more tomorrow than today. Oh, darling, I have found the solace I needed in Israel. Such peaceful rest lays over my mind.'

'Perfect, baby. Let this be our moment forever. I love you more than life.'

'I will send you a video by Aqua. Ha-ha, I think you need to mark up your shoes a bit in a funny style. Jump around as a Candyman. A little sweet, fast candy power for my Candyman from Bounty Land.'

We say goodbye and end our conversation, and I shut down my computer. As I take a shower and go to bed, I'm pondering of my mysterious conversation with Drake. *Hmm… It's sweet, although Drake is suddenly Jesus, and I am unexpectedly Mary Magdalene in his mind! Interesting!* But to me, it implies; the fake Jesus must have taken one hell of a blasting cocktail of speed or LSD, since he has such a Holy imagination and hallucinations of himself.

LSD or not! I love him so much and feel he's my best love ever and treasure his many sweet words but am also afraid if too much of it is too good to be true. I have never heard such devoted words before from any man. I'm ready to take a bullet for him, only to be with him, now and forever. If he asks me to jump from a bridge, I'll jump. My love for him is total affection, and nothing will ever rip this apart for me. But I'm also confused about the way he talks to me, because he can be as a rollercoaster. One moment, it's all about wealth, and the next, its intense tenderness, so this might also be one of the classic dangerous red flags I'm ignoring. Don't ignore such! Though, I allow myself to continue in this pleasant devoted moment, with the feeling of the power of beauty and serenity around me, which gives me a peaceful feeling in my soul of his love. Perhaps it's me who is on an LSD trip.

With the beauty of peacefulness, I go to bed and with a smile on my lips, I contemplate, once more, he is filling up my narcotic love cravings with his affection to me—a dangerous fix I get every day in my hope for the big dream of eternal happiness! So, I stay in the glorious moment of him loving me more than life. I know I'm blessed with my trip to the Holy Land and Drake's eternal feelings to me. As a warm-blooded woman, I lick the sweet honey the buzzing honeybees is producing in my mind, his many declarations of a great devoted spirit. What do you think? Will you do the same? I'm a warm-hearted, passionate woman and not an "ice queen" or heartless. If such sugary talk doesn't melt my boiling blood in my veins, running to my heart and soul, then I'm the icy queen. I get even more captivated and fall more and more in love with him, while my boiling heart melts at the many moments of passion and is weakening my soul with fiery lava. From my jeans pocket, I grasp for my silver rosary, which I've bought from an Israeli artist, and then I kiss and squeeze tenderly the cross of Jesus. I use it many times during the day of our prayers.

Tonight's sleep is horrible, and I feel restless with strange, upsetting dreams about Drake being Jesus, who walks the earth and tells me about many secrets we have in the desert. When I wake up in the morning, I'm not rested, and it is difficult to get back to myself. I shower, dress, and then go for breakfast and prayers together with the rest of the pilgrims, praying our love will last forever.

The following day, we have an amazing sightseeing trip to Gethsemane Garden, adorned with many beautiful olive trees. The location is so stunning and sorrowful for the soul. Here it was that Judas betrayed Jesus, where they arrested him, and where his apostles the night before had their Last Supper and prayed before Jesus' crucifixion. Between the many olive trees, I can glimpse the Church of All Nations, and the picturesque Russian Orthodox St. Mary Magdalene Church which shines as glitter in the universe when the Sun hits its seven gilded onion domes. It is a dreamlike moment for me. We drive to Hebron, thirty-six kilometres away from Jerusalem, which is a

Palestinian city in the southern West Bank, which was David's capital for over seven years until he took the power of Jerusalem. Hebron is one of the oldest inhabited cities in the world and is sacred to Jews, Christians, and Muslims.

The experience of the churches is fantastic, and believe me, we see many of them.

Including the Church of the Nativity in Bethlehem, with its very low opening. The Grotto of the Nativity, where it's told Jesus was born, is an underground space which forms the crypt, so you must humbly bend your head to enter this site. The church's fortified building is partly the work of the crusaders and many crusader kings were crowned here. They wanted not to be crowned with gold in Jerusalem, where they crowned Jesus with thorns. The Birth Cave, with its big fourteen-pointed silver Star on the floor, bears a Latin inscription which translates, "Here was Jesus Christ born by the Virgin Mary." Close by the Nativity Church is also St. Catherine Church, where every Christmas Eve they hold the big Mass and broadcast it to the world. The bright modern church belongs to the Franciscan order, and there are altars for the Virgin Mary, Francis of Assisi, and Antonius of Lisbon. At the south wall, a staircase leads down to the Chapel of the Holy Innocents, where they honour the massacre of the children, commanded by Herod. It feels as if the tours will never end, and we go to the chapel of the Shepherd's Field, where an angel appeared to the shepherds and preached the birth of Jesus. The local shepherds still guard their enormous flocks of sheep's here. Jericho, Haifa, and the Dead Sea is a magical event, as is the terrific trip to Bethlehem (Beit lehem), which in Hebrew means, "The house of bread" where we have our dinner and taste the famous bread. Relaxed and captivated, I watch the picturesque surroundings of the landscape and its ancient olive groves while passing the many minor villages of thirty-five thousand inhabitants. They also mention this location in several pages in the Old Testament. Then our many trips end, and the last night in Jerusalem, before I go to bed, I talk to Drake of the spiritual and moral support I'm receiving from pastor Jonas.

'Hi, darling love. My last call before I go to bed. Pastor Jonas told me an important story about Lot. A patriarch in the biblical book of Genesis. A sweet story. When I was talking with him about my marriage. He pointed out that I don't have to act as Lot's wife.'

'Nice, baby. We must hold all the good things we are about to experience together.'

'I vowed under the word of the Lord that I will not do so. Only look forward.'

'Good! Amazing times goes so fast. Every moment is precious. We must try to keep track of where we are and what we do. We will throw all the bad things of the past in a box and burn it. Now comes the most gruelling time for us.'

'Yea, I know. Listen! Lot met two angels at Sodom's gateway and offered them overnight in his house. First, they answered – "No" - but surrendered and went home with him. The men in the city surrounded his house. They wanted to lie with the angels. Lot hides them and instead offered his two virgin daughters.'

'How can he do so? Sweet, beloved darling, you will go through purgatory if you have not new strength from your trip.'

'But I have. That's why this story is so important. The men were about to blow up Lot's door when the Angels pulled him aside. Then they stroked the men with blindness. The angels asked Lot to take his entire family out of Sodom. Then they would destroy the entire city for their sins. Lot took his wife and his daughters out of town. The rest of the family thought he was keeping them as fools, as the Lord wanted to spare them.'

'That we met each other must also give us the strength to go through what may come. There is nothing we cannot solve together. When we are together, we will win.'

'Yea, we will. When they were all taken out of the city, the Angels told him; 'Run for your life! - Do not look back! - Do not stay anywhere in the Jordan Valley. Bring you to safety in the mountains, if you don't want to lose your life!'"

'Oh ... As I'll bring you to safety. Wow! We are now two in one. You must not forget it, my little girl. We have so much to give each other.'

'I know, darling. When Lot came to SOAR, the Lord poured Sulphur and fire on Sodom and Gomorrah. He destroyed the cities and the entire Jordan Valley. But Lot's wife looked back. Damn it, she turned into a salt figure. (Genesis 19:1) Sweet, right?'

'Ha-ha, yea! Now that you soon must go home, other pressures and demands will come to us. You know that. Right?'

'Darling, I promise with my heart, all the stars of heaven and the universe, that I will not act as Lot's wife did.'

'If we talk about them together, we will find the solutions together. Always!'

'I don't want to live my life in a burning city. Not where it rains with sulphur and fire.'

'You must understand that Flopper (Paul) will be desperate not to lose you. He will try to persuade you to stay so he can get control over you again. He is a control freak.'

'Darling I only wanted to tell you this story to give you and me peace of mind. It means a lot to me. To my soul and conscience. Especially with all the help I get from you. And the Church. Also, from the priests.'

'You know Flopper certainly won't lose face to his colleagues. Or his business associates. Now you can score big. You are great at writing. And can thus easily get a book published. Remember, in divorces, all tricks apply.'

'I hope you understand my faith. It's something sacred when I give my promise in marriage to God. That the Catholic Church doesn't approve of it is of great importance to my future opportunity. I can keep on receiving my sacred sacraments. The Church supports me so much.'

'Baby, when you get home, remember to get all your bank investment accounts. Also, papers of bonds and shares. The pensions. And owner-occupied properties appraised. And the value of the boat.'

'No worries. I hope you don't think I'm a radical within Catholicism. Though it's good to have faith. Ha-ha, now I also have you!'

'Yea! Baby think about what you want to have with you. Remember, you must find all your debts and tax returns. Take pictures of all the valuables in your home.'

'Okay! I'm looking forward to a life with you. I will never let you disappear.'

'Just remember, don't get mad. Get everything. Ha, ha, ha! It's the best advice from your best friend. It's the next chapter of my declaration of love for you—my Mary M.'

'I love you from earth to the shiny guardian Moon. Oh ... and to the blinking Stars. Then all the way back again. Bye, love.'

Shaken, I ponder, *Is he only my best friend? What's that supposed to mean?* And I see that he always uses the word 'baby'. I'm not a baby. What does he mean by that? Maybe it's an American expression for one's beloved? What does a Danish blonde gal know about that? We don't use that expression in Denmark, because a baby is a baby child! The enchanting trip to Israel is about to end, and I'm packing my suitcase ready for departure.

As I get back to Denmark, I will be busy preparing all these things he has advised me, because we have created a firm foundation for the beginning of a high-spirited relationship, in deep love. I don't have the slightest sense of who I am. Am I Mary Liz? Catherine in her stormy relationship with Heathcliff (*Wuthering Heights*)? Or am I Mary Magdalene, who has walked with Jesus through the desert?

What can I expect for my future—both good and evil? Drake expresses that our lovemaking is sheer magic, but I must admit, the trip to Israel has contained the most fantastic and sheer magic moments in my life.

CHAPTER 25

THE PING-PONG GAME

> How do you spell love?
> You don't spell it ... you feel it.
> —Piglet and Winnie the Pooh

It's a freezing cold autumn day and raining in Copenhagen on my return from Israel as relatives pick up the people from the group, while I stand there alone. I'm disappointed no one has picked me up, so I go outside to grab myself a ciggy, next I grab a taxi, sitting on the backseat at the car and sweating with nervousness to meet Paul again. My heart is pounding up to my throat, while I'm shaking like crazy because I need to tell Paul about my decision. Upon arrival, the driver takes my suitcase out of the trunk, I pay him, and stare at the massive black gate as I don't know if I want to go in. I lock myself into the entry, walk to the other large front door at the building, and take the stairs up to the third floor to our flat. Paul stands in the kitchen drinking coffee and smoking out of the window, and ignores me, while his body language shows clear angriness and lack of care for my arrival. I prepare a coffee, light myself a fag, and stare nervously at him. I become sorrowful, and it scares me seeing him so unfriendly because I must tell him about the divorce. With a fast, nervous beating heart, and with my brain beating like irrational jungle drums as I try to figure out how I best can state the merciless news, and stammer through the conversation. My inner soul desires not to be unfriendly with him, but the many discussions end up in awful high angry notes between us. We are yelling at each other, slamming doors, and throwing cups through the kitchen in rage and desperation. It's as an overheated angry monkey zoo when we shout at each other as furious animals. Often, we stand with angriness, nose to nose, and stare at each other as two fuming bulls in the arena, to see which one of us can win the next battle. Both of us behave ruthlessly, and the following weeks ends up in awful nightmares with gruesome conversations.

When we go to bed, we sleep as two crossed children, back to back, without kissing or saying goodnight, which we have never done so before. To irritate him, I often play deafening music on my iPod at full blast, usually Enigma, so he can hear the loud drumming sounds from my earphones. *Boom... boom... boom...* and truly, it's not always pleasant for me, but I don't care. Then I turn around hundreds of times in my bed, kicking my legs hard on the madras or kicking my duvet on and off so he can't fall asleep. Every night, I find some new-fangled ideas, as getting up several times to go to the bathroom, turning on all the lights, or accidentally slamming the doors. If I can irritate him, I feel successful. Oh my gosh, he gets so furious because he has trouble falling asleep, so I partly accomplish my cruel mission. That's my punishment for him, hoping it will exhaust him the next day and hoping he will come home earlier and not spend time with the other woman because he's tired. But the tricks don't work perfectly, so at the end of the day, I'm more tired than he is. Our home then resembles a war zone, as if World War III has erupted at full blast.

Paul then spends most of the time at work, so I feel alone and abandoned. I can't get back on my feet before he starts a new hateful discussion about money, the divorce and his denial of the other woman. All the time, he tries to make me decide what will happen in terms of the apartment, loan, marriage or if I will move to Spain. Suddenly, he says it isn't his intention to divorce, and it will be of no financial benefit for him in the event. I'm confused, dizzy, and scared, and I can't think properly. Then I ponder, *is it all only about money for both these men?* I try to talk about our economic situation, but no matter what I tell him, he doesn't take me seriously. I'm in a chaotic mess and heartbroken, because in the deepest part of my heart and soul, I want to stay with Paul, but also get rid of the damn other woman and having him stop lying to me.

His way of handling the situation only makes things worse, so the lawyer must take over, because I have no more power to fight. I'm exhausted. The bond between Drake and I get stronger, even though I also have problems with him when I don't stand up to his commandments. He often panics if I don't answer him, and for many days he does not understand what's going on, so he gets jealous. My inner spirit has locked down, and I've retreated into quietness and don't want to talk to anyone. Depressed, stressed, and distressed, I read the many angry, panicked emails Drake keeps sending me.

> What the hell is wrong with you? Where are you? I can't reach you!
>
> I'm incredibly upset! Are you okay? I don't like that you are with "Flopper". He's a dangerous man and tells the kids you are taking everything from him, so answer me NOW!
>
> Why don't I hear anything? You only write when you are whining and complaining. It's upsetting. DL..
>
> What have I done to you? I'm very sick today, so answer me. I hate the thought you sleep in the same bed as Paul. When are you leaving him? Drake.
>
> Dear ML I don't feel well. I'm awful sick again and have gone to bed. I have taken penicillin this morning and a sleeping pill so I can get some sleep. Hope you make it through the night. Love and kisses from DL.
>
> Sweet little girl, I sent a message on Skype. But I know too well that's difficult to get hold of the one you love, but you must NOT think at all that I'm not dedicated to YOU and ONLY you. Never doubt it. I slept too long this morning and I have an awful sore throat. Too much cold

air conditioning as they use too much here. Love and kisses
Drake L.

And so, it goes on with lots of brief sweet and angry emails, text messages, or talking over Skype. It's as thunder balls, many erupting volcanoes of craziness sent to my head, so I don't answer him. I've just about gone nuts and have daily headaches, as blistering thunderstorms. My entire body hurts, and I can hardly take it anymore, so I'm on the edge of a nervous breakdown. I feel I'm sinking into the sucking gloomy quicksand of deep depression, and I only want to escape and travel back to Spain.

* * *

The first thing I do the next day after my homecoming is to ensure if the secret money is still there. In a panic, with a pounding heart, I search in all my boots, my lingerie, in shoeboxes and blouses where I believe I have hidden it. Well, shut up! The cupboards are well-stocked with expensive clothes, bags, and footwear of exclusive brands. Oh dear! What to do with all that stuff? Do I sell it or give most of it away to charity? I breathe in great relief and calm down again to normal breathing! Super! Paul has luckily not found the cash, so I throw it into my backpack, and muse; what to do next? The following day I'm pacing nervously on the street we live on; I turn right on the first alley and then next turn left on the other major street until I reach the bank. Oh my, I'm sincerely scared of getting robbed with such a vast amount in my bag, so I sneak closely along all the facades of the buildings and look carefully to ensure no one is following me. In good faith, though I feel identical to a criminal, I take an immense amount from the backpack and give it to the cashier to deposit the amount into Drake's account and do this several times during the week with different amounts deposited into different banks. Almost thirty thousand dollars I deposit into his tax-sheltered account, and I don't even know if such accounts exist. How reckless of me, but I have full confidence in him. I have accepted his amazing bank idea and transfer my hard-earned savings, and when I need them, Drake has promised I will get it back. The perfect idea, and he has once more helped me in a shitty situation. I believe! I'm certain not everybody is as gullible as I am.

Stop! Stop! Stop! You didn't?

Yes, I did! When I had done the last transaction, I sent him a message: 'Subject: Some coins transferred to you. Now you have them all in your account. Hugz, Mary.'

Wham-bam, crazy banana boat, and I'm afraid if it turns all the wrong way. Oh my gosh, unquestionably, the mother-fucking piece of shit must have laughed himself into impudence of victory as he made his way to the bank, when all the money is in his account. And now the chivalrous dancing bird-of-paradise has flown and perfectly settled in his fresh Asia adventure.

Dear reader, you must Google this "bird-of-paradise." It truly exists and has a funny dance he does for the female bird.

Thus, I lose control of the damned savings, I'm afraid it all will disappear as fast as I have transferred it to his account, so will I ever see the money again? So heedless! I should not rely on a man who kindly let me deposit money into his account. But I do! Slam! Bam! Scam! Serious red flag! The cannonball has smashed me right in my naïve, pretty face.

Well, everybody says, 'This will never happen to me', but you don't know Doctor Drake, Lucifer Bates. If you did, you would discover how skilful the charming paradise bird is as he swings women around his handsome little soft feathers. Women drown in his lovely dance and his brown eyes, and they melt in his tender hands when he caresses them with his smooth feathers or hugs them with his embracing stunning tender wings. Your flesh rises in goosebumps when his hands are on it, and he knows exactly which buttons to push. Women get mesmerised and blindfolded by him. He is *that gifted* in his way of manoeuvring you. I don't even dare to say the words *trust me* anymore. I trusted in a person I believed I can trust, and I don't know yet about his cruel game, but Drake fit so well into my perfect escape of a fresh euphoric adventure. He loves me, I trust, and gives me tenderness, and I love him, and this is what every woman wants. Love! Tenderness! And a handsome guy. But he's also lacking patience and sometimes, I get *not so nice* mails from him, and then I call him in despair. In good faith, and because I believe he's an honest man, I forgive him too many times.

'Hi, darling, I get so hopeless when I can feel such panic in your e-mails or on the phone. It's a gruelling time for me. I've many things I need to do before my departure to Spain. Did you get all the money?'

'Hi baby, at last. Yea, all is safe on my account. You are in a situation that's hard to come by but reflect on it; *this too will pass—and soon.*'

'I do whatever I can to keep in touch. Sometimes I don't understand why none of us don't give up. For you, the easiest thing will be to say, "This is something I don't care about. It's too burdensome". I can say, "I might as well stay in my inferno of hell. My darling angel will probably give up soon." I can't manage this total mess of chaos.'

'For your sake, you must do things right.'

'I need to remember my moments with you. I need peace. And tranquillity for both of us. But as you often wish for a gift, just as often, you don't get it fulfilled. What I thought could be a simple matter turns into an inferno of letters that none of us really want to bother with.'

'Baby, you do so well. You stood your ground.'

'Sorry I involve you in my horrible life. I draw off your energy. I drink all your nectar. I'm drained of energy. And now, there is a distance between us I don't want to exist.

I can feel that you are not the same as when you left. Our energy is being drained in our struggle to complete our task.' I'm on the edge of crying.

'Paul goes through twists in his head because he has lost control of you.'

'Let's not delve further into this dull topic, I will tell you something else. I've reviewed all the papers from the bank. If you don't mind, I can send you copies of it. You can have a look at it. Paul has looked at it all. Immediately he claims that the bank has not done it properly.'

'He will go through many more complicated twists in the coming time. He's insecure. He can't handle it to be insecure and out of control. Let's talk about that.'

'I believe it's because he knows I'm watchful. I think he's afraid I'll discover he's trying to get me into a financial trap. I feel I can't trust him.'

'I know it's hard for you. I want to be there and give you the support you need.'

'He says I can easily have faith in him about the economic part. What do you think?' I'm desperate and no longer know what to believe.

'Baby, you might ask the lawyer.'

'No matter how Paul turns it, all the papers go straight to the lawyer. Besides, he also stated that if I go to a lawyer with everything, he will move his own financials, pension funds, and everything to another bank without me on the papers.' Panic spreads in my head.

'Ask her if she can find some time sooner. Then get it fielded.'

'What he tells seems suspicious, doesn't it? Not such a brilliant move on his part! Well, I'm not that stupid. Once bitten, twice shy. I've written everything down. He keeps on commanding me around in the circus ring. As am I, an untrained bear who doesn't understand shit about anything. Maybe I don't.'

'Baby, hurry, make the appointment with the lawyer now.'

'But I need some money back of those I transferred to you.'

'Baby, you can safely pay her by credit card if it all goes well quickly.'

'Hmm … Can you transfer $10,000 back to me?' I feel as begging to get my coinage back.

'I've not the option to enter my Internet banking now. I can't find my passwords. I'll transfer ASAP.' I don't think about his strange answer.

'It frustrates Paul with his trouble to control me. I must hold on to my opinions and views. Sometimes he's humble and tries to see if I will hug him. He feels my hugs are not mutual.' Though, I believe I hug him as I always do. It's more him who distance to me.

'I don't want you to hug him. Then Flopper thinks you will stay.'

'Calm now, Drake. I don't cling to him. There is always distance between our bodies. I only want to get it all over with. I'm so afraid he will find the secret phone. I need you so much here. And now.' Tears run down my cheeks.

'I'm glad for your confidence in me and that you want to share all this with me.'

'I can't stand it anymore. It makes me miserable and painful.'

'I must give you my opinions—good and bad—but I'm pleased to help you. As I understand it, he has made a financially gainful deal for himself. Not for the children and you. Their child savings don't look so impressive either.'

'It's strange. I can't see or feel what he wants.'

'Good and rational debate sounds like this. You have him in trouble on several points. If I were him, I would be distressed about the book you are writing.'

'Huh? Book? Out of the blue, he is withdrawing from apartment number two in Spain. Maybe it's also for the best? I most of all want to step away from it all. I don't know if I'm losing everything.'

'Does he not lose his fifteen thousand dollars deposit if you do not complete the transaction in Spain?'

'I don't know. It feels undeniably long until I'm in Spain again. I consider whether I shall leave now instead of waiting.'

'Baby, you must keep the apartment you have there. Then you have an address. A residence after the break. It's wise to keep. If sold, it probably won't bring in as much as it's worth.'

'I need peace. I lose the desire for everything around me. I have a hard time concentrating on my math and other subjects at school. I want to get it all done as quickly as possible. Thank you for the wonderful time with you on Skype.'

My life is a constant escape from one country to another. Neither do I know which of the men I shall choose, and there is no rest in my body or mind. Millions of fire ants are crawling and fire-pissing on my burning body, and it's all black, white, and grey when I feel I'm thrown into the fire of hell. Paul won't agree to a quick divorce, so he begs me to stay and promises to change. But I've no longer confidence in him, because he has given me promises before, and for me, trust is like glass. Once the fragile glass is broken, it will never be the same, and we can no longer heal up our lives. I don't care about all my materialistic goods and wealth. I only wish for a good life with my husband, but I can't get that.

It's all in vain, and I'm only an object for him. Oh, my gosh, too many times, I've forgiven him, and every time, it's hopeless and in vain for me! Those are the millions of thoughts that run through my confused head.

Few days after Drake calls me.

'Hi my sweet baby. Are you okay?'

'Oh, hi. Yea, because your presence is my freedom. You give me spiritual freedom.' I feel happy having him on Skype and glare at his loving smile. 'It makes me not afraid to walk fresh unknown paths with you. Darling, it doesn't make me afraid of my worries and fears about others.' And I sense I'm in great condition with my feelings for him.

'I have hit on an idea this morning. A brainwave; it's actually very clever.'

'Oh, well, I see. Let me hear it. You give me the courage and power to do what I have feared many times before. You draw me towards what has always been my spirit. I hope that your noble spirit draws you to me.'

'It does, baby. Basically, the phase you go into is financial. You will need your lawyer to handle the negotiations.'

'Thanks that you are helping me with my burden. It makes me brave and strong. I'm strengthened by your daily strength as you send me through the blue universe. And the Stars of the clear sky of the night. Hi, hi, I know you always are blinking;-) and shining on my path. Every night when I sleep. When it's daytime in your country.'

'Oh, baby, you're so poetic.'

'Your strength is my power. My power is your strength. Your spirit is my drive. My motivation is also yours.'

'That's why we must talk about the split.'

'What split?'

'The ninety percent he has promised to you. Get it in cash.'

'Get it in *cash*? Impossible.'

'Yea. If the amount becomes too large, you can get all your securities as part of the settlement. He can just buy new ones for himself afterwards.'

'The appointment with the lawyer is at two o'clock tomorrow. Phew! We sure go through the path of some suffering. Most is love. We go on the right track of our future love life. I long so much for you.'

'Yea, we are on the track. But get money on your account. Decide for how to deal with them in the future. If the bank can't do it well enough, we can move them.'

'What? Move them? I'll bring all the documents to lawyer. I have prepared the economy for the divorce. I have revived the entire banking concept. I've sent you everything. You now know about everything we owe. Housing, will, shares, marriage settlement, pension savings, yes, all private financial matters. Did you get the bank statements?'

'Yep. I can recommend to you a few banks or brokerage companies. They can make them flourish for you. I will manage it for you. Get it to China.'

'Get it all to China?' Has the alien gone completely out of his mind?

'Baby, I have good contacts in China and Macao.'

'It's a gigantic unwise idea. It's not possible.' It's locked in the bank system until my retirement. (When I'm a hundred years old and dead). Kidding! I can get them at sixty and paid out in ten-year monthly instalment. I suppose that's why they call it an instalment annuity. 'Don't you know I cannot move it?' Oh, sorry, he is Swedish, so maybe the tax system is different there. 'Darling, it will cost 60 percent in *tax* if I withdraw the money ahead of time.'

'Baby, I will figure it out for you. No worries.'

'Darling, I long so much for your warm embraces. Your great love.'

'Baby, I long for you too.'

'I miss your hot affection for me. Let it only be me who may love you. My heart only belongs to you.'

'Sweet little girl, my heart also only belongs to you. Listen, I think it's important that you get the shares and other securities as your personal portfolio.'

'I don't have a damn clue about trading shares! Paul usually handles all these matters. He is good at it.' And Paul is a financial genius, that's why he does so well with his company.

'Don't talk to the bank about it. I'll help you so you can get a good divorce settlement,' he promises, and truly, I believe Drake is a genius with money and tricky papers. I've not dared to talk to my bank adviser about it, because I am afraid they will tell Paul about my plans. Drake is giving me all bits of advice, and I wonder if this is the best advice I can get.

'I have turned my back to all that hurts me during my bumpy life. I know that you are the only one who loves me right now.'

'That's right! Baby, when you publish your book, you can sell Flopper's company's shares. It's best before you release the book. While the portfolio is in a high course.'

'I don't understand why that is so important. I will lose too much money on it.'

'No, no. The idea is; you might buy the firm shares again a short time in that event they are low. Then you have it in cash.' I'm totally lost in the space of his suggestions! Alien attack! In my naivety, I believe in most of what he tells, though.

'Darling I only want to live for—and with you. Let's not talk more about wealth.'

'Baby, there is a price for not writing about Flopper's perversions. Perhaps money-wise fearful affairs in your book you must assess the value of. You can only have the real talks with him. Insurance! You must be a recipient of unfitness-for-work insurance on your husband. Especially if he does not pay your settlement in cash and securities.'

'But I don't know about such a thing. I don't even know if I'll write the book.'

'You will. Trust me. Just wait and see. Therefore, you need your personal bank account with credit cards. As only you control those.'

'But I have only shared accounts with Paul.'

'Get fresh ones. Remember, your private accounts are yours—not common ownership. All your gifts and personal values are yours. Cars, art, jewels he has given you, etc. Good luck tomorrow. It will be a great day for you. Bye, bye, baby. Mwah!'

'Thanks, darling. It's just so hard to wait for my meeting with the lawyer. Talk to you tomorrow. Bye. Huggee! Mwah!' Then, I realise I had given him total access to all the documents. Perhaps it's *not clever*! No! No! No! Please never do as I did. I cannot imagine how I was such a fool and executed this plan as carelessly as I did. That's why people need a lawyer! Paul even pleads with me to stay in the marriage, so I have the best and most thankful opportunity to forget all about Drake. But I lost my trust for Paul, so instead, I'm conned into performing all that I do by fully trusting Drake. For heaven's sake! How unwise and immature can I as a woman be? I believe I'm a wise and clever woman, but apparently, I'm not! Will this be the biggest mistake of my life? Women think too often with their heart, and men think mostly with their pecker to trick women. So, none of us are using the wise part of our brain. Paul gets conned by a gold-digger, but that's another story.

CHAPTER 26

Let's Get Floppers Money, Babe

> They may hate us together, but they can't stop us!
> —Bonnie & Clyde

Many years ago, I stopped working to support Paul's massive career, so I take care of the house, the children, and all my husband's naughty wishes. Then I realise during this devious life mess that I don't have any rights regarding the divorce, and what bullshit is that? Paul is impossible to deal with, and the kids are constantly demanding over unreasonable things, simultaneous Drake is pushing hard at the other end. Life really sucks! The country is cold, selfish, and rude, and life is in a disheartening state. My education is outdated, and I must start over if I want to work again. So, what the hell is this nit-picking with Paul and money? Getting some nickels and dimes from him for a life's hard work is not okay. He must pay and take care of his wife and not give me pennies on the dollar. Damn it, the dude can afford it. Besides, *he* is the *culprit* of adultery and has put the entire marriage at risk by dipping his one-eyed-wonder weasel in another woman's pussy. In frustration, I appeal to Drake about women's lack of rights and men's power over wealth. Jeez, his creativity doesn't lack any imaginable suggestions.

In tears and desperation, after I leave the lawyer, I call Drake over Skype. Heartbroken, panicking, and angry, I weep dry tears of frustration, as I stand outside in the freezing cold on the well-known walking street in the middle of Copenhagen, as people pass by me with surprised gazes, shaking their heads, and likely think I'm drunk or on drugs. But the prince on the white horse is, as usual, ready to help.

'Wow! Six hundred dollars for a one-hour meeting with the lawyer. It's depressing and appalling. Just another rip-off. But I know it's important to do things in the correct order.'

'Baby don't gloom. In your case, a serious breach of moral contract happened when Flopper committed adultery. It led you to want to take your own life.'

'I most of all want to be with you. Just forget about everything at home.'

'Stop such baloneys, baby. Now you must fight for your freedom.'

'Sometimes, I understand why people just disappear into thin air. And don't want to be found again. This is how I feel.'

'Flopper has a lot to think about. If you can arrange all this amicably and he pays you fair and square, I will take my hat off to you.'

'You are right. He also has a lot to think about. Vis-à-vis what is happening to me.'

'The reality is, that one part—and it will be him in this case—will twist and try to act to avoid paying. Didn't he promise you an improvement in the form of financial solutions?'

'Well, he tries to do as much as I want him to do. Perhaps only for me to stay. Shall I maybe stay with him?'

'No, baby. Don't. He promised you a personal support. But those documents you only have partially written. Not legally witnessed. You have them not registered.'

'Perhaps it's me that's ahead on points. Maybe it's been a long time since he lost control of me. He realises it now for the first time.'

'With long-term payments, it will be a pestilence for him. It will constantly deprive him of having to punch out. Cash is king. Don't forget that.'

'He asked me if I had another man in my life. Shit, I got nervous. Because of our chat the other day about Jesus and Mary.'

'Why? Did he see you chatted with me?'

'No! But when he entered my office, I couldn't stop writing to you. He asked, "What are you doing?" Snapping, I replied, "I'm chatting with someone in Spain." He stuttered, "Well… hmmm… I see… maybe this is your new guy?" Oops! Bossily, I answered, "Yes, of course it is. What do you think?" and he replies, "Okay, I'm sorry to disturb you."'

'Wow! That was close.'

'Yea! I was thinking deeply about what we talked about regarding Jesus and the Virgin Mary. It was so intense. With such powerful forces between us. It was as if you were sitting on the other side of my screen.'

'Babe, I love you more and more. I'm only pleased to help you. If I can. You have become a special patient. A friend whom I value a lot. More than you may know.'

'Huh? Only friend? Gosh, when we chatted, I could feel the touch from your tender fingers on the keyboard at the same time as I typed my letters. As you were tenderly stroking my hands. It was magical; even though we were over nine thousand kilometres apart. Geez, it felt as it was only nine micrometres between us.'

'You can go right into one's heart. Meeting such a warm and lovely personality as yours is rare.'

'Darling, you are deeply in my heart. I ponder if Paul is only trying to lure me into a trap!' I stroll to the nearest café and buy myself a coffee and water.

'By God, I do not understand why Flopper has not properly looked after you. I wish I had met someone like you before I got married.'

'No, I don't get it. I miss you. I feel your aura and spirit close to my soul every day and night. What shall I do?' Being sad and slurping from my coffee.

'Don't worry. You know I'm helping you with a plan. I'm thrilled to help with my knowledge.'

'Shucks! The dude didn't even leave the room. I grunted, annoyed, "I don't want any of your gawking over my shoulder when I do something on my PC. Shoo! You must allow me to have some privacy. Darn! Without you constantly wanting to know what I'm doing. Shoo! Shoo!" The discussion ends, and he leaves.'

'Well, I can't do anything about Flopper's inability to understand. Or empathise with how good and caring a person you are.'

'What do you mean? I didn't ask you to do such.'

'I know that's not what you're asking me to do.'

'It's unreasonable conditions of women's rights for a divorce.' I sob.

'Women always stand as the loser. With no choices. What the heck! The man stands with all the aces in his hand.'

'Jeez, I'm desperate. Paul has meant nothing for me the last half-year. Not since I found out about his betrayal. Yet I love him so much.'

'Babe forget him. NOW! In your current situation, when you realised he would not follow up on his promises, your situation worsened. Financially and emotionally.'

'Shit! It's mostly in favour of the man. Damn! He can take the entire fortune without sharing with me. It shucks! I fight all the battles alone. With no support.'

'The basis for this option for women is to restore the opportunity for fairness between two married people. I have based it on your relationship. I'll send you the PP. You must set the relevant figures. Can you do that?'

'Maybe. I discovered the law has recently changed to the man's favour.'

'Huh? How? Baby, I offer this solution so you can take up the thread at the event of yours. Back two years ago. I let that year be the first in the result. Look at it when you get home.'

'Fuck. Shame on those stupid politicians; it could only have been a man who came up with such rash new rules. Scumbags.' I'm upset and angry.

'Calm baby. Had I not known you, I would think you are an attorney who is used to settling divorces. Where did you get all that knowledge from? You surprise me again and again. You are doing extremely well in terms of your planning.'

'Hmm, I believe you must be my guardian angel.' I don't feel as an attorney.

'With my principle, the woman receives a wife's salary based on one-third of the current income.'

'What? I don't understand what you are talking about.'

'You must deposit the money into your private account. Only you control it, in the form of a separate estate.'

'I understand some things you say, but not all.' It sounds as the worst hocus-pocus.

'The man gets an account with one-third. One-third goes into a common account. There you will pay for the joint expenses.' He talks only of capital.

'Damn! Paul has never had the finger on the pulse of his marriage. He thought he was the king off the top. Now he spoils it all. Bloody hell! Just because of a stupid bitch who wants his rotten pink wiener and his dough.' My anger is vast.

'Ha-ha! Baby just have in mind that bonuses and board income from Flopper, you get the 50 percent. The pension fund, you get the 90 percent. Remember, he promised you. And 10 percent to him.'

'It's so fucked up. Why does he only think with his stupid heat-seeking moisture missile? Damn, the dude has a wife who loves him entirely. Whatever is in the man's name is now, by law, his sole property.'

'When is the law efficient? Will you not get any of it?' He sounds disappointed.

'Soon. I'm pissed off. Such hocus-pocus!'

'Well, this stuff's latest creation must ensure that there are no wrong and unreasonable splits of a divorce. Neither by death nor to prevent mistakes by smoothing the process of separation.'

'I do not understand.' Funny business he presents to me.

'Babe, it's simple. Flopper promises different "repair mechanisms". He must include it in the formation of your new foundation.'

'Bloody hell. Now it's my turn to cheat. He will lose. I don't get it with men.'

'Calm baby. You must later divide the income that you enter according to the promised distribution key. It will surely provide some scrumptious amounts to your account. But that's also what he has promised!'

'Yea! However, it's always the wife who is the loser when another woman enters one's marriage. The dude gives a shit and fucks around. It's seen too often when they enter their panicky age.'

'Baby, you must hurry. Before the new law becomes effective. Let's get Floppers wealth, babe. I made a fairness principle throughout the presentation. Danish laws do not understand how to consider the woman proper.'

'It's normal to split everything. Fifty-fifty. Also, to get alimony over some years. Ha, ha, if the women get anything—you never know.'

'Let me finish the other plan. Additional securities, stock and bonds, in case of divorce, where you have deposited profits will go into each of your own accounts. 50 percent to each. You appoint a joint account administrator. You will do this task.'

'Huh? What? I do not understand it.' My angry thoughts are more about why Paul has put his foolish bratwurst into another woman's thick yellowish infected smelly pussy.

'It's easy. Any payment over a certain amount (e.g., $3,000) from the common account you must get it approved with a signature by both parties. A sharing of all this you make it so that there can be no doubt about what belongs to whom.'

'Darling, it sounds complicated.' And my brain is not in the direction where Drake wants me to be.

'No, no. I help you. You make debit cards for the common account. Use them for the daily operation of the home. There is always an insight into the joint account.'

'I don't find any of it valuable. What does it all mean?' I scratch my neck and stare at him, me, resembling an alien, jumped down to earth from outer space, not knowing how I shall use his creativity.

'The system starts with negotiation about what you consider as joint responsibility. Meaning; of what you must pay from the mutual fund. You make a precise inventory with pictures of things in the home—furniture, art, etc., down to pots, pans, and tableware. You record everything.'

'Hell no, Drake. I think it's best to keep the Spanish apartment. I can move in ASAP. Then think about what to do. You can always visit me there.'

'Baby don't give up. My plan is simple. You update the list with pictures for each time you purchase new items for the home. That's credited to the spouse who either buys it for himself or agrees to common ownership. Or if it's a personal gift. The value of these lists you must legally register as being a separate estate. Both of you can only make complaints about use in writing once per month.'

'Forget it. It's too complicated. When a man like him climbs to the top of the throne, it's never too long before he falls and hurts himself. Especially when he falls hard.'

'They make Danish law only to create a wife's proletariat. The man can always replace the old wife with a much younger model. Flopper has ensured his own economic stability. The "worn-out" wife (you) must look then at the "poorhouse".'

'Poorhouse? Why?' He lost me there.

'You will live your life without the same opportunities. It's not so often that an older woman as you can score a younger man. Maybe if you have something *very* special to offer. As you have. Then it can happen. Get everything!'

'Wow! You sure have the nerve. Goddamn it! Grr, calling me *old*! A genuine gentleman would never say so.'

'Ha-ha. Of course, a beautiful woman as you can perhaps find a fit older gentleman (me) to shack up with. But then you must be able to do so with your economic situation in moral order.'

'Huh? What? I still don't understand it. Are you joking? It seems to be a solution that other married couples can use.' And I don't bother to fill in the numbers.

'Baby, you are always welcome to contact me. I believe that you rightly see my task. Although there is a vast gap between us, I will answer ASAP when you need it.'

'Thanks darling. I have never had such a powerful love as the one I have with you. Never leave.'

'As for the kids, it will probably be best they live with their father.'

'I want them to live with me in Spain. Basta!' Fuck him, I muse.

'Baby, this will allow Paul to take care of them. Now that diapers, shitty butts, crying babies, and breastfeeding are no longer concerns. You, as a mother, gave them the best life and child-raising.'

'I can't leave my children.' Is he fucking nuts?

'You are not leaving them. But dad must now give them a start on adult life. They will soon fly from the nest, anyway. Then he is free again. This will not be as long for him as the one you have had to go through. That's how life is! So unevenly distributed!'

'Fine, let me see what I do. I'll think about it. And get back. I love you with all I have in me. With all I can give you. Take care. Huggee, huggee, mwah! Bye.'

'Hugs for you too, you little heart-warming precious human being.' We end the conversation. Sadden Bonnie walk home without her Clyde on a sunny, chilly autumn afternoon. I'm passing many of the trees in the giant roundabout, decorated with small light garlands, and stroll further to the famous seafront promenade buzzling of hectic activity.

Arriving at home, I lock myself into the apartment, go into my office, and check Drake's exceedingly creative power Point, as chills go through my skin, and feels as loving hugs from his tender hands. The goosebumps on my body get many more goosebumps on top of them, so the intensity I have with him every day is near the most achievable I can get. When I squeeze my inner soul, it feels as he is inside my body and tenderly hugging it, despite the distance between Asia and Europe.

I prepare myself with every bit of advice and instructions from Drake, though I can't imagine the craziness, even more ideas and suggestions come from him as were we Bonnie and Clyde, robbing every penny from Paul. Drake *never* stops!

The next meeting with the lawyer; who gladly takes my case is ready to fight, although she is not sure I can get all my wishes fulfilled. Everything ends up in awkwardness and hopelessness, so disappointed, I'm ready to give up, as the process also takes ages, and I don't get anywhere with the divorce. In the meantime, the lawyer retires, so, I must start from scrats and find a new one. That angers Drake because things are not going fast enough for him.

Being fifty and knowing Paul is having an affair with a twenty-eight-year-old woman is not a stress-free task. The last year has been a terrible downward slide, and nothing works out for me anymore, so it's necessary to change life into something better and more cheerful. Family is the most vital for me, and the children and the dogs are my only comfort in my lonely life. The importance of life together with Paul is lacking, because I need *love, respect,* and *honesty!* The confusion is gigantic, and the pressure from Drake is as a non-stoppable run-away train, so I can't concentrate on getting my marriage on track again. Hundreds of loving emails, phone messages, and e-cards fill my e-mail inbox every day, so he makes it attractive to choose him. He inspires me, and I have a constant focus on him and not Paul, who doesn't care about my absence. Having in mind of the romance Drake radiates as he seeks to start a new, captivating adventure together easily persuades me, when I read his many love declarations.

> My precious MM, I love you with a passion that I have never felt before. You are made for me—we are made for each other. Yours forever. DL. Eesa.
>
> My sweet MM, I'm so delighted and happy for you in my life, and you fill me up with love, my precious darling. Yours forever. J. Eesa.
>
> My sweetest darling MM, I am so much filled up with love for you. It is so inflamed, and you will be so pampered by me. My delightful and lovely darling. I miss you too much. Hugz, DL.
>
> My loving sweet Baby, I am always with you and I will take worthy care of you, my little darling. No one will ever hurt you again with me by your side. In the name of the Holy God, I love you so much, my Mary Liz. I always did and will always do! Yours forever, J. Eesa.
>
> My dearest sweetheart I would love to embrace and cuddle up with you. I want to take extremely good care of you and make you ecstatic. Kizzez, Drake.

His compassion makes me overjoyed, and I believe he knows he is about to lose me, as I am on the edge of regretting the divorce. Receiving such affection makes me more flattered by him, and he changes my mind to his advantage. I'm as the ping-pong ball he plays his game with, and Drake is as Doctor Hannibal Lecter, who manipulates my brain. Though he is no killer, he is a damn good psychological predator who defeats me, so I can't resist him. Being utterly in his power, the ping-pong game begins, and I no longer deny him anything. The unique enchantment when I'm in contact with him is increasing the quality of my self-esteem. His massive influence, despite the nine thousand kilometres between us, is so convincing, and there is a great weakness on my part. His caring words drag me deeper into his magical wonderland, and I get in deeper than I expect it. So, I keep on talking to him and sending him love letters and plenty of messages. Only once before I have experienced such fascination, and that was on my wedding day, a fantastic fairy tale of a prince and a princess in deep eternal love.

'My dearest darling. There is so much tinkling inside my body when I think deeply of you.' I tell him when we secretly talk over Skype.

'My precious baby. I also feel strange inside. As I can't breathe properly through my lungs. It feels so strong with love.' He seems deeply in love with me.

'Oh, all those sweet words you tell me. My need for you is gigantic.' I'm swept away by his sweet-talk.

'I have such powerful feelings for you, baby. Throughout my entire body. It is telling me this is something crazy we have together. What's wrong with us? Can it be true?' He flatters, and I melt in his brown eyes and sweettalk.

'It must be true. My love for you is massive.' And so, we continue in deep love.

'Isn't that just something we imagine? I'm sure we soon will know, my baby.'

'I wish you were here. I wish my life were not such a mess.'

'Chang called me. He asked if I can go together with him to the hospital to visit a patient I must help.' He of the sudden changes the conversation to something different. 'He is the first patient I will meet. He is a powerful and wealthy man in Hong Kong and Macau.'

'Sounds exciting, darling.' Though I rather want to talk about our love.

'Yeah! Mr Stan Horace fell a while ago. Shucks, the dude knocked his head. Phew!

Bugger, now he sits in a wheelchair. Ha-ha, the patient says he can no longer walk. Ha-ha, because his leg muscles have fallen off.' And why is that so funny? I muse.

'Fallen off. How come?'

'Ha, ha, funny way to express himself. Chang Chen will try to talk to his doctor.

But it's not so easy to get close to Mr Horace, as you can probably imagine. He is extremely well protected by bodyguards.'

'Bodyguards? Is he a mafia boss?' Scary chills run along my spine.

'Well, we must see if I can—or will—treat him. After all, I must be cautious.'

'Why? Be careful, darling.' I get massively nervous.

'Yea. I cannot take too much responsibility in this country. It can cause many problems with the mafia.'

'Mafia? What? Oh, my! Hmm, it sounds dangerous.'

'I have thought wisely about the conditions in your small fucking country.'

'In which way?'

'The politicians have destroyed it. It is intolerable to live there. With divorce and women's rights, I'm not surprised it's that bad. You can't anymore get surprised by them.'

'Yea, jeez, it's so ... fucked up. Let's see what the lawyer comes up with.'

'I didn't sleep after our last talk. I felt you needed help to find solutions.'

'Darling, you already do so much.' So, what is "Clyde's" next move?

'I have a fresh creative plan. I will send it to you. You must fill in the numbers in the fields. I don't know them. It is in principles, flow, timeline, and percentages.'

'Jeez, Drake. No more plans. I more need to feel your warm, firm arms around my body. Not numbers. I need you to comfort me. Have your passionate kisses on my lips.'

'Oh ... baby, you are so dazzling. You are my one and only darling. Gotta go, baby.'

'I love you, my darling. Bye. Mwah, mwah. Huggee, huggee.'

'Baby, I only want—and love you. Mwah, my precious little girl. Ta-ta, my love. Huggee.' Oh, he is my man, filling me with love songs, sweet messages, and honey declarations flying in constant transit within seconds through the magical universe between Europe and Asia. I'm bombarded with tons of loving e-cards, Skype calls and mails, and the only thing my soul wants, is if Paul will fight for me like that. Then an e-card pops up:

> My eternal love,
>
> Couldn't it be nice to have fun here? Us lying on a crystal white sandy beach in Bounty Land, with Hawaiian flowers, palm trees, and coconuts on it.
>
> Love and kizzez,
>
> Drake L.

I would love to be floating in Bounty Land with him, Next morning, the next e-card pops up. My heart is in a sweltering desire for him, and the goosebumps tingle with excitement on my entire body.

> Good morning, my precious love,
>
> Oh, baby, I slept like a dog all night and even woke late. I needed you to cuddle up with you all night. Even though I love you with all my heart and wanted to have you longer on Skype, but my body needed rest last night. I feel so much better now. Today will be a better day than yesterday. I will perform with sharpness. I love you no less for having been without you for a few hours. I love you more and more each day. I must rush and will catch you later.
>
> Yours always,
>
> Drake

Imagine the constant, immense pressure from him, and getting five to eight love letters a day and messages that constantly pop up on the phone as hundreds of uncontrollable eruptions of hot volcanos. The sizzling love lava comes daily, as a floating red-hot steam in my inbox, and my computer is about to melt from his millions of blazing honey mails. I'm possessed of him, and I'm no longer rational and can't resist him!

The ping-pong game goes on for a while until he is certain that I'm trapped in his cage and he has won the match. Together with Spotty, I'm back in Spain, being broken and exhausted, so I feel strangled by the fight with both men. I go into deep silence for almost a week and have only been sleeping, smoking, drinking coffee and walking the dog. 6 kilos have already disappeared on my fragile body, so I appear as one who suffers from anorexia. In my despair of loving Drake and missing my husband, I, after one week's silence, open my computer. Mamma mia, it booms with loving e-cards and harsh negative mail. For heaven's sake, it is a terror attack of good and evil on the screen from him.

> My darling, just a little fun card to make you smile your beautiful smile. You are mine forever, DL.

> My darling love, here I send you a bunch of flowers, and each one is a token of my unconditional love for you. I love you with all my heart. Yours always, DL.

> My love, here is another nice card for you so you know I love you and I am thinking of you always. Yours, DL.

And in between I read the many harsh angry mails. Geez, Drake keeps on swinging as a maniac cracked pendulum from sweet to furious. But no emails from Paul. The frustration is massive for me, with Drake's frustrating mails and letters of guidance, as he seems desperate and obsessed with my divorce. How can he question me? He has all the damn financial papers, and I trust him. And now I must read all his fucking hogwash.

DAMN IT! Where are you? Answer me! NOW!

It's crazy. What happened to you? I'm going NUTS! WRITE! CALL!

So sad that we once again must resort to not being able to speak to each other. Have you dumped me?

Why don't you answer me? Are you not doing the divorce? GET RID OF HIM!

What are you doing? Are you with Paul? Don't have sex with him. I'm worried?

Have I done anything wrong? Any news of the divorce? Answer NOW!

Dear Mary,

Thank you for trusting me and for sending your financial data. At first glance, it looks fucking bogus. But with Floppers way of trading, he is trying to recapture you. I don't like it at all that you are together with him. GET RID OF HIM! It breaks my heart knowing you are still in the same bed as him. But I suppose it's a way for you to avoid facing the economic situation right now. In which situation does that put you? Is that a separation might give him the advantage? If you move to Spain, I mean. Because there are no agreements between these countries. Then you can pay much less tax, or none. So, it is easy to turn this to your advantage. Move now. DON'T STAY WITH HIM! You can also deduct interest expenses and many other items from wherever you post them. You must have an accountant to manage it for you. If you stay in Denmark, as Paul suggests, then he can put his money into tax-favoured savings and thus keep it all. I don't like it if you stay. It makes me resentful. They will tax you very high by a special tax mafia if you withdraw the money from a closed special account. You will only get a small amount, and he will keep the rest, so he ends up winning. Does he mean that you should only have *so little*? Why this trivial bank's savings to you? What about sharing your values and securities? How

> will he pay you out of it? Frankly, I can only see his proposal as a simple scamming merchant account to keep you there. It does not take you into account when separating. I'm distressed! ...

The fact is, there is no longer a double-taxation agreement between Denmark and Spain. In a worst-case scenario, this can mean they can tax me on income in both countries, but I don't know all the rules. Does Drake know what *he* is talking about? It might be he is luring me into an utterly and unforgivable expensive tax trap. I must find out.

He continues:

> One of my friends in the US made a similar deal with his wife, after the lawyer figured it all out, and she ended up getting four times as much, and ended up on the Forbes list of the richest in the US. Thank Paul for the scamming "shoemaker's bill", and you will think about it. Get the lawyer to make a new calculation. Don't forget Ivana Trump's wise words: "Ladies, don't get mad. Get everything." Lots of hugz to you in this troublesome time.
>
> PS! Just an update. It goes forward amazingly for me here. There is a vast American medical group who would like to build a substantial clinic platform around their speciality and mine. Yeeha ... I'm on my feet again and earning loads of cash. I love you, baby.
>
> Drake

For my American readers, it's impossible to compare Danish and US laws, and it's not how Drake describes it.

CHAPTER 27

THE SHADY ANGEL ON THE WHITE HORSE IN MACAU

> 'It's possible.' said pride.
> 'It's risky.' said experience.
> 'It's pointless.' said reason.
> 'Give it a try.' whispered the Heart.
>
> —idlehearts.com

Since my childhood, I have believed that women get fascinated by the fairy tale of the prince on the white horse. However, this is only a phantasm of a fable and not reality. He does not exist! Nor does the true fantasy of my real-life shady angel, because I've noticed he also speaks with two tongues.

Drake's departure several months ago was probably the worst of it all. After my spiritual support from my pilgrimage and next to my hell, when I was back in Denmark, Paul's ignorance hit me so hard in my soul that I travelled back to Spain. I've eaten into my reserves and need to remember my moments with Drake here. I'm beyond happy in my heart at the thought of leaving, and hopefully, happiness will stand with me now. Together with Drake, I feel it is easier to get past my tormentors, because his warmth and amazing heart will take me through one of life's hard phases.

Although it's autumn, the weather is lovely today, with twenty-five degrees and with amazing sunshine, as I drive downtown in the late afternoon and park my car close to the beach. It's dark now, and I'm dwelling in the memories of my time with Drake on the same beach. The bright full Moon and the mesmerising Stars shine intensely and glitter over the water of the Spanish Alboran Sea. I sit at the same spot where we sat in the golden sand a few month ago, and watched the waves splashing with smooth movements up to the golden shoreline, while dragging the small stones and shells in, and then back to the ocean. When my body gets settled, after taking some deep breaths, I feel as if he is next to me. It's as if my body melts completely into his body, while I'm listening to the heartbeats of the calming waves. The rhythm of my heart and breathing slows to a comfortable pace as I imagine his angel-like phantasm, sitting next to me. Though, I realise he's not next to me and it's only an imagination in my head and heart. It's quiet and a little chilly on the beach, and no people longer play in the sand or bathing. The dazzling Sun is long gone, and only the magnificent bluish Moon shines glittering at me while I'm listening to the smooth waves and the rustling of the gentle wind hitting the leaves of the palm tree next to me along the peaceful beach. Sometimes I see a dusky cloud in front of the peaceful, luminous Moon, and he blows the cloud away. I can again see the beauty of the glorious shiny light of him, while he smiles sweetly at me, as Drake does. The Moon likes it when I get mesmerised by him and feels when I'm in a magical heaven when I make imaginary love with the enchanting Moon. It's as if he is blinking and smiling at me when I think of Drake, so I blink back and send the lovely Moon a kiss. As usual, I'm so drawn to the Moon, so I ponder about monsters and werewolves, sneaking around on the beach. But don't be afraid, I tell my imagination, I'm safe on this amazing strand, despite I can see them crawl around in the distance on the golden coastline. Ha, ha, none of them can reach me, I muse, because I'm protected by the angel in my mind, as it tells me, 'none of them are stronger than you. You can defeat them with your magic.' One bastard tries to get me, and I give the sleazeball an uppercut and a hard, feisty kick to his crotch, so it screams as a wounded pig and runs off with the rest of the sneaky pack. Don't worry, I'm not insane, only in love and possess a foolish vivid imagination.

On this scary, beautiful, ghostly night, I can suddenly see some small fishing boats waiting for me to finish my story about the shadowy angel on the white horse. I must hurry in my imagination so the fishermen can get the sealed bottle with my imaginary fairy-tale. They have promised me to bring it to Drake, with my special letter describing how my angel is embracing me with his amazing sensitive wings. Before I leave my spiritual inner fantasy world and the beach, I stick the message safely in the flask as a genie in a bottle, throw it in the ocean, so I can ship it by sea. I hope he has got it by now and has taken off the cork, then sits in peace while reading the scary yet interesting, loving part of my life.

It's getting late, and I must drive back to walk Spotty. Next, it's a bath and straight to bed to get my beauty sleep. The newly washed white silk sheets smell of lavender, and I cuddle the soft duvet when I'm resting my head on the nice soft white goose down pillow. In my head, thoughts swirl of Drake while I'm gazing at his picture, sending healing powers through my soul, and I think it's positive that tomorrow will again be a great, loving sunny day. However, some of my dreams of a brighter future drives me silly. Why do my mind and heart keep on thinking about him? My inner imagination keeps on seeing the fantasy picture of how intoxicated I am by the dark angel's crawling fire ants, pissing on me! I am worn out in my mind and body by this constant phantasm that haunts me, and mostly, I want to forget all about Drake and be with Paul. Instead of pondering of that, I honour my body with a deep, relaxing, resting meditation music before I fall asleep.

Drake has quickly figured out how important he is in my life, and he uses this knowledge to his massive advantage. He keeps sending mammoth amounts of email, which constantly pop up on my computer, and calls me every day over Skype, so it's difficult to forget him. I'm too powerfully attracted to the shady angel, and I suddenly can't survive without him. My journey of peace begins with his presentation of inviting me to many novel adventures with him, which began on the beach this enchanted heated summer night. There is no turning back for me, and I don't know where else to go. Whatever he ponders, he writes or says; I trust in him and I'm trapped blindly as I navigate his maze in perilous darkness. For me, he's the genuine dream of a man, a spellbinding phantom of my shining white saviour on a white rescue horse.

It's morning, and the sunlight is streaming through my windows. The past with Paul becomes to an illusion, so I want to forget about it and erase everything. The present is a nightmare that I must get through safely, as my blissful future is about to start with the fallen messenger. He got a new-fangled idea of me to explore the exotic part of the world, and somehow, he has the impressive skills to plant seeds of ideas in my silly head. His newest idea—of an amazing opportunity for a great fresh future, of a loving life for me in Asia—takes me by surprise. An unexploited adventure only he can give me, which he places in front of me to say yes or no.

'Good morning my dear Mary.'

'Morning, my love.'

'I've a suggestion for you. With all the stress you go through. Take a vacation. By that, I mean away from your husband. Your children. Yea, everyone in your circle.'

'Hmmm... you have a good point there.' I love Spain, but you also must adapt to their culture. I have few friends here, and everyone else I know thinks only of themselves, except for Lucy and Cliff I frequently see. Even I do the same. I have also become a little self-seeker, thinking only of me, me, and me. Hmm ... then of course, I'm also seeking after the shadowy spirit, and I'm a runaway from all my responsibilities to my family.

'Baby, you need to concentrate on *you*! And it's *not* in Spain that you will find peace.' Flashing with his Bambi eyes and smiles.

'Why not? I like it here.'

'Because it's depressing for you. Nobody thinks about you. I do! I care for you and only *you*! Go to an exotic country you've never dreamt of seeing before.'

'It's a tough time for me. I don't know where I should go.'

'Try checking out the site with The Ritz-Carlton Hotel in Indonesia. They say it is as luxurious as can be. You can get a good deal there.'

'Indonesia? Wow… but it concerns me if the country is dangerous. Volcanoes? Terror? Kidnapping?'

'It's not. It will excite me if you can come over to me.' He tries to lure me.

'I'm honored. I know we should enjoy each other more. I hope my soul and love will never disappear from your soul.'

'Then come to me. We can then experience Jakarta together. I will soon be over there and teach my topics.'

'Oh my God! I'm so in love with you. Is it just a dream? Jakarta scares me. Last year, they found another bomb in front of the Ritz-Carlton and Marriott. Terrorists attacked them.' Both hotels are American companies, with a broad portfolio of hotels. In 2009, sadly, several people died in three previous attacks that year, so I'm afraid it can happen again. The Ritz-Carlton Hotels Company manages resorts and luxury hotels around the world, so in my view, they are a terrorist target.

'Baby, it's not dangerous. You can spend the time there. I'll instruct you in my speciality. Let's talk about that.'

'No, no, I'm not sure if I want to take that risk. Many thanks for your invitation. I'll consider the tempting offers. For me, Spain is perfect.'

'Little baby girl, the climate is warm. They can well pamper you in their world-

class health spa.' Who doesn't want to be pampered?

'To be honest, I should probably say, "Fuck it" to everything. Just travel. Hmmm…'

'Do it! You can later come home with renewed resources and energy.'

'Might be you are right! I'm also tired of the cold. Yikes, the snow, rain, and wind. I need Sun, warmth, and pampering.'

'When travelling to the Eastern countries, as the Orient, you get perfect service. You get smiles purely because you are there. Their service is sacred. They have it in themselves.'

'Do you really mean I should go? I don't know if it will be possible for me. I'm doubtful.'

'In my younger days, when I was severely stressed, I went alone, without the family. Mostly on an extended weekend to an exotic country.'

'I don't think Paul will allow me a stress-leave vacation. It's too expensive. Even he earns good money.' Although it will be good and interesting to get to know more about new cultures.

'Fuck him. Just leave. For me, the Cayman Islands were the ultimate realm.'

'Wow… marvellous country! I'd rather go there! I have never been to the Caribbean before. It was there in my dream with the white wooden house. With the sandy beach. And the palm trees. The orchid fields. The butterflies.'

'I came back with renewed energy to withstand the rough Nordic weather. Mostly I went during the fall. Yuck, the winter is worst for me. I went off to the Caribbean again.'

'I get hooked. I would love to go there. You're so wonderful.' And I melt as butter.

'There is something about Scandinavia that makes one depressed. So, you need other climates. As often as possible, to survive.'

'Perhaps this is what I need. I've never healed completely inside my soul. I don't know if I ever will.'

'Do it! I don't understand why someone even bothers to live in such cold, rough countries.'

'No, I cannot, Drake.' It's unnecessary, my common sense tells me, but I'm not always rational! In fact, I'm often too impulsive.

'I can highly recommend that you gather the necessary forces for the final sprint.'

'We will see! I must think about my dull situation. Maybe I'll visit you.'

'Bye the ticket. I'll help you. Flopper will prefer that you stay home; then you are within reach all the time. Then he can be sure of having control over you. Geez, and call you a hundred times a day. You don't need that!'

'A hundred times a day? Paul never calls this often. Oh my, no—he is too busy.'

'He only wants to talk about finances.'

'Only talking about finances. No, you are wrong.'

'Little girl, Flopper will manipulate you to stay.'

'No, no, I'm no longer an interesting matter in his life.' I slightly sob.

'Let the lawyer negotiate for you so that only she can get in touch with you.'

'What do you mean? It is only me she needs to talk to.'

'If your children want to get in contact with you, they must go through the lawyer.'

'Huh? What the fuck? Between me, my children, and the lawyer?'

'Yea, you can create a special hotline that allows her to fix the connection between you and them.'

'Hotline? You must spin loco in your head! My children must always get in touch with me. And with no middleman.' Oh, dear me! As if a lawyer will even play mediator or nanny like this!

'Baby don't worry. It can be a mobile phone that she has. They can dial through her.' Where does he get such cracked ideas from?

'What in heaven's name are you talking about?' This is too much! His methods suggest we are in a war zone. 'Grr, that will not work, Drake.'

'Hmm, okay. You are more than welcome to visit me in Macau first. They will soon have the Formula Three Grand Prix here. I can help you with a superb hotel. At the right price. Okay, I mean, if you want to visit me.'

'I have never been to the East before. I have always dreamt about it—Macau rather than Indonesia. Drake, I can't allow myself to go. I have promised my kids I will soon be back.' Turning off the love fire is tough; it is so difficult to control, and the deprivation is so damn evil and painful. Tears roll down my cheek when I glance at the pictures standing on my table of us kissing, and I wish he were here and not so far away.

'But do not take this as me pushing myself on you. Especially in this tough time for you. It must be hard.'

'Had I been able to stop time before you left, you would still be here. It pains my heart that you are not here.' It is agony not holding his hand when I need him most, and the thought tears up my heart.

'Baby girl, you are the only one in my heart. You are deeply embedded in my soul. Come over to me.'

'I'm just Googling the nation; it looks interesting. It sounds as a great idea.' Macau is an autonomous community (SAR) on the southern coast of China, across the Pearl River Delta from Hong Kong. Until 1999, it had been a Portuguese trading post, before they transferred it to China. Macau is the last existing European area in continental Asia. The realm reflects a mix of ancient Portuguese culture and modern time. It has many gigantic casinos and lots of shopping malls, and the Cotai Strip connects the islands of Taipa and Coloane. They then nicknamed this area as The Las Vegas of Asia and abounds with luxury hotels.

'Just a crazy thought! But I want to be honest that it will honour me very much to see you again, baby.' He does his Bambi trick and flashes slowly his eyelashes.

'I'm glad for your invitation. I'll thing about it.'

'I miss you, my little baby girl. You are so lovely in every way.'

'Oh, darling, I've spent many moments of memories about you. I have taken so much of your energy. I've drunken all your nectar so there is almost no more left of you. We are both drained of power. I sometimes feel that neither of us are the same.'

'Darling girl, I am so glad you love me so much. It is in every way reciprocated.'

'Yeah, our energy is totally eaten up in the struggle for my divorce. I'm also glad you let me drink from your nectar. It nourished my body, instead of me giving up.'

'Yeah, babe. God created you only for me. I am only yours. We are meant to be.' Again! "We got created and destined for each other". Even in the past, during Jesus' time in the desert. Reunite, he says all the time! Christ, he pushes me a lot.

'You are amazing. I'm thankful that I have put my life in your arms and hands. You are so much missed. My love will never stop for you. I trust you love only me.'

'We have been there in the ancient past. I'm waiting for you. My eternal MM.'

'When my divorce is a reality, we can start a life that suits us two.'

'I fully honour you, babe. Now we must reunite. I love you more today than yesterday and more tomorrow than today.'

'Likewise.'

'Think about it. Let me know ASAP. Bye my everlasting love. Mwah, huggee.'

'Maybe I'll visit you. Bye my darling. Mwah, mwah, huggee, huggee.' Shall I do it? I miss him, and it sounds so tempting. I rejoice in having him deeply incarnated in my soul and do not want to let him go again.

CHAPTER 28

ROLL OF FAT, AND HONEYMOON UNDER THE CHERRY BLOSSOM TREE

> The honeymoon phase always ends, for everyone.
> —Rose Leslie

I'm amazed at the courtesy of the Eastern people towards each other and towards Westerners. In Copenhagen, when excursion buses unload Japanese tourist at Langelinie Pier, an extensive park and promenade in central Copenhagen, they are humble and friendly as they greet you. The Little Mermaid statue has her home here, and in the park, there are at least two hundred cherry blossom trees (*sakura*, in Japanese). Despite its short lifetime, it depicts the patience of life and represents the brief life—a major theme of Buddhism, as it then became associated with religion and the aristocratic feudal Japanese warriors adopted it. It came to represent how the life of a warrior is and a symbol that a light breeze can cause flowers to fall off the crown of the tree—as a warrior also can easily fall in war, making them realise that although life is beautiful, it is also brief.

In King's Garden, in the heart of Copenhagen, they have planted many cherry blossoms trees, adorned with their pink flowers, and fifty different species of the tree at Assistens Cemetery, an important green space for the citizens and a burial site of many Danish notables. Many leading figures of the era of the nineteenth century lay to rest here, such as fairy-tale teller Hans Christian Andersen and history/philosophy writer Soren Kierkegaard, and both characters are used in my book. The Nobel Prize–winning physicist Niels Bohr and some American jazz musicians, such as Kenny Drew and Ben Webster, lie to rest in this amazing area. One of our prime attractions is Bispebjerg Cemetery, with a stunning avenue of Japanese pink trees forming a long, a pink tunnel. It's the most popular zone in the vast area and resembles more a park than a cemetery. People walk there every year in blossom season, a picturesque tradition that originally comes from Japan. Guests make it a day trip, looking at the pink trees and having their picnic under the stunning, massive trees. The tradition has its own name *hanami*, and you can enjoy it every spring, around mid-April until the beginning of May. So, there is also something great about Denmark, but to experience such a view in Japan, when I'm that close to such a fascinating country is one of my biggest dream. I imagine it will only take a short flight from Macau to Japan, so why not travel to Asia and explore my dream together with Drake?

I haven't seen him in several months by now, and I miss him so much. Oh, what shall I do? I consider about the trip for several days. 'Do it anyway,' says my heart. 'Don't do it,' my good friend Lucy tells me, but I don't listen to her advice and tell her, 'I'll soon be back again.' I surrender to my craving heart and buy a business ticket to Macau, so, this becomes my first trip to Asia.

As I sit and listen to calm lounge music while crazy *Drake ions* spin around in my head, with thoughts of the wonderful weeks in Spain and about my spiritual experience in Israel, my distress gets worse. I call him to tell him the splendid news.

'Hi darling. I have grand news for you.' I joyfully smile.

'My sweet, beloved darling. Oh, there she is.' And he flashes with his brown eyes.

'I hastily have purchased a flight ticket to Macau. I will love to cuddle in your gentle embrace again.'

'Oh, my precious love, you are so intense. It's so great to feel you and your soul again. It seems so good inside my soul. Finally, you come to visit me.'

'Thanks. I deeply look forward to being in your arms.' Oh, I can't wait for him to give me the most wonderful hug. To have his warm kisses with his lovely soft lips on my lips.

'I know I have felt this before. Once, many years ago. During our holy desert walk in the ancient past.' Hmmm! Clearly, he still imagines he is the Holy Spirit and believes he can save me. He nearly ruins my joy. What a show-off! That's weird.

'I want to snuggle in your lovely lips while you're holding me tight.' And I hope he will tell me how much he loves me.

'Yeah! Yeehaw! Then we can feel the warmth and love again. I look forward to seeing you again. To feel how strong our bond is.'

'Yep, I want to hug you to my heart.' I feel how rapid and solid my heart beats in a second over the joy to meet him again.

'I'm sure we'll get many beautiful weeks together. Sadly, they will run fast.'

'You are the one I need most. You are the most sacred to me.' I float in his eyes as I gently and lovingly glance at him.

'We must enjoy every second we have with each other. We must waste no moment.

It must be so that when you leave me again, you leave your soul with me. And I move into yours.' He has already moved into my soul and devilishly possessed me!

'You are the only one who matters to me.' Oh, my goodness, he does such wonderful things in me.

'I'm so pleased you will come to me.'

'You are my great joy. My hope. My eternal true bliss. I must come.' With him, I feel sanctuary, and an inner peace.

'You know it's your husband who left you alone in misery.'

'Yea. That's why you give me strength. Darling, you are my wisdom. My gentle angel.' Least, he gives me renewed power for my fresh path of life.'

'Even you say you love Flopper; you know you do it because you are jealous. It frustrates you. You feel cheated as he preferred a younger woman.'

'Yea! I am glad that you have patience.' I sense my renewed beauty is because he makes me beautiful and lovable.

'You do not, and did not, ever love him, babe. Flopper is an asshole to you. He only ill-uses you.' His voice changes to more serious and controlling.

'Darling, you are my guardian angel. My eternal life. You give me energy. It strengthens me. Thanks. I know Paul is shit.'

'Yet you stayed true to him through your painful hell. I feel for you, my darling.' I don't need him to feel pity for me, and I feel uncomfortable with his controlling speech.

'Together we can face the big test. I cannot breathe with Paul. My heart can no longer beat if I not have you with me.'

'Baby, you deserve so much better. I promise to take care of you. I will send you the confirmation of the invitation to Jakarta. I hope it will be a success. Use it to reassure your children.'

'Huh? If we help each other, we can have the happiness and joy we seek. Then live our life in love, in what we both seek in each other.'

'They will surely understand that their mother wants a safe future. That she needs an exciting and rewarding *metier*. With me as a mentor, when you complete the divorce.'

'I'm proud of you, that you will be my mentor.'

'We both need peace now. They can't interfere while you are here.'

'Who will interfere?'

'Your children. We will travel to Jakarta a week after your arrival in Macau. There, you will learn about the speciality, together with the others. I will send instructions on what to do before you are travelling.'

'Great, thanks. You are my love and mercy. You are the one I miss the most. Even while I sleep next to you. When we eat together, I miss you.'

'Tonight, the Chinese have invited me to a special Hennessy Cognac promotion dinner. Trust me, it's with my *actual* important friends.'

'Wow! What do you mean? Which new important? friends?'

'You are more than welcome. Please know. My friends own this peninsula. They and I will look well after you. Tonight, I will taste some of the world's most expensive bottles.' *Show-off!* 'I hope I won't get drunk.'

'Yep, better you don't get drunk.' Can I trust him?

'Chang Chen and the others are afterwards, as usual, continuing to a brothel.'

'Eh? What? Don't you dare to go on a brothel with them. In that case, we are so much done.'

'Argh, baby. Don't worry. I go home alone. I think only of you. You are the sexiest woman. The only one in my life. Love you wildly and deeply.' I remain nervous about the brothel part, and my stomach tells me I can't trust him. (I will get back to that.)

'Little girl, I must prepare a lecture now for the many professors coming in a few minutes. Bye. Love you passionately. Mwah!'

'Bye. Love you. Mwah.' I'm sitting left with the thought; if it was me, I have prepared my lecture a long time ago. Why has he not finished it? Such things don't take five minutes to prepare!

I'm thrilled about the fresh adventure and the next important step for my life, although I have no idea of what the future will bring. The stormy honeymoon phase begins, and a loving relationship with a narcissist typically develops in three stages: the *honeymoon phase*, the *devaluation phase*, and the *discard phase*. My relationship with Drake is in the gentle start of the enchanting honeymoon phase. If the reader doesn't know the meaning of the *Honeymoon phase*, then allow me to tell you what a narcissist is in this stage.

Be attentive of the **bold** words.

Honeymoon phase

> It all begins so well, and the relationship is on high peaks of **stormy infatuation,** with prominent emotions at stake.

The narcissist is a **terrific actor** and knows what it takes to get what he wants. He wants to get the **woman hooked** and make her **fall in love with him**, then **appear as the ideal partner** and is an **expert in courting, seducing,** and **enchanting** her. He reads her and gives her what *she wants and longs for*. He does not see it as a problem he repeats the same courting with several women, and he even calls them the **same nicknames.** He is **attentive, gallant, helpful, enterprising, charming.** The woman is well **pampered** and **adored,** while he gives her **gifts, flowers,** and invitations to exciting **experiences** and **travels.** He whispers to her he has never had such a powerful feeling for any other woman and tells her how much he loves her. **You are meant to be.** He paints the most **beautiful future dreams** for them, **seems empathetic** and **interested,** and immediately has **glorious plans** for them. For him, it cannot go fast enough. He will always be with her because he cannot concentrate, sleep, or eat when she is not there. She is **always receiving a multitude of messages, calls, wonderful small invitations, and love declarations.** It is no wonder that the woman falls in love with him and dreams of a future with him. (Susanne Møberg, *In Love with a Narcissist*).

Dear friends, I'm sure you caught the point?

Will I discover the many tricks at this stage? Oh… my… gosh, I'm so *overjoyed* with him! Who won't love to experience all these fantastic things he can enchant you with? That's why I fall steeply in love with Drake. **Stormy infatuation! Expert in courting! Experiences and travels! Enchanting! Observant, gallant, helpful, adores me, and is charming!** Yes! He certainly is using them all, and I wonder, if has read the book? Oh no, he can't, because the first edition was first published in 2017, where I discovered it many years after my first meeting with him. I wish I had known the book back then. Has he played such acts his entire life? It seems to be all about him being a talented actor. **Nicknames?** Those, there are many sweet ones: darling girl, precious love, little girl, baby girl, my love, MM, and many other cute names, but mostly, he uses babe and baby. And my pussy; he always calls *Minnie*. Have I fallen straight into a narcissistic, vilely-thought-out love trap?

Yet, I still don't know about the agenda and can't see through his amazing Oscar performance. And he is remarkable in writing love letters and sweeten me with oceans of loving words, including a well described diligent instruction on how to prepare myself before take-off to Macau.

> Darling baby girl,
>
> Exchange to Hong Kong dollars! The ferry costs $360! After arriving in Hong Kong, take the escalator. Perhaps you will need to board the train to the major terminal. Then look for Macau Ferries. Avoid the queue for Hong Kong and take Turbo Jet and buy a ticket in first class. Take off all luggage tags. They will put new ones on by the ferry company. You will then first see the suitcases in Macau. Go aboard the ferry to first class! It includes food and drink in the ticket. Send an SMS telling me which ferry you come with. Fill in the Macau landing card with the Ritz-Carlton as 'hotel'. Upon arrival in Macau, go to passport control, get it stamped, and hand over your landing card. Go to the right and pick up your suitcases and get a porter to help. Give him sixty Hong Kong dollars in gratuity. Then go towards the exit where you will first encounter a few customs officers. If they ask you something, fairly say you are on holiday and going to the casino. They love it, as Macau is a substantial casino city. Then go ahead. I will stand sweating and longing to give you the biggest hug you've ever had.
>
> Love you,
>
> Your forever Guardian angel Drake Lucifer.

A few days before my departure, it surprised me to receive an unexpected business proposal from Drake. This is the part I have not seen coming. What is he up to? I dig in to (in part) his letter

My beautiful baby darling,

As we have communicated, I want to say that I'm impressed by your decision to learn about my know-how. I will teach you in my speciality so you will become a great therapist in my new thesis. But becoming a good therapist requires a lot of knowledge about human anatomy. I can suggest you learn about circulatory disorders, and next about scar tissue and skin problems. There is a lot of money in it, and with that speciality, you can make an excellent practice. I invite you to the course in Indonesia, and I will send you information about where I have the course in Jakarta. You are more than welcome, and I have agreed and arranged with them you will take part. I'm certain this technology will hook you, so if you then decide you want to do this, you will again return to Macau with me. There I will also teach you at the clinic as my intern. The owners are such sweet people, and they work there, so I have checked up with them, and you are welcome, and they are looking forward to meeting you. I, as your mentor, will educate you to become independent so we may do future business together. But you must understand that I am a tough teacher, because I demand that my students do the subject before getting a diploma from me. We need an investment in time and money to reach your goal. Normally, students pay six thousand dollars for this two-week special education, because I'm the only one in the world who provides such teaching. No one else can provide such expert knowledge. For the equipment, you must count on around $56,000. I can offer you the complete equipment I have in Sweden, but we can talk about that...

What? One more investment? Well, this is unexpected! I have already given him $1,600 for the first payment of the equipment he has in Macau! First, he only wanted to borrow the money for the first payment, and then he promised me a partnership in my investment, if I pay every month; which I do in good faith because I'm madly in love with him. Now, he wants me to buy more, and besides; he also has the vast amount of $30,000 from my cash savings.

I know there will be many more equipment invoices landing on my desk, because he told me he owes roughly $70,000 for that machinery, but okay, he has promised to pay it all back. I continue to read (in part) his letter:

> You are a woman who appears to me to have explosive energy. With this, everything will be fine, and I welcome you into my new continent. It is so exciting out here...

I can easily imagine it's exciting for him, and what does he mean by *explosive energy*? Let's see what more there is in the melting pot, so I read the rest:

> I will make sure that you are well picked up at the airport. Then you will not be there as *Little Palle alone in the world*. My driver will wait with a sign bearing your name. I'm sure he'll be able to recognise the beautiful tall blonde woman among all the tiny Chinese. I will then nervously sweat and waiting eagerly for you. Remember to do your fitness regimen before you come so you will get some sexy arms, and you need somehow to lift your buttocks a bit. Not to mention that your belly should probably be a little more trained. You need to get rid of your little roll of fat at the top of the tummy. All I want to add now, which is very important: We are a team, and we belong together, so everyone else can just talk about us and be stupid all they want. It will *never* tear us apart. Spiritually, I felt you tonight so strongly, as if I were hugging you and telling you how much I love you and that you never have to doubt my devotion to you. Please dwell on that thought, and tomorrow, I will love you even more. When you come, you will see it in my eyes when I glance at you. My eyes do not lie. I wish you a pleasant trip. Love and kisses and power handholding, from your angel and I "Jesus" will protect you forever.
>
> Yours always, J.

But did his eyes lie? Did he lie massively? And who the fuck is *Palle*? A famous expression often used by Danes. (Jens Sigsgaard was a Danish writer and psychologist. He is best known for the classic children's book (Palle alone in the world) 'Palle alene i Verden' A little boy wakes up to find that he's alone in the world. A deserted, silent Copenhagen becomes his giant playground. He did what many children fantasies about. He stole a fire engine and drove it fast, drives a steamroller, and flies a rocket to the Moon. Adapting a famous novel, it is a Danish fantasy film for children by Astrid Henning-Jensen, 1949, one of the greatest directors of children, makes an all-time classic of charm and wonder. The film won an award for best short film at the Cannes Film Festival, 1949.)

Nervously sweat and waiting eagerly for you? Why a driver so suddenly? Braggart! Show-off! Christ! Some of his body comments make me explosive and offended, so I nearly lose the spirit to visit him. The *dragon* man doesn't even care about his own roll of fat, and to be honest, I am offended by his critique of my body. Roll of fat? Poor arms? And lift my buttocks? How dare he? Man, look at your own blubbery! I never complain about his blubber. Come on, dude. Cheeky! I train almost every day and tell my fitness trainer, 'It does not satisfy Drake with my flabby arms, fallen buttocks, and fatty belly.' Then she laughs, do the elevator glare at me, and laughs again.

'Ha-ha, fat? Oh, my gosh. No, no, Mary, it's not so.' But, what did I get out of it? Many more unaccustomed exercises! I conclude that the fact about women is that they must have sexy arms, big buttocks, and a firm six-pack. Clearly, it's a top priority for the man. Not to forget we must also have perfect cleavage, big breasts, and be thin like an eel. We must be clever, gosh, but not too clever. Oh... my... goodness. Otherwise, we will figure out men's devious cons. Women must continue being blondes and remaining foolish, so that might be why men like blondes. If you're not blonde by nature, get your hairdresser to colour your hair. The women's makeup must be perfect, preferably including hot-red lipstick. Women must wear sexy lace lingerie, miniskirts, and a blouse that lets the man see most of her cleavage and breasts. Best if you then spice the sexy dolled-up with stunning long red nails and lastly a pair of high-heeled black Prada shoes. She must stroll straight and aesthetically next to the man, head and nose pointing up to the sky, and make him proud. Don't speak, but preferable for the man if you spread your legs on command and fuck with him when he orders it. When you are thirty or forty, you are useless, worn-out, and he will dump you for a younger model. *Lucky woman!*

And the man, what does he do? Bar, pool, beer, drugs, and whiskey. Watching football on TV, while he constantly screams 'goal' or 'fucking judge' or 'off-side' while they root for their favourite team. Or playing, PlayStation, partying with his wild, washed-out dirty baboon friends, next fucking around with their beaver basher and complaining about their own women. When he gets bored, he watches porn all night long, and whacks off what he believes is Krull the warrior king, hanging between his dropping nuts. The beer makes them fatter and fatter until they look like fat men. Then *Big Daddy* captures another young woman with his great *fatness* of charm, showing off his wonderful baby-arm, holding two nuts ready to for her to crack them. He doesn't even bother to exercise, so he's somewhat floppy and obese. But I don't care about Drake is a little chunky; in my eyes, he's a handsome, gorgeous man, because I fell for his charm, not his massive fatness or his dropping nuts and baby-arm.

Though my wealth might captivate him more and not my sexy lace, my beauty, or slim body with a pair of big boobies, when I walked along with him on the street in my miniskirt, wearing my high-heeled black Prada shoes, while holding his tender hands. And I'm not even a real blondie, as I let my hairdresser fix the darkness to blondness. So, at the end of the day, who is more clever and fit? And not every man is as I described it.

The day arrives for my exciting journey, and it takes almost a day from Spain to Hong Kong. Next I must take the Turbo Jet ferry from Hong Kong to Macau, which takes furthermore one hour. Finally, the ship arrives at Macau Ferry terminal, and I'm exhausted and appearing awful, with my worn-out make-up on my way out of the luggage area. Surprisingly, Drake stands outside, with his head at a slightly skewed angle, smiling and gently blinking with his dazzling brown Bambi eyes.

I drop all my belongings on the floor and run straight into his open embrace and hold on tight to him. People stare flabbergasted at us while we tenderly kiss in a hot embrace. But I don't care; I see only him, so I gladly follow the *shadowy angel on the white rescue horse* to my next heavenly adventure.

CHAPTER 29

HE CONSUMED MY SOUL

> The present Catechism of the Catholic Church defines the **soul** as "the innermost aspect of humans, that which is of greatest value in them, that by which they are in God's image described as **'soul'** signifies the **spiritual** principle in man".
>
> —en.wikipedia.org

Dear Mary

I can understand that you are getting involved in something you should think carefully about. I must warn you that you are about to fall into the clutches of a true *psychopath*. Let me tell you what I've experienced in my relationship with a *psychopath*. How it fatally affected me. How hard it was for me to get through it. The same thing is going to happen to you. Be careful what you expose yourself to in your relationship with Drake Lucifer Bates.

One day, I wrote a short story to myself, as if I were writing a letter to my *psychopath*. Christian never received the letter about my innermost feelings and the nightmares I went through with him. Think about it, Mary, after you have read my letter. Maybe you should *not* go back to Drake. Hugs from your friend.

Amy

get a shock, after Amy had sent me the mail and after I had read the attachment to the end:

> Did my *psychopath* consume my soul? Was my prediction a warning to myself? It plagued my joy, warmth and faith in life, as if Christian was abusing my body and violently fucked around with me like he owned my body and soul. Did Christian vastly control me? I was of the sudden unsure if he invented fake stories about me, to give me bad conscience and guilt when other men, according to him, stared affectionate at me. But I loved them glaring at me and wanted to make Christian jealous. Deliberately, I wore my sexy red bra and thongs when I was going to visit my sexy physiotherapist. Damn, it was so calculating of me, only to seduce the charming man who was supposed to relieve my pain of tension. When I cried, my *psychopath* became awfully pissed at me, and grumbled that I didn't hug him enough. When I cried, Christian scornfully and victoriously laughed at me.
>
> Once I was out of my depth, he had total control over me. I felt I was *drowning* when he played between my life and death. I imagined; he threw a life buoy at me as I was dying over his cruel treatment. When I was about to grab it, he pulled it back without me having really reached it. My wet slippery hands lost hold of it and I sank almost to the bottom of the rough ocean. I cried and yelled he should save me. Fuck, Christian stood just at the pier and laughed, while he mockingly watched how I was dying I the rough waves.
>
> Christian had the ultimate power over me. It was as me playing Russian roulette. He played emotionally with my fragile life because I loved him dearly. He loved to torment me and watch me fall deeper to the bottom of the coarse sea.

He loved to see me dependent on him as I got weaker and weaker, until I stood on the edge to a suicide. For each day that passed, he took one more bite of my vulnerable kind soul. Made me insensitive. He emotionally paralyzed me, so I did not care about my own life. I only wished to die. Commit suicide! Slit my wrist. Eat dangerous pills or hang myself.

My heart desperately cried and screamed loud in my head, but my brain could not delete him from my memory. It could not remove his kiss from my lips or remove his tender fingers that have touched me while his fuck stick raped my body. The way he held me against my will, became a nightmare. The way he screamed at me with his scary high-pitched voice into my face and glared devilishly at me with his big, dark ice-cold eyes. He made me freak and scared and insecure. I threw up out of disgust after he touched me and over his massive abuse. I couldn't stand it any longer having his hands on my body. I couldn't breathe the air down to my collapsed lungs. I couldn't any longer look at Christian or glance into his empty brown shady evil eyes.

I screamed loud and I still scream, panicking inside my soul. I often cried. I still cry. In sheer frustration, I feel like throwing things around. I wanted to destroy something, to feel something gets shattered. Get the rage out of my body.

My *psychopath* had cruelly brainwashed and manipulated me. I became an empty soul with many big, deep open wounds that slowly became chilling ugly scars. I no longer dared to rely on other people, especially men. I didn't trust that anyone wished me anything good in life. *Did I deserve something good in life?* I often asked myself. Obviously *not*, since I allowed Christian to abuse me. I allowed him to misuse my body and my kind soul. I shared him with other girls as well. Every time I forgave him. I had allowed him that I believed in all his lies and manipulation.

I was a character in Christian's creepy movie. A surrealistic awful horror movie. I did not understand this. In fact, I still don't understand any of what Christian did to me.

Amy

CHAPTER 30

Who is that Handsome Bastard?

> I'm not a psychopath, I'm a high functioning sociopath.
> —Steven Moffat, A Study in Pink

When I first meet Doctor Drake, Lucifer Bates, he is in his sixties, and for his age, he is a good-looking man, resembling Michael Douglas in his sixties—the ultimate classic leading man of Old Hollywood. With Drake's rasping voice, he reminds me mostly of Clint Eastwood, and Drake often tells me; I'm often told by others that I resemble Sean Connery. But mostly in their mid-age. Drake was born and grew up in Sweden. He has a hilarious personality on the outside and is a fascinating man for many women and men, including me, with his ability to capture an audience.

He tells me and others proudly, 'I am a well-educated and knowledgeable doctor.' Fine, and a well-educated man, with fantastic knowledge, I muse as he continues, 'yea, it's comparable to occupational therapy.'

'What is that?' I ask.

'You see, I completed my certification in the United States. It's as physical therapy. Resembling an osteopath. Or a chiropractor. Though more advanced. It's focused on injuries and rehabilitation of lover back, neck and shoulder problems.' He proudly smirks.

As a child, his mother Gretchen and his father Johann frequently spoiled Drake, and Gretchen gave into the many commanding wishes and dreams of this spoiled brat. Though, she adored this little lad more than she loved Johann, so Drake formed some compelling love bonds with her. People perceived Gretchen as big-headed because she had an *arrogant posture*. Drake adored both his parents, but most of all, Gretchen was of great importance for him, so they had a flawless sensitive and tender relationship. When he got upset, he often searched for comfort from Gretchen by sleeping in her bed late into his childhood years.

In elementary school, the other kids often bullied Drake about being a tiny chubby boy and a bragging smart-ass. One day, he got more than enough of the whoppers and beaten up Michael, the leader of the boy pack, to a pulp. Drake had at that point learned few amazing boxing skills, which he got very good at.

'In my younger days, a boxer taught me to beat first and hard. When the other is down to counting then you must knock him one more on his stupid head. When he gets up several times again, what do you do? Give Michael a chance to swing his arms a little in the air before bobbing him one more hook or another uppercut? No, I immediately gave the stupid asshole another hook. That's how I survived those mean boys,' he says. The rough fight happened in a small backyard near Drake's residence between the mean boy pack, mostly between Michael and Drake. Finally, it ended up with Drake winning the match, so he earned the respect of the other foul boys in town and at school, so no one dared to fight him.

'No one could box as well as I could. I can easily break anyone's neck with my skills I have today. I know a way no others can find out about. That's how they die with a broken neck,' he claims, and back then he didn't hold back for a fight if it was needed. It scares me when he talks about breaking a neck, and I freak out thinking about what he might do to my neck.

Moving forward with his skills as a teen, he had the peace to take care of himself and his schooling. Drake did remarkably well in school and was a diligent student. Everyone called him the teacher's little sleazeball of a pet because of his immense diligence and smirky charm. In class, he always asked too many questions to the great annoyance of all the other kids. In the schoolyard, he was a loner and avoided the other kids. Every day, he walked alone home from school without fear of the bad-boy pack in the area. The brave little lad did his daily homework and grocery job after school and became every mother's dream. As an inexperienced teenager, he worked in a small grocery store, his parents owned, in a mid-sized town outside Stockholm.

'Daily I had to carry heavy wooden beer crates comprising of eighteen bottles. Also, heavy wooden soda crates, comprising of twenty-four bottles up to people's apartments. Geez, often it was up to the fourth or six floors. Stomping up on narrow tiny steep stairways in a building with no elevator.' He proudly tells of his childhood.

What a darn good and strong little guy he became, 'ha-ha, then I got some tips. Two or four pence. I saved them for my education.'

After primary school, he started high school and had a very hard time adjusting to the other students and teachers. He lied and bragged too much and controlled many other students. After the second year and several conflicts, he travelled to America, the land of opportunities, to study further. As an exchange student, he lived with a local family, with completely different norms and rules, which he was not used to. This resulted in many conflicts and problems at school and with the strict family. Yep, it failed. Shortly after, Drake came back to his birthplace, as a sorrowful and troubled person, who had changed slightly, and had difficulties adapting to other people. He moved home to his parents' again and felt blissful when he got reunited with Gretchen and Johann. They let him start at another high school and got him placed in a special class, only with boys. The boys tested each other for absurdity and explored their sexuality and manhood by performing weird sexual activities with each other. That became a problem for Drake, because he came from a respectable family, so he couldn't let the secrets of his heated sexual relationship with Scottie get out in the air. Therefore, Drake could never jump out of the closet and pretended he was madly in love with his first female relationship. However, the scorned devastated Scottie threatened Drake to gossip about them to the other boy's which would become a nightmare for Drake. So, in secret Drake continued to put his little heat-seeking moisture missile into Scottie's narrow heinie, as well he also screwed Sofia, without using a condom. Yuck!

After high school, he became a student of prime grades, continuing to college with a wonderful future ahead. He hoped to become a dentist or a physician, or to become a surgeon. His parents were proud of their only child and praised him for his wisdom and his vast IQ, which was well above normal, so Drake studied medical means. Before completing his medical education, he wanted to study alternative medicine and travelled to London in the United Kingdom. Beforehand, he met his first genuine love, Maria, who also wanted to study medical means. Drake's parents told them to get married before they moved abroad, so at a young age, Drake and Maria made the holy bond to each other. The romance was immense between them, and he played his role well, pretending to have a real deep love affair with her. Together, they moved to the southern part of this vast British Island, between the Northern Atlantic and the North Sea.

They have found a one-bedroom student apartment close by the school and spend (looking from the outside) a romantic time together. Maria got spellbound by Drake, but he had no time for her while he diligently was studying and had only his books in mind. As months went by, it turned out that Maria finds out his secret when she discovered he was more interested in a British handsome fella at the school, than in her. Drake headstrong lied about the affair with James and called James a lying stupid queer. It also annoyed Maria that Drake constantly wanted to know about her first boyfriend Peter and about their sexuality; of how good *Peter* was in the sack. And if Peter had a bigger danger noodle than Drake's. And so, it goes on. Well, imagine how that goes in Drake's head (the same way he constantly asks me the same questions about Paul). Maria never gets sexually satisfied by Drake and she was not allowed to touch him on his one-eyed wonder weasel, so she searched for some other options who didn't possess a baby-arm in his trousers. Maris had a heated love affair with Big Jack, another handsome dark-haired straight man from the school, a gigantic rugby player, and then she divorced choppy Drake and ran off with big Jack. Drake was vastly jealous and showed off with other women in front of Maria, as he keeps on chasing her and pretended the brake-up had shattered him with a broken heart. Disappointed and furious by being neglected by a woman, his broken soul made him lose all confidence in every woman. He was so upset and decided no other woman should ever do this to him again. After the painful breakup with his precious wife, he couldn't reconnect in any normal, proper love affair with any other female again. His agonising life made him into a hunting womaniser instead, and he emotionally abused every woman that came into his life. Left and right, he bangs around with any female who falls into his "lady-killer" trap. With no empathy, he became a callous predator who brusquely always dumped his prey in the worst gutter of shit. The women's grief, tears, and pleading did not help them, because as Drake said it, 'I don't give a damn.' Because he preferred a firm hunk of a man most of all. But in the sixties and seventies, he couldn't jump out of the closet, so instead, he went to the next women. He was only using them for his own benefit to get sex or show off that he could catch any female primate he wanted to have. Drake was and still is, a stunningly good-looking man, with full, sharply drawn cherry-red lips, as a prima donna. A beautiful feminine face, dark curly rich hair, and smashing brown Bambi eyes, resembling James Dean or Paul Newman in their younger days.

At school, Drake got into many problems with students and teachers, so he never completed the medical or alternative medicine exam in the United Kingdom, because he was dispelled. He got himself transferred to a school in the United States instead and lived with another US family, one that helped many exchange students. Many problems arose there too, because he tumble-down the couple's marriage entirely, by flirting with the wife Susan and having wild sex with the husband William. While Drake was studying diligently, he found his mentor in one of the world's leading person, Doctor Miles Horeb in Illinois. Drake completed his exam and quickly established himself as a recognised certified doctor of complementary and alternative medicine, after he had been in rotation as an intern with his mentor, Doctor Miles Horeb. Drake got quickly in trouble at the vast clinic and fled back to Sweden.

Doctor Miles Horeb had built the largest facility in the world, with a clinic of over twenty thousand square feet, comprising a vast waiting room to seat more than a hundred patients. Ten treatment rooms, X-ray facilities, a lab, and a lower level to hold seminars, so the place became the most renowned facility in the world. Next to the mentor's new clinic, he builds an almost eighty-room full-service motel to accommodate the clinic's numerous long-distance patients. Doctor Miles Horeb and his fellow staff members attended over three hundred patients daily, as many patients were seeking for help from the dedicated doctor, whom worked from eight in the morning, often until midnight, six days a week. His massive dedication made him often to work every Sunday afternoon, so he could help everyone. Doctor Miles Horeb developed his own seminars and taught the philosophy of his famous treatment procedures.

Quickly Drake learned all the skills and got the desire to be the *world's most famous*, surpassing his mentor. However, I'm only a child and don't know this so-called world's famous (Dragon) man, as he called himself "most famous" in Sweden. He started his first clinic in a small facility on the fourth floor in his apartment, in the outskirt of Stockholm, where patients used the narrow steep staircase as a waiting room. As Drake's dream expanded and he grew (in his own opinion) more famous than Doctor Miles Horeb, Drake quickly got established and earned a great reputation among the Scandinavian patients who were seeking his help. The business exploded, and the narrow steep staircase as a waiting room was no longer a satisfactory solution for the patients or for him. As a diligent person, he had from the first day saved money for a new and larger clinic. His new-fangled idea of his enhancement got born when they on the drawing board, illustrated in the first architectural drawings for the innovative clinic, and his dream was about to come true, as the massive building project began. Again, he wanted to surpass his mentor Doctor Miles Horeb, in the clinic size Drake wanted to build, so three years later, he opens the world's largest and most grandiose clinic, nearly thirty thousand square feet, outside

Stockholm. It was an exact copy and exceeded the clinic size of Doctor Miles Horeb's clinic. ('A copycat is like a poor amateur. Just another rip-off'—Knisztina.) Drake's clinic comprised a gigantic waiting space for four times more patients as his mentor's clinic. About twenty treatment rooms, X-ray, four laboratories, a larger conference room for lectures, and an Olympic-size swimming pool, and a massive rehabilitation centre. Shortly after he had over three thousand patients in his protocol, who came from Europe and Scandinavia, equalling many more patients than his mentor. He had many employees and over four hundred patients daily. (When I met Drake, he claimed he alone had treated over forty-five thousand patients.) In connection to the clinic he had built a hotel, with fifteen double rooms, which could accommodate the clinic's many long-distance patients. His French restaurant served daily healthy dishes, such as vegetable and fruit beverages, to patients and staff. This was very unusual for the seventies. Drake worked every day from early morning to midnight and every Sunday from morning to late afternoon. There was no doubt it was an exact copy of Doctor Miles Horeb's clinic in the United States. 'Be authentic, not a copycat.' Debasish Mridha, quote.

In Drake's younger days he had a severe temper, and he detested incompetence, and felt under enormous time pressure throughout his clinical career and learned to not accept waste of time and caused some of his lack of patience with small talk and his staff. He did not fancy to pay for nonsense and non-performance by his staff and got angry when they tried to cheat him, according to his philosophy, they did. Often, the staff did not get paid their salary, especially not their holiday allowance, so they saw him as a ticking bomb, untrustworthy, and lying, when they asked for their money.

His parents were an important part of the vast company, and Johann was a skilled craftsman who took care of all the practical tasks inside and outside the buildings. Gretchen was a skilled nurse and got hired in the rehabilitation centre as the firm boss, presiding over many other employees in her strict department. In alliance with Drake, they got many patients to function physically again, and he had significant success. The family was together under one roof, and everything seemed joyfully, as they had created the golden egg, and Drake became filthy rich and a trusted man, until four years later, when it went in the wrong and destructing direction.

Beforehand the clinic was built, he met Laila and settles with her in a country house outside Stockholm. One night he needs to lift his burden about Laila and their life as he scornfully tells me, 'I only got married to Laila out of decency.'

'Oh, what do you mean?' I curiously question.

'I felt obliged to do it. Darn, I didn't want to get married. I felt pity for her.'

'Why then marry?'

'They pressured me to continue. Before I went to the church, I realised my whopping mistake.' While he gazes at me sadly, telling me his tragic moment. 'Babe, can you imagine me eyeing at myself in the mirror while I'm dressing up?'

'Hmmm, no, I can't.'

'I had the massive urge to escape. Shit, yea to run from the impending marriage.'

'Why so? Was she not your love of life?'

'The compassion we had, yes. But we never understood each other. Therefore, we never achieved synergy.'

'How come?'

'From the very beginning we started out on the wrong foot. Damn, it ended up doing what I have always told everyone else *not* to do. *Not* to marry because of a child.'

'Eh? A child? Was she pregnant?'

'By missing harmony and deep love, we doomed our relationship to failure.' He mentions and I have a hard time fantasising that a man will elope from his wedding. His elegant wedding suit made him appear as a handsome, slim bridegroom, with a well-trained body and tanned skin. His strong dark curly gleaming hair and his amazing brown eyes glanced gently and invitingly, as the gaze of a deer, when he showed me his wedding picture. I bet; many women must have thought this handsome bachelor was a dream of a hunky man. But was he gay or not?

'I must do it out of respectful manners. We are expecting our first child.' I pondered that day. 'Baby, it was awful for pity me.' By taking the step into this small wooden white Swedish Village church, he chose not to step away from the woman he didn't even love.

Perhaps it was all about practicality for Drake.

Laila appears as a stunningly tall, slim Swedish woman in her twenties and walks up the aisle in her fine white wedding dress wearing a France designer lace veil over her pretty head. She resembles Agnetha Fältskog a Swedish singer, songwriter, musician and actress, who reached international stardom as a member of the pop group ABBA, from the seventies. Laila's long light-blonde hair was set beautifully for the day's event, and her gentle bridal make-up shone on her smiling face. No one knew what the actual reason for this wedding was, because it didn't show she was pregnant. Everyone believed it was about love, because she loved Drake deeply. Leila's father, Gustav was a typical tall, dark-haired Swede, whom walked her up to the aisle and gave her away with a gentle fatherly kiss on her cheek, before Drake took Laila's hand. The young blonde, beautiful flight attendant and the dark-haired man proceeded with the exciting matrimonial ceremony, yet his lips vibrated nervously while his nostrils open and closed in fast, anxious moves, as a fuming bull. He glanced at her, then dreamt eagerly of becoming the runaway groom, as he wanted to leave her alone and devastated in her fine wedding dress, crying out her tears. *But I must stay*, he muses, irritated, and tormented himself to say yes to this marriage. Is this love by the altar where the priest was uniting two people who didn't wanted to be in holy marriage?

In time, it proved to be an awful, unhappy, and fatal decision for both. She became one of the many victims of his merciless behaviours, as the snake in the grass offered her the poison apple, so she slowly would die in sorrow. As a cold-blooded lizard, he couldn't even get it into his obnoxious head to leave her in decency and give her the chance to be happy with another decent man instead. Is he, therefore, a selfish fool who dared not to say, 'Laila, I don't want to marry you?' As a talented actor, he played the flawless Oscar role of the sudden victim perfectly, by telling me, 'They forced me to marry her.' Shall I feel sorry for him? Is it's all a gigantic lie, what he told me? Over the years, Laila became deeply unhappy and lonely in the miserable marriage. They got two children and many years later Drake's son Ricardo told him, 'You are the worst father I have had in my life. I was always afraid of you. Even Rosalyn (Ricardo's sister) is afraid of you.' The proof that Ricardo may have been right came as a blasting bomb when Drake saw on Facebook the happy pictures of the family in the USA, celebrating Rosalyn's marriage, without having told Drake about that joyous occasion.

'They would only leave a person who they completely disliked out of such an enormous event. That was me.' Drake weeps in sorrow. 'It deeply hurt me. For a long time, I had thought of the moment I would walk Rosalyn up the isle to give her to Berry.'

'I'm sorry to hear, darling' as I take his hand in mine to comfort him.

'Ricardo describes me as an angry person. That I'm unstable. That I resemble a ticking bomb that could go off at any time. He describes me as being irritable. That I would get angry at anyone who would oppose me. Worst he says; *I am a sick sociopath!*' He angers, and that subject I will get back to later.

Drake cheated on Laila countless times, with his secretaries, women around the world, and his many female patients. The aware reader perhaps remembers his sentence: '*Trust me.* Given the many years I've treated women, I've seen a little of everything. Nicely shaped breasts. Ha-ha, and hanging breasts. Bare butts. Ha-ha, yea even full naked bodies.' I wonder why he had seen that.

Times were slightly different in the seventies and eighties, so why marry when you don't think it's the right thing to do? Both parties ruin something in their life, and Drake had ever since regretted the matrimony, though, he was selfish and wouldn't have anyone considering him as depraved if he said *no* to Laila.

'I believe it would have created a lot of trouble.' He complains in self-defence. 'Man, all the guests had arrived at this idyllic, beautiful Swedish church. Everyone sat and watched me while I was waiting for my second bride to arrive.' After the ceremony, they had gathered guests from near and far for the grand party at a romantic boutique inn. A romantic part close to a lovely lake a little outside the vibrant city of Stockholm. I have visited the region with Drake once on vacation without me knowing that this was the hotel, he once had his wedding night and party. He proudly brags with a radiant smile on his face, 'Baby, this is the same suite I had my first wedding night with Laila.'

'Oh, my goodness.' I am flabbergasted, but it doesn't bother me so much. I remain unbiased and want only the best out of the stay with him.

'Baby, can you imagine how angry she was at me that night?'

'No, I can't. Why?'

'She was in madness on our wedding night by hitting me crazily with a pillow.'

Immediately I picture Pauls and my wild wedding night, as we had fun with a crazy pillow fight, chasing each other in the vast suite, before we ended up in the sack having the greatest sex ever. It was awesome.

'Huh? What? No ... come on! Such a night is important.'

'She was mad at me for having danced once or twice with her girlfriend after the dinner that evening.'

'Come on, Drake. You don't get mad because you dance with another woman.'

'Christ, there were feathers all over the room.' As there was in Paul's and my wedding suite. We destroyed several down pillows.

'Did you bang her so much with your pecker?'

'Fuck no! We did not make love that night.'

'Oh, well, I do not understand it.'

'She never understood me either. Ha-ha, or maybe also she just feared me. Ha-ha, as with the kids.' He sarcastically laughs.

'Wow. Sounds serious. Why did she do so?' I'm dumbfounded over his story.

'She claimed I was flirting with one of her girlfriends.'

'Ha-ha. Did you?'

'No, no. Of course, it was all in her cracked imagination. Over the years we kept on failing to connect in the marriage. Bloody hell! All I felt I could do was to leave her and the children.'

'Where did you go?'

'I wonder if she was afraid of me. Perhaps I caused psychological harm to her. Perhaps it's therefore we never could resolve our problems?' He scornfully smirks. I'm sure they have changed the beds and pillows since that time, he-he. Giggles. But in this instant moment, Drake is all I sense, and I'm madly in love with him, so instead, I enjoy the romantic spot with him, with its breathtaking and dreamy, idyllic scenery. The story of the gorgeous natural surroundings of the romantic boutique inn goes back hundreds of years, when couples were in love and were visiting this amazing spot. Many pairs chose, therefore, to use this location for one of their most important events in life, having their wedding dinner and night at this specific hotel. Drake and Laila had made the same choice, and the bride's family had arranged the entire wedding at this idyllically located setting, close by Royal Haga Park, only a short walk to the city centre. The hotel and its classic restaurant serve traditional Swedish cuisine in these historic surroundings, with a view of the Brunnsviken Lake's calm, shiny water, while I continue to listen to his life story.

For a few years, he had success with his clinic in Sweden, until he was accused of being an impostor of a doctor and of damaging several patients. He also flirted with younger female patients or had affairs with his staff, mostly secretaries. The great clinic time was over, and the golden goose was more than dead. To avoid any court case between him and the health authorities, he fled to an exotic island in the Caribbean and did dubious building business with the government.

'Baby, I told the buyer of a shipment of constructing materials that it was lost during a tropical storm on its way to the Island. All building materials were on the bottom of the sea. I wanted them to pay again for a new shipment.'

'Wow, that sounds tragic. Did you not have any insurance?'

'Shit, no. Rapidly the government expelled me as an imposter. It was not even my fault. They tricked me.'

'Darling, that's horrible. Who tricked you? Where did you go?'

'The government. Next, we immigrated to the United States.' During his time over the next twenty-five years, he worked with many strange business concepts instead of his actual doctor profession.

'Bloody hell!' He shouts snappily. 'Suddenly, banks, IRS and people sue me for fraud. What the heck is that about?' he angers more. 'Shit I lost my entire fortune.'

'Wow, what happened?'

'I have not the farthest idea. I got swindled by several people.'

'Huh? Wow! How so? Oh, my God, what then? Did you move from US?'

'No, no, but for a while I worked illegal in US. Damn, I had lost my Green Card.' He seems very convincing and I believe the entire story. 'At one point a Swedish guy must have prompted an action to defence himself in a strange sort of way.'

'How? I do not understand.'

'He prompted an investigator to search for me.'

'Wow! Why? Did the police search for you?'

'It was to claim fraud against me. Fucking hell! This private investigator has lately sent me an e-mail with a copy to Ricardo.'

'Huh? What? Awful. No, that can't be true. Can it?' I'm shocked.

'Those halfwits wanted me to surrender to the police. What? I am darned. Claiming that I had committed fraud. If I did not surrender at once they would consider me as a fugitive. Bloody hell, *a fugitive???*' he shouts. 'Can you imagine me with a warrant for my arrest hanging over my head everywhere in the world?'

'Darling, I'm utterly speechless.' Though I realise that suddenly it's the California inquisition that seems to be very fishy, according to Drake's opinion, yet he is anxious about such a warrant.

'Baby, I acted in good faith. I have defrauded none in USA. I struggled with my own demons. Anyhow, I moved from the United States.' Yea, by leaving behind his kids and his wife, shattered and poor. And now he has achieved to do his damage control straight to my face, to minimize his reputation and credibility caused by his scandalous revelation.

'Ricardo once wrote in his way that I was financially irresponsible. The fact is that I had made lots of money. I also had the misfortune to lose it again. I always tried my best. Sometimes I failed in what I did. Jesus Christ, yea, despite all valiant efforts. I became more and more frustrated. I lost my good luck. Christ, I had a hard time dealing with that. I needed help. But there was no help to get from Laila. Or anywhere.' He complains, pitiful

'Oh, darling, I feel so sorry for you.'

'We had no future together. I wanted to move on. Unfortunately, I had no money to offer Laila. All I have made since I moved back to Europe has gone into the deep black hole of the house. Yea, to support her life the best I could.'

'Well, you did brave, darling.' I praise him, not thinking about the inconsistency there is in his many stories.

'Yea, I think so. I was trying to start a fresh life from scratch. Therefore, I cannot pay any alimony to her. I wanted to sell the house. The problem was that she never had time to clean it. She never kept it show-ready. So, we could not have potential buyers come to see it. I wonder if she remembers the constant room full of her boxes.'

'What? Boxes?'

'Jeez, it was awful. Her general state of untidiness I felt the house was a problem.

All the hope for a life in the USA for me disappeared. With all the stabs I had gotten in that country over the years. It was foolish for me to think anything would change for the better.'

'Oh, so that's why you moved to Spain?'

'Yea, I got divorced from Laila. I had some short love affairs afterwards. I saved another woman from violent abuse,' he proudly brags as were he the hero of the year.

'Oh!'

'Babe, I've invented and patented some golf clubs. Also, an honest communication platform. You know? Internet.'

'Wow. Interesting. What do you mean about honest?'

'Yea, I want to start up the business again, Let's invest in it. We can make a fortune selling it in Macau and China. The engineers and the

Swedish investor ended up stealing everything from my company that I had created,' he peep sorrowful.

'What? That sounds bad.'

'Yea, they left me dead in their tracks with *nothing*. So those slimeballs could move on with their own plans. I was a *victim* of a venture that failed.' Oh, my, he appears so convincing, that I fall for his trick.

'Why? What happened?'

'Merely because of external greed. Not of managerial incompetence. Human ugliness. But they never got all my secrets and the patent,' he proudly smirks. Though, I discover it's not his golf patent, but it belongs to another famous golfer in the US. Why did he lie? But I don't want to question him. I get the feeling that when Drake fails, and the business goes bankrupt, everybody loses all their money. Does he never lose? It seems to he gets rich and gets out of all his devastating debts on other people's behalf.

'Everyone wanted to have what I had. The people around the world are difficult to deal with. I did not know how crooks worked,' he smirks. 'In the USA and in England I have met lots of them during my learning process. You see, baby, it's not my fault I failed.'

'No, it seems to they have scammed you vastly. Terrible, darling,' I pity him as I jump right into his trap.

In psychological terms, such people are what you can call a dangerous, narcissistic sociopath with no means. The amazing way of playing such acts, as a charming and understandable person, is the way of their living.

Drake came to Spain few years before I met him, and as you know by now, that's where I meet him for the first time. That year I met him is where he also runs from Spain, with a stupid, lame excuse: 'I'm needed elsewhere with my vast knowledge. My brain is worth millions.' But he needs a woman, and most likely a woman with money, because maybe he is broke. Short and simple! So, is it therefor he is seducing me with his many love letters and sweet honey word? With his amazing way of being. will I sincerely get into business with him? Has he trapped me because he has borrowed money from me? Perhaps I allowed myself to let him catch me in his massive spin of influence, then in time I might have to pay the price for my ignorance. And that's where I am now, with my lovely prince in the shiny armour on the shady white rescue horse.

Studies have shown 3 percent of males are such psychopaths, whereas only 1 percent of women are like that. This means women are truly the victims of such men.

Below is information from research and conversations with other victims. I have protected all names, but the author known the victims.

> He is crazy in his fucked-up mind and should be locked up and no longer be able to have patients. I have no doubt at all anymore. He is out of reach and a man who thinks he is the navel of the world. He is loaded with lies and has no conscience. He has psychologically abused and manipulated me. I was grossly sexually harassed by him, and he has behaved insanely and appropriately to me many times. From the start, I was upset at his gross behaviour. I'm terribly traumatised by that idiot and had to go to a psychologist. She was deeply shaken! He acts like he is Jesus. He fumbles blindly with his treatments, creates false stories, and has a generally nasty way of being. He commented aggressively on my body and sent inappropriate glances at me. He looked at my big breast all the times. 'Are yours of nature?' he eagerly asked. He kept saying, 'Such a beautiful woman like you deserves to be well, and I must help you' and 'You must be very sought after and every man's dream'. He was hardcore in his flirting from the beginning and thought I was hot. He said, 'You are something very special, and as beautiful as you are, we must get such a lovely girl like you well. You deserve it.'

* * *

I thought he was weird and very sneaky.

* * *

You might as well not try to understand such a nasty guy. He was sickly bragging a lot of his knowledge and equipment. Such a manipulative, lying moron.

* * *

They are crazy at that clinic, most of all him. I wish they banned him from treating people. He also believed that he was the only one who could treat a royal family member as they should have the best treatment in the world. He thought he was the best. His sense of reality is otherworldly. Megalomania! He's a nasty old man with a dark filthy soul.

* * *

CHAPTER 31

REFLECTIONS FROM KATE

>He is not to be trusted as a friend who illtreats his own family.
>
>—Aesop

I'm exhausted, tired to the deepest of my bones and sick of so much bullshit in my life. While staring at my moving boxes, I open one of them and find one more picture of Drake. I still have a lot of feelings for him, and I can't let go of him, even our relationship is confusingly. Then he is there and then he is not. Massively, I miss him, but I know I must get my broken pieces together and I believe he is still the only one.

He looks cool in the picture, with his hands folded and raised behind his neck, and then his amazing gorgeous smile and shiny eyes. He appears so happy, and I understand nothing about my present unhappy situation, from the time when he helped to get me out of my troubles, six years ago. When I moved to UK in 2016, Drake gets a new-fangled idea.

'Let's set up a fresh company and a clinic in United Kingdom. Then we can start a renewed life,' he suggested.

'I don't know if I want too.' Because he has cut my heart into two shattered pieces, with pain and misery. Instead, I did plenty of research on him to get my puzzle into one united picture, so I spoke with other women from his past.

During that upcoming winter, I went on a well-deserved vacation to Spain again, and randomly I briefly meet Kate on the street for the first time after our catastrophic meetings at the clinic in 2010. I friendly greet her and unreservedly, yea, humbled and embarrassed, I have the guts to apologise to her.

'Hi, Kate, it's so nice to see you.'

'Nice to meet you too, Mary.' She glares surprised at me.

'I owe you a sincere apology.' Is the first thing I say.

'Thank you for your apology. It's accepted.' She looks great, with long dark hair and is now athletic and slim.

'Do you have time for a coffee?' and we sat at the local café downtown. 'I have many questions.'

'So do I.' She smirks

'Yea, I can imagine. Among one of them is Stockholm.'

'Oh, ha-ha, the jerk never went there.' She laughs.

'He said he did. When you were in Copenhagen with him.' I'm frustrated. Yet I had the feeling he never went there.

'Jeez, more lies on the list of his many magnificent lies.' That's her reflections of his betrayal.

'Ha-ha. Trusting a man is the most dangerous thing one can do. I need some answers concerning his behaviour. Also, some closure between you and me.'

'I broke up with him when I realised what he was doing to you. I did not understand how roughly he could exploit others.' She wrinkles her nose.

'I'm sorry. I didn't know about you and Drake.'

'I had my suspicion that the doofus was seeking you.'

'I'm so sorry for interrupting your relationship. He told me later about you and him.'

'Mary, the dummy is a sociopath. A dangerous acquaintance. Dump him.'

'What do you mean about he is a dangerous person? Well, I have noticed he likes to swirl with grandiose greatness and madness. As he believes he is the most important person in the centre of the universe.'

'I met a resident who told me I should be glad to be free from him. He knew him. He told me that dunce is a psychopath.'

'Well, then you are lucky to get rid of him.' I ironically smirk.

'What a sucker he is. And have been! Hopefully, you get your self-esteem back. I know it can take a long time,' she nervously says and seems genuinely content with our meeting.

'My friend Lucy in Spain told me you were angry at me. I must clean the air with you. If I have the guts.' The waiter comes to our table and we order breakfast, coffee and water.

'At first, I was mad. Later grateful. It has truly upset me he broke doctor-patient ethics by hitting on you with his mad flirtations.'

'I understand your angriness. I believe it's good for both of us to get our self-esteem and understanding cleared. What do you think?' I ask, while she listens carefully.

'He knew it was a time when you weren't strong mentally. I hope you are better by now?'

'Yea, I'm okay. Though, I have gone through several dangerous paths over many years. Alas, I was on the verge of suicide. You're right in your remark.'

'I know about your misery. He broke the patient confidentiality.'

'How?' Have I not listened to my gut feelings and ignored the red flags?

'He told me all about your life. Again, as you see, he broke patient confidentiality.'

'Huh? What? Oh, my goodness! He promised not to tell. I'm shocked.' It's appallingly, when I hear Kate's words, he must have forgotten his promise by breaking the confidentiality between doctor and patient! That hurts deeply, and it breaks my heart!

'I'm sorry you became the victim of his sick manipulation.'

'I trust it's good for both of us to talk about what he did to us. I'm reaching out for your understanding. And forgiveness.' And the waiter plants the coffee on our table.

'It was gross, with his tenderness to your feet. It was too much for me. I think he expressed it, "They are tiny and sweet, like mine."

Come on. Doh! You were his patient! Gross! I knew it was a vulgar exploitation of you. Yuck!'

'Yea, his "sweet little foot" comment was indeed inappropriate. Strange.' I'm glad she remembers the foot fetish part. Breakfast arrives, and we pause the conversation, smear our bread with butter and strawberry jam and slurp the coffee

'He told me you were no longer welcome in the clinic. Is that correct?'

'Yes, it's true. What the heck? The half-wit banned me!' She angers and continues. 'But only when he treated *you*. He told me it was *you* who banished me from the sessions.'

'What?' I glare dumbfounded at her.

'Yea, that you hated me. I became so mad at him. It helped me to throw him out.'

'When you stopped, all the flirting began hardcore. I don't like it when people abuse my weakness. First, they play good cop. Then they trick you,' I slurp my coffee, and gnaw some of the toasted bread.

'You were the perfect victim of his sickly urge for dominance.'

'He raped me few days after both of you came back from Denmark.'

'WHAT???'

'Yea, then he claimed it was because I wanted it myself. I've a hard time to believe that. But I forgave him, because we had our first bang the day you went to Denmark.'

'Fuck, that's why he was in such a hurry to get back from the airport. Christ, Mary, you fitted perfectly into his alternative plans.'

'Wow! Perhaps you are right.'

'He needed your money. Also, for you to fall in love with him. Get rid of him!'

'Do you think I was an easy victim to him?' I glare shamefully at her.

'Yes! He was desperate to get you to divorce your husband. He Googled both of you. He found out you were among the high society.'

'Eh? I don't get it. Why?' I'm shocked.

'He knew you would get a lot of money from the divorce. He didn't get money out of me.' Kate seems offended of his cruel way of behaviour.

'Perhaps I adored him too quickly?'

'I can recognise the part of *adoring* him. I got wildly impressed with his talent as a doctor. That's what I fell for.' She says. The temperature is bearable this morning, and the Sun shines from a blue sky in the end of November. I truly enjoy getting away from the cold and rainy British days, and now I sit in the blistering Sun and talk to Kate.

'I fell for his outstanding talent. I got captivated by his charm.' I glare at the surroundings, and realise I have never visited this place before, although I've often walked past it.

'His complaints began on his birthday. Remember when we went for this fishing trip?'

'Yea, he was rude.'

'He grumbled about how badly I treated him. That he had never felt comfortable or welcomed by me. That he had to live up to all my strange house rules. He had no private space because we lived and worked together.'

'Huh? Holy moly!'

'He must have known that he could use you.'

'Oh, do you think so?'

'Yep! I knew it instinctively.'

'Why didn't you warn me?'

'Hmm … I should. The truth must be that he was angry. I was costing him money.

And not the reverse.' She pauses and glances downwards as she is pondering of something.

Then I notice she is about to cry but keeps her tears back.

'He was insulting me for my body. My cellulite and yelled at me. "It will be best if you dangle upside down. Then you will look nicer," he mockingly laughs.'

'Oh, horrible. Oh, my. Creepy dude!'

'He criticised me, and shouted, "you smell from the crotch when I'm lying in the same bed as you." I got traumatised! "I can't stand to have sex with you." And I got crushed! "I'm sure you have chlamydia. Yikes, or some other ugly diseases in your female parts," he shouted.'

'Oh… my … God … Yikes! He has told me about it.' I feel sad for her and back then I got flabbergasted over his rude words about her.

'With his ugly criticisms, I went to the gynaecologist. She got furious about his horrible accusations. Now I think about it! I should have kicked the bastard out after the first time we had dinner at my home.'

'But you didn't? Why? What did he say to you about me?'

'On the first date he sat and admired me wildly. Suddenly! Smack! The head-loose grabs my non-existent wrinkles on my cheeks and mockingly smirks. "A little surgery will do you good her", suggesting I must have a facelift! What a *prick*!' She is getting upset about these gruesome things he has taunted her with, and I notice a tear in her eye.

'He blasted that my tummy was fat. My butt and arms were sagging. It was shortly before I went to Macau to visit him.'

'What?' she shouts. 'Look at yourself. You look good. You were stunning and well-trained, I remember.'

'Ha-ha, well, that was his opinion of it. Why does he then want to be together with me if he has such negative thoughts?'

'He tried to take advantage of me. Big time. He made a *storm* flirting over the phone. Then invited me later for a trip to London.'

'Yea, he enjoys complaining. Was he not earning good money here?' Which I thought they did.

'He came with tons of business suggestion half a year before we broke up. He didn't get any money out of me. But he destroyed my self-respect.'

'It's not so much the money. But I feel that he is misusing his charming power over me. That he allowed me to fall in love with him.' And damnit, I'm still in love with him.

'He only accepted me and my financial demands because the clinic was based on my fame. I had many business contacts in the area. I got all the clients. I had important access to the media.'

'Did you feel he only takes from others? That he gives nothing back?'

'Indeed! The fool is dangerous, Mary. Watch out for him. He had to get totally out of my life,' she jabs.

'But I adore him so much. I don't see all the flaws.' I excuse myself to rectify myself.

'You will! If I disregard the damage my soul took, then he hasn't cost me so much. On the contrary! I have had many travel experiences at his or other's expense. But I was *never* overjoyed with him.'

'What about your trip to Macau and Japan?'

'What trip to Macau? I was never in Macau with him. He went there after we broke up. I was only twice in Japan with him. Last time was in the spring same year we met you.'

'Oh, but he told me you guys went to Macau together.' And I ponder, is he a liar, a cheat, and a fraud?

'It's unbelievable what women find themselves in. What they will do financially for a scammer. Jeez, and a sociopath as him.' She glances at me and smiles.

'Hmm!' I grumble and shake my head.

'Everyone speaks about, he can only talk about himself, himself, and his work.'

'Yea, he does. Ha-ha. And a lot.'

'He complained over the rent and said, "I might as well sleep in the clinic because it's free." Imbecile!' She says sarcastically. 'He's nasty! I should have thrown him out.'

'Why didn't you?'

'Hmm ... Something infatuated me with him. Hmm ... Financially! Oh, boy! He has a lot to catch up after the time with me. With you, Mary, it seems he got the money out of you quickly.'

'Yea, I have paid a lot of money.' It frustrates me I 'm too besotted with him. Damn! I feel so dependent on him. Am I an unwise woman?

'One of my girlfriends didn't understand what I saw in him physically. He is a sick chump. Disgusting! It must be difficult for you to understand his gross exploitation?' she glances at me with pity.

'Gross exploitation?'

'Yes, it's many years of humiliation which require us to build us up afterwards. What I find difficult to understand and forgive myself for is that it lasted some years with that birdbrain.' She gazes at me as if disappointed with herself.

'Do you know about a woman who bought some equipment from him?'

'Yea, she paid for some of his fake education, but not for equipment. Do you know the authorities do not approve of his education?'

'No! Wow! Do they not? Oops!'

'Nope!' She shakes her head steadfast.

'He also said that the two machines mysteriously disappeared from her clinic. Puff! Into outer space! Maybe it's two different women.'

'Perhaps. About disappearing machines. Hmmm… I'm not sure if it's hers,' she glares speechless at me, sips some water, and we order more coffee and water.

'Strange! Biggest mystery in my life.' The café is filled with locals, and some of her friends have arrived and greet her. I realise she speaks good Spanish, which leads me back to my Spanish message I had sent to Drake. And she had seen it. Her friends leave, and she continues talking to me.

'Oh! He told me his education is valid.'

'They are *not* valid!' She says resolute as I stare flabbergasted at her.

'He wanted me to pay $6.000 for a 2 or was it a 3-week course in Indonesia. And roughly $60.000 for a machine identical to the one you had in the clinic.'

'What? No! Are you serious?'

'I've many questions, so I'm trying to do some research on him.'

'Someone threatened and forced the dummy to pay this one woman back her money for some education she couldn't use for a shit. I believe it was her farther who called the jerk. The sucker had to pay it back in several instalments.'

'Wow! Do you remember why Drake came to Spain?' I question, curious.

'He came from Sweden, where he was working. Well, you never know if he is lying. He spent a lot of energy on telling me how bad his staff treated him. Also, of a court case. I believe it was with the union.'

'Oh, I see. Wow!'

'He learned his new skills from a colleague. Then brought it to Spain. Jeez, the fool believes he's the best in the world. Probably he believes he's God!' She laughs at her great comment.

'Ha-ha, yea, he believes he is Jesus. The Chosen One. And the best practitioner. He has told me you reported him in Spain and Sweden for tax evasion.'

'What! That's not true. He ran a clinic here, probably without permission.'

'They had frozen his account, he told me. I wanted him to pay back my $30.000. I needed them for my lawyer.'

'What? Are you crazy? Did you get them?'

'No, but he used this Tax evasion as an excuse. He had no access to the bank, he said. They froze the money. Then other stupid excursuses popped up.' My stomach is turning up-side-down in despair.

'Christ! No, patients were always paying in cash. I'm sure you remember that?'

'Yea, cleverly done by him!' And she gets miffed over his horrendous accusations.

'He told me shortly before he left Spain, that US tax was after him. I don't know what then happens. Then he left for Asia.' While she talks, I glance at her great fresh look.

'You look much better and happier now. I remember you appeared more depressed. I understand why! Terrible what he has done to you. Chilling!'

'Well, it's understandable. I looked like a dragged, hung cat.' She smiles.

'Apologies for not having had positive thoughts of you.'

'Why didn't you see me with positive eyes if I only rented the idiot a room, as he told you?'

'Yea, hmm ... I don't know. It saddens me I've been a part of the terror against you.'

'Oh, my goodness, men, I still have a hard time believing in them.'

'But in considering what he told me, that you guys were not lovers. Hmm ... I can't have known better,' I excuse myself with pain in my voice.

'Shortly after our break-up, he wrote me an email. Such a retard! He wanted to pick up his knife. Jeez, and a potato masher and six dish mats at my home. Have you seen it?'

'Yes, he forwarded the mails to me afterwards,' I answer embarrassing.

'I gave him the cold shoulder and wrote back to him, "You must be a complete *idiot* if you don't understand that I *don't* want to communicate with you. Or your family or their remnants." Imagine, he had the nerve to ask me to contact you. That goes over my head.'

'I remember he was furious. "You had gone completely from your sanities. How could you allow yourself to give—or throw—away *his things?*'

'Such a donkey.'

'You were selfish *not* to remind him he forgot them that night when all his things stood outside your building. It was unworthy of you. He wanted you to promptly to hand over his items to me", he thundered.'

'He commanded me to call you. He said you would pick it up.'

'Ha-ha, yeah, but I was not interested in doing it. He also told me you spoke rudely about his family.'

'Fathead. I've seen them one or two times. Never really spoken with them.'

'Also, he had only dealt with you and your family properly. He didn't need such an outburst from you. Your life was over with him.'

'Such a dope! His actions before and after his departure showed me he was a moron who I'm more than happy to get rid of.'

'He continued to thunder. "It also suited him perfectly to be free from you. He didn't need what you had in you," he roared.'

'Geez, well, lastly the moron wrote, "Stop bothering me. There is no room for such bad vibrations your presence brings", Prick! Such a twerp!' She maddened.

'Christ, he went wrathful and told me, "it's clear to him what a cold bitch you were. You had never given his soul anything of value." I thought his words were foul.' I felt shameful to tell her all this. Should I stop? But I couldn't.

'The last I wrote to that fuckhead, "It's the last time I opened an email from you," and I opened none of his mails and blocked him,' she roars in rage, and I fully understand her.

'Yea, he said he also wrote, "you were a plain selfish person." I pondered, wow, this is awful. What will he say about me if he dumps me and finds a new woman?'

'Mary, truthfully, others have to see him enough in action to believe that someone can fall for what he does.'

'True. Then he drags me into his creepy darkness and tells me, "It filled you with resentment. That I was *the fresh breath* he needed in his life. Yours and his life were dead for a long time ago." He was so furious and yelled for hours about you. Did you get a mail where he wrote to you, "I was more than worth it all? Even more than you were. That I'm extremely generous. I had a much bigger heart and soul than you." Can you imagine how shaken I was at his accusation against you?'

'But I don't get why you spent so much money on him. And you stay with him.'

'I don't know. I should have seen the red flags there. He intended telling me he wrote to you, "I'm a great friend who he always could trust. That you *not* possess such qualities as I do." He ends writing, "goodbye to you and thank you for the nothing you gave him." Then he ends up bragging with the last thing he wrote to you, "You have only given him a terrible life. He will *not waste* his lovely, joyful, and harmonious life on talking or writing to you anymore." Did you see it?'

'No, I didn't see it. And I don't want to see it.'

'Wow! I was speechless when he told me all this. I imagine he wanted me to feel pity for him. Make you look as an awful woman.' I'm embarrassed after I have told her those ugly things he has barked about. I even felt ashamed when he angered during his stay in my apartment.

'Sorry to say, if people know nothing about you, they will probably think you are a stupid blue-eyed woman with flaps covering her eyes.'

'Perhaps I am.'

'It's *not* the impression I have of you. You seem to be a smart and clever woman,' she sweetly smiles. Our talk has continued for more than an hour, then I try to end our conversation. It has been difficult for both of us, so I don't want to drag it into some meaningless long-haul shit.

'I'm grateful for your understanding. For our meeting. Not in my wildest vivid imagination have I dreamt that any human being could do so to others.'

'Mary, I think it's good for my self-understanding and forgiveness that we met.'

'Yea! I didn't believe such people existed. I should forget all about him.'

'It was a great initiative you took for both of us,' she kindly smiles.

'Take good care of yourself. Maybe we meet again.' I reciprocate her smile.

'Thanks to you and likewise, sweet Mary. Dump him. Get rid of him. That's my advice.' And we pay our bill, hug, and say bye-bye. Her friends are still sitting at the other table, and she walks over there, as I stroll to my car. Our meeting has eased my conscience, and it was nice we cleared the air between us, though it was only a minor part of the enlightening for my understanding. So, who is Drake? I was often tired of being treated as a tiny, useless, fragile, stupid Barbie doll by both men. Though I might still be unwise for getting deeper involved with Drake. Let's jump back to the *Honeymoon phase* and where he has invited me to Asia in the winter of 2010. I wonder if I'll be so inanely that I get trapped into his dangerous psychological spin, unaware of the danger I might put in my life. Therefore, as Mother Teresa so wisely says, 'We must be the voice of those who have none' (Proverbs 31:8).

CHAPTER 32

THE PUPPET MASTER.

> Never regret a day in your life.
> Good days give you happiness, bad days give you experience, worst days give you lessons, and best days give you memories.
> —Lesson learned in life

What does the puppet learn in Macau and Indonesia, in the year of 2010, from the day when Drake stands outside in the arrival zone at the Macau ferry terminal? With his head at a slightly skewed angle, smiling and gently blinking with his dazzling brown Bambi eyes, I drop all my belongings on the floor and run straight into his open embrace and hold on tight to him. People stare flabbergasted at us while we tenderly kiss in a heated, amorous embrace. But I don't care; I see only him and sense a deep perception of emotions from his love, coming from his stomach over to my body, ending up in my brain. The deep aura of infatuation between us, makes us not aware of no one's presence in the space except for our own, as noises, sweaty smells, screaming children, and crowds of people disappear in my thought and mind. Perhaps it's my own hot and sensitive emotions I transfer from my heart and soul, down to my tummy and into him, and makes the hug so meltingly intensely. The embracement rapidly put me into a calm and deep relaxed state, as I'm more than ecstatic, and inhale steady, deep breaths through my nostrils and exhaled calmly through my mouth in a massive relief of being in his arms again. My heart is pounding steadily in calm, blistering rhythms, eager for his tender adoration, an in relief, I rest my head on though, I can't hear his rapid beats. We let go of the embrace and I gladly follow the *shadowy angel on the white rescue horse* to my next heavenly adventure with him.

This is the beginning of my fresh journey, of the deep release of my relaxation because of my fresh life with Drake, as this is the specific, actual romantic existing and prospect I wish for. Hopefully, I'll find the answer if my dream with him will be good and true, as the many promises he has given me. Will this be the ultimate illusionistic dream, as the one I have dreamt about in my Caribbean fantasy? Will this adventure turn out to become a vital reality for me? What I have not seen yet is him as my future invisible puppet master, because I believe I'm dealing with a cosy, normal, amusing, and grave person, although I don't know who he truly is. He has only told me he has set up a company and has several interested investors abroad. Everything feels perfect, and I have a righteous gut feeling that I will be joyful with him, as the novel Far East adventure will help me in ways through my unhappiness and insecurity. The shadowy angel will make me shine again, as a glowing Star, and my gladness will be enormous. This is one of the best times of my life, though the surprises will appear when I least expect them.

Carrying my suitcase in his one hand and holding my hand with the other, we go outside the terminal.

The private chauffeur is not there, so we grab a taxi from the ferry terminal to the hotel on the Cotai Strip, the City of Dreams. Wow, left-side driving—what is that about? I have never tried that before, and it feels strange. Well, I don't have to sit behind the steering wheel, I ponder, so that is someway safe! Ecstatic, I glue my body to him and hushed; we clench our hands, feeling breath-taking warmth between our fingers. In a snug and devoted embrace, he holds me tight while he talks of the different places and casinos we pass on our way to the hotel.

I won't let go of him for one second, and I'm so excited about being in his embrace again.

'Are you hungry? Or thirsty?' he gently asks.

'No thanks, darling. I'm good,' I smilingly respond, and all my distress disappears in a delightful, relaxed state of peace with him. It's only a short drive before we arrive at the impressive hotel, and I am stunned by such a mind-blowing skyscraper in the centre of the City of Dreams. Two gleaming tall buildings appear blueish in the late hours of the day. The dusk hangs over the city in bluish colours, and the dark blue sky makes the giant fountain in front of the buildings seem enchanted with its light, and water jets splashing in soft movements. Only the green grass, the palm trees, and the hundreds of red-light strips on the building break the light of the beautiful warm blue glow of dusk. As we enter the entrance, one more spectacular vast splattering water fountain appears in front of us. The giant golden ball in the middle, with tiny holes splashes the water up in spectacular, elegant silence. Over the ball dangle hundreds of crystals, reflecting the spotlights in many directions and performing a captivating play as where it fragments from a massive kaleidoscope. As millions of giant diamonds, the lights hit the crystals, sending small fascinating and shiny colourful particles around the extensive area.

While Drake gently holds my hand he proudly guides me to the gigantic white marble reception for my check-in. His elegant walk fascinates me as he puts one foot in front of the other, having his back in a perfectly upright position. He appears compelling, proud, and flawless, so I am mesmerised by his attractive and mystic way of strolling; it's identical as of what happened in my Caribbean dream many months before. Is this my mysterious déjà vu? I muse in the seconds I watch him.

As the friendly staff welcomes me, they prepare all the paperwork, and in the meantime a sweat lady brings a refreshing cold drink and a little wet towel to refresh my face and hands. I get my key-card for the room, though Drake has already checked in the day before, so he has one already. Sweet and cheerful, his arm ends around my wrist, and as two newlywed people, we snatch the massive golden elevator up to the Grand Executive Suite on twenty-second floor. Oh gosh! I enter a massive room with floor-to-ceiling windows, overlooking the breathtaking Pearl River Delta. As I'm watching out of the massive panoramic windows, I notice millions of small and big boats, with their colourful light in red, green, and yellow, while the blue Moon is shining cheerfully in the calm water of the dazzling river. They have adored the eight hundred square feet room with a stunning archaic luxury, with a great en-suite bedroom comprising a giant double bed and adjoined private bathroom, so there is everything the heart can desire.

'In the morning, we have a free breakfast. You can choose between Chinese and Western selections in their stunning restaurant.' Drake informs me about the practicalities, and continues, 'During the day, we have plenty of refreshments. Afternoon tea. Evening cocktails and canapés.'

As I enter the bathroom I stare at the awesome white sculpture bathtub, with golden taps and next to it is a grand rain shower, so I immediately want to jump in the tub. Everything seems striking, and in my dreamy head, I picture us jumping into the vast tub, right now, and bathing naked in a hot devoted embrace with him. It's the only thing in my head, while we next can cuddle in the soft white bathrobes. Nicely and inviting they have placed plenty of luxury toiletries, so I want to use them right away. Drake takes me by the hand and guides me into the living area and turn on the TV with over hundreds of satellite channels.

'I will have a quick peek at the latest news,' he mumbles. Damn, and the romance suddenly fades in my head. I go to the kitchenette and want to make a coffee but grab a water instead from the free minibar.

'Do you want anything from the minibar?'

'Yes, please. Give me a whiskey and a beer.' He shouts.

'If you want to see a movie, we have free Internet,' he yells, and I give him a surprised glare and bring the drinks and my water bottle into the room.

'No, thank you. I didn't come to visit you to watch movies. I only want to sit next to you and hold you tight,' I lovingly say with a massive smile on my face.

There stand two tall slim glasses, a bottle of champagne on ice, some fresh fruits, and some strawberries dipped in chocolate on the glass dining table, as I stop glaring at it with enormous eyes.

'Oh, dearie me. This looks nice. Can we drink that and eat the strawberries?' I smile contentedly and notice the remarkable mahogany chairs along with the table and the tremendous fat white lounge sofa, they have encircled by the same variety of wood.

'The sofa is impressive. Looks comfy.' I laugh.

'Yeeeeeah! Babe snatch the icy champagne. I take the glasses,' and he gets up. 'Also grab the strawberries,' he laughs cheerfully and instantly sits on the nice, comfy sofa. I first give him his drink and beer, put my water on the table, and grab the champagne and the fruit. Oh gosh, I'm busted and want to relax the travel bustle out of my system, so I downright slam my corpus into the comfy sofa out of exhaustion.

'Cool!' I peep blissfully. Most of all, I first want to have a sweaty bang with him and next to fall asleep in his arms and relax by his side. I browse around with my curious eyes and muse, *Gosh almighty! He has given it a gigantic notch up with luxury.*

'Seems you already have brilliant success. Are you earning some good dough!' I question and glance at him.

'Huh? Yea! Well. Hmmm ...'

'Well, I'm so glad for you. It's so great,' I acknowledge. 'I want it honestly to work for you.' He gazes at me silently, and don't comment on my praise, but pours me a glass of champagne, grabs a strawberry and hands it over to me.

'I'm so convinced that you will do amazing here,' I rejoice.

'This suite must have cost at least twenty-five hundred dollars for four days.'

He glares, amused at me, with a loving smile on his face. 'Babe, don't worry, Mr Chang Chen is paying.'

'Wow!' It's overshadowing all my worries within a moment, so I'm proud of him!

'Are you happy for me?' He cheerfully and proudly asks. But dear reader, let's not celebrate the good spirits too quickly. Even it feels great to follow my happy heart and not fear any judgement of Drake. Is there something he has not told me? He knows I have peeked deep into my heart and followed it as never before. I'll get back to that.

Although I'd like to remain a little longer in my lovely moment of happiness and genuine adoration. Suddenly, while we sit in peace and relaxation, enjoying the icy bubbly champagne and eat chocolate strawberries, he jumps up as a chased rabbit from its murky hole. He sticks one hand in his trouser pocket and sits down in front of me.

'Oops! Surprise!' he laughs while I gaze speechless at him with loving eyes and a pounding heart, pacing as fast as the rabbit was running out of his hole.

'What are you doing suddenly on the floor?' I ask, curious, while he is rooting for something in his jeans pocket. Then, with his head slightly tilted, he flashes his brown eyes at me, and licks his lips wet and shiny.

'My sweetest little darling girl. Now that we finally are together, I must ask you something important.'

'Huh? Important?'

'You know I want to be with you forever. Right?'

'Yea, I know.'

'I love you more today than yesterday. And more tomorrow than today.'

'I'm happy. Likewise, darling.'

'Will you marry me?' he sweetly requests.

'Whew!' I go into a total daze with surprise. 'Eh? Hmmm ... What?' I hesitate, but I am over the Moon in my amazing moment as he lifts his hand with the ring in between his fingers. He is holding up a massive rock of a diamond, embedded in white gold.

'Oh, my gosh!' I yell with fake amazement. 'What are you saying, my love? So romantic you are! Thanks very much? Darling, I'm overwhelmed.' I'm sure he thought it looked like a million, and maybe it does! Softly, he takes my hand and puts it gently on my right ring finger, where my wedding ring sits. The golden ring has never been off my finger for the last twenty years, unless when it went for cleaning at the goldsmith. My heart pumps in fast pounding rhythms and humph... oops! Shame on me. Close up, it's not what I thought at first. I stare, disappointed, at the fake ring! Sorry, but I don't even like it, and it's not my kind of ring. Frustrated when it's sitting on my finger, it no longer sparkles as a million-dollar authentic one carat diamond.

'Don't you like it?' he questions, disappointed, and I'm sure he can feel my frustration. Silently I muse, *Am I worth that little to him? A fake ring?* But I smile nicely, glare surprised, and try to answer kindly.

'Yes, yes… oh … my … it's lovely. But I think it shall sit on my left ring finger.' I once again peek at the fake diamond ring, which doesn't appeal to me. I switch my voice to something more serious and concerned. 'But don't you think it's a little too early? I believe we first must get to know each other a little better.' I worry and can feel a strange discomfort in my stomach.

'Of course, you get a genuine and much bigger real diamond later. I only had time to find this Swarovski for you,' he tries to excuse himself.

'No, no, darling. Wow, it's stunning.'

'Sorry, but I had such a brief notice of your arrival. I promise you we will find a beautiful engagement ring together while you are here.'

'Eh? Why? Don't you like it yourself?'

'Baby, marry me, my beloved sweet darling!' he begs on his knees and continues, 'We belong together. We are made for each other. We are meant to be for eternity.' I glance disheartened at the one-hundred-dollar fake ring. Ugh… I know! Shame on me. It's not the price, but the thought!

'Hmm, honestly, *this* I'm not prepared for!'

'Baby take your wedding ring off. And wear only my ring!' he insists.

'What? No!' That I *can't* handle, and my mind turns into a confusing spin of depressing thoughts at his command.

'That's too much to ask. It stays where it always has been!' Disturbing thought runs through my mind.

'Come on, babe. Take it off? At least as long as you are here with me.' He eagerly insists.

'Why? Oh no!' Taking it of frightens me; what if you lose it Mary?

'Yee-haw, now we are husband and wife. Therefore, it doesn't belong there anymore.' He seems jubilant as he changes his mood.

'I'm delighted you have proposed. Hmm, but is it not somewhat bizarre?'

'Bizarre? What do you mean?'

'You know I'm still married. It's not normal. I have yet not filled my divorce,' and perhaps I'm still clinging to my marriage, so why the rush? Oh, I'm sure the aware reader remembers my words: honeymoon phase—**stormy infatuation. Pampered. Adored and wants to get married.** Unethical! Not gallant! And then in the middle of my excruciating situation. The prior bed is not cold yet! Damn it! But politely I must find an answer.

'It doesn't matter. A man can ask whenever he wants.' He smirks.

'Hmm. At this moment, it's difficult to marry you!' I show sweet and smile, refusing to give him the yes he wants. Anyhow, he needs some answers, so I tenderly hug him, take his soft hands, and glance mildly at him, because I love him.

'Let me finish my separation. Then the divorce. That can take up to a year.' I try to turn it around to my advantage because I sense something isn't as it should be. It confuses me, and I turn it down, thinking we should get to know each other first. I am not a bigamist; I do not believe in multiple wives for one man or several men for one woman! Besides, I'm not ready for another marriage. I take matrimony as sacred and serious.

'So, what will it be? I can't sit on my knee all night long.'

'Darling, when the times come. Then let's talk about it again. Then we can get married. But thank you. But no thanks. I cannot give a promise I can't keep.'

As I want to kiss him, Grumpy irritated turns his head away, and disappointed gazes at me and let go of my hand.

'Wow! Wow! Wow! Let's not talk more. I'm tired. I want to go to bed,' he snaps, and we sit in silence on the couch for a little while more.

While we spend time in Macau, he does his utmost to court me even more, so I enjoy being so adored and feel cherished as never before. I'm not an ice-cold queen or a polar bear, so my inner chaos is turning to something positive instead of listening to its negativity. I'm blessed to have Drake in my life, and we talk about our grand future, but he never gets a yes, and the funny thing is he always presents me as his wife. Okay, I must admit it, as I play along with the game, and in my passion, I imagine that he is my husband; in some countries, you must appear as married if you share the same bed. Later, though, I change the ring to my left finger instead, so for a long time, I am temporarily the fake Mrs Bates.

For the next half-hour, we sit chit-chatting, drink our champagne, and eat all the strawberries.

'Let's have a shower and then go to sleep,' I cheer because I'm tired.

'Okay, come on then,' and the warm bath under the rain shower brings us together again in a passionate embrace. The Frangipani fresh scent on the silky white sheets makes me happy, thinking of the amazingly fresh-smelling flower. On our soft goose pillows lie yellow flowers, whose blossoms send an aroma through the room as a dream of a tremendous flower field. We warmly snuggled our naked bodies under the sheets, and hug in each other's embrace. Watching from the foot of the bed, I sleep on the right side of the bed, so I'm close to his heart when my head is tugging on his warm skin on top of his chest. *Boom ... boom...* I can hear it in steady, calming rhythms. With a crispy, calm, gentle voice, he talks about what he has achieved in Macau. Our romance and the nude-body feelings get deeply divine and intense with affection. The vibrations of his rasping speech bring me into a sedative meditation, and my fears and anxieties disappear into cosmos, replaced by a space of quietness and peace. Blinking Stars and the shiny milky Moon appear in front of my closed eyes, as his voice hypnotises me until it gets weaker and weaker, and I can't hear it anymore. Knowing he is my spirit, I fall into a calm, deep, restful sleep with my beloved next to me, after our great first night in the stunning land of Macau. Peace and quietness come over my sleeping body, and I sleep in total relaxation with him by my side while we clench our hands all night.

In the morning, Drake wakes me up after a serene rest, while he gently gives me a kiss, and a great sensation goes through my body. For a half-hour, we embrace each other while he tells me of the day's agenda.

'Mr Chang Chen (let's call him CC from now on) has invited us to a gigantic party. He is the investor I'm working for. At 7 p.m., we will take part in this massive venue. A driver will pick us up.'

As we arrive at the great party, the following night, Drake with proudness clasps my hand, him in his dark blue lounge suit, spiced up with a red tie and me in my knee long pleated red dress, wearing glittering high-heeled shoes as we walk straight to Mr CC.

'May I present my wife?' Drake grins proudly when he greets CC and presents me to him. Next to CC stands another suspicious little guy, appearing ugly and scary. The chap stares intensely and ravenously at me, as I reach over my hand to CC and do a polite curtsey in front of him as CC smiles kindly at me. What a stunning tall Chinese gentleman with shiny dark hair; though I have thought all Chinese were short. He is roughly the same age as Drake, possessing a great gentle smiling face, striking brown eyes, with a compelling glance. But it scares me a little because their appearance reminds me more of the mafia than normal businesspeople. Yet, I'm kindly welcomed by them, however I'm somewhat petrified, as a chill runs down my spine when I notice the one dude is carrying a gun and the other one has a knife in his belt.

'CC has based most of his business in Hong Kong. It's his party. The guy is filthy rich,' Drake tells me as we walk over to our table.

'Oh, what kind of business?'

'Several hotels and food shops in Macau. Including gambling. All these business associates here—I guess there are five or six hundred guests—are serious businesspeople, or partners to CC,' he proudly continues. We sit together with twenty other guests from China, Japan, and Macau. I have yet not comprehended what the party is about, but two hundred round tables decorated with plenty of amazing colourful flower decorations, in reddish, yellow and orange colours adorns the massive ballroom in front of the vast scene. CC gets up and presents the evening's program and welcome greeting in Chinese, and later, he has another long speech, spoken in Mandarin, also call 'Putonghua'. Next to him stands two sworn interpreters, translating it in Japanese and Portuguese. I don't understand any of, but it seems CC is the main attraction, as he appears hilarious, because people fancy him, and so do

I. It's blasting loud in the hall during the entire dinner, with shouting and laughing, while guests gets drunker and drunker and gulping the great Asian specialities. During the dinner, CC and his, yuck, yikes, oh, my God, scary followers, whom came many times to our table while they are in a massive drunken eccentric mood.

'Cheers! Drink!' CC shouts and laugh.

'It's as if he is trying to get us drunk,' Drake comment.

'Yep, ha-ha, I think so,' I answer, and this goes on continuously.

'Babe, no worries. It's their special drinking ritual,' I realise when Drake tells me. 'It's always like that.' He adds.

'Ha-ha, well, at every "cheer", I drink twice the amount of water. I only sip the wine. I don't want to get drunk,' because I dislike drunkenness and being out of bodily control. I have had enough after my latest drunkenness with Drake in Spain.

'Ha-ha, ha-ha, and blah ... blah ... blah ...'

Laughing and cheering, Drake is about to enter a jubilant, self-absorbed alcohol phase. In a precise, proud manner, he tells everybody about the business dealings he has with CC Honestly? Geez, oh, my goodness, he's so big-headed and acts as he is the centre of the universe when he boasts about his many achievements.

'Babe, you must do me a favour!' He smirks, when he unexpectedly, glances at me with a naughty grin, and a hot-headed impulse catches him in his stupidity. I'm sure he is about to get a little too tipsy and heedless.

'Okay!' I glare devoted at my beloved, while he continues with his blabbermouth.

'Definitely, CC will ask you how good I am in the sack.'

'Huh? What?'

'Yea, ha-ha, the fella frequently asks me.' My sweetheart laughs teasingly, and I stare oddly at him.

'Oh, for heaven's sake!' I'm dumbfounded. 'Why ask such a foolish question? Is it a competition?' I teasingly question and smile mockingly at him.

'No, no! But if he asks. Hmmm, please say that I can fully perform.' He grins seriously and strangely.

'Eh? Okay. What a weird question!' I respond, and want to deny him such stupidity, but in the same second, it strikes me, 'are you having a competition to see who has the greatest manhood? Gee, men and their beaver basher!' as I stare strangely at him. Oh ... my ... God ... I am glad there are no Swedes or Danish people around us who can understand this strange conversation.

'What? Eh? What do you mean about competition? Greatest manhood?' He laughs at me, 'ha-ha, ha-ha, geez Mary.'

'Yea, why? Honestly. Isn't that a man's thing? Such an unusual thing to ask me.'

'Please, do it for me.'

'Come on. I'm not sure I want to go there.' I worry and wrinkle my forehead, so my eyes squeeze a bit. But he insists that I help him with this nonsensical matter, and my next question is 'Why? We have hardly had any sex yet.' Pondering, oh, boy, he was not that good in the sack the first time in Spain.

'Sometimes we go downtown. Every time, he has offered me prostitutes.'

'Ay caramba! He hasn't?' I'm about to burst out in laughter. I mind my manners.

'Yea, he has. Each time I explain to him, I don't want to take part.'

'Okay. That's the most bizarre to suggest to you.'

'Babe you know I love only you,' I told CC that. 'Then he thinks I can't get it up,' the big bull of a mortal Adonis mumbles, embarrassed, only able to stare shyly down to the floor.

'Did you go with them?' I question. I am extremely nervous. I'm observing him seriously and he gazes weirdly at me, as if he has a bad conscience. Dear friends, what do you think he answers? Ha-ha!

'No, no! Are you out of your mind? Of course, I never go with them.'

'Okay ... okay, fine.'

'How can you even so much as think such things about me?' he seriously tries to convince me. I'm not so sure if I can trust him.

'My stomach troubles nervously. My heart says something else, darling.' I stare at him with my one eye squeezed, worried by my thoughts. He glares convincing at me, so I believe him, as he flashes several times with his stunning eyelashes. Well, that part I'll come back to.

'Come on, babe. Help me out.'

'Fine darling. Hmm, if it's so important for you. I'll say you are more than top-notch in the sack. I'll tell him you can perform every day. Big bull!' I mock him.

'Ha-ha, great babe.'

'Honestly, Drake? We have barely had sex yet! I must lie.'

'It doesn't matter. Do it for me.' He smirks.

'Well, fine. I'll do it. He-he, oh, boy, I'll say that your pocket rocket is big.' I eyed at him confused and ask, 'Is it okay if I say so?' I giggle inside myself about this madness over trouser snakes and find it utterly amusing and brainless.

'Yes, yes, babe. Perfect.' He grins.

Surprise! He-he. Who comes to our table next? CC approaches us, smiling, with his two daunting goons, and swiftly, he throws the question straight forward into my pretty face. I'm not sure if this is the normal way he communicates such things with women. With no hesitation, he plants his stupid question to his own big amusement, as I also notice he's about to be very drunk.

'You are a stunning woman,' CC states, giving me the elevator stare. His two bodyguards are following him wherever he goes, and I'm scared of them. They stare again greedily at me, and CC puts his hand on my shoulder and lets out a bogus laugh.

'Ha-ha, ha-ha, are you certain Drake can handle you?' He smirks. Uh huh, yep, CC indeed has a nice, sexy smile and blinking, inviting eyes, though I gaze at him, speechless.

Goodness gracious! Is this a joke? I muse. Men are challenging each other to see who has the biggest, best, and stiffest yoghurt slinger! Gently, I laugh, and give CC a serious glare then replies to his ridiculous and awkward questions.

'Funny question you ask. Ha-ha. Well, yes… yes… Drake is the best!' Next I give CC the elevator stare and gaze directly at the big bulge in his pants and find that he seems to be well endowed for a man. I glance up again with a naughty smile. 'It's nice.' Having in mind of CC's vast pecker bulge, dreaming of a great fuck with him.

With a naughty smirk I say, 'Well, Drake can perform every single night for my great pleasure.' I foolishly say, knowing it's a lie. 'And it's nice and big,' I joke with my typical Danish humour, and glance down, staring directly at CC's vast bulge. Admit it ladies. This is what women do. Stare at men's nice butt and their pecker. Of course, I lie! Oh my God! I wish CC knew I lied as he next is gazing surprised at my quick, naughty answer and the conversation turn around.

'Well, Drake also says you will invest in the clinic.'

'Huh? Eh? Perhaps.'

'I'm glad. Come and meet a few of the other investors,' and contentedly we walk over to the table where Mr Haruto, one of the Japanese investors sits. CC and Mr Haruto perform the introduction in a polite Japanese manner, bowing and bowing until they bring the important formalities to order. Archaic and pleasant, though Mr Haruto appears timid, he is a handsome middle-aged man with straight, shiny black hair, and looks attractive in his dark suit. He is a little floppy and taller than most Japanese men, but very nice and warm-hearted. (Tsk, tsk, also a well-equipped bulge and ass.) We talk about the business Drake has with CC, about the investments and other matters, which I know little about. Of the sudden, Mr Haruto makes the friendly suggestion that Drake should do a seminar in Japan for his many investors. Holy moly! I get excited about travelling to Japan.

The party is about to reach an end when CC asks Drake a weird question.

'Do you want to continue with us downtown? To *our* brothel.'

'No thanks.' Embarrassed, Drake politely answers.

'Come on. We have been there before.' CC smirks, and I overrule the comment, pretending I did not hear it.

After the party, the chauffeur drives us back to the hotel, being exhausted after a long, interesting day. Before we go to bed, we sit on the enormous sofa, having a drink and talking about today's agenda.

Let's make love, Drake says, and wants to know about my sexual relationship with Paul.

'Can I tell you something else first?' I ask. For some strange reason, I need to tell him about the Caribbean dream that has haunted me several times before I met him for the first time.

'Sure. Well, what is it? I'm listening,' he mumbles, uninterested because I'm not telling him one of my sexy stories.

'Darling, listen. I must tell you about a weird dream.'

'A dream?'

'Yea, it has troubled me several times by now.' I gaze nervously at him.

'What is it, my love? Is it bad?'

'I don't know.'

'Okeydokey, then tell me.'

'I think it… hmmm… yes… hmmm… it started about a month before I meet you for the first time in the clinic. It's so odd,' I stammer, and he listens to the entire story of:

"Time Is Just an Illusion."

'Huh? Strange dream. Are you going back to Paul?' he asks nervously.

'No, no! The strange thing with the dream is there are so many things that fit you!' I smirk and I hardly dare to ask him, but do it anyway, 'Is it you? Do I have to be careful with you? Are you a charlatan?' I daringly directly and smoothly test, and then I try to laugh myself out of this odd question. *Shut up!* He gets furious. I should never have done so, as he gets outraged with me. As a furious tiger in a tiny cramped cage, he verbally attacks me. God almighty! I have never seen him so frantic before. This is a part of him I have not expected, and it makes me nervous when he shows a part of his true personality. I never dared to cross him like that anymore.

'What the hell is wrong with your mental health? How can you even ask me such heedless things?' he shouts. 'Are you completely out of your stupid mind?'

'Sorry, sorry. It was not an attack.' I peep.

'I asked you to marry me. Bloody hell, Mary. You have no right to accuse me of being a gold-digger. Or a Casanova. What the hell is wrong with you?'

'I did not call you a Casanova. Or a gold-digger.'

I get somewhat scared of him when he continues. 'You did. What do you know about me, anyway? Oh, my goodness, such bullshit you come with.'

'No, I did not. It was in my dream.'

'Jeez! What sort of demons are you possessed by?' He goes on and on in his lunacy. At last, the puppet master convinces me of the opposite, that I'm influenced by demons. Crazy mind? Instead, I keep on apologising, so it takes a while before he is calm again.

'Listen, babe. I'm a good person.'

'I know, darling. Why do you get so upset?'

'I'm a man who wants to be good and fair to you. Help you. Love you.'

'Yah, maybe I'm imprudent.' I squeak.

'I do not understand what this senseless dream is about. Forget it. It's not realistic.'

'Yah, ha-ha, I get it. Maybe it's stupid.'

'It's just a heedless illusion,' he implores me. Then he takes my hand and kisses me on my forehead. Yikes, it disgusts me when a man kiss me on my forehead. Degrading!

'Someday, I'm sure you will make someone feel disastrous.'

'Oh! Why so?'

'Hmm, for sure also crushes a woman's heart immensely. Oh, my, I hope it will not be me.' He gawks at me.

'Let's have a shower,' and he points in the bath's direction. During a warm shower together, in his warm squeeze while the water drops fall on our naked bodies, we next go to bed as good friends. I trust him, but it's difficult for me to get rid of the dream and thoughts. I still ponder about it, and perhaps I should see my dream as a warning.

'Tell me one of your sexy stories.'

'Which one?'

'Yea, about you and Paul.' So, for the next half hour, I blabber about the man and his neon green lizard. As Drake gets excited, he pressed closer against me. I felt a certain stiffness near my back.

'Is that what I think it is?' And I expect a grand night with my horny bull.

'Yes!' he squeezed closer to me.

As I had finished the story, I expected to get passionate sex, but of the sudden his virility disappeared, as I sneak my hand to his phallus and realise he first was excited, but not so motivated that I get a grand bang from him.

The perfect night's sleep gives me renewed strength, as today is an exciting day, when I will visit the "vast" clinic. While we walk along many small cobblestoned streets, we pass many small shops and some stunning vast casinos until we arrive at the clinic's front door. I am disappointed as I stare at this basic location, with only Drake and a secretary working there. Strange, because he has told me it's a "huge" clinic, though it's not! Two minor treatment rooms, a kitchen, and a minor office. *Huge?* I ponder. It's not even nice or decently clean.

'I must treat a patient.' He utters proudly, and I notice it's only this one patient who waits in the treatment room for a cure that day. Drake manages the session while I wait and watch the treatment. The rest of the time, he guides me around in Macau, as we pass the Wynn Palace, the Plaza, and the Venetian casinos, and he has access to enter one casino without paying because CC owns it. It's the first time I ever visit a casino, and it looks impressive, however, it's not my style of game, because I dislike gambling; it doesn't appeal to me. There are millions of Chinese and other nationalities in there, and of the sudden, we hear a couple yelling and screaming at each other, while they are chasing each other. Have they lost all their money in gambling?

The weather is amazing today, with a clear blue sky and the Sun shining powerfully. It's a little cold, around ten degrees, so I'm freezing slightly, as we are trolling to the facade icon of a church and the religious museum of Saint Paul's seventeenth-century ruins. This is more of my cup of tea, to enjoy the local history. Coloane is where Macau has temples, churches, parks, beaches, and much more. It's stunningly beautiful, and we pass a woman sitting on a chair, playing fairylike music on her flute. I notice the birds in the nearby trees watching her, as though they love the gently falling notes from her flute.

Yee-haw! Shopping! Not to forget. We pass many great boutiques, and I buy myself a Vivienne Westwood dark coat, purple scarf, matching belt, and a purple handbag. In another great shop, I buy some sexy lingerie, and next to that is a great Prada shop where I buy myself a pair of short black Prada boots and a new black bag. Wow, sexy mama! We never end up in any jewellery store to see for an engagement ring. With all my expensive paper bags containing my stunning purchases, we pass lots of fish shops, where they sell shark fins, abalones, and other local delicacies. Yuck! The fishy smell is awful, but the locals have displayed it breathtakingly as is it lined up with a ruler in the tiny shops. Some days, we dine in the cafeteria where CC has one of his major business. Interesting, because as tall as Scandinavians, we receive curious glances every time we arrive. The food is delicious, served in stunning small bowls and always with green tea and hot and cold water. In a corner, I observe some men chewing loudly. Eww, next, they burp and fart after they have finished their eating.

'Eww!' I say to Drake.

'I know. It seems sickening. But that's how it is. It's normal. Not seen as rude here.'

'Okay, but it's still disgusting to fart and burp at the table.' And at the same second they serve us the shark-fin soup and abalones. They consider both dishes as delicacies, so we try them.

The fishermen cut the shark fins off the living sharks, as I read about it later in an online article, when I googled it. Horrifying! Afterwards, they throw the live sharks into the sea again without their fins. Grotesque! Animal cruelty! I never eat it again after I read this. Abalones are a small group of small or large saltwater snails where they eat the meat either raw or cooked, depending on which Eastern culture is preparing the dish. When you see them in the shops, they look as an ugly, petrifying vagina with a fully-grown bush of hair. Only the eight legs of the abalones would miss, if they had such, but then they would appear as the venomous Brazilian Wandering Spider.

Scared, I stare at these hairy vagina beasts, and I'm sure I'll never forget how they look—frightening! Otherwise, Macanese cuisine is quite unique, deriving from Portuguese sailors and settlers who brought their favourite dishes here. Many of the ingredients came from South Africa, India, and Malaysia, and the Cantonese cuisine, is primarily based on fresh seafood. Then we try some other specialities, such as a bird's nest, where we eat vomited bird spit, I'm told. Eww! I try it—been there, done that, and will never taste it again. But I'm a curious person, so I always attempt many of the local dishes. Eating with chopsticks is the funniest part, which I must learn because no one anywhere gives me a fork and knife. However, I become a well master at it with those two wooden sticks.

After less than a week, the trip is about to end, and the next adventure for us is in Indonesia. We pack our suitcases and grab a taxi to the ferry terminal and sail on the hour back to Hong Kong Ferry terminal, then take the train to the airport as we next sit in the flight, with Garuda Indonesia, on our way to Jakarta.

CHAPTER 33

Now I'm a Bloody Secretary!

> Happy is the man with a wife to tell him what to do and a secretary to do it.
>
> —Lord Mancroft

As we land in Indonesia, the humidity and heat immediately cause us to sweat. It's my first time in Jakarta, a massive capital on the northwest coast of the island of Java, and a deafening city, often with a humidity over 80 percent. Unbearable! Indonesia is primarily Muslim and 5 percent Christian, as the rest is a mix of Hindus, Buddhists, and other religions, with a population of nine and a half million people in the capital of Jakarta alone. The people consist of a mix of Javanese, Chinese, Arab, Indian Malay, and European, whom most of them have, over time, influenced the architecture, language, and cuisine.

Mr Barney's secretary Jeni welcomes us at the five-star luxury Ritz-Carlton. Drake presents us as a married couple, otherwise, we can't stay in the same room. The staff accommodates us on the twenties floor in a six-hundred-square-foot room, with a comfy double bed and a medium-sized desk. From the window, we have a view of the stunning pool area, with lots of green plants.

'You have free Internet and daily international newspapers. Free minibar. Coffee- and tea-making facilities. There stands an incredible fruit basket at your disposal. You have a delicious continental breakfast. Everything is included with your stay.' Jeni informs us.

'This will be our base for the next three weeks.' Drake grins.

'Amazing!'

'You have your first meeting with Mr Barney at 8 PM.' Jeni says and walks away.

'Yea, it will be while I'm teaching my special therapy for you and the two physiotherapists,' he says proudly and smirks compellingly.

'Tough dude! I'm nervous. Also eager at the same time for the fresh future for us.'

At least I will finally experience how talented Drake is at his profession! I hope! After we have settled, rested, and bathed, we go for the arranged dinner meeting with Mr Barney and his wife, Ambar. He is an appealing medium-aged man of Indonesian ancestry and the owner of the clinic and Hotel. A tall, dark-haired, well-dressed man, wearing a typical batik shirt, dark pants, and black shoes. Ambar, a beautiful dark-haired woman wears a *kabaya*, a traditional blouse dress, and a pair of tight pants underneath, dressed up with a pair of stunning high-heeled black shoes.

The next morning, two energetic therapists at the clinic welcomed us—Ms Mawar (meaning 'rose') and Ms Indah (meaning 'beautiful woman'—and gosh, is she ever). Both sweet and educated women.

'I want you to make film recordings daily. Take pictures and notes every day,' Drake commands, referring to the four patients there.

'Piece of cake. I will do my best,' and take all the medical records, even though I'm not used to doing such things.

The first patients are Mr Barney, a diplomat, an owner of a tobacco company, and a young boy. Little Raajaa (meaning 'king; prince; ruler; monarch') goes straight to my heart. Gee, he's such an awesome little kid, with cute, stunning, big dark eyes. Swiftly, we create a unique bond between us, and then he calls me his "golden angel", though he is Muslim. His mother, Amisha (meaning 'pure, truthful, and with a heart of gold') tells me about this sweet angel thing and buys me a breathtaking angel as a present from the boy. I can't understand Indonesian, but I understand the body language between Raajaa and me. How sweet. Eight years later, I fly back to Jakarta only to visit him, his family, and the therapists at the clinic. It was a great heartfelt moment to meet everyone again, and there was a great joy in Raajaa's eyes when we meet.

Getting back on track, those become the few patients we treat in the first three weeks. Yes, believe or not! Now I'm a bloody secretary? Shut up! That's not the plan! So, I miss a lot of the lessons and have basically paid $6,000 to be Drake's secretary. He should pay me for the work, but I'll do anything for my beloved, of course, so I never protest! Three weeks of being an assistant and watching him doing his lecture is tolerable, and I'm somehow impressed by what he does, and I learn some. It's interesting, and the treatment protocol along with the technical use of the machinery captivates me, so I want to learn much more, and as a secretary, I can learn a lot. One thing is not so good, though. By now, my three-month acquaintance with my shady dragon angel has cost me roughly $60,000.

I recall the words: *'But you must understand that I'm a tough teacher. I demand that my students complete the subject before getting a diploma from me. All I want to add, right now, and this is very important, is that we are a team—you and I together.'*

Over the weeks, I notice Drake's cruel behaviour of punishment; as he is an unreasonable, sharp, commanding teacher. If he has an antipathy towards his students, he often becomes angry at them and conducts a smear campaign against them. That happens to me sometimes, up too many times a day. One day, I'm his most *excellent* student, and the next moment, I'm awfully *dumb*. I feel most sorry for Ms Mawar because she experiences it daily when he speaks disparagingly about and to her, and she often ends up crying during the sessions. He *hates* her! He is so mean to her I can't bear it in my mind. Let's see what else waits for me in the melting pot.

Daily, we do our duty, but I'm about to go stir-crazy, only being in the clinic or at the hotel room. I need to get out for a walk, explore the world, so I go outside the hotel zone, walking around the surrounding streets. Keep in mind that I'm used to my many daily hourly walks with the dogs, so I miss them, not to mention my family and the dogs. I *must* get out! No one knows where I am, and Drake, Mr Barney, and the hotel prepares a search for me without my knowledge. For four hours, the tall blonde Danish gal strolls content around as an unsuspecting tourist, with no mind for how dangerous it is for her. As I come back to the hotel, everybody sighs in great relief, and Drake is raging at me.

'What the hell are you thinking?' Shouting at me in front of the staff.

'Huh? What do you mean?' I'm dumbfounded.

'Are you completely out of your stupid mind?' The boar roars.

'Eh? Why should I be?' Glaring at him innocent.

'Do you realise they can kill you? Or kidnap you.'

'Who would kill me? Kidnap me?' I stupidly question and glare flummoxed at him.

'Stupid of you walking around, flashing with your long blonde hair?' He bangs his palm to his forehead, as I am stupid.

'I was careful.' My voice peeps.

'Jeez, everyone can see you're a foreigner. How imprudent can you be?' While he is waving his arms angry in the air.

'Calm, Drake. I'm not the only foreigner her.'

'Grr, grr. Stupid woman! There has been a massive search for you,' he screams.

'I've not properly considered the danger.'

'Stupid. Stupid.' The dragon roars and spits fire out of his nose.

'I believe I'm walking in not so dangerous areas. There were loads of people. I'm sorry. Heartfelt sorry if I messed up.' Humbly, I apologise to our host, to the receptionist, and to Drake.

Mr Barney honours us later with a relaxing extended weekend. Four days in Bali. A resort in Nusa Dua, all paid. Luxury! Amazing! Bali is an Indonesian island known for its wooded volcanic mountains and its iconic rice fields, stunning beaches, coral reefs, surfing sites, and yoga and meditation sanctuaries. On Bali, lives mostly Hindus, very friendly, destitute, heart-warming people. The hotel is next to a snow-white sandy beach, with swaying palms, shells, and cones—precisely as I've experienced it in my dream. They have placed a beautiful fountain with a big jar in the middle and surrounded by many big black stones, in their vast reception area. From the distance, I can hear the water coming up from the minor holes, and it gets louder until I'm standing in a relaxed position, right in front of the fountain, which makes it stun in a mysterious and cosy way. At the white marble reception, the friendly Bali staff welcome us with an exotic drink during our check-in. I have never experienced such kind, smiling people before, petite, stunning, and sweet. So, it's not all bad in my relationship with my angel, as we also have many glorious moments.

In the morning, as the sunlight is catching the water in the sea in front of our window, the sight calms and inspires me to be on the beach today. It's overall relaxation every day, and here we can walk in peace along the beach and the promenade. Relaxing in the sunbeds in the white sand with the shade of the swaying palms or parasols, we hold hands and enjoy exotic drinks with fresh fruit in the glass and tiny paper umbrellas on the edge. What a magnificent life. I feel the salty water on my face when it leaves tiny crystal droplets on my cheeks and lips as we walk hand in hand into the sea. I'm sensing the sharp taste of salt when the drops end on my lips while glancing at Drake clenching my hand in his, as we wildly splash in the water.

'Let go of your worries and physical tension,' he whispers and holds me tightly in his warm embrace while he walks softly and slowly around with me in the warm water of Benoa Bay. Breathing shallowly and deep in my thoughts, my chest moves into deep relaxation, and I let go of all my worries. Back and forth in a comforting cuddling embrace, as a baby monkey, I'm clinging to his body while he gently rocks me. My lips, jaw, and head rest in peace on his shoulder, as I wrap my legs securely around his body and hold my arms tight around his neck. All the tension in my body relax bit by bit and melt into an enigmatic comfort zone. We can't get enough of touching each other, so I'm completely convinced that I've made the right decision with him.

As we enjoy our unimaginable lives to the fullest, he gets in his very romantic corner, and I feel as the world's happiest woman in this gorgeous paradise with him. At night, we sit outside on the beach with candlelit dinners, drinking beer or cooled white wine. The service is the upmost top class, and the beautiful Bali women in their stunning traditional *kabaya* sarongs, bustle around us. One night, during our romantic dinner, we watch the magnificent scenery of the Balinese Legong dance, a striking moment, watching the colourful and breathtaking women and men, dressed in their beautiful clothes as they perform the fine, slow moves of their dance. Our hands are always touching, and the sparkling energy of hot tenderness surges through our bodies and souls.

There are pros and cons to our ecstatic life in paradise. Drake is also very content with one specific thing: I have stopped smoking. The good thing is, his kissing becomes much more passionate than before. Hallelujah! I have achieved one satisfying thing in my life.

'I'm so thrilled.' As he clenches my hand and smiles.

'About what?' I ask curiously.

'Baby, I want to make love to you tonight.' He unleashed something deliciously dirty in him.

'Wow! I'm imagining a sweaty bang with you,' as my pussy gets wet, ready to climb him and be greeted with multiplied orgasms.

'My libido is much greater when you don't smoke.' He dangerously smiles naughty, licking his lips wet and moist.

'I'm glad to hear that.' I smile, satisfied and gasp for my breath in excitement.

'Yea, I can no longer smell the tobacco on your skin. I noticed.' He chuckles contentedly and squeezes my hand. In that moment, I want a fag desperately.

'I understand it to the fullest. Smoking is not good for my health.' His promise makes me ecstatic, and wow... I'm excited to gett some great sex with my foxy boyfriend.

As I'm tossing around in the bed, naked, I'm eagerly waiting for my lover to begin the sex act. I ponder, *where did the libido of Adonis go?* We have consummated no sex act together since my arrival, except that he has trained my "Minnie" in multiple orgasms, as he promised me. Every time I try to have more intimate contact with him, he seems to have problems getting his Willy in the strong, upright position.

'Don't touch there,' as I trace my hand on my way to the area around his his one-eyed wonder weasel, then he removes my hand. Has he forgotten his Viagra pills?

I whisper dirty, sexy words in his ears about things I whispered to Paul, or what Paul used to do to me during our erotic experiences.

'Oh, baby. I get enormously excited. Tell me more stories about you and Paul,' he whispers back, even though I find it difficult to feel his hardness of his schlong in his boxers.

I crawl under the sheet and want to give him a blowjob. Gosh, it's a long-lasting performance and does not work.

'Am I doing something wrong?' Instead of giving up I take control, though it's a tough job to get his meat thermometer hot and hard, and when he becomes horny and stiff, it lasts only a short moment. I'm sucking so much on his floppy cock, so my lips become blue. The muscles in my mouth get exhausted from the damn hard work I perform on his dead snake. Still, it doesn't scare me off, because I'm a tolerant and understanding woman. *Give it time*, I muse, and I try all kinds of stimulating, dirty tricks.

'I don't know what is wrong with him.'

'Calm, darling, you're not twenty-five anymore. I do not expect you to be a tough, sexy, horny wild bull between the sheets.' But he brags so much about his sexuality that I'm certain he can still perform to the utmost.

'Get up from there. Lie next to me,' and he uses his fingers on my little wild pearl. As a sweet little cockleshell, she opens the cleft for the touches of his soft, teasing fingertips. He drives me crazy as he plays with tender strokes on the pearl inside. My sex drive is ecstatic, so I want to have sex with him almost every night. But what a bummer! That is not possible, so only little Minnie gets pleased by his hot, tender touch, so I become addicted.

The vacation is a perfect, blissful, affectionate time, though it's about time to pack our suitcases and travel back to Jakarta, where we have several meetings with Mr Barney. Plenty of proposals come on the table of what the opportunity can offer us in Indonesia, as Mr Barney wants to build a new and advanced clinic, with him as the sole investor and us operation the clinic afterwards. Magnificent prospect, and I believe in the vast chance to learn more about the treatment. Maybe my investment will pay out, and Drake gets enthusiastic, so we must decide if we want to stay or not.

Though, Drake has a conflict of interest with Macau and his business agreements with CC which do not fit into the plans. How can he do both things at the same time? Both of us have a return ticket the following week to Macau. A week later I will leave from Hong Kong as I must get back to Spain and he will stay in Macau. Problem! What do we do? I don't know, and then he becomes sneaky, secretive towards me. Days before, he sat for many hours with his calculator, trying to figure out the economics and devise a new-fangled plan. It's frustrating for me, as he gets often irritated at me.

'Maybe I will not do it that way, Drake,' or 'Maybe I think it's wrong, darling.' I sometimes comment on his ideas. He doesn't like my head-on confrontations, so I must find a gentler track for my sharp tongue.

'Why blame me for your foolish mess?' I say on the last day, after we have treated the last two patients in Jakarta, before we travelled back to Macau. Over the next weeks, he must solve the problems before the seminar for Mr Haruto, I met earlier at CC's party.

'Do you want to go with me to Japan?' He tempts me.

'I would love to.'

'Then don't go back to Spain. Stay with me,' he pleads with a lovely, seductive smile.

'Oh, my. You know Japan is my dream.' I'm ecstatic and shine as a shooting Star and suddenly I was faced with the hardest decision of my life.

'Then do it. Fuck Spain.' He entices me and I don't know if I should risk my heart by remaining in his life.

'We must wait a little until we can be together forever.' I had few rules, one was not to move in with him immediately, and the other was to accomplish the divorce first. But rules are meant to be broken, right?

'We can stay forever from now on.'

'Oh, no. Darling Christmas is close. I have some obligations to my family.'

'Don't you want to stay with me?'

'Of course, I'd prefer to be with you.' I was prepared to lose everything, but not my children.

'I don't believe you.'

'Darling, please.' I beg to his understanding heart. 'I must pay attention to the children. I promised to spend Christmas with them.'

'Babe, they have no interest in you. Damn, then you will stay with Paul.' He sounds very jealous and is threatening to destroy everything we had built.

'Yea, and so? I have my return ticket to Spain, next to Denmark.'

'I'm very jealous. Forget them all, baby.'

'Oh, my, that I can't. We might consider whether we shall meet again.' I get nervous and ponder of Lucy's warning not to fall for him and about his shadowy past.

'Bloody hell. I knew it. You don't love me.'

'Calm now, Drake. I love you more today than yesterday. And tomorrow I will love you more than today. This is how it continues every single day.'

'I don't believe you. You ruin everything for us.'

'No, I don't. Love simply goes around in a circle. It never stops.'

'I think you are breaking up with me.' He grumbles as the sour dwarf, Grumpy, from Snow White and The Seven Dwarfs.

'No. The circle is as the round bracelet you gave me. It sits as a symbol of love on my arm. Day and night.' I smile and touch the bracelet. I only take it off when I take a bath.

I grab his hand and want to kiss him, but Grumpy turns his head away.

I am sure that the attentive reader is aware of the deepest layers in the plot into which I have fatally fallen. I know I can blame only myself for being naïve and a people-pleaser, so thank you so much, Mary, for not taking care of yourself. However, such dangerous connections should only be in fictional novels and not happen to a person as me. I'm caught in a dangerous, cynical cage of love for Drake and have not realised that I am dealing with the worst and most drawn-out suicide of my life. This duel I will have with him is massive until the day I discover how intriguing a psychopathic behaviour can be. Will I, future wise flee from him in a broken state to a veritable hell of grief and depression? Though, I'm in deep love with him, and yet I can't find out if he has a wicked plot for me. Will the future dream help me discover the true devilishness?

The gloomy day arise as he drives me to the airport, and we stand in the pouring rain as he dropped me off at Hong Kong Airport, and I broke down before we said goodbye. Wet from the rain I'm following in his steps at the hectic, noisy, packed Airport, with millions of rushing people heading to their destinations around the world. I can only see him among the crowds of people and want to scream my heart out as loudly as I can to him. I want to stay with him—not fly back home. The words are screaming in my head. *Let me stay with you, my beloved*, but the verses can't get out of my mouth, and in my grief, I am speechless, weeping inwardly. We hug intensely, while I have tears in my eyes, and he kisses me tenderly goodbye and let go of my hand. As he turns around he takes his last graceful steps while I watch his stylish figure disappear, without him looking back. With cries in my eyes, I continue to watch him elegantly fade farther and farther away from me with hasty footsteps, as a shadow over the horizon, as if it has all been a dream in my head.

Though it was real-time—I cried as earlier; I'd held him tight to me, and as I'd clenched his lovely soft hands before we said goodbye in an emotionless and insensitive, unimportant loud Airport. Resembling an opaque shadow on the horizon, when my beloved ghostly disappeared.

Drake makes me cry, and usually, I never cry. Something my tough childhood had taught me ever not to weep. 'Tears are worthless. They don't help a miserable state,' I had often been told. 'Brave, sturdy girls don't cry over spilt milk—and not over a man.'

A Japanese idiom says, 覆水盆に帰らず. 'Spilt water will not return to the tray.'

It's another way of saying, 'No use crying over spilled milk'. Only water, fittingly, turns out as a way less significant loss than milk.

Twenty-four hours later I sit on my empty balcony with my loneliness, on a chilly winter's morning in Southern Spain and faced with my hardest decision of my life. Should I run from my previous life with Paul and stay in my enchanted romance and remain in Drake's strong arms?

Or did I just imagine the entire fairytale? Was the romance only a ghostly dream?

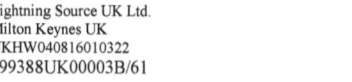
Lightning Source UK Ltd.
Milton Keynes UK
UKHW040816010322
399388UK00003B/61